Wilde Mountain Time

By
Siobhan MacKenzie

Edin Road Press

1508 Continental Square

Lexington KY 40505

publisher@edinroad.com

Ebook/Print edition: February 2015

The characters and events of this book are fictitious. Any similarity to real persons, living or dead, is coincidental and not intended by the author.

Cover and Layout design by Lorrieann Russell

Story and copy editing by Foery MacDonell, Christopher L Jones, Rosa Sophia, and Lorrieann Russell

Published in the United States

Wilde Mountain Time

Siobhan MacKenzie

Edin Road Press

Also by Siobhan MacKenzie

Short Fiction

His Man Friday
His Man Saturday
His Man Sunday

Anthologies (published with Wicked Seductions Press)

Stranded with a Billionaire Boxed Set
Hot Soldier Boxed Set
Wicked Fairy Tales: The Curvy Collection Boxed Set
Gods and Goddesses (Boxed Set)

ACKNOWLEDGEMENTS

Writing a book is a very close approximation of giving birth. The book is the child, newly born and innocent. It takes nurturing and discipline to raise that child from a concept to a fully fleshed out novel.

There's an old saying that's been attributed to quite a few cultures – It takes a village.... Truer words have never been spoken. And it was one hell of a village that helped me get this book ready to present to you, my darling reader.

Special thanks to Lorrieann Russell and Jacqueline Druga for being my beta readers and helping me to get the story just right. Lorrieann gave me all the details about New Hampshire and hiking that an author could use. She was my best expert in the field. Jackie is a great story teller and she had some wonderful insights in the plotting.

More special thanks to my editors who caught my mistakes in grammar, spelling, and punctuation – Foery McDonell and Chris Jones.

Even more special thanks to Seraphina Donovan, Donna Macdonald, and the ladies of the Kentucky Independent Writers Network. My beautiful Seraphina has given me more insight on how be a bestselling author than I could ever imagine. All of the ladies of the KIW have been so very supportive. And I'll never forget that.

All of them are just as responsible for this story as I am. And I am, and always will be, eternally grateful.

Yes, there really is a Mt. Washington Hotel and no, I've never been there – well, I've never been inside. I have actually been to the hotel and it's an amazing place to see. Yes, the hotel is really haunted by the late Caroline Stickney, wife of the late Joseph Stickney. They designed and commissioned the hotel to be built near the President's range and at the base of Mt. Washington in 1902. They loved that hotel so much that they still walk the grounds today, she more than he.

I took liberties with the internal layout and rooms of the hotel to serve my purposes for the story. One of these days, I hope to stay in one of them, just to see how close I came.

Table of Contents

1

*I*T'S A HELL *of a night, hobnobbing with the rich, the famous, the politicians. Heady stuff for a guy like him. Someone who's come from a pretty poor background. And yet, here he is. In his salad days and feeling fine. Talking to them as if they were old friends, listening to how much they love his music. How much they all love him. He smiles and shakes hands with senators, congressmen, the governor. Yeah, they all love him.*

His senses are full of the night air and the scotch, both in copious amounts. All he has to do is put out his hand and a tray appears with glasses of the stuff. Pick one up and leave the empty behind in its place. Oh, how this scotch is so smooth down the back of his throat—honey water that still tastes of burnt oak, aged for twenty-five years. Maybe more.

He and Phil, working the crowd like two pros. And the booze is pouring and the money is flowing. Just two buddies, hanging out and having fun. The colors run together in taffeta dresses and silk ties. Someone warbles familiar tunes with the air of a cabaret singer and the cigarette smoke wafts around him.

The smoke gets thicker as he goes. Not grey any longer, it turns blacker with each step he takes. But he can still feel an arm wrapped around his, still hear the laughter of the crowd. He's still walking, still making his way somewhere. Where is he going? Where is...he...?

His head is getting more befuddled; the alcohol is catching up to him now. But another glass is thrust into his hand, and then another and another and another. Darker and darker. The taste of the scotch is too much now; he's practically choking on the flavor. It's thick like molasses and the burning oak is clawing at the back of his throat. His head is beginning to throb.

The voices fade; everything is black now. He has the sense of moving fast, of flying with the wind flinging his hair back and out of his face. He can't see where he's going but he's not afraid. Should he be? He knows he's not alone but he's too busy feeling the cold air against his cheeks and forehead to wonder who it is.

It happens so fast and seems to go on forever. He's no longer flying; he's smothering in a white cloud that's appeared out of the blackness. His body is tossed this way and that, his headache turns into a brutal assault on his brain as he smacks against something hard and cold. Something grips him across his chest; it feels like he's being cracked open like an egg.

And the sound of screaming. Screaming and the smell of burning. The sound of metal folding in on itself. Louder and louder and louder, the screaming. Who's screaming? What the hell is going on? Why can't he see? Who the fuck is screaming? The sound of screaming and the taste of scotch and blood in the back of his throat. And his head aching, his chest aching; every part of him is in pain.

Screaming...the pain...the taste of the blood....

Then, nothing again. And when he wakes in the morning, all he'll remember is the sound of the screaming and the taste of the blood and scotch. And vomit.

And the feeling that it was his fault.

2

Thom's head pounded; nothing like a migraine to remind him that he'd stayed up way too late chatting up that pretty blonde. Too bad he still had to sleep alone; she'd have warmed him up and kept the loneliness away. But he'd slept alone, slept too deep, and then overslept. A harbinger of the coming fiasco, he'd been dragged kicking and screaming into sunrise and the migraine only made it worse.

A forty-five minute flight turned into three hours because of a problem with the plane's hydraulic system. And of course, the flight crew couldn't find this out *before* they'd boarded the passengers—oh hell no, they had to wait until *after* everyone was in their seats, checked in and carryon baggage stowed. He hated sitting on a damn plane, waiting and with nothing to do, but the attendants wouldn't let them get up to move around, nor would they let him visit the cockpit just to meet the pilots. "Too busy," they kept telling him. It ended up taking an hour and a half to fix the problem, along with another forty-five minutes to top off the fuel tanks, before they finally got in the air.

To add insult to injury, Thom and his staff were late checking into the hotel, so the manager had given his suite away. That was absolutely unacceptable; he was Thom Mitchell, for Christ's sakes—maybe his name wasn't as big as it had been in the past but, goddamn it, it was still big enough to get a decent hotel room. Now, he had no place to rest while his crew set up the next gig. Okay, the hotel staff had hustled to find other accommodations for him, but he wouldn't have them until *after* the show. So instead of napping on a nice, soft mattress, he was stuck here in a green room—painted the ugliest shade of green there was—and forgoing the nap that would have refreshed him.

He was already exhausted from this tour; this was the icing on the cake. Then his business manager had dropped the mother lode on him as soon as he'd walked in the door—an extra and unexpected show. It was just too much to ask.

"Look, I don't care what the damned contract says! I'm not doing it and that's that."

Thom yanked open the door of the small refrigerator and pulled a bottle of non-alcoholic beer from the shelf. He flipped the cap with a practiced thumb and took a long drink from the bottle. This stuff was nothing more than beer-flavored water, as far as he was concerned, but it kept him on the straight and narrow. After enough time, he was used to it. But it wasn't helping his mood.

"Thom, come on," Malcolm whined. "Be reasonable."

"To hell with bein' reasonable," Thom snarled. "I'm worn out and sung out. Just because you're getting stuck for PR."

Malcolm recoiled as if he'd been slapped. "This isn't *my* damned PR. It's yours. Show some gratitude!"

"I don't have to show shit." Thom took a long hard pull from the bottle, letting a quiet burp whisper from his lips. "Since I'm the one paying your salary, you better remember who's the boss! And who's the employee!"

Thom put the bottle down, instantly sorry he'd opened his mouth. Malcolm scrubbed his face, looking entirely defeated. Thom *was* tired—completely worn out from a tour that was still drawing the faithful but without the hype that had been his for twenty years. Completely worn out from all of the other work he did with his foundations. He'd been on the road for ten months nonstop and it was enough. He just wanted to melt into the background and rest.

Malcolm took a breath, slumping his shoulders a little. "I know, Thom. I know. But *Wild Mountain Thyme* just isn't selling like we wanted. We *need* this gig."

"What are you talking about?"

Mal crossed his arms and avoided Thom's gaze as he answered. "I got a call from the suits. Your album peaked at twenty and it's falling off the charts. If you don't do something that gets you noticed, something that's going to sell some CDs, you're finished with Electra. And I have that from the number one man!"

The fight left him as fast as it had come. He felt old and used up. He was only fifty-three; it wasn't supposed to be like this. All he'd ever known was singing, making his music. In the thirty years that he'd been in this business, he'd outsold any other act on the company's label. And they knew that. But they were slowly ousting him without one word of gratitude or acknowledgment of what he'd once been for them. Forcing him to do a country CD when it wasn't his style. Firing his longtime producer to work with a kid who was untried and unknown, a rookie. He'd done it their way, recorded their damned country music, only to find that the label refused to promote the work at all.

"I'm sorry, Mal," he muttered. "I'm just burned out." He felt the hand on his back, rubbing his shoulder.

"I know, Thommy," Malcolm answered. "But, we *need* this gig. Look, you do this one and I swear I won't book anything else. You got my word, okay? And you can get that nice long rest in New Hampshire—a whole month—before *The Tonight Show* gig in June."

That sounded promising. He could get away and refresh the batteries. He could hike the Whites; maybe finally get to the big one that he'd always wanted to try. He could spend time on the golf course. Get in some fishing. Photograph the wildlife. It might even be enough to write some music, something he'd not done in a very long time. Thom squared up his shoulders and mentally pulled himself up by the bootstraps. "Yeah, Malcolm, okay. But I got a condition."

"Sure, Thom. Name it. Anything."

"Book me into that place I always stay at, the Mt. Washington Hotel. Book me there." He nodded, more to himself than anyone else. "Yeah, that'll do. No one will bug me there. It's quiet and perfect. Book me a suite and then forget you know where I am."

Malcolm nodded with a will. "Sure, Thommy, sure. I'll go do it right now." He relaxed his fists into hands again. "Look, there's a sofa over there; it's not a bed but it looks comfy enough. Why don't you lay down on it and try to get a nap in. I can let you know the arrangements for this charity thing after the show tonight."

Thom nodded in return. A nap would be just the thing, even on a lumpy green room sofa. Maybe it would even get rid of this fucking migraine. "Hey, Mal?"

Malcolm paused, looking over his shoulder. "Yeah?"

"I really am sorry I snapped, man."

Mal's grin was worth it. "How can anyone stay mad at you? It's cool, Thommy. Let it go and get some rest."

Thom shooed them all out of the room. A nap was just what he needed before tonight's gig. He'd do this show, then that charity show, and he could head off for the hotel with an easy conscience. Hell, he might even see that ghost up there. The Mt. Washington Hotel was supposed to be haunted by the woman who helped her husband build and design it. The more he thought about it, the more he loved it. Just some peace and quiet, no intrigue at all. Just golf and hiking. Maybe even hit the big prize—Wilde Mountain.

Yeah, that's all I need, he thought. That's all I want.

3

WHEN THE PLANE was an hour late taking off from the Vegas airport, Thom began popping the ibuprofen like candy, indulging himself in a chocolate milkshake. It was better than heading to the bar, which is what he really wanted to do. No, what he really wanted to do was start screaming at anyone in the appropriate uniform. But he managed to keep that famous grin on his face, laughing and joking with the flight attendants, signing an autograph for a couple who actually recognized him. Mal was gonna get an earful later for booking him on a commercial flight, even if it was first class.

When he barely made his connecting flight in Chicago, his disposition didn't get any better. He managed to survive on a can of orange juice and another can of sparkling water, sitting quietly in his seat until the plane landed at the Nashville airport. When the law firm's liaison was a no-show, the black mood descended on him and his fists stayed clenched.

Okay, he wasn't looking for the star treatment but damn it, that Micarello guy had told him that the charity coordinator was going to be there when he got off the plane. That's the only reason he'd told Malcolm to book the later flight. Mal was going to take care of getting his vacation plans for him, and then follow along to Nashville. Thom spent twenty minutes standing at the gate before *someone* finally came along to collect him.

The airport manager apologized all the way to his office, volunteering to contact the law firm and the liaison. He escorted Thom to the Executives' Club and told Thom to help himself to anything while he made the calls. Thom decided to take advantage of the wet bar and helped himself to a bottle of seltzer water. His hand poised over the nip of single malt for the briefest of seconds before moving on to the ice bucket. He dropped a few ice cubes into a tall glass and poured the water, enjoying the fizz as the bubbles splashed up against his skin. The sound had the desired effect.

He felt the anger draining away and started to mull options. He could go ahead to the hotel since Mal had confirmed all of that before Thom left Vegas. He knew *where* he was supposed to go, if not the room number. He could go check in and wait for the moron there. He drained the glass and decided to have another bottle. Yeah, that would do it. Have the manager get his bags for him and then call the hotel limo. He'd just go there and leave whoever this jackass—who had no clue about time or punctuality—to sweat a little.

The door burst open just as he brought the glass to his mouth. He turned to the door, the rim of the glass still resting against his lower lip, and got his first glimpse of the woman as she burst into the room. And immediately, any irritation or bad mood was completely replaced with a growing lust.

She was tall, he noticed approvingly; had to be somewhere around five foot ten or so. When she turned to close the door behind her, he glanced at her feet. She wore a pair of low, black heels, the kind that put the heart in her shapely calves. She was wearing hosiery and he indulged in a moment of speculation on whether she was wearing pantyhose or a good, old-fashioned pair of stockings. The black suit wasn't exactly form fitting but did nothing to hide the voluptuous quality about her—she was hardly overweight but she wasn't stick thin either. His eyes followed up, approving the swell of her bosom that looked almost Raphaellian.

There was something so deliciously attractive about a natural red head. Her hair was long, pulled back into a French twist on the back of her head. She had the most intense blue eyes he'd ever seen, combined with the cupid's bow of her lips. For a moment, he could imagine having her in bed; her hair like fire across his skin, her body wrapped around him, and her lips swollen with his kisses. Thom smiled over the top of the glass, taking another deep drink of the water. If he played his cards right, the old Mitchell magic might just score him an entertaining evening.

The woman took a moment to catch her breath; she looked rather harried as if she'd run the entire way. Her expression quickly relaxed, the smile on her lips was very genuine as she put her hand out towards him. She shook hands with a firm grip. "Mr. Mitchell...."

He set the glass down on the counter top and clasped her hand in both of his, smiling back at her. It was time to turn on the charm. "Call me Thom."

The flustered look returned as she began to apologize. "Uh, Thom, then. I'm Joanna. Joanna Hayes." She took a deep breath before continuing. "I am so sorry for being late. I got hung up at the office and then there was an accident on I-40 and...I am so sorry."

He decided that the southern accent might just be the sexiest thing about her. He grinned at her, giving her one of his best stage smiles. "Not at all, darlin'." He was still holding the hand that she'd offered him, making sure to look only into her eyes. "Now that you're here, it's quite fine." He was so caught up in those eyes that he barely felt the tug in his grip. He just kept smiling, holding on to that lovely hand.

"No, really. I feel terrible," she told him, closing her eyes and finishing with a huff. "I really wanted to be here to welcome you at the gate. You must be so angry."

The fact that he had been was pretty much over. "Don't worry about it, darlin'. These things happen," he assured her. "You can't help traffic." But he was really thinking, *never thought about checking a traffic report? News on the radio? Damn good thing she's lovely!*

She smiled, a little nervous, and he felt a definite tug between his hands. He arched his eyebrows, indicating he was waiting on her to say something.

"Uh, would you like to go to your hotel now? Freshen up a little?" Her eyes darted down to his fingers, then back up. "You'll have about two hours before the press conference set up for 5:00 PM. You'll be on the local 6:00 PM cutaway show, *Nashville Tonight*. We'll have the limo pick you up about 4:00 and...uh... then afterward...um...the limo can take you to the hall for the show...uh...."

Thom knew he needed to say something to put her at ease. A compliment always did the trick. "That sounds great, Joanna. I can tell I'm in good hands. You're a friendly girl; I know you'll take real good care of me." He winked at her, trying to show her that he meant it.

That didn't seem to do it, though. Her shoulders squared off and her back went ramrod straight. Her eyes were suddenly steely and the tone of her voice was frosty. "Mr. Mitchell?"

"Thom, please, okay? Please?"

"Thom...." She cleared her throat, no longer smiling. "Can I have my hand back, please?"

For a moment, the sound of her voice took him by surprise. It sounded more as if she was giving an order rather than making a request. And something in the eyes hardened as well, no longer friendly. But he released her hand as asked. He was, after all, a gentleman.

"Thank you." She stepped back, putting some distance between them. She went on, no longer irritated but still distant and cool. "Now, the show will be held in the small concert theater downtown. But afterward, there will be a reception at the country club. There will be a few speeches by the—"

He shook his head. "Afterward won't matter to me, little darlin'. I'll be heading back to the hotel."

Her brow furrowed a little. "You won't stay?"

"Is there a reason I should?"

"I beg your pardon?"

"I'm here to do a show, honey. What else is there?"

The hard edge returned to her voice. "Joanna."

Something wasn't right here and the Mitchell smooth wasn't working. What the hell was her problem? "Excuse me?" he asked.

"My name is not honey or darlin'. It's Joanna."

He cocked his head to one side. "I'm...uh, okay. Sure, whatever you want. Joanna."

"Thank you," she answered, terse and now very formal.

Whatever had put the burr in her saddle, she was taking it out on him. For a liaison, this Joanna left a lot to be desired. "So, is this your southern hospitality?"

That brought her up short. She pulled herself up to her full height, tilted her head back, and had the gall to look down her nose at him. "Excuse me?"

"Well, you're biting my head off all of a sudden and I'm a bit curious. Did I do something wrong?"

"Mr. Mitchell, I'm not sure what you were told but you're not just here to do a show!"

He crossed his arms and took his own stance. If she was going to play this game, he could play it too. "You know, I have no idea what you're talking about but, okay. Educate me then. If I'm not here just to do a show, then why *am* I here?"

She exhaled, sounding as if she was merely humoring him but he was being a total jackass and should have known this. "This is a fund raiser," she answered, annoyed. "You're here to raise money for the Cloud Nine Center for Abused Children. I don't really care about your music, to be honest; I've never heard of you nor do I care. But what I *do* want is your ability to talk to people, raise money. And perhaps make a contribution of your own!"

Thom swore under his breath, turning to lean on the bar and shaking his head. "I should have known! I damn well should have known."

"Known? Known what?"

He whirled on her, infuriated. Nothing ever changed in this business. "It's never 'just play the music, Thom.' There's always the goddamn dog and pony show. Smile, Thom; be a good dog, Thom! Meet the mayor, do the interviews, smile for the camera. It's never about what matters to me, only what you can get out of me!"

Her eyes flashed and she balled her hands into fists. "Why you son of a—"

He didn't let her finish. "Listen, sweetheart—excuse me, *Joanna.* I got roped into this gig because my manager said I needed the PR. I'm on way to a nice month of sleep, relaxation, and no stress. I would be there already except for this. I did not come here to pitch for cash. Especially for a bunch of snot-nosed brats and some redheaded bitch who wants to sharpen her claws on my back! Get it?"

Her face paled, her lips disappeared, and her nose pinched up. Her chest rose and fell in shallow breaths. She acted as if he'd struck her. To be honest, he felt as if he had. It was the rudest thing he'd ever said to a lady. He gave serious consideration to making a quick apology, but the look on her face told him that she probably wouldn't accept it. Or understand it.

She seemed to get control quite quickly. "Well, I *did* come to pitch for those children. But since it's such an inconvenience for you—and trust me, you're not the only one missing out on a vacation—we'll just get you to where you need to be with a great deal of speed and efficiency, shall we?"

She did a military turn on one heel and stormed out of the office, not even trying to wait for him. Thom took off at a gallop—raising a hand to the Airport manager and tossing off a quick thanks as he ran out the door—and tried to keep up with her. She was quick, sashaying through the concourse on those heels like a pro. By the time he'd reached the limo, she was already in the jump seat and waiting with a ramrod straight back. He stepped into the car and sat down with a heavy sigh.

His conscience was still pricking at him and he truly felt like a real ass. It was a charity event—he knew that. And he'd worked enough of these to know that the obligatory meet and greet always came after. Besides, this was for children. *Abused* children. What kind of monster would call them snot-nosed brats in front of her when she was deeply committed to them? Even *he* could see that. She stared out the window to avoid looking at him, still wearing that pinched expression on her face. He waited until the limo had taken off before making the attempt.

"Look, Joanna...."

Her blue eyes turned the frigid gaze at him.

"I'm sorry. I said some really nasty things and I was way out of line." He smiled his brightest smile, hoping to thaw her demeanor. "It was a rotten flight and I'm having a bad day, but that's no excuse. I behaved like a real jerk. Of course, I'll be glad to stay after. For the children. And yes, I want to give a donation for them. You think $50,000 would be enough to get things started?"

It worked. The look dissolved, her lips relaxed. "Thank you, Mr. Mitchell. That would be gratefully accepted."

He nodded. Yeah, it was shaping up to be a hell of a day.

They didn't go to the hotel right away, much as he wanted to. Her suggestion of a nap was a great idea but that would have to wait. His routine at any gig was to go straight to the hall and check out the acoustics. Thom was a hands-on performer when it came to sound check. He liked it that way; he could get a feel for the place.

The crew already had his gear set out and most of the set dressing. He stood in the center of the stage, tuning and re-tuning his favorite twelve-string. When he had it just right, he stepped up to the microphone. He and his sound engineer talked for a few minutes about the acoustics, comparing notes. Joanna came in and sat down, watching him intently. Inside, he felt the satisfaction. *She'll know me now, damn it.*

"Let's play one for the lady, Mark."

Over the loudspeakers, he heard, "Sure, Thom, you're live on the mike and speaker nine."

Thom started to play, fingerpicking the intricate introduction of an old Scottish tune that he'd recorded on the latest CD. It had been one of his favorites because it was one of his Mom's favorites. He'd sung it since he had first learned to play the guitar, sang it for every date he'd ever wanted to impress. But this time, he kept focused on the song, really feeling it for the first time. For once, he was actually feeling the music. He forgot about the hall, the sound engineer, the stage—he even forgot about Joanna. He closed his eyes, let the fingers find the strings, and opened his throat to sing.

Oh, the summer time is coming,
And the trees are blooming,
And the wild mountain thyme
Grows around the blooming heather.

Will you go, lassie, go?
And we'll all go together
To pull wild mountain thyme
All around the blooming heather,
Will you go, lassie, go?

The old expression about music having charms to soothe savage breasts didn't lie this time. By the time the song was done, he could see that she'd thawed considerably. And for some reason that he wasn't sure he understood, it was important to him that she had. Why her? He could have any woman he wanted and if any other woman had treated him the way Joanna had, he'd have sent the bitch packing and moved on. He was too old to play those kinds of games and he had no taste for them. So why her?

She took him to his hotel with an hour left for him to rest and freshen up for the show. They'd laughed and joked the whole way, and he was feeling hopeful about things. By the time she'd dropped him off at the front desk with his luggage, he'd invited her backstage to watch the show. She'd accepted with a slight blush and a smile. She stayed in the wings the whole time, while he played and sang his best. Of course, he couldn't watch *her*, but he could sneak looks. And he did. She danced and clapped, smiling as she did. He smiled too.

Just as promised, he worked the crowd with his New England charm and hospitality. He sweet-talked more than a dozen of them into sizable checks. All the time, she was watching him. Never took her eyes off him once. And he never wanted a woman so much in his life. It took him a while to work his way over to her. But he got to the bar where she was standing, wearing a low cut dress that revealed the most delicious breasts and a curvy figure that would make a man want to lay down on the ground and be her carpet.

"Can I buy you a drink, Ms. Hayes?"

"It's an open bar, Mr. Mitchell."

"Thom."

She had the most beautiful smile that made her eyes sparkle. "Okay. Thom."

"Now, how about those drinks." He motioned to the bartender by pointing at her glass and his own. "So? How'd I do?"

"You were incredible," she gushed. "How could I have missed this?"

"Miss my music? You mean you've never heard of me?" He raised a mock hand to his heart. "I'm crushed! I've only outsold every—"

"Group or solo artist on your label, winning four People's Choice Awards, two Grammys, and the Windstar Foundation's 'Humanitarian of the Year Award,'" she finished for him. "I took the time to read up on the internet."

"Why, Joanna. I do believe you're blushing."

She turned a shade of scarlet that only whetted his appetite more. God, she was beautiful when she blushed. He took the opportunity to move a little closer until he could feel one of those perfect breasts against his arm.

She didn't move. But she did look up at him suddenly, the blush quickly fading away. "Uh, Mr. Mi—"

"Thom. Remember?"

"Uh...I think you've...uh...."

"What? What is it?"

Now she appeared flustered. "Yeah, I...uh...look, I...."

"Look, we're getting along fine," he murmured. "After that ruckus earlier, this is a chance for us to get to know each other a bit better." The moment he had put his hand on her back, he knew he'd screwed it up big time. She pulled away so abruptly that he almost got pulled along with her.

"And just what do you think you're doing?"

"I...I ," he stammered. "I thought we were getting to know each other a little better, getting a little friendlier."

"Oh. Oh, I see." She slammed the glass down on the bar. "You thought you could liquor me up and do your charming rock star crap on me."

"What? Huh?" He shook his head, trying not to snap back at her. "What are you talking about?"

"I am here to represent my firm and assist you through the concert and reception," she answered, punctuating the last word. "That's all you get, buddy."

"Hey, look," he started.

"I don't believe this," she muttered. She whirled around as if she was going to walk away, then wheeled back on him with fury in her eyes. "You think you can just come in here and every woman's gonna fall at your feet, don't you?"

"Look, lady… ." He felt the flush on his own face and gripped the glass in his hand a little harder. "All right, yeah, I was hoping we were going to have a nice evening, have a little fun."

"HA!"

"What are you talking about?" The fatigue, the rotten day, all of it caught up with him and he bit back. "I'm just trying to make a little conversation here, have a nice evening with a lovely lady. At least, I thought you were."

"Oh, horse feathers," she spat. "You just want another one night stand."

The fact that this was exactly what he had in mind didn't help the situation. But he wasn't going to let *her* know that. "Lady, I don't know what put the bug up your ass—and I really don't think I want to know. But any idea I had about spending an evening with a beautiful woman just went up in smoke."

"Good! Because I'm not some groupie."

"I *never* treated you that way, sweetheart." He raised his

hand quickly, stilling any protest that was about to come out of her mouth. "Excuse me, *Joanna!*"

"No! You can call me Ms. Hayes."

He placed his glass on the bar and put his hands in his pockets. Something that would help him get control again and keep him from throttling her. He leaned into her, to make sure that no one could hear what he was about to say.

"Well, Ms. Hayes, if the truth be known, yes, I was attracted to you. And yes, maybe we'd have made love later. I wasn't really thinking that far ahead." He swallowed hard and pushed on. "But after your bullshit today, I wouldn't go to bed with you now if you were the last woman on the planet." He shot her a look that matched the earlier steel that she'd given him. "And quite frankly, if it wasn't for the children, I'd be out the door."

Her face was priceless as she sputtered, trying to say something even more ridiculous. "You...you...."

"You got me, darlin'. I believe in the children and I worked my ass off here for them. But I also did it because I was quite attracted to you. And no, it wasn't going to be a one-night stand!" He stood with his fists clenched in his pockets, his legs wide. "I had every intention of giving you my cell phone number, so you could call me when you wanted to. I was going to get your cell phone number so we could talk, get to know each other." He stepped back and took the check from his pocket. "But since you're so sure that I'm just out for a one-nighter, I'll just save you that embarrassment. If you'll excuse me...."

Thom slapped his check down on the bar, grabbed his half-drunk glass of club soda, and stormed off. To be honest—and he had to be—he was also embarrassed with himself; he'd been far too transparent and had just blown something. He knew it in his heart. She might be a handful, he thought to himself, but I could fall for that kind of handful. He looked ruefully down at the glass in his hand and dropped it on a table as he left.

4

THOM ROLLED OVER, pulling the covers with him as he did, and opened one bleary eye. According to the bedside clock, it was 7:30 in the bloody morning; that was too early for him to be awake and mentally functioning. The phone was ringing, a chirpy buzzy tone that was flat out annoying. He groaned, closed the eye, and slapped around on the bedside table, finally grasping the handset. He pulled it to his ear and grunted.

"Good morning to you too, sunshine. Did I wake you up?"

"Don't worry about it, I had to get up to answer the phone anyway," he grumbled into the handset.

Malcolm was far too cheerful, his laugh barking through the phone like a seal. Thom was sorely tempted to slam the damned handset down and throw the phone across the room. But that required too much energy and he still wasn't fully awake yet. He growled again.

Malcolm could be a real pain in the ass but he wasn't stupid. The laughing stopped and his tone was immediately conciliatory. "I'm sorry, Thommy, but I had to call you. Make sure you got checked in okay. Make sure everything was cool."

Thom rolled over and sat up, pulling the sheets over his naked middle. There was no one in the room to notice but it was an old habit. He'd always slept in the nude, even as a child.

All throughout school, college, his career, and two marriages, he'd shucked his clothes to go to bed and he wasn't about to change now. However, he usually had someone coming into the room to straighten it or read his schedule for the day. Far from being a prude, he was more concerned that the other party—usually Malcolm—would be uncomfortable. Malcolm never said a word, although *his* assistant had a tendency to blush. But she was a former nun. It was to be expected.

"I'm fine, Mal. Just tired."

"How's the room? You get checked in okay?"

"Jared is checked in just fine, thanks," Thom answered.

Jared Thomas was Thom's cover name for what he called his "off duty time." If he had to fly commercial, if he was on vacation, if he needed to rent a car, or anytime he needed to travel incognito, all arrangements were made under that name. This time was no different. Malcolm had booked the hotel room under Jared's moniker and the hotel manager greeted him with a wink. The only folks here that were aware of the deception were the hotel staff. He'd stayed at the Washington Hotel so many times that they were well aware of his alias and kept it quiet.

"Good," Malcolm said. "Did you sleep okay?"

"I guess," Thom answered, still struggling to kick his brain into alert.

Malcolm was quiet for a moment or two before asking, "The dream again?"

"Yeah." Thom rubbed his eyes, trying to focus them. "Again."

"Thom...."

"Mal, I don't want to worry about it, okay? Just let it go."

"Okay." Mal prudently went on to a different area of

conversation. "So. Whatcha got planned for today?"

"Oh, hadn't made up my mind about today." He stretched, feeling every muscle tighten and then relax, every joint popping comfortably, which refreshed him into full coherence. "But I'm definitely gonna score a hiking guide and check out some of the trails around here before I leave. Maybe go up a few east trails before I hit Wilde."

"That sounds lovely. I wish I could be there."

"What's stopping you?" Thom asked, feeling a little more charitable now that he was fully awake. "You need a little 'R and R' too, you know."

"Think so?"

"I know so," he assured Mal. "You're my manager, but you're my friend, too. I care. Come on, what do you say?"

Malcolm hesitated before he answered. "Yeah, sure. Okay. Give me a day or two to get loose ends tied up. I'm in the middle of something, something big. Something that'll help your career. Then, I'll be there."

Thom smiled. It would be good to have a friend with him. He hated being alone almost as much as he hated being bored. "Well, I think I'll head on down for breakfast then. Check out the golf course today, maybe have a go at eighteen holes."

"You do that, my friend," Malcolm said, chuckling. "Get some shopping in."

Thom laughed along. "Sure. I need some new ugly shirts."

He could almost see Malcolm grimacing. Thom's collection of tacky Hawaiian shirts and colorful sweaters were notorious in the music industry. Some had geometric designs in bizarre color combinations; some had day-glow colors. A few looked as if they'd come from some poor man's *Hawaii Five-O* wardrobe.

It was a given that during any review of a show, the reviewer would make some comment about what Thom was wearing. What started out as a wardrobe choice turned into a game with the press. And a love of shopping on Thom's part.

"Do me a favor, Thommy."

"Depends on the favor."

"Just find a sexy little tart and have a tumble. The perfect cure for insomnia."

"No tumbles on this side, buddy," Thom answered. "I don't need the entanglements, thank you. Just rest. Hiking. And eighteen holes. That's all I need."

But that was a bit of a lie, really. Joanna Hayes had gotten under his skin and he *needed* her. That fiery temper, the smell of her perfume. He wanted to feel that red hair draped over his groin, his thighs. She'd gotten under his skin as deep and as sure as if she'd been a chigger. But there was no cure for that particular itch and, for once, a substitute wasn't going to scratch it either. He really meant what he said; the best thing to do was to forget her as best as he could.

His belly rumbled and he figured that, as long as he was awake, he might as well go get something to eat. He showered and changed into a pair of slacks and a polo shirt, then left the room. He got off the elevator at the ground floor and turned for the dining room. He wasn't really watching where he was going when the man ran into him. The force of the blow bounced him into a sideboard, bruising his hip and narrowly missing his crotch. He turned around to protest to the hastily departing figure of a dark haired, somewhat stocky man. But before Thom could say anything, the man turned a corner and was gone.

Shake it off, Thom. Just some tourist. No big deal. He rubbed the place on his hip until the pain had subsided into a slight thudding ache and went on into the dining room. The place was huge and stunning, and this time, when he ran into the person, he made sure he stopped. Until he got a good look at the person, and it turned out to be *her!*

The shocked look on her face was priceless. "*YOU!* Oh God, tell me I'm dreaming. Oh hell, not *you!*"

He was just as stunned, if not a little secretly pleased. "Hello again, Ms. Hayes."

She turned red, jerking out of his grasp. "Are you following me?"

"Ms. Hayes, I promise you, I'm not," he answered. "If I were going to follow someone, it would a person with class."

"Go to hell!"

Thom felt the twinge. He took a deep breath, held up his hand in conciliation, and tried again. "Look. Ms. Hayes. I'm sorry for the way I acted back in Nashville. It was rude and boorish, and I was completely out of line."

Her anger seemed to dim a little. "Completely."

Thom gave his best smile, hoping it would pour oil on the troubled waters. "Well not *completely* completely. I meant what I said about you being a very lovely lady."

She had a suspicious glare.

"Look, Joanna." He shifted a little on his feet, rubbing the back of his neck. "I am sorry if I came across like a jerk. I was out of line and I hope you can accept my apology." He looked into her eyes, trying to find something in there. Something that meant he had a chance to make it up to her. "Please. I promise, no funny stuff, no monkey business. Can we just have breakfast and talk?"

She seemed to relax at that and a small smile appeared on

her lips. Thom waited while she worked out what she was going to say to him.

"I guess I owe you an apology too. I'm sure you think I'm some kind of...I mean...." She sighed heavily. "You must think I'm totally deranged."

"I never thought so," he answered. "I still don't."

"You should, you know," she told him. "I owe you an explanation for all of that."

"Only if you want to." He grinned at her. "Over breakfast?"

"I've eaten already."

"Then just sit with me. Please?"

She answered right away, her smile dazzling and very genuine. "All right. Sure."

He led the way to the table, pulling the chair out for her.

"Thanks...Thom."

He sat down next to her. "I have to tell you, I was a bit confused."

"I know, and I'm sorry for that." She looked so downcast and he was willing to bet it wasn't a look she wore that often.

"Want to tell me?" he asked.

She nodded. "Yeah. See my boss is...uh, well, he's okay to work for. I mean that. It's just that, sometimes he can be a real chauvinist pig."

Thom laughed and waved in the direction of the server. "I know what you mean."

"No, you don't," she told him. "See, when he told me I was arranging the whole concert and party, he made a few rather rude suggestions."

"Like what?"

"He told me to use my feminine wiles and, uh...." She made

air quotation marks with her fingers as she added, "Be friendly."

Thom did a double take. It wasn't that he'd never heard of such a thing; he got it all the time in his line of work. The "friendly" types were all over. He just hadn't expected it at a charity event. It finally dawned on him what had sent her over the edge.

"So when I said I knew you'd take care of me, and—"

"I thought he'd said something to you and you were expecting me to—"

"Take care of my needs *that* way."

She nodded, looking more than a little sheepish. "Yeah. See, I think you're very attractive, too. But I'm not a groupie. And I don't sleep around just because my boss says I have to, so that I can keep my job."

He desperately wanted to take her hand in his. He really did understand, and he wanted her to know that. But how to tell her. "Tell you what," he finally said to her. "How about I call him and tell him you took care of my needs just fine and we'll just let him work his ass off trying to figure out what that means."

That did it; that broke the ice. Her face lit up, the blue eyes began to twinkle, and she broke out into the most delicious giggles he'd ever heard. They were almost musical the way they rose and fell in something close to a perfect musical scale. He laughed along with her; he'd mended the breach.

The polite cough to one side caught their attention.

"Well, hello there," he said, grinning broadly.

"Hi, I'm Missy and I'll be your server." Missy was blonde with green eyes and a very sweet smile. She was tinier, more petite than Joanna.

He winked at her. "Well, good, Missy. I think we're about

ready. I'll be the only one eating." He turned to Joanna. "Unless I can entice you with some of their famous streusel coffee cake? A lovely blueberry muffin? Made with blueberries from right here on the mountain?"

Joanna nodded, still smiling. "You sold me. Sure."

Thom ordered his breakfast and a treat for her. Missy wrote it all down and promised to be right back with their coffee and orange juice. She scurried off and left them alone again.

"So...." It was a rather lame beginning to the conversation but he honestly didn't know where else to start. "You're staying here too, are you?"

She sat back, smoothing the cloth napkin over her lap with graceful hands like butterflies over the material. "Yeah, all thanks to Larry Micarello for arranging his charity soiree. The law firm is picking up the tab."

"Ever been here before?" he asked her.

"Nope. First time. You?"

He gave his best professional smile. "I love this hotel. Great place to hide."

"Ah. You come here a lot?"

"Oh sure," he bragged. "They love me here. I even stayed here after a show once. They know how to treat a guy."

Her face pinched up again. "I'm sure they do. Unfortunately, I'm just a lowly attorney, so I wouldn't know about the pop star treatment."

He stopped, shaking his head. "I don't believe this. I'm doing it again."

"Doing *what* again?"

For a change, he dropped all of his usual celebrity façade. It just didn't feel right with her and all it did was irritate her.

And maybe that's a good thing. Anyone else but her. She deserves better. "I'm trying to impress you," he said honestly. "You said you didn't know anything about me or my music and uh...."

The expression in her eyes changed. "And what?"

"Well, it hurt. It wounded my ego. But at the same time, it was okay. Because it meant you'd be honest with me, not tell me a lot of sh— I mean, tell me what I want to hear because of who I was. Who I am."

She put a hand on his arm and it felt both electrical and calming. "I'll tell you a secret, if you think your ego can handle it."

He nodded. First, she winked at him. Then, she leaned in to whisper to him and he leaned in to hear her.

"I really don't listen to the radio all that much. If it's not Shubert or Sibelius, I'm afraid I'm an idiot about music."

He covered her hand in his. "That's okay. It means I can just be me."

"And who is 'me?'" she asked him. Her eyes seemed to be penetrating deep into his soul, looking to find him.

"My real name is Jared—Jared Thomas Mitchell," he confessed, not even knowing why. Something about her made him open his mouth and let his life spill out on the table. "Thom Mitchell is just my stage name."

She pulled the hand from his arm and stuck it out before her. When he took it in his, the grip was inviting and gentle. It took him a moment to realize, they were both smiling at each other.

"Well, Jared Thomas Mitchell," she said. "Let's just start all over. And I'm right pleased to make your acquaintance. My name is Joanna Catherine Hayes."

This time, he did something smart. He just shook her hand. "Very pleased to meet you, Joanna Catherine Hayes."

Missy arrived with a large tray and set it on the table next to them. She served up the food as the conversation continued.

"So, what are you planning on today?" Joanna asked.

"I was thinking about some golf. They've got a great course around here. So, eighteen holes and beautiful sunshine."

"Well, that sounds like a full day."

He laughed. "The only kind I like. What about you?"

Joanna took a nibble from her muffin. "Mmm, this is really good." She picked up the knife by her plate and added a small amount of butter to the warm muffin. "Well, I was thinking about some shopping. Do you know anything about the stores around here?"

"I don't normally come here to shop," he answered, smiling. "But I could do with a little bit, myself. What are you looking for?"

"Oh, something that will remind me of the place. I promised myself to do souvenir and knick-knack shopping while I was here." She sat back as Missy set the cups and coffee carafe down between them. "I don't know anything about the area."

"Oh, I can help you with that," Missy broke in. "I know all the really wicked craft shops in the area. If you want, I can write down the names for you."

"I think that would be great, Missy," Joanna said. "I should be able to find my way around then."

Missy poured the coffee and left them again.

Before he had even thought about it, the words were out of his mouth. "Would you like an escort?" He watched her face, nervously hoping she wouldn't shoot him down. "I'd be glad to volunteer."

She smiled, the coffee cup poised halfway to her beautiful mouth. "Yes, that would be lovely. Thank you."

He felt his insides light up, warm and full, as he basked in the warmth of that smile. "Good, then. After breakfast, we'll go shopping."

"What about your golf game?"

Thom shrugged. "I can golf later. Or tomorrow. I don't get to escort lovely ladies shopping very often." He winked at her. "Besides, you'll need someone to carry the bags for you."

She winked back at him. "We'll see."

"Mr. Mitchell?"

They both turned around to see Missy standing with the paper held out.

He flashed a toothy smile at the young lady. "Darlin', all my friends call me Thom. You are now officially a friend."

Joanna was alternately amused and annoyed to see the girl blush a pretty crimson as she handed him the paper.

"Um, these are all the best craft shops in the area, some of them right here in Carroll," Missy told him. "If you need anything else—"

"As a matter of fact...." Thom turned back to Joanna. "Do you hike?"

"Me?"

"Yes, you."

"Um, well," she started. "To be honest, I like to walk but I don't know that I'd call that hiking."

"Missy, darlin', any shops in town where I can get some gear? Maybe find a guide?"

Missy laughed, her eyes practically sparkling at that. "You

forget where you are. This is a hiking Mecca. I know a great shop with all of the latest gear."

"You do?"

"Sure," she exclaimed. "It's called *The Mind of God*. Great little shop. They sell everything you could want for hiking and climbing. Rappelling ropes and cleats, carabiners, shoes, backpacks, all the goodies. You'll love it. I can give you the address, too."

"Great. They know any guides?"

"Oh sure," came the chipper reply. "My boyfriend Walt. He's a hiking guide, the best in the business. Knows every peak in the area."

He thrust the paper back to her, winking as he did. "Give me the name, the address, and the number, darlin'."

Missy wrote the information on the back of the paper. With a shy smile, she handed him the paper again, took off to go back to her work.

"You mind, Joanna?"

She crooked an eyebrow at him. "Not at all. I'm intrigued now."

He paused for a moment, cocking his head. She was just watching him, a half smile on her face. After a moment, she shook her head.

"What?" he asked, truly baffled. "What is it?"

She shook her head again. "You. Nothing, never mind." She smiled again. "Let's go shopping, sir."

He took her arm, leading her on the way. And then stopped. She stopped with him; this time, both of her eyebrows rose in question.

"Jo, uh… " He faltered around for the words. It was a bit of an embarrassment to ask the next question but he was going to be forced to do so.

She watched him, never once laughing at his obvious discomfort. "Thom?"

He sighed and bit the bullet. "You, uh...you mind driving?"

She laughed with that musical giggle of hers. "You didn't bring a car?"

He grinned and shrugged. "Didn't really plan on going anywhere that I needed a car. If I needed to, I was going to hire a limo. Besides, I don't drive."

"You don't drive?" she asked, her eyebrows practically meeting her hairline.

"Nope. I don't."

"Why?"

Thom put his elbow out instead, inviting the lady to take it. "Come on, we can talk about that another time. The shops await the fair lady and her beast of burden."

The conversation made itself—nothing deep and penetrating, they were just two people vacationing in the same place and enjoying the time together. Thom signed the check and they made their way out of the dining room.

Neither of them saw the dark haired man get up behind them and follow them out.

5

"You're joking, right?" Joanna plucked the sweater out of his hands. "You can't be serious about this."

Thom burst out laughing and took it right back. It had to be one of the ugliest things he'd ever seen in his life. And it was perfect! "I'm real serious about this one," he managed to blurt out between his spate of giggles. "This is great!"

She groaned, rolled her eyes, and shook her head. "Thom, it's...wow. I've seen loud in my time but that takes the cake. No one will hear your music over that scarlet and violet monstrosity."

He restrained himself from an obscene remark and blew a raspberry instead. "I like it. I'm going to get it."

She snatched it out of his hands one more time. "Give me a break. Please tell me you're not that big of a fashion idiot. This is just flat out ugly."

Thom stared at her, his fists shoved into his pockets and his fingertips digging into his palms. How could one woman be so brilliant and so obtuse in the same breath?

It took her a moment before she realized that he wasn't answering. She stopped in the act of tossing the sweater back onto the heap. "What?"

"I am *not* an idiot," he fumed. "And I resent you treating me like a child. It's *my* goddamn wardrobe and I'll wear what I like.

Now give me that goddamn sweater!"

Her cheeks pinked at that and her lips compressed together. "Fine! If you want to look like a reject from a pack of playing cards, it's your career." She threw the sweater at him and turned to stomp out.

"Shit!" he muttered under his breath and reached out for her arm. "Jo, wait."

She gave him a dirty look but she didn't pull her arm away. "What?"

Thom let go very quickly. He squirmed a bit on the inside, trying not to let his temper take control of his tongue. God, she did know how to bring it out of him, didn't she. "Look. I'm sorry. You're right; it's loud and it's ugly. But, it's a stage thing."

She had a wary look on her face as she asked him, "What do you mean?"

"See, I like to wear these kinds of shirts and sweaters on stage because they're really colorful and catch the light better. When folks are sitting in the back of the theater, sometimes that's all they can see—the color."

"Oh," she said, the angry red leaving her face.

"Besides, it's a bit of an idiom. It's what people expect, my ugly shirts."

She blushed again this time but for a different reason. "I am so embarrassed."

"Embarrassed? Why?"

"I just made a total ass of myself," she confessed. "And I...I'm sorry, Thom. You're right, you're a grown man, and you can choose your own clothes. I didn't know."

He took her hand in his and kissed the back of it. "Never heard of me, remember?" he asked with a grin. "I'm sorry I got snippy about it."

"I'll forgive you if you forgive me," she said, smiling at him.

"Done."

"But do me a favor, Thom. Pick another one?" She shook her head at the garment in his hand. "That one is just...well, let's just say there are 'ugly shirts' and there are '*ugly* shirts.' And that is just putrid."

"Okay, find me one," he told her and handed her the red and purple sweater.

"Deal," she answered. She refolded it and added it back to the pile.

She went digging through, meticulously looking at the patterns and colors of each one before turning around and showing him a geometric pattern done in maize, puce, and orange. It was perfect! He loved it. She cringed and laughed. He bought it anyway. Everything was healed and it was fine again. His heart was at peace.

It turned out that the clothing shop they were in was right across the street from the next shop that they wanted to visit. They stopped long enough to put everything in the back of her rented Saturn, then crossed the street and entered *The Mind of God*. The shop was everything and nothing like he thought; it was hiker's heaven with a bit of biking, climbing, and running thrown in to match. From the moment he walked in, it felt like home. The only thing stopping it from being perfect was the lack of golfing equipment.

He managed to zone out, looking at everything. Picking up things that piqued his interest. For a moment, he'd forgotten her. Until he heard her speaking at his side.

"What's that?" she asked, holding something in her hand as

she turned it over a few times in her palm.

He held out his hand and she gave it to him. "This? This is a carabiner."

Joanna leaned over his arm, staring at the metal object in his hand. "So, what does that do?"

Thom held it up again for her, demonstrating as he talked. "This is mostly used in climbing. You use one of these to hold your ropes. See? You wrap the rope around this and it'll pay out slowly. You can also use it to hold your other equipment-hooks and such. Clip this to your belt—" He clasped it to a loop of her jeans. "—and there you go."

"Cool."

"And this." He picked up a small device, the size of a wristwatch. He turned it around in his hands. "I'd say this was a GPS but it's too small."

"The miracles of modern technology, my friend," said someone standing behind them. "Nothing like a silicon chip the size of a pinhead. Stick that in your pocket and I can pick you up all over the state. With a satellite, all over the world."

Thom and Joanna turned quickly, in time to see the tall man standing behind them. His black hair was glossy, curls tendriled around his face and shoulders.

"Hi," the new guy said. "I'm Walt. How can I help you?"

"Oh good." Joanna turned back to Thom. "Didn't you say Missy told you to look for a Walt?"

"Oh yeah, she said you'd be in. You must be Thom Mitchell."

Thom smiled and nodded. Before he could do no more than turn around, Joanna had jumped in. Hand extended, she breezed into her own introduction.

"I'm Joanna. But you can call me Jo."

Walt was a little bit *too* friendly when he took her hand. "Nice to meet y—"

"Excuse me," Thom broke in, getting back to the point. He was here for a professional, not a buddy. "I'm interested in some hiking gear for me and the lady here."

Walt nodded, seeming to understand. "I think I can hook you up fine. You know what peaks you want to hit around here?"

"Well, just me, I'm thinking of Washington, maybe some of the northern presidents," Thom answered, thoughtfully. "If I've got a good guide, I really want to try out Wilde."

Walt whistled through his teeth. "You *are* a brave man. Why Wilde?"

Thom shrugged. He'd asked himself that question more than a few times. "It's a challenge and a personal goal. I've always wanted to climb that one."

Walt looked a bit dubious at the idea. "You do know the stories about Wilde, right? I don't mean the legends, I mean the news stories."

Thom bristled; this Walt guy was second-guessing him in front of the lady. "Yes, I know all about Wilde—"

"Wait," Joanna interrupted. "What's wrong with that one?"

"That's a tough one," Walt explained. "Wilde has claimed quite a few lives of some pretty experienced hikers and climbers. Isolated, very rough terrain and nasty cliffs. It's not for a beginner."

"I'm not a beginner," Thom grumbled. He stopped himself from making another scathing remark. This Walt kid was just trying to be helpful. "I'm sorry, Walt," he said. "That didn't come out right. What I mean is I've done some rock climbing as well as hiking some major peaks in the country. I've climbed the Rockies both in the US and in Canada, hiked some of the presidents."

"Then, it sounds like you know what you're doing. That's great. Especially if you want to head up Wilde. It's just my job, you know? Make sure my customers are equal to the job. I'm sorry if I insulted you."

Thom flashed his famous grin in answer. "No insult taken, don't worry about it."

Joanna had a puzzled look on her face. "So, Wilde is...."

"Wilde Mountain is full of hundred foot drops from some steep cliffs," Walt explained to her. "See, trails are ranked so you know what you're getting into. There's the easy ones like Crawford and Jewel. Easy because you don't need a lot of experience or endurance training. Mostly mud and stair-step trails, easily marked."

Thom jumped in, feeling the spotlight drifting away from him. "Wilde Mountain is ranked difficult," he interrupted, savoring the taste of Walt's surprised look. "It's got a lot of forty-five and fifty degree inclines. In some cases, a sheer rock wall or two that you'll need the ropes and cleats for."

"Cleats?" she asked. "Like what's on your shoes?"

"No," Walt answered with a chuckle. "Cleats are what you hammer into the rock face. They hold your weight and help you climb." To Thom, he asked, "Are you rope trained?"

Thom crossed his arms over his chest, rocking on the balls of his feet. "Absolutely," he bragged.

"Good then." Walt smiled and clapped his hands together. "What do you folks need?"

"Well, we're not going climbing, but we *are* planning on some hiking." Thom put his arm around Joanna's waist. "I've brought all of *my* gear. But the lady needs some."

"Cool." Walt looked back at Joanna. "Have you ever done any hiking?"

"Oh sure," she said, just a little too quickly. "Yeah, I've uh...I've done some walking. I go with friends to a nature preserve down around Nashville.

Thom held his tongue and let Walt handle this one.

Walt just nodded. "Well, that's not quite the same thing but it's still a pretty good way to go. So let's get you set up here. You need shoes to start, I bet."

She smiled warmly at the younger man. "Got it first try." She looked down at the deck shoes that she wore. "These are all I have with me and Thom says they are definitely *not* trail worthy."

Walt nodded, looking down as well. "Nope. Those are great for a boat, but lousy on the trails." He grinned. "What size do you wear?"

"I wear an eight and a half, medium."

"Great. I got a few pairs that I think you'll love. Be right back."

Walt went off to a back room, leaving the two of them alone.

"So, maybe some clothes?" she asked.

Thom turned back, momentarily confused. "Hmm?"

Joanna put her hand on Thom's elbow. "Clothes. I take it the dinner outfits I bought won't work any better than my shoes?"

Thom smiled and winked. "I think some hiking clothes would be a good idea. At some of these altitudes, it gets windy and cold. You need some layers to wick away the sweat and keep you dry."

"Okay," she cheerfully agreed. "You're the expert. Show me what I need."

Thom plucked a few pairs of hiking shorts and some shirts, helping her to choose at least three outfits. They took them to the register area and made a pile.

"Here we are." Walt crossed over to a bench and gestured with one hand. "Ma'am, if you'll come sit here."

"Just call me Jo," she said. She sat down on the bench and had her shoe off in a flash. "This is my bigger foot, use this one."

Walt slipped one of the boots over the thin sock and up over the heel. Thom felt a twinge at the familiar way this Walt guy was touching her ankle, easing the foot into the hiking boot. It was the guy's job but *he* should be doing that.

A female voice interrupted his reverie. "What do you think?"

Thom blinked a few times, clearing the thought away. *Don't be an idiot.* "What?"

"The boots, Thom," Joanna reminded him, pointing at her foot. "What do you think?"

"Uh, they, uh, they look great. But you need to walk around a bit. Get a feel for them."

"Listen, you really need to try those on with the socks you're going to wear," Walt told her. "And I've got a great pair for you. Keep your feet from blistering, wick the sweat away so you can walk in comfort. Shoes are great but socks make the rest of it."

"All right."

Walt stepped away to another display. Thom came over to join her, carrying another pair of boots. He'd found a pair that were like his, a brand that he thought was more comfortable than the ones Walt was showing her.

"I like these better."

She looked up at him. "You think so? I like them too. But he said these are a sturdier boot."

He said, he said. Shit, like I'm some idiot off the street. "Well, see which pair feels better on your foot."

She reached out for the boots Thom had. "Okay, I'll try these, too."

Walt returned at that moment with a thick pair of grey socks. "Here, try these," Walt said, handing them to her.

She did as she was told, talking as she did. "Oh, Thom, why don't you ask him about the other thing while we're here?"

"Ask me?" Walt turned around towards Thom. "Ask me what?"

"Oh, uh, nothing."

"Oh stop that." To Walt, she said, "Thom's looking for a guide for *us*. I know he's asked you to take him up Wilde, but I've never done anything like this before. And I trust him but I'd sure feel a whole lot better if I had two of you to keep me safe. Thom, would you mind?"

What a way to put him on the spot. But she was right. "No, not at all." To Walt, he said, "She's right. You know what you're doing and we'd be a lot better off with a guide. And these trails aren't all marked. I could get us lost."

Walt nodded. He smiled at Thom. "I'll be glad to. To tell you the truth, I need a break from this place. I need the great outdoors. I don't get nearly the amount of hiking time I love."

That settled that, then. "You available to take me up Wilde?"

"Sure am." Walt stood up. "I've been up there a few times and I'm a certified guide. And for you and Jo, I can get you through some really nice trails that won't be too tough for a beginner, get you some great photo ops if you like that."

"That would be great." Thom grinned broadly at the suggestion. "I brought the camera, in case I see some wild life up there."

"You'll see plenty where I'll take you," Walt told him.

Thom was pleased with the transaction. "Good, you're hired, then."

"Great," Walt said. "How about tomorrow? And we can start with Crawford Path. It's a pretty easy trail compared to the rest of them. We can take the part that heads up Pierce. I think your lady can handle that one very well."

Thom shook hands with the young man and they agreed on a time to leave. Jo took the boots that Walt had picked out but she was going to wear the clothes that Thom chose for her. All in all, he had the better end of that bargain and that made Thom very happy. They bought the trail mix, clothes, shoes, socks, and everything they'd need, and then headed back for the Hotel.

6

THE DARK HAIRED man sat hunched over in the front seat and stared out the window as the couple crossed the street. As soon as they went into the shop, he pulled the cell phone out of his pocket and dialed the number. A gravelly voice answered.

"Hey, it's me," he muttered.

He gave a brief recap of where the couple had been for the morning, ending in where they were right now.

"There's a chick with him?" the gravelly voice asked.

"Yeah. Does it change anything?"

"No. Just gives us another witness but as long as we're careful and she don't see us to identify us, it'll be cool. All she can tell the cops is that we took his sorry ass."

The dark haired man grunted his understanding. "So? What do you want me to do now?"

"Nothing. Just follow. Ross hasn't given the word yet. Until he does, we just follow and keep track of the asshole's trail. You dig?"

"Whatever. It's just stupid. We should be *doing* something instead o' sitting with our thumbs up our asses."

"Just do what I tell ya, okay?"

"Whatever," the dark man answered. "We're getting paid, right?"

"Right."

"Then I'll follow."

He did exactly what he was told, waiting until they came out of the shop and then, following them back to the hotel. This was going to be a hell of a payday.

7

"I CAN'T DO THIS. I can't."

Thom was behind her, encouraging her and being as supportive as he could. "Come on, Joanna. You can. Just a little further, then we can sit and have lunch. I promise. Just a little further. You can do this, darlin'."

She was huffing and puffing but she wasn't stopping. Even with every muscle in her body screaming, every joint feeling like ground glass held together with baling wire. She was to the point of feeling her heartbeat pounding in her toes. She was only half-joking when she said, "You're a sadist, Walt! You know that, don't you? A real sadist."

Walt laughed, a full throated, deep laugh that was so different from Thom's. "Come on, you can do this. Like the man said, just a little bit further."

"Jo, honey, I'm right here," Thom said, giving her back a pat and the slightest little nudge to help. "Another fifteen feet. Come on, we're almost there.

She was pouty but she was going. "You're both sadists! You lied to me, Walt. You said this was an easy one!"

They'd had to fight her at first. She'd tried to bring a few bottles of soda, but Walt tossed those fast. "They'll dehydrate you," he had told her. "You need water." She'd wanted to bring candy too and both men had to convince her that candy was just empty calories. She was going to need something a lot more substantial. Thom had made sure she brought the trail mix and protein bars that they'd bought instead.

Walt had brought these backpack sort of things that he called camelbacks, one for each of them. He helped them fill the bladders with water and store them in their packs, clipping the hoses conveniently to their shirts so they could slurp as they walked. He had also brought along three of what he called his 'famous peanut butter and banana sandwiches on whole-wheat honey bread.' They had enough food and water, but he'd brought a filter and iodine drops for that *just in case* scenario. They'd be passing a few ponds on the way, he said, plenty of places if they needed a refill of fluid. He'd also packed his GPS device in the front pocket of his pack. Always better to be safe than sorry, he'd told them, and he'd be prepared.

"Come on, Jo," Walt called out to her. "You're almost here. And it's gorgeous. Wait 'til you get here. Come on. Come see."

"Any place to sit?" Thom asked.

"Yup," he answered. "There's a flat place up here, with some rocks to sit on. We can sit and eat and rest."

For something that was working her to the point of pain, it had been an amazingly beautiful walk. She was a city girl, not used to the open spaces and fresh air that she found on this hike. And there was plenty of it. There was no hint of car exhaust or the crowd of bodies packed tightly together. Here, the air smelled sweet and pure, with the scent of the pines and aspens, the occasional smell of an animal. The only things close to her were the two men she was with, the trees, and the blue, clear sky. And the view.

They'd taken a path that meandered, up and down over a hard packed ground. The ground was carpeted with wild flowers of such beauty. Pink, white, and violet petals bloomed up around her, some so delicate and small that they looked as if they shouldn't be there at all. In the distance, she could see the rest of the mountain range looming up as far as the eye could see. Great, huge tops that looked misty in the distance but still had character and strength, the trees melting into a cover of dull green, navy, and purple. The clouds danced over the tops of some of them, dressing them in white gauze.

With a deep sigh, she pulled herself up by the proverbial bootstraps and renewed her effort. Thom put a hand under her elbow and they made it up over the small rise to the summit. True to his word, Walt had found a place where they could sit and relax, mostly rocks and scrub, but there was shade provided by some of the taller boulders of granite, huge grey things that had to weigh an easy ton or more. They were cool to the touch and the shade was glorious.

Jo dropped more than sat, with both Walt and Thom helping her down. They doled out the food and began eating in silence. She took in a lungful of the cool air, leaning against the smooth surface. Her feet throbbed in time with her heart, the slight pain in her knees starting to get more and more uncomfortable. "Good grief. And you two *enjoy* this?"

Walt chuckled. "You get used to it after a while. Keep walking and you build up stamina. Besides, it's amazing out here."

"Yes it is," Thom agreed. "I've never climbed this particular peak before. The scenery is incredible."

She could see the mountains more distinctly now. There were a few, much closer to them, which teemed with life as the birds flew in and out of the trees. She could hear the sounds of wildlife off in the distance, the sound of one coyote calling to another. There were other animal calls, sounds she couldn't identify any more than she could name the flowers in the grass. But it didn't matter; the beauty was still the same.

"It is that," she reluctantly replied. "But good grief, I'm frying here. I'm hot and my knees are killing me."

Walt reached into his backpack and pulled out a couple of plastic bundles. "Here, you'll want to use these."

"What are those?"

"Collapsible poles." With a flick of his wrist, he had one extended. "You use these to walk with. Takes a lot of the pressure off your knees by giving you something to balance with. You can use these to probe the ground ahead and make sure it's stable. You can lean on them coming down and it helps keep your knees from absorbing the shock."

She gave him a dubious look.

Fortunately, Thom confirmed what the younger man had told her. "It does, darlin'; trust him on that. That's why we're both carrying one."

"I don't want to carry anything," she insisted stubbornly. "I like having my hands free."

"I'm sure you do, Jo," Walt answered. "And these are collapsible; so when we're on a flat and level ground, you can put them in your pocket or pack. But we're not right now. We're going up and down some swells. These can be your best friend."

She thought about it for a moment. Her eyes met Thom's, receiving a nod of his head. With that, she shrugged and held her hand out.

Walt grinned. "Good girl. Here." He had already folded the stick back on itself, handing her the bundle. "You put that in your pocket. But I bet you'll be using it soon enough. You'll see the difference."

She nodded. "Thanks, Walt. I know you're just taking care of us." She went back to nibbling her sandwich. She was more thirsty than hungry but since he'd gone out of his way to make the sandwiches, she didn't have it in her to refuse hers. She didn't want to insult him.

Thom had polished off his and was working on a bag of the trail mix, looking around in a state of awe. "I'd forgotten how wild and free it is up here."

"Yeah, I think so too." Walt gestured off in the distance. "Now, if you want, I can lead you out there on some of the really wicked peaks. Those have some great scenery if you've got a camera." With a sideways glance at Jo, he added, "But they're not for the beginner, I'll be up front about that."

She held up her hands in mock surrender, still a bit grumpy. "Not me, babe. I'll enjoy the pictures he takes. I can't believe you said this was an easy trail."

"I'm sorry, Jo. Compared to the others, it really is." Walt smiled at her. "Hey, you said you'd done some serious walking around your area and I figured you could handle it. And you *are* handling it. I'm impressed."

Thom put a hand on her knee. "You're doing just fine for your first, Joanna. I'm very proud of you."

She felt the glow rising on her cheeks and grinned broadly at both men. What the hell; if they thought she was doing so well, who was she to argue. She took another sip of water, shaded her eyes, and looked over to Walt. "Hey, can I ask you something?"

He shrugged with a smile and nodded at her. "Sure. Ask away."

"Your shop. The name, *Mind of God*. Where did that come from?"

Thom smiled at her. "I was curious about that myself." He turned to Walt. "But I think I know."

Walt grinned back. "I bet you do." To Jo, he said, "Well, my partner and I are both serious hikers. When we decided to open the place, we got the name from an old saying around here."

She tilted her head in question. "Old saying?"

"Yeah. The saying goes, *to walk in the mountains is to walk in the mind of God.*" He rocked back on his heels, crouching as he pointed out in the distance. "Only God could make this kind of beauty and walking up here makes me feel like I can understand why he would want it like this. To know creation and the beauty of it. To feel the love of nature. The mind of God."

"It is beautiful here," she said, relishing the whole of it all. The food tasted better, the air smelled better. For that moment, she could understand it herself. This had to be what God felt like, knowing that he had created it all. Knowing the splendor and the grandeur. "Mind of God." She nodded. "Makes sense to me."

They didn't talk much on the rest of the hike. Walt slowed them down to match her pace, so it took a while to finish the last four miles of trail. By the time they hit the parking lot again, Joanna felt like she was going to cry from the exhaustion but she was smiling too—she'd done it; she'd done the whole eight miles. She'd also used the poles Walt had given her. When she handed them back to him, she did so with a great deal of gratitude. "You're right," she said to him. "They did help."

He winked at her as he took them back. "Hey, I'll never steer you wrong."

"Missy was right about you," she told him.

"Oh?"

"You *are* a nice guy." Jo eased into his SUV and heaved a deep sigh of relief at *finally* being off her feet. She gave him a weary smile. "And to think I'm used to power shopping on the weekends.

Walt dropped them off at the turnaround. Thom paid him in cash for the outing and the rest of the gear Walt had brought along for them. Jo managed to gingerly get out of the SUV. She was in more pain that she could ever have imagined; everything was sore and tight but it was a good feeling. If anyone had told her that she'd be climbing mountain peaks like a billy goat, she'd have told them to piss off. And here, she'd just climbed one. She could handle that kind of pain.

Thom helped Walt unpack their gear as she watched. Watching him, she felt an overwhelming sense of absolute admiration. He might be a monumental pain in the derriere, stubborn, know-it-all, and, occasionally, full of himself— but damned if he wasn't the most charming man she'd ever met. Thom had kept her going, kept giving her words of encouragement. Several times, he'd told Walt to slow down or stop so that she could rest. He'd taken care of her, never letting her give up.

He chose that moment to lean into the back of the SUV to reach something. Joanna noted, with a great deal of lusty satisfaction, that he had a truly marvelous backside—perfect globes filling his spandex hiking pants quite nicely. When he stood back up, she took stock of his back—perfectly muscled. For an older man, he was trim and in fantastic shape. That gorgeous ass, the well-toned legs, that sexy grin that made his whole face light up, those beautiful chocolate brown eyes—

Whoa, girl. You better stop that right now. Mr. Pop Star isn't interested in you! You're just a vacation distraction, nothing more.

That was too bad, because Thom Mitchell was just the kind of guy that she could get used to having around. Full of himself, pain in the butt, and all!

Thom gave the bellboy a tip and asked him to take the gear to his room. He turned the most gorgeous grin to Joanna and gave her his arm to use for support. "You all right there, lady?"

"My legs are never going to be the same," she told him as they started for the door to the lobby.

He laughed at that, but kept his hand under her elbow. "You know what you need, don't you?

"Do tell."

He grinned at her, his hand under her elbow. "Your room has one of those big old fashioned bathtubs? The claw foot kind? Deep and made for a long soak?"

She brightened at that. "Oh hell, yes. I totally forgot about that."

"Then, I recommend a long bath, followed by an excellent dinner tonight. My treat."

"What should I eat, oh, learned one?" she asked, acting the dutiful pupil.

He opened the door for her, helping her in. "I recommend a really good T-bone steak. With all the trimmings. If you don't mind an old fart for company."

She turned to face him, standing as close as she dared. Close enough to smell the spicy sent of his aftershave. "You're *definitely* on!"

"Thommy!"

They both pulled up short as a man came toward them,

grinning from ear to ear. She had time to note that he was taller than Thom was, dark haired and fuller in the chest. He looked like an athlete.

Thom had an even bigger grin on his face, leaving her to dash over to the guy. "Mal! You made it! I didn't expect you 'til this weekend."

"You think I'm gonna let you stay up here all by yourself? I got lonely."

Thom laughed heartily. "Can't have that now."

They reached each other at the same time, pulling each other into a hearty embrace. The man held Thom back, looking at him as he beamed.

"Coming or going?" the man asked.

Thom clapped him on the shoulder. "Just got back from a hike on the Crawford, went up Pierce."

"By yourself?"

At that point, Thom turned around to face her and held his hand out. Joanna forgot the pain and plastered a smile on her face. She stepped forward, still keeping her eyes on the other man but allowing Thom to pull her close until his hand was resting on her hip.

"Nope," Thom answered. "Malcolm, I'd like you to meet this lovely lady formally. I don't think you two got that chance at the fundraiser. This is Joanna Hayes."

She nodded at the man.

"Joanna, I want you to meet Malcolm, my dearest friend and manager"

"How do you do?" She held her hand out to Malcolm to offer him a handshake.

He took her hand and gave her a warm gracious smile.

Without warning, she sneezed several times in rapid-fire succession. What a time for her allergies to kick in. With a blush, she let go of his hand and pulled the tissue out of her pocket.

"Excuse me," she mumbled. She blew her nose in as close to a lady-like way as she could.

For his part, Thom's friend just chuckled and ignored it. "I'm very pleased to meet you, Joanna," he said. "I'm sorry I didn't have the pleasure the other night. Nice to see you and Thom have been getting...acquainted."

"More than that," Thom jumped in. "We've been doing some shopping and having a grand old time." He smiled at her and winked, then turned his attention back to his friend. "Tell you what. I'm gonna walk the lady to her room. How about I meet you back here and we can catch up over a cup of coffee in the dining room."

Thom's friend laughed, tossing his head back. "Sure, it's open?"

"If not there, then the hotel bar has coffee."

"Okay," the man answered. "I'll wait for you."

Thom took her hand again. "I'll be right back."

Thom's friend looked at her, the smile still on his lips. But there was something about his eyes—they didn't light up. As if the smile stopped at his nose. With a pleasant voice, he said to her, "I'm very pleased to meet you, Joanna."

"Likewise, uh...."

"Call me Mal," he said, the expression never changing.

"Mal, then," she answered and turned to follow Thom.

Thom led her slowly to the elevator and they stood waiting for it come down to the first floor.

"He seems nice."

"He is, darlin'. Me and Mal go way back; and I do mean *way* back." The doors opened and he led her in. He pushed the button and the doors closed on them. "Twenty-five years, as a matter of fact."

"Wow, that is a long time. You must have been a baby." She winked at him.

Thom laughed, his cheeks turning a bit pink. "Well, I'm really a bit older than he is, if you want the truth."

"You don't look it."

"Thanks."

They stepped off the elevator when they reached her floor.

"You know," she muttered, as they walked to her room. She was barely able to stumble by that time, everything from her hips down in pain. "You could at least have the decency to wince a little. Pretend that something hurts."

He chuckled at her, wrapping his arm around her waist again. "How do you know I don't hurt in places that men don't discuss in polite society?"

God, even her neck hurt. But she managed to give him a glare. "Like what?"

He did more than chuckle at her expression, which made her want to smack him. "My hips, darlin'. My hips and butt are sore. Better?"

She gave him a rather satisfied smile. "It's a start." It had to be true, she smugly thought; he was actually walking a little slower than he had been before. Maybe he was getting just as stiff as she was. *Good!*

"Listen, I want you to go get that soak, okay? And take some ibuprofen. The desk can get you some if you don't have any—"

"I have some in my purse."

He nodded. "Good. You take an extra tab or two to help. I'll call you for dinner."

When they got to her door, she handed him her key card and let him open it for her. She paused, tentatively placing her hand on his chest. "Thom?"

"Yeah?"

"Your friend is here and you want to spend some time with him." She leaned against the doorframe to hold herself up. "To tell you the truth, I'm really wiped out. I'm thinking of taking that bath and then just going to bed. Would you be terribly insulted?" She wasn't lying about that last part; she *was* exhausted. Right now, all she wanted was the ibuprofen, the bath, and the bed. And she'd be lucky to stay awake through that much.

But he looked very disappointed; it almost broke her heart when he asked plaintively, "What about dinner?"

"I'll get room service." She reached up and stroked his cheek. "Go on. You and your friend can have some guy time."

The smile was worth it, so different from Mal's smile. Thom's smile lit up his eyes, brightening his whole face. She stared into his eyes, basking in the way they seemed so deep and warm. His cheeks were pebbled with the stubble of his five-o-clock shadow, the lines highlighting his smile, crinkling in the corners of his eyes. His jaw was square and strong, the mouth sensual and full. His face was so friendly, so strong and handsome.

"You get some rest, Jo," he told her, stepping close enough that she could feel the warmth of his skin. "I'll call you in the morning."

"Yes. Please."

Afterward, she was never sure why she did it or where the bravado came from. It wasn't like her to do something so impulsive, so unabashedly romantic. He bent his head as he made to kiss her cheek. Time slowed to a crawl as she turned her face to meet his lips with hers. Neither one moved, letting the pressing of their lips be the only contact. It was soft and sweet, lingering and fulfilling. And when it finally ended, she felt as if his warmth had spread into her body.

The smile never left his lips; he said nothing more. He only kissed her on the forehead and watched her go inside. She closed the door and went to the tub with the memory of his kiss still on her lips.

8

TRUE TO HIS word, he called her the next morning. She wasn't quite as chipper as before but then, she'd probably just woke up. He suggested that she take another hot shower and more painkillers. He also suggested a game of golf. He didn't get the answer he expected.

"Excuse me, but are you insane?" Jo blurted out.

He stopped for a moment, actually staring at the receiver in his hand. He put the hand set back to his ear. "Uh, no, I don't think so. What, you don't like golf?"

She groaned in answer to that.

"Darlin', golf is like my religion. You can't hate golf!"

Jo started laughing. "You think this is because I hate golf?"

His question was tentative but the little stab wasn't. "Isn't it?"

She laughed hard, a slight harsh edge to the sound. "Thom! I'm in more pain than I can imagine and you're telling me to take another hot bath or shower. *Then,* you ask me if I want to play golf. You're totally deranged!"

He tightened up, feeling the fuse lit inside again. He stayed quiet, balling his free hand into a fist and trying not to snap at her.

"Thom?" When there was no answer, her tone changed. "Oh, Thom, that's not what I meant. No, I don't hate golf. I *like* golf. I do play."

He relaxed, feeling like a bit of an idiot. Once again, he'd jumped on the wrong bandwagon. "Sorry."

"No, *I'm* sorry," she added, laughing again. "I just hurt so badly; I don't know if I can walk a golf course."

This time, he was laughing with her but his laughter was more from relief than he wanted to let on. "Jo, trust me on this. You go take that shower, take some more ibuprofen, and we'll have some breakfast. Then, walking is just the thing you need. Get back up on that horse. It'll work the kinks and stiffness out. I promise."

It was funny, in a way, how they could push each other's buttons like that. Only one other woman had been able to do that to him, Angie. Angie could drive him absolutely insane, make him want to put his fist through a wall, and then distract him from whatever it was that had set him off to begin with. That distraction usually kept him from embarrassing himself or doing something stupid. Angie knew those buttons so well and he hated her for it. But God, how he had loved her. She knew him inside and out with an almost psychic connection. And she knew how to piss him off. They'd do it to each other, to get each other back for something said or done.

But, Jo just knew how to push the buttons, intentionally or not. She knew how to say the wrong thing at the wrong time and then make it all right again in the next breath. With Jo, it wasn't a revenge thing; it was just a Jo thing. She wasn't afraid to speak her mind, to say what she was thinking and damned be the consequences. She was a free spirit, he could tell. It had to be that red hair. Whatever. Didn't matter. She was wild and free, curvy in the right places, a smile that made him want to drop to the ground at her feet.

He wanted her. And it didn't matter one bit that he did. When the vacation was over, she was going back to her world and leaving his behind. She just wasn't interested in him. And that hurt.

After the walk to the course, she was complaining about her feet hurting. After yesterday's trip around Crawford Pass, he wasn't surprised. Thom insisted that they take a golf cart to shuttle around—she drove, at his request. He also talked her into a pair of shoes at the rental office; she was still wearing the same deck shoes.

"How can you play golf and not have shoes?" he teased.

"I wasn't planning on playing golf while I was here," she answered in that dry, matter of fact tone that he was beginning to understand as her 'I think you're missing the obvious here' voice. She pulled the three-iron out of her bag and set up her shot.

"Oh? What were the plans?"

She hit the ball squarely, sending it off the tee and out over the ground. While she watched it soar, she answered, "Well, I was going to read contracts, watch some TV, and maybe read a book or two. I don't know. I guess sleep a lot and rest some more." The ball bounced a few times, taking her onto the green. When it had landed solidly in a good position, she took her eyes off it. "What about you?"

"Oh, I planned on golfing," he answered. He picked up her tee and handed it to her, and set up his ball. "There's rest and then there's golf. And golf is the finest rest I know." He addressed the ball, setting his feet firmly in stance. With the driver in hand, he took a mighty swing and connected. Both tee and ball went sailing; the tee landed a few feet away from him.

The ball landed on the green, closer to the hole than hers did. He smiled and winked. "Except for hittin' the trails."

She nodded her head. "You know, except for being stiff and sore, I had a great time yesterday."

They walked back to the cart and put their clubs in the bags. Thom climbed into the passenger side of the cart, feeling the vehicle settle a bit with his weight. "Really?"

She sat down behind the wheel of the cart and flicked the switch to turn on the power. "Yeah, really," she answered, smiling.

He back in the seat, resting his arm behind her. "I hear Gatlinburg is a fantastic place to hike the mountains, see some nature."

"So, I hear. I just hate to go alone, you know? I suppose I could find the time, but...alone?" She shrugged.

Thom took her hand in his. "Well, maybe I can find some reason to come visit. Then you won't be alone, will you?"

She squeezed his fingers, that beautiful smile on her face. "No, I won't."

"So? Would you like to hike a few of the peaks with me? We'll do a couple easy ones, if you'd like."

She nodded at him, her smile broadening into a 'come hither' grin. He wasn't sure if he was keeping his outside as cool as he should but inside he felt everything start pounding at once. Like the little kid, he was dancing inside.

"Sure, why not. As long as it's not *too* tough, I'm up for it."

That was it; the rest of the day could just stop now.

It was mostly chitchat thereafter, sticking to the game and focusing on their scores. He managed to shoot a very respectable sixty-five but she wowed him by shooting a new course record of sixty-three. Her form was impeccable; her swing was a thing of beauty. He'd been thinking he was going to teach her a few tips and it turned out to be the other way around. He gladly bought the 'root beer'—tonic water with a twist for himself, and a vodka and tonic for her.

"Root beer, huh?"

He laughed at that. "It's an old joke," he told her. "A good buddy and I played at least once a week. Was in those days when we were hiding out from the wives; they didn't like us drinking, you see. So we told 'em the loser bought root beer." He chuckled again. "I don't think the girls believed it, but you never know."

She sat back in the chair, her arms on the rests of the chair. She was so casual, so different from any other woman he'd ever know. She just watched him, that half smile on her lips. "You're very old fashioned, aren't you?"

He looked up from his glass at that. There was no button-pushing intended. It was just an innocent, straightforward question. "Why do you ask?"

"Oh, calling your wives 'girls.' Every female is 'honey' or 'darlin'.' It's an old-fashioned thing to do. My grandparents were like that."

He smiled ruefully into the glass and took a sip. "I'm not *that* old."

She laid her hand on his arm. "No, you're not old, that's for certain." She sat back again, still watching him with those blue eyes of hers. "You were married twice, right?"

Thom shrugged. "*You* looked me up, you tell *me*."

She hesitated for a moment or two. When she finally answered, she sounded like she was quoting whatever web site she'd found his bio on. "Thom Mitchell, married and divorced twice. First wife, Angela Dumont; two children—Allan and Lisa. Divorced after fifteen years. Second wife, Sandra Mortenson; one child—Michelle. Divorced after four years."

"You know all there is to know about me."

She gracefully crossed her legs. "What happened?"

"Oh, my fault on the first," he answered in as honest a fashion as he could. "We, uh...hit a hard place. She decided that she was going to stay home to raise the kids and I decided that I—Well, I was getting big in the business and I let it go to my head—the booze, the ladies, the drugs."

"You cheated on her?"

"Yeah," he admitted. "I did. She got tired of it and divorced me. But karma being what it is, that's okay. My second wife screwed around on *me*. Once with my best friend, once with my brother. A few dozen other times with men I don't know." Thom shrugged again. "Doesn't matter."

She held his hand in hers, a look of concern on her face. "I'm sorry, Thom."

"Shh, don't be," he said, warmed by her genuine caring. "I'm just a lousy husband."

"I doubt that." She picked up her glass to sip her drink.

She had pulled her hair back into a ponytail but one stray wisp had broken free of the scrunchy that held the strands. A short tendril, growing from the forehead and laying across the outer corner of her eye. It was the color of burnished copper and rich auburn, shimmering against the softness of her skin. It was all he could do to restrain himself from reaching across to smooth it away from her face. Instead, he raised his own drink to his lips, watching her over the rim of the glass.

"So," he said, finally breaking the silence. "What about you?"

"Me?" She seemed genuinely surprised at the question.

"Yeah, you," he teased. "You know about me from the internet. Come on, quid pro quo. Unless I can look *you* up there."

She waved her hand in the air, as if to dismiss the thought entirely. "No, I'm not internet worthy, I'm afraid."

"Okay, tell me about you."

Her giggle was the nervous kind and still managed to sound like a finger strumming the strings of a harp. With a shrug, she gave in. "Well," she started. "I'm a contract lawyer; I specialize in government funding and 301K accounts—uh, what you'd call "not for profit." I live alone with a tank of tropical fish because I read somewhere that it's good for your stress level and blood pressure."

"I'll have to remember that."

She tossed a napkin at him before continuing. "Um, I love to read; historical fiction mostly."

"What?" He slapped the table in mock surprise. "Not a romance reader?"

She snorted. "If you mean those bodice rippers with the helpless females weeping about paying the rent and the broad-chested men who arrive in the nick of time with the gold, uh... *no!*" She leaned forward and, with a conspiratorial whisper, said, "I'll tell you a little secret."

He leaned close enough to get a waft of the lavender shampoo she used. "What?"

"I don't find rape sexy in the least."

He whispered back, "I don't either." It was enough to earn him a smile and he warmed in it. "Married?"

"Nope," she answered, an enigmatic smile on her lips that

practically dared him to find the right question. Or the right answer.

"Engaged?"

"Nope."

He took another sip from his glass and signaled the server for another round. "Tempted?"

Her face sobered. "No, divorced."

For a moment, he was taken aback. It had to have played out on his face, because she smiled again.

"You asked me if I was married, I said no. I didn't say that I had *never* been married."

He grinned at her. "All right, you got me on that one." The grin faded as he asked, "Mind if I ask you that same question?"

She took a quick sip and set the glass down. "What happened?"

He nodded.

She sat for a moment, twisting the empty glass in her hands. By then, the server had arrived with their fresh drinks and she surrendered the empty one to the young man. When he'd left, she sat stirring with the swizzle stick. He could feel something coming off her in waves, but he wasn't sure what it was. He reached out and took her hand; the gesture pulled her back and the blue eyes met his again.

"You don't have to tell me if you don't want to," he tried to reassure her. "It's none of my business."

She took a breath, slowly licked her lips. "No," she answered. "I think I want to. I'm just not sure what to say."

"Only what you want me to know and after that, I don't care," he assured her.

She opened her mouth to speak and closed it again. Just

as he was getting ready to change the subject, she decided to answer. "I guess you could say he just wasn't a very nice man, that's all." She started tracing a pattern in the tablecloth with her free hand. "I made my share of stupid mistakes, I'll admit it. I didn't make things easy, maybe. But...."

"Look, let's not talk about it, okay?"

She nodded. "Thom?"

"Yes?"

"Why don't you drive?"

That question came out of the blue. He *had* been the one to bring it up originally. Thom looked into her eyes, trying to foresee the result of telling her. He decided that, maybe, an abbreviated version might be the best idea.

"I had a black period in my life, one I'm not real proud of."

"What happened?" she asked with a great deal of innocence.

Come on, darlin', I know it was on the internet. How could you miss that one? "I'm a recovering alcoholic," he stated, quite baldly. "I will have a nip now and then after a show, but I mostly stay away from any alcohol."

Evidently, this was something she'd *not* found on the 'net. "What happened?" she asked again, this time less of a question and more of an opening for him.

He took a deep breath. "I got really drunk and blacked out at this fundraiser for an environmental group I supported. I still don't know all of the details, really. Not. . .well, I woke up a day or so later, at home with a mild concussion, a totaled sports car, and about thirty six hours wiped from my memory. My friend Phil wasn't so lucky. He was out driving too; I guess he had a one-car collision with a moose and it killed him. He was as drunk as I was."

Her brow furrowed in concern. "That must have been so painful for you."

"You'd think I'd have learned from that but no," he confessed. "When Angie and I started having the problems, I started drinking again. I still have empty spots, holes in my memory where I was so damn drunk that I blacked out." He started to drift, feeling things slip out of focus as the elusive answer tried to slip away again. "I have this dream...."

"What dream?"

"Everything's black. And I can hear...." *No, no, don't do this, idiot. You don't want her to think you're nuts. Cool it. Come on, she's looking with that pity look. Come on, Mitchell; get it together.* He smiled, shaking it off. "I don't drive. I never got behind the wheel again. My family and friends gave me an intervention and I started going to AA meetings regularly."

"And you only drink sparkling water?"

"The usual—sparkling water, coffee, that non-alcoholic, beer flavored water. A little brandy now and again before or after a show; it helps my throat, calms my nerves. But that's about it. Brandy gives me a migraine if I drink too much, so it's pretty safe."

"And you don't drive."

He shook his head, waiting for her to say something—*anything*—reassuring to him.

She took his hand in hers. "I'm really proud of you for that. You did something very hard and made it through, turned your life around. That's amazing."

He felt his chest start to glow. "Yeah?"

"Yeah," she said, nodding with conviction.

"So, how about dinner tonight?" When her beautiful face lit

up, he thought he was going to float away.

"Absolutely."

"Good," he declared. "I want Malcolm to get to know you. I want you two to meet."

There was the slightest hesitation in her voice, almost a crack. "Uh, sure, okay. Yeah."

"Something wrong?"

"Well, uh, I mean...."

"What...oh," he said, the concept finally dawning. "You wanted it to be just us."

That relieved look came back quickly. "Yes, exactly."

He swallowed hard. "I would really like you to meet him. He's a great guy. He's been with me through it all, my best friend. I can tell him anything. It's important to me. I want you to like him. And I want him to like you."

"Oh. Well." The smile was warmer, more sincere. "Then, by all means. Dinner would be great. I'd love to get to know him."

They decided that a nap was in order; the walk around the course had tired them both. He walked her back to her room, making plans to meet in the dining room about seven for dinner, reassuring her that Malcolm would love her and vice versa. But leaving her at the door was hard. He was lost in the blue eyes, the curve of her smile. The details of her face etched themselves into his memory. The softness of her hair against her shoulder. He snapped himself back before he could embarrass himself completely.

"I'll call you later?"

"Sure," she answered, smiling. "Have a good nap."

"You too."

He turned around and headed back towards his room, humming all the way.

9

"YOU TWO ARE gonna love each other, I swear it."
Thom rose up a little from the seat of the chair, sweeping the dining room with his eyes again. She was a little late. But that was fine; in his experience, a quality lady always showed up late. They loved to dress and pamper, primp and polish. So they could make *an entrance*. The wait would be worth the vision that came in. He just knew these things. He thought.

Malcolm sat, stirring the olive around in his martini.

"Hey. Mal."

Malcolm looked up.

"It's okay. I mean it. You two will love each other. She'll think you're great. Just like I do."

Mal shook his head, keeping his face blank and expressionless. One thing he was good at, hiding his feelings or what he was thinking. Until he was ready to talk about it. "It's not that, Thommy. I worry about you. I'm worried you're moving too fast on this."

Here comes the mother hen act. "Mal—"

"You don't even know her."

"I know enough," he answered, trying to reassure his friend. "Besides, we're not talking marriage here."

Malcolm didn't look convinced. He took a sip of his martini

and just shook his head.

Thom leaned forward. "Look, she's a nice lady. A *real* lady. I've not been with a woman like this in a long time. She doesn't care who I am or what I do for a living. She actually cares about me. *Me*. Okay?"

Malcolm lifted a corner of his mouth in a weak smile. "I know, Thom. I just worry about you, that's all. You're important to me. Like a brother." He turned his gaze back to the glass. "I love you."

Thom smiled. Mal could be a bit melodramatic sometimes, but he was still a good friend. "Back atcha, buddy. That won't ever change. Okay?"

Mal's grin was more than enough, but another sight caught Thom's attention and made him go suddenly weak in the knees. He saw the vision at the door and desperately tried to remember how to breathe.

Joanna was wearing a dress of dark forest green, her auburn hair swept up in a simple roll, but with tendrils falling around her ears and forehead. She stood there, looking over the room. When she saw Thom, her face lit up in a sparkling smile. She had the most graceful walk, gliding her way across the dining room floor. Thom was on his feet, brushing the linen napkin off his lap and onto the table. As she got closer, he saw the emeralds against her skin and ears. It should be diamonds, he thought to himself, then reached forward to pull the chair out for her.

Malcolm also stood and nodded to her.

Thom tucked her and the chair up to the table. Malcolm signaled the server to come and she ordered a sparkling water with a slice of lime.

Thom bent over to whisper in her ear. "You look amazing."

She blushed, smiling down at the table. "Thank you," she whispered back.

Thom sat down, still grinning from ear to ear. "Menu, lady?"

Joanna accepted the offered parchment from him, then said hello to Mal, who said hello back. It was going to be a great night, he could tell. Thom opened his own menu and started peering over the selections. "Man, you're gonna love the food here, Mal. It's great stuff. All the New Hampshire delights and more."

Malcolm smiled. "I can't wait, Thommy." He immediately buried his nose behind the covers. "Joanna, my dear. You look lovely."

"What, this old thing?" She gave a naughty wink at Thom. "Thank you, Malcolm."

Thom laughed immediately. Malcolm didn't even smile. Thom figured he was just hungry; Mal had no sense of humor when food was his focus.

"So. Thommy." Malcolm had the menu flat on the table, his finger running down the list of entrees. "What's good here?"

"Gotta try the lobster, man," Thom answered. "They have a stuffed lobster here that'll turn you upside down and make you beg for more. And the seafood chowder can't be beat. Buddy, you're in the land of seafood and they do it right here."

"What about crab cakes?" Jo asked tentatively.

"Ah, that's Maryland, darlin'," Thom answered her. "Here, we are the lobster kings!"

Her giggle was nervous, but she nodded. "Well, then, I know exactly what I want. That lobster salad looks incredible."

"Excellent. Mal? What about you?"

"You pick for me," he answered. "You know what I like."

That was Mal; when he was at a loss for something, he'd let Thom do it. Thom smiled and gave the server their orders. He knew *exactly* what Malcolm wanted. There was a lull in the conversation for a few minutes. Thom waited to see if Jo or Mal would fill the space. But they were both looking at him.

"How's the room, buddy?"

Malcolm nodded. "Great, really comfortable."

"You get a good view?"

"Um, can I ask you question?" Jo was looking at both of them, her eyes darting back and forth.

"Of course," Thom told her. "Ask away."

"So, how long have you two known each other?"

Malcolm seemed to relax a little with the ease of the question. *Good*, Thom thought, *they'll get to know each other now. He'll like her; I know he will.*

"Oh, Thommy and me go way back. College."

"You went to college together?"

It was Thom's turn to laugh. "What he means is the college circuit. That first group I sang with, we did a lot of colleges and universities."

"I taught at one," Malcolm said, picking up the thread. "I was teaching economics and Thom's group...what was the name?"

"Mitchell, Ramsey, and Rivers."

"That's right. Anyway, they played the local watering hole, doing acoustic covers of old folk and Dylan tunes."

"Covered some John Denver, too."

Malcolm grinned at that. "I remember." To Jo, he went on. "Anyway, I went to a gig and thought Thom here was the next pop sensation. I was sold enough to want to manage his career."

Jo seemed amazed. "You went from teacher to manager? Just

like that?"

"Just like that." Malcolm sipped his drink. "Smartest move I've ever made."

"Made all the difference in my career," Thom agreed. "He hooked me up with Oscar, my producer, and the rest is history."

Malcolm eased back into the chair, staring across the table. "Only mistake I ever made was introducing you to the second ex!"

Thom laughed it off. "Only mistake I ever made was not letting you *have* a second ex!"

They both laughed at that one. Joanna looked puzzled.

Thom smiled at her. "Oh, Malcolm is a love 'em and leave 'em type. I keep him too busy for things like romance." He winked at his friend.

"That doesn't seem fair," Jo answered.

That tugged at him; that she seemed to care about a man she just met. Enough to worry about his happiness. "You're right, it isn't fair," Thom answered. "I never really thought about it but you're right.

"No, she's not," Malcolm interjected. He was smiling at Thom. "I never felt deprived of anything, my friend. You're special; you're my best friend. I'd do it all again, give everything to be by your side."

He'd never thought about what Mal had sacrificed on his behalf, what his friend had given up in terms of a personal life. It had always been the two of them, Thom making the demands and Malcolm fulfilling them. Thom on stage, Mal in the wings. His friend had done more for him that he'd ever acknowledge. He stared at Mal and felt an enormous sense of gratitude under the guilt.

Malcolm must have sensed it, because he leaned forward

and rested his hand on the table. "I mean it. Really."

That mollified Thom somewhat. Enough to let it go. "Okay, Mal. Thanks."

Malcolm turned his gaze back to Joanna. "The truth be told, we've had a great life together. I don't think there's anyone we're closer to than each other."

Thom beamed at the man. "Closer than anyone else in my life." He chuckled. "Well, with an exception or two."

"Very few," Malcolm added.

It was a little awkward, Thom could tell. But it was going to work itself out. They'd share stories, get Joanna talking, and his best friend would get to know the lady he was attracted to. If those two hit it off, Thom knew everything would be all right.

"Excuse me, sir."

He turned around to see their server standing, his hands clasped behind his back.

"Yes?"

"Mr. Mitchell, I know we're not supposed to bother you but...."

Thom smiled. "Not a problem, uh...."

"Daniel, sir."

"Not a problem, Daniel. What can I do for you?"

"It's just that we're all really huge fans, sir. And um, Mr. Waterhouse—he's our manager here—was wondering if he could get a picture of you and maybe an autograph." Daniel chuckled. "We wanted to do a group picture, but you know how it is."

Thom flipped his napkin up in the air, folding it neatly on the catch. "Hey, I know and that's fine. I'll be glad to do this."

"Thommy? You're on vacation."

Thom waved it off as he stood up. "Mal, I don't mind. I love this place. It's the least I can do." To Daniel, he smiled and said, "Lead on."

He paused long enough to kiss Joanna on the top of the head. "I'll be back before dinner is served, you two. So, don't run off on me now and elope!"

He laughed at his own joke as he walked away, following the server. In fact, this was a great idea after all. Jo and Mal could sit and talk without him for a few minutes. Get a chance to relax and get acquainted. A much better idea because he wouldn't be there to make them nervous.

He gave a quick look over his shoulder before leaving the dining room. For a moment, the stiff posture worried him, but he just attributed it to nerves.

They'll be okay. He went into the office to greet the smiling Mr. Waterhouse. He didn't spare them another thought while he did his best self-promotion.

10

JOANNA WATCHED THOM greet the manager of the dining room. She could tell from the way the other man was smiling that Thom had said something jovial. The time had come to admit that she'd been wrong about Thom Mitchell; he wasn't the average pop star with an overgrown ego. He was actually a decent man, a warm and giving person who was just as real as he seemed to be.

She was too suspicious; she knew that. Divorcing Roger had done that to her. He'd tried to manipulate the proceedings to his own ends and a female judge had rebuffed him at every turn. When that didn't work, Roger had taken to battering her reputation with a multitude of her sins, real and imagined. She'd walked out of the courtroom a free woman getting no alimony (sorry, *spousal support*)—which was fine, she hadn't wanted it—and fully convinced that men wanted only one thing, the royal screwing in both literal and figurative terms.

Two years later, she was still distrustful of men and held them at arm's length. Certainly, Larry Micarello and his insistence that she be 'friendly' to Thom hadn't helped. Larry was just another man who thought a woman's place was on her back. He had no choice but to accept the women on his staff as equals, the law demanded it. But he always had that implied expectation from the female lawyers. And as the boss felt, so did the male staff. It was a shame that the job paid as well as it did and had such great benefits; the men in the firm were assholes.

But Thom was different from the men she worked with, pretty much the only man she could tolerate being around. Thom treated her with respect, an old-fashioned respect that dictated that a man held the door for a lady and seated her first at the table. Okay, he called her a 'girl' on occasion, and 'honey' and 'darlin'.' But she was used to that, it was just a southern thing. The difference was that Thom meant them; they weren't just words to him.

It was a moment before she realized that Malcolm was speaking to her. She whirled away from watching Thom. "I'm sorry, what?"

"I asked you what brought you to New Hampshire."

Joanna looked at the man across the table from her and sized him up. He had the kind of face that would stop a woman dead in her tracks; the masculine curve of the jaw, the high cheekbones, the hazel eyes that were full-lidded with long eyelashes. His wasn't a classic beauty because of his stocky form, yet he certainly was handsome in a rugged way. But there was something in the way he was looking at her, as if he was studying a bug under a microscope. There was a smile teasing at his lips, but it seemed to be so cursory. It was as if the smile was just for effect.

"Oh, um," she stammered a bit. "Well, I came up for a vacation."

"Oh?"

"Yes."

"Nice hotel, too."

"I had booked here but I was originally just going to be

here for a week. My stay got extended, thanks to my boss. He's actually paying for it."

"Nice boss."

"I took care of Thom for the fund raiser."

He took another sip from the glass before him, never taking his eyes off her. When he finally spoke, the tone of his answer was just odd. "How very kind of you to do that. I'm sure it was appreciated."

She was starting to feel like a fly just before the hungry lizard snapped it up for dinner. "Well, it was my job, of course." She giggled, trying to cover her sudden insecurity. "We didn't exactly hit it off right away, Thom and me."

"I'm sure," he repeated. "But you seem to be getting along famously now."

Joanna smiled. "Yeah, you could say that. We talked things through, got it all sorted out."

The corners of his mouth went up again, the expression still not moving beyond his mouth. "He's a good man. And I should know."

"Yes he is," she agreed. "He's easy to talk to. I really like him. A lot."

"Mmhmm."

"He's been taking me hiking and shopping."

He waved his hand, dismissing the idea. "He does that with everyone. He took you golfing, too?"

The wave of his hand wafted his cologne in her general direction, starting her nose to tickle again. She made a pretense of wiping her mouth with her napkin, to stave off the sickeningly sweet scent. "Yes, he did."

"I thought so." He sat back in the chair, shaking his head.

"Another notch in the bedpost."

She furrowed her brow, feeling the bottom start to burn. "What do you mean?"

His laugh was genuine this time, almost friendly. "I've known Thommy a long time and I've seen him go through a *lot* of women. That's his pick up routine." He leaned closer again. "You know when he's looking for some action. A little golfing and hiking for himself, a little shopping as foreplay for you and he's got you."

Surely, he wasn't suggesting what she thought he was suggesting. "But he...."

"You really didn't think he was doing all that out of the goodness of his heart, did you?" When she didn't answer right away, he asked again. "*Did* you?"

"You're wrong." She was indignant, wondering why she had to protect Thom's reputation at all with this guy. Or her own. "He's been nothing but a gentleman to me. He never once tried to hit on me. You're way off base here."

He laughed again, a humorless sound. "Let me guess; the shopping was *his* idea. Told you he liked to shop, said he wanted to help you carry the bags. Am I right?"

She couldn't quite believe him but at the same time, why would he say this to her? Not wanting to betray the sudden doubt, she said nothing. She just nodded her head.

"And of course, he's been telling you the small intimate details of his life; his sins, so to speak. To show you what a jerk he was and how he's reformed into a sensitive, caring guy."

She nodded again.

"I love the man, don't get me wrong. But I know his act better than he does." Malcolm took another sip of the martini. "The thing is he means every word. He really does. But I've heard it all before...uh, Joanna, is it?"

"Yes," she whispered. Was it true? What this man was saying? Was it?

Malcolm finished off his drink and pushed back from the table. "My dear, I can see you care about Thommy. So I think I can be honest with you."

"Please do," she said, her heart suddenly leaping into her throat. The mouse has nothing better to do than bait the lion, just before being eaten.

"Thommy is a good man, really. But after his second divorce, Thom stopped trying to meet his next ex-wife and decided to play the field. He's not looking to get serious. He told me all he wants to do while he's here is to play golf, hike, and if he meets anyone, he's just in it for the sex. That's it."

Damn it! Just when she was starting to trust the guy, starting to believe that he was sincere. "He's playing me for a sucker, isn't he?"

Malcolm shrugged.

She sat for a moment, her face flushing with her anger. This Malcolm person was keeping his distance because he knew better than to get chummy with the boss' current piece of tail. That's why he was being so distant, so cold. Okay, she could understand that. But, Thom. The bastard was trying to get into her pants; that was all this was. It was all so perfectly clear now. She'd seen him with others; he was so friendly and personable. It was all just an act.

She suddenly felt like the world's biggest fool. She never looked up again, not wanting to see the pity on that man's face. She simply tossed her napkin to the table, stood up with her purse firmly clutched in her hand, and left the dining room.

Joanna made her way to her room, her lips pressed together hard and one hand gripped so tightly to her bag that her fingernails were leaving impressions in the leather. With a quick flip of her wrist, the card key gave her admittance to the room. She slammed the door behind her and threw her purse across the room, smacking it against the cheap copy of a seascape painting.

"That son of a bitch!" She started pacing, a full head of steam percolating inside of her. "That conceited son of a bitch! How dare he! How freaking *dare* he."

She paced and paced, calling that no good pop star everything but a child of any god she could think of, cursing him in at least three languages—only one of which she was fluent in—and making up a few more as she went. When she got tired of pacing, she went into the bedroom. Still verbally questioning the humility factor of her should-have-been date, she pulled off the fancy dress she'd bought for the occasion and tossed it unceremoniously on the chair. She changed into her jeans and favorite sweater, still fuming and still making disparaging remarks about the parentage of one Jared Thomas Mitchell and the lack of matrimonial status at his conception. Then when the anger wore off, the depression set in.

"Damn! And I liked him, too," she said to her mirrored reflection. She studied her hair, her face. She pulled the sweater up to look at her breasts and abdomen.

"Fine, so I don't have six pack abs. And I'm a damned C cup. That's not so bad. Is it?"

With a huff, she yanked the sweater back down.

"Stupid son of a bitch! Just in it for the sex, huh? Think I'm gonna just lay down with my heels behind my ears because you're Thom fucking Mitchell, the famous singer!" She put her fists to her hips, glaring at the mirror. "Well, if that's what you think, then you've got another think coming, old buddy!"

And with the last burst, she was done. The anger and hurt left her. And in their place came the confusion. She'd spent three days with him, three wonderful days of going places, talking, sharing meals. They'd sat at night in either his room or hers and watched old movies. And every moment, he'd been nothing but a gentleman. That one kiss at her door. He had held her hand. That was it. But he'd never made any kind of untoward overture.

She met her mirrored eyes again. What was wrong with her? Wasn't she pretty enough? Wasn't she attractive enough? Didn't he like redheads? Or maybe she'd sent the wrong signals. Maybe she'd been too shrewish, or maybe she was just too independent. Maybe he'd been sending the signals and she sent something back saying "screw off, not interested." So, she paced a little more, trying to make sense of it. And nothing was coming.

She was starting to get a headache and the room was shrinking. She just wanted some air; maybe a turn outside would help her think. She went back into the living room and pulled the card key from her purse. She would take a short turn on the veranda and just let the cold night air clear her head. *Hell, he probably didn't even notice that I wasn't there for dinner. Stupid ass probably didn't even miss me! He and his good buddy, the football player. I hope he choked on his frigging salmon!*

She grabbed a heavy coat and slammed the door behind her as she left. Pulling the coat around her, she made her way back to the lobby and out the main doors, still muttering to herself.

If anyone was watching, she hoped whoever was getting a good show. She stuffed her hands in her pockets and let her feet carry her out onto the wooden decking.

It was freezing; a typical New Hampshire evening, she supposed. There was a diffused light coming from the windows, as well as a full moon overhead. It gave a soft shimmer to the world around her, lulling her into a peaceful calm. She remembered a snippet of song about shadows and lullabies, and watched the clouds flitting over the face of shining orb above her. The world outside was bathed in an otherworldly glow and she lost herself to it. Her breath made tufts of smoke, blowing out of her lips into the night.

Joanna walked over to a railing and clutched her coat a bit more tightly around her. She wouldn't be able to stay out here long; it was freezing that southern fanny of hers. But it was so worth it. She listened to the hooting of an owl, a plaintive and lonesome call. She could see why he had fallen in love with this place and it had nothing to do with being born here.

The light behind her got brighter as the door opened, then dimmed as it closed. She heard his boots as he walked across the deck to where she stood. She had absolutely no clue what she was going to say to him, absolutely none.

"Jo?"

When you don't know what to say, don't say anything. She just stood, quietly waiting.

"Jo, are you alright? Is something wrong?"

She was going to give in; she felt it coming. His voice was so concerned, so vulnerable. How could he be faking that? But he had to be, he just had to be. What his friend had said, about the whole thing being a way to have sex with her, with any woman. She let her hands slip back into her pockets and dug her nails into her palms. She relaxed every muscle in her face and turned to him, thankful that the diffused light hid what was inside of her.

"Thom. Yes, I'm fine. Thank you for asking."

He seemed confused, his brow furrowed with a slight frown. "You left dinner. Are you sure you're okay?"

"Why would I not be?"

"Malcolm said you maybe didn't feel well. I wanted to.... Are you angry with me?"

She gave a small snort at that. She just needed to play it cool as a cucumber. If he wanted a sex partner, he'd have to find someone else for the job.

"Don't be silly, Thom. I just needed some fresh air. I guess I stayed too long."

"I missed you."

"Oh, I doubt that. You and your friend seemed to be having a great time."

He moved closer to her. She could practically feel the heat radiating from him, smell the woody scent of him, an aroma of balsam and pine. Right now, all she wanted was to feel his arms around her and hear him tell her that she was the only one that mattered. Right now, all she wanted to do was get lost in his hair, his eyes, his kisses.

Right and be one of a thousand other women he's slept with. No, I am not gonna be another notch in his guitar case. But she didn't exactly move away from him either.

"I wanted him to get to know you, for you to know him."

She purposefully made her voice stay neutral, emotionless. But with Thom standing so close, she didn't know how long that was going to last. "Thom, really, it's not necessary. It's not like you're taking me home to meet your mother. I'm sure you don't do this with *all* of your conquests, do you?"

That had stung him, she could tell. "All of my conquests? What's that supposed to mean?"

She wanted to take it back. She opened her mouth to do it. But a flash to her left caught her attention and she turned toward it.

Just in time to see a body dressed in dark clothes and a ski mask hurdle up the steps in two bounding leaps. The metal of a watchband stood out on the inky form, reflecting the moonlight, as what surely had to be male took a flying tackle at Thom. Thom turned his head too late as the other man connected, both of them flying backwards onto a settee. Joanna watched in horror as the dark figure began to pummel Thom with fists flying.

Without thinking, she started screaming as loud as she could. But she wasn't just going to let this bastard hurt Thom. A quick survey of the veranda yielded an old standing ashtray. She grasped it in her hands and wheeled around, holding it like a baseball bat. By now, the dark figure had managed to subdue Thom and was pulling something out of a back pocket. Still screaming, Joanna went into action.

She swung with all her might at the assailant, catching him on the shoulder and knocking him flying. "Get away from him, you son of a bitch!"

The figure had managed to jump up and Joanna took another swing. She missed as he jumped backwards. For a moment, she was sure he was going to charge at her but the main doors flew open at that point. The light was blinding to her, but it was enough to scare the assailant. As several men—including Malcolm, much to her dismay—came spilling out, the man in the mask simply pushed her back into them and ran off.

The place turned into a melee. Three of the men that had run in answer to her screaming chased off after the attacker, including one of the guards. Before she could move, Malcolm and the hotel manager had collected Thom and whisked him back into the lobby. It was the last sight she had of him before the other guard had her elbow.

"Miss? Miss, are you hurt?"

"No," she answered, her voice shaking just as hard as her knees were now. "But I think I need to sit down."

Joanna felt his hand clutching at her elbow, leading her back inside the hotel. She let her mind go blank and thought no more of Thom Mitchell as the aftershock began to sink in.

11

JOANNA HAD A fitful night, dreaming of the moonlight, the cold air, and Thom standing close enough to smell the balsam on his skin. Only in the dream, she told him everything. In the dream, he didn't care. He leaned forward to kiss her again. And the man jumped from the darkness to attack him. Except, in her dream, the attacker would do more than just hurt him. She would jolt awake, her hands gripping the pillow to her mouth to hold in the scream. She would force herself to remember that he was okay. They'd stopped the bastard and Thom was okay. She would go back to sleep only to start the cycle again.

Daybreak seemed to take forever to dawn over her windowsill. When the first light finally came up over the mountaintops, she was up and in the shower. If she couldn't sleep, she might as well get a crack on the day. Joanna decided that she'd have breakfast first, then come back to her room and wade through the briefs she'd brought with her. She promised herself that she was done with Thom Mitchell. Damn musicians were all alike.

Or were they?

Unfortunately, her feet didn't take her where she wanted to go. With card key in her back pocket and her purse slung over her shoulder, she made her way to the elevator just as two of the housemaids got on. They pushed the button to go up and since Jo really didn't feel like waiting for the bloody thing to pick her up, she got on to ride.

"I heard it was awful."

"Really? Who told you?"

"Marybeth. She's got his floor, you know."

"So what happened?"

Jo realized that they were talking about Thom. She said nothing, waiting while the elevator took its damned sweet time making it up two frigging floors. But she listened to them, giddy over Mr. Pop Star.

"Somebody attacked him. Right here. Right on the front veranda. Mr. Guilford is furious at security."

"Geez, and he's such a nice guy."

"I know. I told Marybeth she's so freaking lucky. He tips really great."

"Yeah."

"You going up to his floor?"

"Yeah, I gotta pick up his breakfast dishes for the kitchen."

The other girl giggled. "You oughta stop in and give him some TLC."

"Don't tempt me."

The car came to rest on the fifth floor. "Here's my stop."

"Don't molest him, now. Remember, he's wounded."

Without thinking, Jo followed the young girl out of the elevator. She didn't want to like him anymore, this Thom Mitchell Pop Star. He was a womanizer, a cad, a liar. *You know, you're taking one man's word...and you don't even trust the source.*

That brought her up short, that voice in her head. No, she didn't care for Malcolm whatever his name was. It was nothing she could put her finger on, just something that put her off. The way he kept looking at her, the way he'd talked to her the night before. She could tell that he genuinely cared for Thom. But he treated her like—

Like a groupie, don't you think?

That's exactly how he was treating her, like a groupie.

And he doesn't even know you, does he?

No, he didn't. Maybe that's why he'd said those things. To make sure she wasn't just using Thom. She sighed. She disliked Malcolm, maybe unfairly. She'd also let a bunch of bullshit get to her. *Thom's not that way.*

She had to know how Thom was doing, how badly he'd been hurt. She had to know. To hell with what that Malcolm idiot thought. Thom was the one she was concerned about. She would go to his room, knock on the door, and talk to him. Listen to him, to what he had to say. See if it was all true. Hey, she was a lawyer, a damned good judge of character—

The girl she'd been following stopped and knocked on the door to one of the suites. Jo felt the clutch in her throat and quickly hid behind a large potted plant in one corner. She peeked around in time to see the door open and a too-perky Missy standing in it. For a moment, Jo was almost speechless. *And what's she doing in his room?*

"Morning, Glo," Missy chirped. "Did you come for the dishes?"

"Yeah, Guilford sent me. Said you were busy." The young girl chuckled knowingly. "So, how was he?"

"How was who?"

"You know! Come on; dish the dirt, Missy. And here I thought you were totally devoted to that Walt of yours."

Joanna wanted to throttle whoever this Glo was with both hands. She acted like this was funny. It wasn't funny; it was disgusting. A man of his age chasing after a young girl like that. She heard the giggle again and reached through the boughs to part them enough to see through.

"Gloria, damn it! I am devoted to Walt. Thom is a really nice man; it's not like that. I mean it. I just came to help out after he got hurt last night."

"Uh-huh." Gloria giggled salaciously again. "Got the cart ready?"

Missy disappeared long enough to wheel the food cart out into the hallway. "Not that you asked, but he's still sleeping," Missy answered. "The doctor was here earlier, said Thom's gonna be just fine. He just has a bump on his head and a black eye. Otherwise, he's cool."

"Oh. Really."

"Yeah, really." Missy rolled her eyes reprovingly. "And *nothing* happened."

"If you say so, hon," Gloria said, pushing the cart in front of her. "But I think you're holding out on me. See you later, Miss."

Jo watched Gloria push the cart to the elevator and get on with it. Missy closed the door, going back into the suite. Jo stood there, clenching and unclenching her fists. Given what that Malcolm person had said to her last night, a too clear picture was starting to form. *Methinks the lady doth protest too much. And so does he. That manager creep of his was right after all.*

She turned on her heel and went back to her room, breakfast and anything else forgotten. She inserted the card key into the lock, flinging open the door and letting it slam behind her. Right now, Joanna felt every other inch the fool. She flung her purse over onto the sofa and then her body on the bed. She'd almost convinced herself that she was wrong about the man and last night. She wiped the tears from her face, wondering what the hell was her problem. How could she be so damned gullible?

She stared at the TV for a while, letting it distract her mind, before she took a nap after the local news at noon. And in her sleep, she dreamed of a tall mountain and a path edged in that wild mountain thyme.

And Thom Mitchell picking some to give to her.

12

MALCOLM BLINKED HIMSELF awake. A bleary look at the clock told him it was an hour after lunch. He and Thom would have to split the room service since the dining room stopped serving at one. He forced himself into a sitting position and realized that he was alone on the bed.

Escorting Thom back to his own suite, Malcolm had made the decision to spend the night. Thom was too shaken and in too much pain to be left alone. He'd also raised a stink to get an on-call physician up to the room, just to be sure. The doctor had given Thom a clean bill of health—well, except for the bruises and black eye—but Malcolm wasn't going to take any chances. It was Thom's insistence that he sleep in the other half of the bed, so that's where he'd slept.

Thom looked like hell, but all he worried about was that damned woman. Asking if she'd been hurt, had someone helped her, where was she? Malcolm had deflected each one with the same answer; he didn't know and didn't care—Thom was his priority. Thom finally stopped asking and only because he had planned to go in the morning to see her. Malcolm managed to deflect that too. He told Thom that he'd arrange it first thing in the morning if Thom would see a *real* physician—as if the other one hadn't been—and get a more thorough exam. Thom agreed and went to sleep like a good boy.

Mal dozed and tried to think what he could do. Ms. Hayes

was going to be a problem; he knew it. Why? No clue. Just that sixth sense that said she was. After as many years as they'd been together, he was a better judge of a situation that Thom would or could be. And that redhead was more trouble than she was worth. Thom probably wouldn't believe him but he *knew* it.

Thom was wide awake at the butt crack of dawn, wanting to call her. Malcolm reminded him of his promise and started searching for a doctor. It turned out to be easier than he'd dreamed when Thom suggested the young girl from the dining room. She knew exactly whom to call. She even brought the doctor up and then stayed to hear that the singer's hard head was still hard. Thom insisted that Malcolm back to bed. Missy had offered to answer the phone and anything else that needed to be done, so that Thom could take a nap, if he needed. The two of them had crashed in the king sized bed again, and Malcolm had surrendered himself to the dark peace behind his eyelids.

A quick look out the door into the seating room and he saw Thom sleeping on the sofa. He'd either decided to give Mal some privacy or he'd left to get some real rest; Mal had the misfortune of being a rather restless sleeper. A few repeat bedmates had learned how to keep him pinned enough to spend *most* of the night in deep slumber—but there were very few repeat bedmates to begin with.

He reassured himself that Thom was fine, gently touching the man's face. Malcolm took a light blanket from the bedroom and laid it down on the sleeping form, then stepped into the bathroom to take care of a physical need. He closed the door behind him for privacy—and to muffle the noise—and began to urinate. Too many things ran through his head now.

Thom was fine; things could progress normally. And if he

worked hard enough, he could actually carry this off. The truth was that Thom's career was foundering. The sweet young things like Missy were becoming far too rare and they weren't buying music. Thom hadn't had a hit in a long time; wasn't going to have one thanks to the label dropping him. Malcolm had seen this coming.

He sat down at the small table in what passed for a dining area. Missy had left a carafe of coffee on the table, cold but still fairly drinkable. Malcolm poured a cup and sipped as he brooded over his next move. He heard a moan behind him and turned to see Thom's eyelids fluttering. Thom was moaning softly, twitching in his sleep.

"Thommy?"

He waited, watching the singer convulse and moan in his sleep, while he argued with himself about waking Thom. It was a *Catch-22* situation; if he woke Thom, he ran the risk of a tongue lashing from hell—Thom did *not* wake up gently—and if he didn't, he'd have a grumpy Thom for the rest of the day because of that damn nightmare. Fortunately, the decision was taken out of his hands. Thom moaned once more before he blinked himself awake.

"Thommy? You okay? You awake now?"

Thom pulled himself into a sitting position, scrubbing his cheeks with both hands. He stuck his tongue out a few times, looking like a dog that was clearing peanut butter from the roof of its mouth.

"You okay?" Malcolm repeated.

"Yeah," Thom answered. "My mouth tastes like... We got any coffee?"

"Just this cold stuff."

"Pass." Thom groaned and dragged himself off the sofa. "God, these things are uncomfortable."

Malcolm chuckled and took another sip of the horrid liquid. "That's what you get for sleeping on the sofa."

"You snore, man." Thom reached up to the ceiling as he stretched the muscles of his back, twisting this way and that to work out the kinks, then exhaled loud and strong. "You sleep any?"

"I slept all I needed, Thommy."

Thom wasn't convinced. With an arched eyebrow, he asked, "You sure? Your eyes still have dark circles under them."

Malcolm waved it away. "I'll take a nap later. Want me to call room service?"

"No. Thanks. I'm not hungry."

"You alright, Thommy?"

The smile was slight, but it was there behind the corner of his lip that still showed the traces of knuckles splitting the skin. The brown eyes twinkled a bit behind the bruises. Thom dropped into the other chair at the table, running a hand through his already tousled hair. "I'm getting real sick of this dream."

"You ready to talk about it?" he asked, watching Thom with a certain amount of trepidation. His friend hadn't exactly discussed the details of this nightmare but from the few details that Thom had let slip, he was beginning to get an idea.

Thom changed the mood quickly, clapping his hands and rubbing them together. His injured face lighting up with a mischievous grin. "You know what? I *am* starved."

"Me too," Malcolm agreed.

"Good. Tell you what, call room service and order me the

biggest, thickest cheeseburger they got, with everything. And a big plate of french fries and catsup. I'll go get dressed."

"Sounds good," Malcolm told him.

And in that moment, Malcolm felt as if time had stopped and he was staring at an alternate future. That moment stretched out, making him question his decision. Okay, maybe it was a right strategy—as long as nothing pointed back to Thom or himself. Okay, it could work. It could give them both what they wanted. *Am I making the smart move here? Is this really the right thing to do?* Suddenly, he saw things going wrong. Thom was a man who never forgot and seldom forgave any slight or disagreement. Could he ever understand this? Malcolm felt the dagger digging into his chest, in that place where his heart was going stone cold.

Then, time sped up again and Malcolm came to in the middle of Thom's sentence.

"...don't understand what happened."

Malcolm blinked, clearing the thoughts away. "Hm? What?"

"Jo," Thom repeated. "She didn't come by, didn't call to ask. And I thought...." He sighed deeply.

"What, Thommy?"

Thom shrugged in that halfhearted way he always had, when he was dismissing something that mattered, that had hurt him. "I really thought we had something, you know? I thought there was a chance...."

"A chance for what?"

Thom met Malcolm's gaze. "A chance for something real. I like her, Mal. I care about her. She's smart, sexy, funny; she's everything I've ever wanted. I thought she felt that way too." He shrugged again and said no more.

Malcolm shook his head. "She's not worth this, Thommy. She's just not."

"But, Mal," Thom insisted, "she *is*."

"Do you love her?"

"I don't know," Thom confessed. "But I know she means something to me."

This was getting dangerous. "Go on, Thommy, you take your shower first and get dressed. I'll get us those cheeseburgers and they should be delivering by the time you're done."

Thom smiled at his friend, patted Malcolm's shoulder before heading off to the bedroom and the shower.

Malcolm ordered the food while Thom rustled about in the bedroom. His mind was going a hundred miles an hour. With luck, this would all be over within a few days and Thom would be the darling of the media again. Selling plenty of CDs and back to packed houses and back the Grammys. As long as that meddling woman stayed out of the picture. Taking another sip of the cold coffee, Malcolm thought to himself, time to get this show on the road. But first....

13

THE CHEESEBURGERS WERE fabulous, rich with gooey cheese and the meat was medium rare—his favorite. They ate the thick cut steak fries with plenty of catsup and a melt-your-socks-off ale provided by a local microbrewery. They had laughs and great conversation and played chess until the sun was low enough to kiss the top of the mountains. But Thom's mind wasn't really on the game or the discussion. It was elsewhere—on *her*. On Jo.

She had changed so quickly. He wasn't crazy; they *had* been getting very close. He knew she was feeling what he was. There was attraction and she wanted to be with him, that wasn't just his ego talking. But she pulled away again. It was as if the last three days hadn't happened at all. He had to know why. He had to know what happened, why she changed. He had to ask her. Even if she told him to go to hell, he still had to ask her.

By the time he and Mal had finished the first game, Thom knew what to do. By the end of the second game, he had an idea of how to do it. But he didn't want to tell anyone. After all, if she shot him down, he didn't want witnesses to his humiliation. So, after the fifth game, he just told Malcolm that he wanted to take a walk and get some air. Mal was readily agreeable about that. Then he told Mal that he wanted to do it alone. His friend was much less than enthusiastic about that one.

"Thommy, someone tried to hurt you last night."

"Mal, I'm not—"

Mal didn't get pushy that often, most of the time he was willing to go along with Thom. But periodically, he would dig his spurs in and when he did that, the tone was insolent and dictatorial. "You're not listening! I said—"

"I *heard* you the first time." Thom swallowed his irritation. He didn't need to snap at his friend. "Mal, thank you for worrying about me. But I can't stay a prisoner in my own room because someone got crazy."

"Thom...." Malcolm shook his head, hands on hips and looking up at the ceiling. When he met Thom's gaze again, he had a determined set to his chin.

Thom didn't give him a chance to continue that thought. "Mal, they've got more security added. You talked to the hotel manager, right?"

"Yes, but—"

"Then, I'll be alright. I won't go out of the hotel alone. They'll see me."

"I'm going with you."

Thom mimicked his friend's posture, standing almost nose to nose with Malcolm. "I'm a grown man and I can do things by myself. There's security and I'll be where people can see me."

Malcolm's laugh was very sarcastic. "Small comfort when they do nothing as some asshole shoots you dead."

Thom reached out his hands, taking his friend by the shoulders. "Please. I will be fine."

"Thom—"

"Mal, you're gonna have to trust me. Please! Let me have some 'me time!'"

Malcolm finally threw up his hands. "Fine, you win. Against my better judgment."

Thom breathed a sigh of relief. "Nothing will happen. I'm just gonna take a walk."

"Thommy, I don't like this. You'll be out there and exposed," Malcolm warned.

Thom couldn't repress the grin. "I'll keep my jacket and pants on." He patted Malcolm's shoulder. "You look like crap."

Malcolm just nodded. "I feel like crap. I think I'll just go to bed early. Call me when you get back from your walk, will you?"

"Of course I won't," he said. "You'll be asleep by then."

Mal was not amused. "That's the deal, man. You want alone, you call me when you get back to your room. And be glad I don't give you a curfew."

Thom narrowed his eyes, tilting his head. "You're kidding, right?"

"Nope! I mean it."

Thom threw up his hands in surrender. "Fine, okay. When I get back to my room." He put his hand over his heart. "I swear!"

That appeased Mal enough that he headed off to his room without grumbling. Thom watched him go and then headed to the elevator.

What was it about her? Why was she so different? If any other woman had treated him this way, he'd have just walked. Shown her the back of his Porsche and just gone. He had his pride; he didn't beg or whine. And he damn sure didn't bend for anyone. If it was just sex, he could have any woman he wanted. They still flocked to him, still thought he was sexy. Well, maybe not the ones he wanted, but he could still get women. He kept his body in good shape. Maybe there was more snow in the hair than blonde, but it still looked good. So why was he trying so goddamn hard for her?

Because she was different somehow. She was sure of herself, uncompromising. She didn't take crap from anyone for any reason. There was an outer beauty to that redhead, but there was an inner one too. She was smart, for one thing. Not just in a bookish way, but in things that mattered to him. In the short time that they'd been together, they'd discussed everything from the environment to the political hot buttons of the day. At no time did she skip a beat in the discussion, never raised her voice, seemed to be caught up on the latest news or issue.

She had the most intense blue eyes that looked into his soul, seeing everything. Thom was firmly convinced she *had* seen everything inside of him. Her hands were so graceful, flitting like butterflies when she spoke. She had the sweetest backside of any woman he'd ever met. The thought came unbidden; those long legs wrapped around his waist, her hair draped over a pillow or soft and silky against his skin. He shook that thought out of his head before his body could betray him in public.

He finally found her, out on the deck again. He stood for a moment, holding the door open. There was a lot of trepidation about going out there again, after last night. But his need to talk to her was greater than his paranoia. He closed the door behind him as he stepped outside to join her. Her hair was loose around her shoulders, curls blowing in the slight breeze. The sun was glinting off each strand. She was dressed in a dark purple sweater and jeans, a light coat thrown over her shoulders. She just stood there, hugging herself as she stared out at the mountains.

"You must love this spot. This is the second time I found

you here."

She didn't even jump at the sound of his voice. "I thought that was you."

"I, uh, I wanted to take a walk. Get out of that room for a while."

She just nodded her head.

"Um, how are you?"

She shrugged. "Same old, same old."

He wanted to turn her around, make her look at him. "Jo?"

Still not facing him, she seemed to pull an invisible something around herself, cutting herself off from him. With a guarded tone, she said, "Look, Thom, I really need to go in. I'm a little chilled now."

"Jo?"

She opened her mouth to say something, turning in his direction, and just stopped cold. The shock registered on her face.

"Jo?"

"Oh God, Thom," she breathed. Her fingers lightly brushed the bruise above his cheek.

"I'm fine."

"Your eye. Oh my Go—" She stopped herself, her hand dropping down to her side. The look of concern and sympathy was gone. The shield was back. "Well, I'm glad you're okay then. I need to go."

He took her shoulders in his hands, making her face him. "Jo, I want to know how *you* are."

The cold look never wavered. "Why?"

"Why?" He shook his head. "You have to ask?"

"Yeah, I do." She took a deep breath. "Why? Why do you

care? I'm just another lawyer to you. Just another woman."

"Hey." His brow furrowed. "That hurt. Come on, I never treated you that way."

"No, that's just part of the Mitchell charm, isn't it? Treat every conquest like the love of your life?"

"You're not another conquest, not to me."

"Well, that's not what he...." Her eyes glanced away.

"He what? He *who*?"

"That's not what I heard."

"Well...." Thom let go of her shoulders. "I can't deny anything. Yeah, you're right. I've had a lot of women who were just one night stands."

"Well, there you go."

"But that's not it, Jo." His fingers cupped her chin and, gently, he turned her face to him. "They used *me,* don't you see? Not the other way around. I was either a one-way track to fame and fortune, or it was a way to brag to their friends. 'I made it with the great Thom Mitchell, ain't I special.'"

"You didn't say no," she answered with a stubborn set to her mouth.

"Would you?" he asked her. "I spend three hours making love to an audience with my music. An incredibly sexy woman comes on to me, you think I'm not gonna take her up on it?"

She looked affronted at that. "Is that what you think I did? Come on to you?"

He shook his head, faltering as he spoke. That's not what he meant; damn it, he was saying this all wrong. "No. I never thought you did and I still don't. It wasn't that, okay? I mean you talked to me. You treated me like I was just me."

Her mouth opened and shut a few times before she finally

spoke. "Look, Thom...."

"Jo, whatever it was I did, I'm sorry." He still held her chin in his hand, now using the thumb to stroke her cheek. "I don't think of you in a cheap way at all. I think of you as a real lady, someone I've enjoyed being with."

"And Missy?"

"I told you. Missy is a kid. A pretty one, I'll grant you. But she's young, immature."

"She was in your room this morning."

Thom felt the warmth flood his heart and chest. She *had* come to see about him after all. "Malcolm asked her to find another doctor, not the hotel medic. She stayed around to clean up and help Mal. That's all."

Jo's eyes narrowed.

"I swear it, Jo!" He made an "x" shape over his chest, before holding his free hand up in his oath. "Mal was with me. To be honest, he never left, said he wanted to stay close in case I started convulsing or something. I made him sleep on the other side of the bed only because he wasn't leaving me all night and because that sofa is too short for a tall man."

"You..." she stuttered. "You...she..."

"She came in this morning. He called down about eight or so and asked for her. The front desk can confirm that. I swear it."

He watched her face, waiting patiently. She would either believe him or not. That feeling came back, that feeling of symmetry with her. But there was just enough doubt that his palms were sweating a little. Which would she choose?

It didn't take her long; her smile was pure sunshine over her face. "I'm sorry," she said. "I got stupid jealous." She ducked her head. "I can be a real idiot sometimes."

"Hey, you're not an idiot," he reassured her.

He took her into his arms and she came willingly, reaching around his waist and resting her cheek on his shoulder. The mere closeness of her, the smell of her perfumed skin; it was enough to drive him crazy. And yet, he was more than content to just stand here holding her.

"I wasted an entire day," she muttered against his chest. "I thought...." She left the rest unsaid, burying her face against his shoulder for a moment, before laying her cheek there again.

"Darlin', when in doubt, ask me. I won't lie to you."

"I will; I promise."

"Good."

She pushed back until she could see his face. "So, what do we do now?"

"How about watching the sun set?" He pointed over her shoulder. "It's setting over Wilde. See it?"

She turned around, still wrapped in his arms. "Where? Show me?"

She leaned back against his solid warmth, watching the slowly dimming light. Everything felt normal again; she was his again. He wrapped his arms around her waist and she laid her own on top of them. His cheek rested against hers and they watched as the sun started its 'peek-a-boo' game over the top of the mountain range.

"See that one? With the sun like fire on the summit?"

One hand left the pile of arms around her middle as he pointed off into the distance. She closed one eye and sited down the finger to see which mountain he was pointing toward.

"Yes," she answered. "Is that it?"

"That's Wilde."

She smiled, giggled a little. "That doesn't look so bad."

He pulled her closer, burying his face in her hair for a moment, then continued. "There's a story about it, you know. About Wilde."

"Yeah? Tell me?"

"Well," he started. "The mountain is named for Alexander Wilde. He came here in the first wave of Scottish immigrants, transported here after the uprising in 1745. They were sent here as prisoners, to serve as slave labor."

"Oh my God, that's terrible."

Thom chuckled and said, "That was war, honey. Anyway, old Alex wasn't having any of that. He lasted about six months before he ran away. And he headed right for that mountain, too. They searched the area for a month or so before giving up. Figured if he'd gone to that mountain, he was as good as dead. See, it had a bad reputation because of the Indians and the animals—man eaters, see."

"What, the Indians too?

"Yup. Most of the settlers believed the yarns that the trackers would tell, see. They were just trying to give the tribe its peace away from the white man, so they told tales that too many ignorant settlers believed."

"So what happened to Alexander?" she asked, caught up in the tale now.

"It was ugly up there at first, real ugly. Because of the steep incline and the bears and coyotes and wolves. Back then, there were more critters than you could shake a stick at and they weren't real afraid of men. They'd eat you as soon as look at you. But old Alex, he stood his ground. Built an old two room cabin up there that they say still exists."

She could see it, too. Closing her eyes, she imagined a tall, red haired man fighting the elements and the creatures. The forest primeval, with all of its fury and untamed glory, swallowing him whole to harden him against its harsh beauty. She could almost smell the scents of the animals, the trees, the grasses. But the face she saw wasn't a generic Scotsman—it was Thom's. And she had a moment to wonder what he would look like in a kilt. With his long hair, wild across his shoulders and blowing across his face.

"Anyway," he continued. "One day, he was hunting deer out in the forest, when he came across this bear sniffing around a tree. He started to run away until he heard this whimper and when he looked up in the tree, there was this woman."

"Oh no!"

"And without thinking, Wilde attacked that bear and they battled together—the highland warrior and the creature. Wilde was badly wounded but he killed that bear with his dirk. The tribe was grateful and he took the woman as his wife. The tribe also let him stay on that mountain and he's supposed to be the only white man ever to tame it. Which just means that he managed to live up there and not get killed by it or the wildlife."

She smiled, turning in his arms to face him. "Did he love her?"

Thom smiled at her again. "Oh yes he did. They say he had ten children with his Abanaki wife. And took many skins. Became a brother to the tribe, became one of them. For her."

Wrapping her arms around him, she sighed, "How romantic." She caught herself, rolling her eyes. "Would you listen to me, all dewy eyed. That's just disgusting."

He watched her, amused at the way she dismissed the

comment. "Hey, I like that dewy eyed," he told her, kissing the tip of her nose. "You want me to fight a bear or two for you while I'm up there?"

"Nah! But I'll settle for you coming back safe, if that mountain is as bad as you and Walt say it is."

"Tell you what," he said. "How about I bring you back some wild mountain thyme? It's thick up there and it's not an endangered plant, so I can pluck a few sprigs and no one would complain."

"Well then, sir, I think that would be fitting tribute for the maiden fair that I am," she teased. "I will accept that from you— and a song."

She turned back around to watch the sun continue on its way behind the mountain. They watched, saying nothing more and listening to the sounds of the birds and crickets, before they went in to dinner.

14

"You ready?" Thom picked up his backpack, shifting it around one shoulder. "Can you get yours?"

"You betcha," she told him, lifting it off the floor with a tiny twinge. She hoisted it over the opposite shoulder, then turned back to face him. "And I packed it right this time! I'm going to amaze you!"

He chuckled at that, leading her out of the dining room and into the employee's corridor that lead back to the kitchen. "You'll do just fine. This trail isn't too bad this time. It's an old carriage trail. We might have some obstacles along the way, the occasional rock or tree that's fallen over. But the elevation isn't too bad and the view is spectacular in places. ."

"I can do it," she assured him. "As a matter of fact, I plan on holding my own and then some!"

He grinned at her and winked, carrying his own pack slung over his shoulder like hers had been. "That's my girl. Tell you what, if the elevation doesn't put you off, then we'll see if Walt will take us on the Avalon trail that crosses it. It's a little more difficult and we might have to do a little climbing in places. But I think you can handle that. I'll help you along."

She nodded, slipping her hand in his. "Cool. Let's go."

Walt pulled up at the kitchen entrance, with Missy in the big four by four with him. Thom waved to them, then took Jo's pack from her and started around to the back of the car. Walt jumped out of the SUV and went to join him. Missy opened the window and Jo stood by the door.

"I hope you don't mind that I invited myself."

"Not at all," she answered, grinning. "You a hiker too?"

"Oh, I dabble. I'm not the hiker Walt is."

Jo relaxed a bit. "Good, I won't feel so overwhelmed. Those two are so out of my league it's not even funny. I'll be nice to have a casual hiker like me around."

Missy tossed a glance over her shoulder at the two men. "Walt said he and Thom sorta pushed you a little too hard."

Jo winced, the memory of the sore stiffness was still there two days later. "A little. But I survived. Thom says it'll help if I get up and get to it again."

"In here, Thom. I've got room for your packs. And I brought extras in case you need anything."

She caught Thom's raised eyebrow as he moved around behind Walt to stow the packs.

"Nice skirt," was all he said, his tone suggesting that he was trying not to laugh.

"Kilt," Walt corrected.

Jo craned her neck to see that Walt *was* wearing a kilt, a jaunty plaid of blue, black, and purple wool that draped around his hips and ended above his knees. *If there was ever a man that made that look manly and sexy, it's Walt. Good lord, I'm practically drooling.* She looked out of the corner of her eye to see Missy giving her man the same appreciative look. Jo quickly pulled it together and looked elsewhere.

Thom turned a blank look to Walt. "Sorry?"

"Kilt, man. You don't call a kilt a 'skirt.' That'll earn you a few nasty looks and a name or two around here."

"Why?" Joanna interrupted. "Just curious."

"Because New Hampshire is very proud of her Scottish heritage. See, a lot of the Scots fleeing the Culloden massacre and famine landed here. They fell in love with the Whites and said this was just like the highlands of home. So, they settled here."

"Really?" Jo asked.

"Really," he answered. "New Hampshire has her own tartan, too. You'll see it on the state police as their dress uniform. They wear the kilts everywhere."

"You're Scotch?" Thom asked.

"Scottish," Walt corrected. "Scotch is the drink. And yeah, I am. Beaton is my last name and my family came from the St. Andrews area of Scotland."

A smile grew on Thom's lips. "St. Andrews? Really? You have golf in your blood?"

Walt laughed and flashed a toothy grin. "Are you kidding? My grandfather caddied the British Open when he was just in his teens. He moved here and married my grandmother. Taught my dad how to play and my dad taught me. Next to hiking, it's my favorite. I've got a handicap of twenty-five."

Thom whistled in appreciation. "Mine's about nineteen or twenty. How long you been playing?"

Walt wrinkled his forehead, thinking about it. "Let's see; I started playing when I was nine. So, about sixteen years, I think."

Thom grinned. "I think I found my new best friend."

And with that, they headed off for the trail. It was a pleasant drive on a twisty two-lane road. Huge pines and maples lined the road and Jo kept looking in them to see if she could spot any wildlife. The air was scented with the sap of the trees and the musk of the wild things that lived within. While Walt drove, Missy pointed out landmarks and little sights along the way. It didn't take long before they were in the parking lot and Walt was turning off the engine.

"Okay, we're here." He helped them all into their packs, making sure they had the collapsible poles and their camelbacks secure. "Ready?"

They all nodded.

"Now, we're going to take the Mt. Willard trail. It'll lead us through some beautiful forested areas and straight up to the cliffs. We'll also pass by the Hitchcock Flume, which is a pretty amazing sight, too."

"Thom said something about the Avalon trail?" Jo glanced at Thom to confirm. "Wasn't that what you said?"

"Yes, I did." Thom turned to Walt. "I thought if she was doing okay, we could cut over that one. What do you think?"

Walt chewed on that one for a moment. "I don't know."

"Why? What's wrong with it?" she asked.

"That one might be a bit over your skill level," Walt explained. "The trail is overgrown in places where no one's been keeping it up. And it's a bit like the last trail." He shrugged and told Thom, "Look, you're paying me and you can choose. But I thought you might want something that's not quite as strenuous."

Jo watched Thom consider it. He put a hand on her elbow, giving her the decision.

"It's up to you, honey," he said. "How deep do you want to go?"

The lesser trail would give her a chance to redeem herself. She was still a little stiff and her feet hurt a bit, despite the comfortable shoes and socks. But, she wanted to show him that she could do it. "Let's just stay on the Willard then. I'd like to see the cliffs and the flume."

Thom took her hand. "Whatever the lady wants, Walt."

Walt smiled at them, his own arm around Missy's waist. "Sounds good to me." He kissed the top of her head and let her go. "So. Thom, have you ever been up this path?"

Thom shook his head. "First time for me, too."

Walt looked back at Missy, who nodded and smiled at him. He turned back to Jo and Thom. "Well, Missy and I have both done this one, so I think the best thing to do will be to buddy up." He pointed to the camera around Thom's neck. "Missy can point out the photo ops along the way."

Thom grinned and nodded. "Thanks."

To Jo, Walt said, "And I can show you some of the flora and fauna around here, things you won't see anywhere else and definitely not in those guide books."

Jo felt any doubt fade away. "Well then, let's get moving, Sparky. The morning's a-wasting."

Walt turned back to the other couple. "Ready?"

Thom gestured Missy to walk in front of him. "We're ready."

They decided that Walt would be in the lead and Thom would take the rear. They took off at a steady walk. Walt pointed out various plants that were indigenous to the area, the fragile ecosystem that formed the White Mountains. The natural sounds of the birds and a wafting breeze were punctuated with the frequent clicking of Thom's shutter as Missy pointed out the perfect shots. They formed a rhythm and pace, walking over the dirt and stone path, periodically stopping for Thom to get his shots and Jo to ask questions about some plant or sight. The day was perfect.

"Here, Jo." Walt pointed down. "Look down there."

Joanna peered down over the edge of the cliff, down into the crevasse below. "What is it?"

"That's a moose; a cow by the look of it. And the way she's acting, I'd say she's got—" He held up his hand for her to be quiet. "Yup, look. She's got her baby with her."

Joanna was entranced, mother and child walking leisurely along the floor of the valley as they stopped to eat along the way. The mother was huge, heavily muscled with dark rich colored fur. For a clumsy looking beast, she had such grace as she walked, sniffing the air occasionally to check for threats of danger. When she was satisfied again that she and her little one were safe, she would put her nose back to the grass and take a mouthful to chew slowly and methodically.

Her calf was gangly, all knees and big eyes, barely keeping its zeal at being out in the world in check. Jo wanted to laugh aloud as the little one would walk only so far, always looking over to make sure its mum was still within running distance. A jay screeched, startling the baby, and it scooted back to the mother and leaned against the cow's side. A few seconds passed and the baby got brave enough again to go a little further. The pair slowly made their way across the valley, repeating the dance over and over.

Thom and Missy joined the two of them, also hushed, and the four watched. There was something so tranquil about the small family as they foraged. There was an almost reverent feel to it all.

Walt moved closer to Joanna, one hand resting on his hip and his collapsed pole in the other. He used the object as a pointer to show where a male deer had just walked out into the clearing; a huge set of antlers hooked proudly over the stag's head.

"You like wild animals?" Walt whispered.

She smiled and whispered back to him. "The wilder the better."

"You know, that stag looks like he's got the right idea."

"Oh?"

"Showing off his manhood there. That rack overhead makes him attractive to the females. He's also showing off to the other males. Show 'em who's boss."

"So. Is it true what they say?" she teasingly asked him. "The bigger the rack, the bigger the—"

He chuckled. "So they say."

"You are very bad, Walt Beaton," she teased. "You could get me in serious trouble here."

He leaned closer, grinning. "Me, too."

She heard a polite cough to her left and saw Thom's tight-lipped expression. In a way, his jealous reaction was a bit insulting but at the same time, it was rather sweet. It made her feel a little better to know that he actually cared about her, probably more than he was ready to let on. She smiled to reassure him, winking at him as she did. He smiled back at her, nodding, then went back to his camera and lining up his next shot.

It was the unspoken communication between Walt and Missy that took her focus away from him. The look that passed between them was tender and it was obvious that they were the only ones standing on that ridge at that moment. And it went on and on, the electricity between them almost palpable.

Jo started to feel very uncomfortable, an unwanted voyeur, and turned her gaze back to the stag, still holding court in the valley below.

"Sorry," came the quiet voice beside her.

She smiled back at Walt, who was wearing a sheepish grin and a little blush still on his cheeks. "Why are you sorry for being in love?" she asked, her voice equally soft. It seemed a sin to speak any louder than whispers in this place.

"Oh, uh...." He scratched the back of his head, trying not to look every other inch the little boy. And failed, because that's exactly what he looked like.

Jo patted him on the back. "It's okay. It's really sweet. How long have you two known each other?"

"Since she started working at the hotel." Walt crossed his arms, smiling with the memory. "I used to work at the Mt. Washington, too. That's how we met. Except I graduated from college a couple years before she did."

"But you two still dated?"

"Yup. We did." He rubbed on hand on the wool of the kilt. "That's why I wore this, because she loves me in it."

Jo peeked from the corner of one eye to see that Missy hadn't taken her eyes off Walt. "Walt, my friend," Jo said, "that's called love."

He nodded. "I asked her to marry me. Did she tell you that?"

"She's not told me anything, honey." Jo turned her attention back to Walt. "Congratulations."

He shrugged. "Well, don't congratulate us yet. She's dragging her heels a little."

"Oh? Why?"

"A lot of crap. See, she didn't come from a real stable family—

her Mom was married six times by the time she was eighteen. Missy's afraid she's like her Mom that way."

Jo took another look at the younger woman, then back to Walt. "Sweety, you just be patient, okay? Trust me; I saw the way she was looking at you. And that young lady is head over heels about you."

Walt grinned. "Think so?"

"Know so," she answered with a wink.

Walt pointed down again, this time at another part of the valley. But she never heard a single thing he said. The metallic pole shot out of his hand, flipping end over end, back and over his shoulder. It was a split second before they heard the crack of a rifle report from somewhere in the forest around them. Moose and deer scurried back into the cover of the forest. The ground at Joanna's feet flicked with a puff of soil reacting to the lead that had disturbed it. Another crack echoed in the valley around them.

"Holy shit!"

Thom gripped Joanna's elbow, pulling her backwards. Everything moved in slow motion at that point. As she turned toward Thom, she got a quick glimpse of their companions. Walt had pulled Missy into his arms and out of the way. Thom was evidently trying to do the same for Joanna, but he wasn't moving fast enough. The collar of his jacket twitched, then jumped as two bullets tore through the material. Two more retorts bounced off the rocks before Thom finally pulled her away.

But they were standing too close to the edge. Thom's face changed from one of grim anger to one of shock as he lost his balance. His arms pinwheeled in frantic circles as he tried to keep from a headlong plummet over the ledge and down. Without thinking, Joanna reached out and grabbed the denim of his jacket. She planted one foot against a large rock and pulled gently. It was just enough to stop the free fall and get him pulled back away from the edge. He fell against her, both of them locked in an embrace as they moved quickly away from the ledge and back behind another jutting boulder. Another series of whining noises greeted their ears as several more bullets struck the rocks, followed by the bang from the shots.

Missy was in panic, clutching at Walt and burying her face in his chest. She was alternately screaming and sobbing. Thom put his hand on Walt's shoulder and the younger man turned an equally grim look Thom's way.

"Don't panic, buddy." Thom's voice was pitched low, trying to reassure.

Walt just nodded. "I'm not panicking. I'm pissed. There's a difference." He pulled out a small device that looked like a cross between a walkie-talkie and a very large cell phone.

"What are you doing?"

Walt quickly dialed a few numbers before putting the contraption to his ear. With one arm wrapped around Missy, he started cooing to her. It took exactly three seconds before he started barking into the handset. "Walt Beaton. Yeah, Reg, we got rifle fire on Willard, around the cliffs. Some dumb ass hunter is in the wrong section. I need the rangers notified and tell 'em to make sure they follow the map I filed." He pressed a button and stuffed the handset back in his pack. His arms came back around Missy and he went back to cradling her against his chest.

"Sorry, Thom, I didn't mean to get short with you."

"What the hell is going on?" Thom sounded furious but Joanna knew that he was just trying to keep it together.

"Probably just some dumb ass who thinks this is open land. It's not. This is federal land we're on and that jackass is poaching."

Thom's face was pale but he was doing better than she was. Joanna was sweating from alternating cold and hot flashes. She could feel her heart hammering in her chest. Those bullets had come too close. Hunters? She was beginning to wonder.

"I think the guy's done, Walt," Thom said as quietly as he could. "It's been quiet for the last minute or so."

"Yeah, well, I'm not going to take the chance." Walt carefully stood up, using the huge boulder as cover. He was keeping *his* voice down, too. "Come on, we're going down a different way. It'll be rough, but I think you folks can do it. It'll get us back down fast. I want distance between us and that idiot."

Joanna felt paralyzed. Her legs refused to do anything and her whole body was suddenly one big 'pins and needles' mass of electric stabs. She was panting, not sure if she had the energy to get up. Walt had Missy quieted for now; she had stopped sobbing but her eyes still had a glassy look.

Thom's hand cut into her field of vision, outstretched and expectant. She looked from the hand, up the arm, into the face. He was smiling, the warm chocolate eyes calm. She'd never really noticed it before, how beautiful that smile was and how it crinkled the corners of his eyes. How the corner of his mouth curled up into a dimple. It helped to see that detail; it helped her get her focus back.

"Come on, Jo. Let's get out of here. I need a drink. How about you?"

She nodded vehemently. "Abso-friggin-lutely!" She took his hand, her eyes never leaving his.

He was strong, even while he was just as unnerved as she was. He pulled her up to a standing position, put his arm around her waist, and kept her supported. "Think you can do this?" he asked, quietly.

"Yeah," she told him. "Just don't let go, okay?"

"Never, darlin'."

Quietly and swiftly, they followed Walt down another trail. True to his word, it was rough—steeper passages, some large rocks to climb over, all going downhill—but it was quick enough to get them back to the parking lot and on their way.

15

THOM REALIZED THAT this was the end of his anonymity, coming and going as he pleased. Walt drove down the long, winding drive that lead to the hotel and passed at least thirty vans and trucks. Each one had a logo of a news service on the side, along with satellite hook ups. And all of the biggies were here; CNN, NBC, CBS, ABC, and Fox—you name it; they were there. Even Al-Jazeera had sent a van. Thom shook his head and groaned. So much for his peaceful vacation.

Walt had called the rangers. The rangers had contacted the local police. The local cops knew they were way over their heads and called the state police. The state police, upon finding out that the incident happened on federal land, contacted the FBI. Of course, every local radio and TV station, along with every newspaper, had a police scanner. As soon as his name was mentioned—even as a has-been—the interest was there.

Walt pulled up to the front entrance and the throng surrounded his SUV. Just as quickly, the state cops had a way cleared and the locals gave the four an escort into the lobby. Thom put a protective arm around Jo and guided her through the gauntlet of shouted questions and flashing lights. The reporters were kept back far enough that they didn't have to shove their way through but they were still close enough to unnerve Jo. He helped her in the door, followed by Walt protecting Missy in the same way. No sooner had they cleared the threshold than two of the local cops slammed the doors behind them and stood guard to keep the press outside.

Thom mentally thanked God for the locals. Crowd control was probably the only thing they had to do in this small town. And they did it very, very well.

The lobby was boiling with the *big* law enforcement, which also included the rangers who had also poked around up on the mountain. Malcolm had called for an ambulance and the paramedics were inside. You couldn't swing a dead cat and not hit some sort of official. They were separated at that point, each of them taken to a different corner of the room. Thom took one last look at Jo before turning to the ranger, the two state cops, one of the two FBI agents, and the paramedic trying to shine that damn light in his eyes.

He was almost normal again, telling everyone what happened. His pulse had slowed back down. A quick exam and no, he'd not been hit by any of the bullets. No, he hadn't hit his head on a rock, or fallen, or gotten hurt. He was just shaken up. He gave his statement to the law officials, let the paramedic feel up his head and poke him in the right places. The paramedic pronounced him healthy as a horse and the cops thanked him for answering their questions.

"Thommy!"

For a moment, Thom thought the man was going to hug him. Mal stopped just short of that, thankfully, but the scared look never left his face. Thom smiled, hoping that he looked normal—even if he didn't feel that way right now.

"Mal."

The words came out rushed and hurried as Mal let his

normally self-assured curtain fall to the wayside. "Are you alright? Did the guy check you out?"

"I'm fine, man. Honest. I'm good. A little shaken up but no damage."

Malcolm surveyed the room, his eyes resting in one place over Thom's shoulder. Thom took a quick glance and saw that Malcolm was staring at Jo.

She wasn't as pale as before, looking as if she'd calmed as well. He gave her a quick smile, hoping for one in return but didn't get it. But she was watching him as well; she nodded in his direction before she turned back to the cop at her side.

"Thommy, you're sure you're okay?"

"Paramedics gave me a clean bill of health. All I got was winded from running and I may have to change my shorts thanks to having something scared out of me. But I'm good."

"But—"

Geez, there were days when Mal was worse than a mother hen. "Look, you know what would do me more good than anything?"

Mal jumped on that. "Name it, man, name it. What do you need?"

"We could all use some coffee or hot tea."

"You want some brandy in that?" Mal asked nervously.

Thom shook his head. "No, man, better not. The press out there watching, the cops inside. Besides, not when I'm like this. Not when I'm still upset. Just coffee or hot tea. For all of us."

Mal nodded. "Sure, sure. I'll go get the kitchen to make a couple pots of strong, hot coffee. I'll be right back."

Thom turned back to see that Jo was now seated on one of the sofas. Right now, sitting didn't seem to be such a bad idea.

So he walked over and sat down next to her. "Hey, there."

"Hi."

"How are you doing there?"

She was sitting straight as a ramrod, her hands nervously working in her lap.

"Jo—"

She sat back, a confused look on her face. "Huh?"

He took one of the hands in his, weaving his fingers in between hers. "Talk to me. What's going on in that pretty head of yours?"

Her face relaxed into a smile. "I'm okay, Thom. Very freaked out right now but I'm okay. I'm coming down off the adrenaline rush."

He kissed her fingers, ignoring the flashes in the background. *Let 'em flash, she's my lady and I don't care.*

Missy plopped down next to them. "Are you guys okay?"

Jo nodded at her. "Yeah, thanks. How's Walt."

She shrugged, a very blasé tone in her voice. Missy was sitting ramrod straight but her shoulders were slumped. Her hair hung in strands around her face as she stared at the floor. "Walt's great, are you kidding? He's always great in a crisis."

No sooner had she said that than Walt joined them. "You two all right? Thom? Jo?"

Thom nodded, sitting back against the cushions "Yep, clean bill of health for both of us."

"Good then. You mind if I take Missy and we get out of here? I'm...." He stole a glance at the girl who was staring at her fingers. "I think just we need to go home and relax. Wait for the after-the-emergency panic to set in."

Thom watched Missy, saw the blank look on her face. He

knew that panic all too well; the safety of falling apart when something traumatic was all over and you didn't have to live on the edge of the knife blade anymore. She looked like she really needed to fall apart and just cry it out. Walt was smart enough to realize that she needed privacy to do it.

"Mr. Beaton?"

All of them turned their attention to the FBI agent, crisp black suit and stern expression on his face, standing there.

"Can I talk to you for a moment, sir? I need your statement for the report."

"But I just gave it to Dale."

"Sir, this is for the official federal record."

Walt sighed, rolling his eyes toward the ceiling. "Yeah, sure."

The ranger appeared beside Jo. "Ms. Hayes?"

She sighed too. "Oh, bloody hell." She squeezed Thom's hand. "You'll wait right here?"

He smiled at her. "I sure will."

"Good, I'll only be a moment and then, we're going upstairs to put you to bed."

Severe fatigue washed over him at that moment, his own adrenaline rush suddenly gone. He decided not to argue. "Sure, darlin'. I'll be right here."

They both followed their respective officers off to separate corners. Thom watched them as they stood talking. Walt was stoic, his arms crossed over his chest and the kilt dirty but still in good order. Joanna, however, was waving her hands. Thom watched her, her animated discourse was like watching two birds fluttering around her face. He could tell she was not as pulled together as she appeared—

"Thom?"

Missy had slight traces of wetness on her cheeks.

"Oh, honey," he murmured to her. He pulled her into an embrace. "It's all right, honey. Don't cry. It's done and over."

She wrapped her arms around him and laid her cheek against his shoulder. "I'm trying not to. I really am."

He hugged her close and kissed the top of her forehead. "You did just fine, honey. You really did."

She chose that particular moment to look up into his eyes; her lips were scant centimeters away from his own. "Really?"

"Really." He kissed her cheek and stroked her hair. "You go home and take a nice hot shower and get some rest. Everything will be just fine in the morning."

She wiped the back of her hand against her nose.

"What is it, honey?"

"We coulda...we...I mean...."

"I know," Thom answered. He tucked the strands of hair behind her ears and turned her so she could look into his eyes. "Now, you listen to me. We're all here; we're all safe. Whatever happened out there is over."

"Over," she repeated, dubious but still holding on in however a tentative way. She was going to be brave, come hell or high water.

He put his arm around her again and they both sat back. He could be hugging his daughter, he thought, and it gave him a bit of a warm feeling despite it all.

"Can I ask you a question?"

He looked down at his side. "Sure, Missy. What is it?"

"How do you know if you're in love?"

He smiled a bit at that. "Oh, you just know."

"But how? Are you in love with Ms. Hayes?"

"With Jo?" He watched Joanna, still talking away with her hands. "You know, I was in love with my first wife. But it wasn't enough. I really screwed that one up bad. And then came my second wife."

"Did you love *her*?"

He turned his head to answer her. "You know, I thought I did at the time. But the truth is, no. I was in love with her being in love with me. If that makes sense."

Missy nodded, watching him and gripping a pillow so tightly that her knuckles were turning white.

"Missy, darlin', one thing I do know." He squeezed her wrist and smiled reassuringly at her. "You'll feel it inside when you've met the right one. And it'll be no bending required. Both of my wives, it's like we were doing a contortionist act." He patted her knee. "Truth is they gave me three great kids and we tied each other in emotional knots from it."

"Does Joanna make you bend?"

Jo turned at that moment to see them watching her. She smiled at Thom, and then went back to the discussion.

"No. She doesn't."

"Sounds like you really love her then."

Thom grinned. "You think so?"

"Yeah."

"Does Walt make *you* bend?"

Missy shook her head.

"Sounds like you really love him then."

"I wish I could be sure."

"You'll know, honey," he advised. "Just relax and don't over-think it."

"He asked me to marry him."

He smiled at her again. "Sounds like he's in love with you, then."

She got up without another word and walked over to where Walt was finishing up. She put her arms around Walt's waist, resting her cheek against his shoulder. They left a moment later, with an escort of police to get them to Walt's SUV.

"Thom." Malcolm handed him a hot cup of coffee.

"Oh, thanks, man." The first sip was rich and hot, relaxing the rest of him. "Did you get any for the rest of 'em?"

"Yeah," Mal answered, pointing around the room. Everyone had a hot cup of coffee and was drinking.

"Thanks, man," Thom told him.

Malcolm focused on Thom again. "You want to talk about what happened? I mean, if you haven't talked it out of your system."

"In the morning, okay? Right now, I'll be lucky to make it upstairs to pass out."

Mal jutted his jaw in the direction of the two or three remaining officers. "Do the cops have any idea who did it?"

Thom shrugged. "No clue.

Jo materialized at Thom's side and sat down next to him. "Thom? Oh, hello, Malcolm."

Mal bowed slightly, his voice formal and neutral. "Joanna. Are you all right, too?"

Thom took her hand. "Jo and I are fine, Mal. It's okay."

Mal nodded. "Let's get you both upstairs and now."

Thom turned his head and in a no-nonsense-allowed voice, declared, "Jo, I want you to come stay the night with me."

She snorted at that suggestion. "What, the post shoot out slumber party?"

"Of course." Thom crossed his arms, shaking his head. "I shouldn't be the only one pissing my pants right now."

"That's all you got? A little pee in your shorts?" Jo blew a raspberry at him before scrubbing her mouth with the back of her hand.

Malcolm had been momentarily forgotten in their repartee, but his interruption reminded them of his presence. "Thommy—"

"Mal, I want her close. Make sure she's fine."

"Thom, it's okay," she said. "I think you need to go sleep. You still look pale and I feel like I need to throw up."

"Then, come sleep on the so—," In mid-word, he changed his mind. "No, on second thought, you get the bed and *I'll* sleep on the sofa." He raised a finger to silence them both. "I'm not taking no for an answer and I promise to be a gentleman."

"Thom, that couch opens out into another bed she can sleep on," Mal protested.

"No, no, I'll get the sofa and let the lady have the room." He pulled his best manners out of the mental closet he kept them in, dusted them off, and bowed deeply. After all, she was a southern belle, used to that kind of thing. Or should be.

Jo laughed, throwing up her hands in mock defeat. "Okay, fine. I know when I'm fighting a losing battle."

"Good." That helped, the color returned to her face. Thom turned to his best friend. "Mal? Come join us. I need to fall apart right now." He pointed out the window to the paparazzi still milling around. "And I'd prefer not to have an audience."

Mal nodded again. "Go on up. I need to get a bottle of brandy sent up to your room and I'm going to insist on this, Thom. You need something to steady your nerves. I'll be right behind you."

"No argument from me. And don't forget the tea," Thom said. He took Joanna's hand. "Come on, honey, let's go upstairs."

Malcolm waited until they'd stepped on the elevator before he pulled out his cell phone. He was going to have a few well-chosen, very obscene words for someone later. But for now, he needed something else. He dialed a number quickly, then held the phone to his ear.

"Milton Detective Agency."

"Milt, it's Mal."

"Hey, buddy! Long time no hear from."

"I have another job for you."

"Shoot, my man. Who's the mark?"

"Her name is Hayes. Joanna Hayes. She's a lawyer with the firm of Roland, Micarello, and Howell in Nashville, Tennessee."

"Got it."

"I want everything about this woman. I want to know every bit of dirt, from her first cry in diapers until the moment she got here in New Hampshire. And I need it tomorrow."

"Geez, buddy. You don't give a guy much notice."

"But I pay you extremely well. Can you do it?"

"It's done."

Malcolm slipped his phone into his pocket. He went to the front desk and ordered the tea and brandy, following the request with a fifty-dollar bill. When the desk clerk assured him that everything would be sent up immediately, he turned on his heel and headed for Thom's room.

16

Malcolm spent the night dozing in the recliner. Thom, true to his word, had slept on the sofa. Well, neither one had *slept*, if he had to be honest. They'd both just dozed, although Thom wasn't aware that *Malcolm* knew that. Mal kept his lids closed just enough to look asleep, but still be able to watch through his lashes. All night, Thom would doze, then jump up as silently as possible to creep into the bedroom. He would stay gone a few minutes, then would come back and settle down to doze for another hour or so.

Malcolm hated that woman with all his being. Thom's two wives had never threatened him like she did. He could keep those women in check, but not Ms. Hayes. She would know what he was and not tolerate it at all. She'd force Thom to drop him like a bad habit. She'd turn Thom's head around and that would be the end of everything. And that was something Mal could not stomach. Or allow.

Somewhere around dawn, Thom had finally passed out into a deep sleep. Malcolm waited until he heard Thom's deep snores, then got up and went to the table in what was passing for a dining area and just sat.

Thom was the best thing that had ever happened to Malcolm. They held a genuine affection for each other, a tenderness that transcended anything as sordid as a relationship. Being with

Thom gave Malcolm a sense of elation and euphoria, a sense of place and being. When he'd long given up on any semblance of a real life, Malcolm always had Thom.

I've nursed you back too many times, buddy. Too many times. From the booze and the pain. I did too many things for you, Thommy. Too many to count, some of them...well, some less than savory. Took care of that union mess and you didn't deal with a strike on that first tour. Took care of the drugs when your drummer got caught with a dime bag. That Mullins thing. You never got your hands dirty on that one. I took care of it and left you spotless.

There was still tea in the pot. Malcolm poured a dollop of brandy in the cup and topped it off with the rest of the brew. Brandy was the only thing Thom could drink in moderation without succumbing to his severe alcoholic tendencies. He very rarely had more than one or two, choosing to put it in tea to help soothe his throat after a show or his nerves before anything huge. After what had happened, Malcolm had made sure it was handy for the latter reason.

I remember when Angie left you; I bet you don't remember that, do you? The night she told you that she was divorcing you and you broke down. Do you remember the rage when you found out that Sandy was screwing around on you? Where did you come? To me. And I listened.

He sipped from the cup, feeling the warmth of the brandy filling his stomach. Thom, lying on his back, looked like such a child. The shock of blond hair across his forehead. The skin smoothing out into peaceful slumber and careless relaxation. Malcolm watched the rise and fall of his chest, listened to the soft snores that came from Thom's mouth.

This bitch is bad news, Thommy. I feel it inside me. She'll upset everything. She can't take care of you like I can. She won't know how to rein you in when you get self-indulgent. Or how to stop your tears when you hit a depression so black that light is only a dream. She won't know how to celebrate your triumphs or bolster you up when you fall. But what can I do? What can I do to make her leave you alone?

She came stumbling into the room, her hair tousled in sleepy disarray. She was wearing a pair of Thom's pajamas, working her hand through her slutty red hair. Malcolm raised a finger to his lips and pointed to the sofa. She nodded. He motioned to the other chair and she sat down in it.

"Good morning," he whispered.

"Is he sleeping?" she whispered back.

"Finally."

"Good." She watched Thom for a moment before turning back to Malcolm. "I need to head back to my room, to shower and change."

He nodded, hearing a soft *whump* at the door. He made his way to the entrance. "Fine. Thom needs to stay in, if you don't mind. I'm more worried about the publicity that this is going to bring now."

He opened the door to find the newspaper laying there. It was lying open, the picture and headline glaring at him. It was all he needed; he saw the answer to everything. He folded it and brought it inside.

"Is that the paper?"

He repressed the smile, acting as if he'd not seen the front. "Yes." Before he handed it to her, he said, "You mind if I use the bathroom before you take it over to change?"

She nodded and he went on, giving her the paper. He

stopped at the door—where she couldn't see him—and watched her as she opened it to the front page. With a malicious glee, he watched her face go pale. She stared, her lips tightening and disappearing as she did. Malcolm ducked inside the bathroom and silently closed the door when he saw her stand up. He waited until the sounds of her dressing and gathering her things stopped and the bedroom was quiet again. He tiptoed out, just in time to see her close the main door behind her.

And that takes care of that, he thought to himself with a smug assurance. But his phone began to vibrate in his pocket. He thumbed the slide on the display screen to answer, stepping back into the bathroom.

"Hey, buddy, it's me."

Malcolm grinned wide as he answered, "Promise me you have information."

"Oh, I got great info, my man. I'm gonna fax these sheets to the hotel and have 'em deliver the goods to you. You're gonna love this stuff."

This day was getting better and better all the time.

17

MALCOLM PAUSED BEFORE the eggs and sausage. "I love this place. They have a great breakfast buffet."

"Oh yeah." Thom stared at the spread with a growing lust before something shiny caught his eye. "Oh, hey, the coffee's down here. You finish filling your plate and I'll go get us a table."

"Okay."

Thom found the nearest empty table to the coffee urn and set his plates down. He filled a carafe and grabbed two cups. By now, the staff was used to him and had told him to help himself when he wanted. Today, he wanted a lot of things. He poured the coffee and sat down to eat. The growling in his belly impressed upon him that all he'd had the night before was two cups of tea with brandy and three more without. He tore into his food with a voracious appetite.

Mal sat down with an amused look on his face. "Geez, Thommy, not hungry, are you?"

Thom chortled through a mouthful of scrambled eggs. He swallowed, taking a sip of the best coffee he'd had in a while. *Or is it just because I'm happy?* "Feels like forever since I ate last," he answered. "I'm making up for lost time."

Malcolm tucked the napkin in his lap. "I'm not surprised. I'm starving too."

Thom nodded and stuffed another piece of bacon in his mouth.

"You look different, Thommy."

The fork poised in midair, Thom cocked an eyebrow. He *looked* different? He thought about that for a moment. Was he different? The slow grin gave away his answer; he probably was.

Mal paused between bites. "And what brought this on? Because you can share, you know."

Thom swallowed the bite he'd been chewing on. "You mean besides yesterday's hike and 'adventure?'"

"That would be enough for *me*."

"Mmm, good coffee." Thom took a sip of his coffee, trying to put it together in words. He wasn't even sure if he could say it the right way. But he had to try. "Yeah, but it's more than that. You know, yesterday did something to me." He paused, staring at the cup in his hands. "I had a hard time sleeping last night."

"I noticed," was Mal's dry response.

So Malcolm knew. Thom shrugged. "You know, whoever that was could have killed me, Mal. Maybe it was an accident, but those two shots came too damned close for me."

Malcolm froze, his fork poised in mid-route to his mouth. Just like him to understand immediately.

"It kinda changed my perspective," Thom finished.

"I'm sure it did." Mal put his fork back down, bite uneaten. His face was unreadable, dark and lost in thought. "I'm sorry, Thom."

Thom snapped his fingers to get his friend's attention. "Wasn't your fault, man. Besides, that's not the point."

"What *is* the point?"

"Mal, I'm a very lucky man. I started thinking of all the things I have—my family, my kids. My friends." He reached out to squeeze Mal's shoulder. "*All* of my friends."

Malcolm smiled at him, the dark look gone again.

Thom sat back with his mug, and drained it. "But there's something else," he continued. "I suddenly realized that I've been missing something. In all of the good fortune I have, all of the friends I've met with my music, I'm missing something."

Malcolm resumed his breakfast. "What's that?"

It was time to say aloud what he'd thought about all night. Taking a big gulp of air, he opened his mouth and let the words flow. "I've met someone. Someone incredible. Someone who wants me for me, not for my career or any influence I might have had at one time. She doesn't give a shit about my star status. She doesn't care about Thom Mitchell. She wants *Jared* Thomas Mitchell. "

For a second time, Mal's fork stopped before it reached his lips.

Thom rushed ahead before he could be interrupted. "No, I know what you're thinking. 'Thom's just on a vacation affair.' I hear you thinking it. But not *this* time, buddy. Not *this* time."

"Oh?"

It all came pouring out of him, almost as if he was saying it in one breath. "She's terrific. She's smart and funny. And she's so honest. She doesn't tell me things just because she thinks I want to hear them. She tells me the truth." He held his empty mug in his hands, looking down at it. "Do you know what that feels like? You're the only other soul who was ever honest with me like that."

Mal's elbows hit the table and he tented his fingers, tapping both index fingers against his chin. "I take it you're referring to the illustrious Ms. Hayes?"

Thom sat back in his chair, an indescribable wave of emotion sweeping him away. "Yes I am. Malcolm, I'm...I'm.... "

"In love?"

Thom considered that. Was he? And if he was, was he ready to admit *that* to the world. He'd just taken a huge step for now. Was he ready to go all out yet? "Mal, I don't know. I'm almost afraid to go that far. But I know how she makes me feel."

Malcolm shook his head. That was never a good sign.

"What? Mal, what is it?"

"Thom...." Malcolm shook his head again. "None of my business."

"No, say it."

Malcolm hesitated first. "Okay, but you won't like it."

Thom smiled. "Don't pull a punch now. I'd think I didn't know you as well as I thought I did."

"All right then," Malcolm answered. He took the last bite, set the fork on the plate, and pushed it away. He wiped the corners of his mouth and laid the napkin to the side of the plate.

Thom watched all of this with a clutch at his guts, but said nothing.

"You and I go way back, Thommy," he finally said.

Thom nodded. "Yes we do."

He took a deep breath before continuing. "I was there when your first marriage ended. Thom, you were this side of devastated. You also went through a series of—."

Suddenly Thom knew where this was going. "Hold on now."

"Thom, let me finish."

Thom nodded and sat back to wait.

"I'm just saying that, well, your choices of companions weren't as serious as you were and you got hurt a lot. You were lonely. And then, Sandy came along. Your friends saw it was a wrong thing—*wait*, let me finish—but you were so sure you were in love. We didn't stop you."

Thom said nothing. Mal was going to drag out his sins one by one and wasn't going to be stopped. Maybe he *did* need to hear it, hear the perspective of the other side of the coin. But that didn't mean he had to like it.

Malcolm laid his hands on the table, linking his fingers. "All I'm saying is just go slow. You fall in love too easy. And have this old fashioned idea that you have to marry the woman if you sleep with her. You barely know her. All I'm saying is take your time."

Thom smiled, trying to keep it as warm as he could. Malcolm really did care; he knew that. But his friend didn't get it, didn't understand what he was feeling.

"Besides," Malcolm added. "How do you know she's not married?"

"She told me she's not."

Malcolm made an odd noise, reaching for the coffee carafe. He poured them both another cup. "She *told* you? And you *believed* her?"

"Yes, I did," Thom asserted. "She's not trying to trick me, Mal. She's honest, *blunt* honest. And I appreciate that. She's not pushing me or wanting anything from me that I don't want to give."

"Just be careful, Thom. Please?"

Thom stirred at the potatoes and eggs on his plate, moving things around without really looking at them. "Mal, you don't get it. She makes me feel young and alive again. It's been a long time since I felt that way."

He felt Malcolm's hand on his shoulder. When he looked up, he saw that Mal really was concerned. "I know, Thommy. I hope

I'm wrong."

"You are, man. You'll see. In the meantime, let me enjoy this. Let me have this. I need it bad."

There was a polite cough behind them. Thom turned to see two men standing, side by side. One was shorter and slight, dressed in a black polo shirt and jeans. He had dark hair that had been cropped above the collar, but still had the spring of curls haloing his face. The other man was taller, blonde hair cut into a screaming short buzz. His dress was impeccable; dark colored suit, starched white button down shirt, a tie that looked as if it had been made by the same tailor that made his suit. Where the darker one slouched a little, this one stood ramrod straight.

"Mr. Mitchell?"

Both men pulled out what looked like leather business card holders. But when they opened them in unison, Thom saw the badges. The darker one spoke for both of them.

"I'm Detective Garrison. This is my partner, Detective Morris. Carroll Police. We're here about the shooting."

Thom stood up to face the men. "Shooting? Wait, I thought we settled all of this yesterday."

Garrison shrugged. "We have some more questions."

"What happened?" Malcolm asked. "Has something changed?"

"And you are?" Morris asked.

"Uh, this is my personal manager," Thom answered. "This is Malcolm Ross."

Both of the detectives nodded in Malcolm's direction and he nodded back.

"So, are you saying this wasn't an accident?" Mal inquired.

Morris decided to answer that one. "Yes, the evidence suggests that it wasn't."

Garrison gave his partner a sidelong glance, then rolled his eyes heavenward. To Thom, he said, "Dude was shooting straight at you folks. I figure, anyone trying to hit an animal ain't gonna be shooting up the side of a mountain. So, me and Tony here are asking ourselves, why would anyone wanna shoot at a bunch of hikers anyway?"

Detective Morris said nothing, just watching Thom as if he were eying his next meal.

"We figure that the dude was aiming at you," Garrison finished

Thom felt punched in the stomach. "Me? Why me?"

"That's why we're here, sir," Morris said. "I think your answers could tell us the reason."

"I don't know much, gentlemen."

"You might know more than you think," Garrison told him. "Anybody with a grudge? Yanked anybody's chain in the biz lately? That kinda thing."

"But—"

"Mr. Mitchell, we would like you to come to the station with us," Morris stated. "So we can get a statement from you, ask some questions."

"Uh...." Thom started to panic; his chest got tight as a drum, his heart pounding in his ears. *Oh, Jesus, no! What the fuck is going on?*

"Please, sir," Garrison pleaded. "It's really important. We won't keep you long, I swear."

"All right," Thom agreed, getting a grip on his runaway panic. He forced a smile and nodded. "If you think this was intentional, then I want this guy caught. I want to know who did this too."

"Right on!" The dark haired detective motioned to the doorway. "Let's go get it on and you'll be back in time for another hiking gig."

"Sounds good."

"I'll come with you, Thom"

Morris looked Malcolm up and down. "No, sir. Just Mr. Mitchell. Unless *you* were there too?"

Mal shook his head as Thom answered. "No, Mal wasn't there. Just me, Jo—shit, Jo."

"We already have Ms. Hayes' statement, Mr. Mitchell." Morris gestured to the doorway. "If you'll come with us, sir."

"I'll call you as soon as I get back from the station," he told Mal. He followed the two men as they headed out of the dining room.

They had barely cleared the entry into the lobby when he almost ran into her. "Jo!" he called out, then grinned at her. His joy at seeing her deflated as soon as she saw him.

She looked terrible, her eyes red rimmed and puffy. In an instant, her beautiful face went from surprise to red-faced anger. He watched the grim set of her jaw as her lips disappeared and her eyes narrowed down. She stood for a moment, visibly shaking and her fist squeezing on the rolled up piece of newspaper in it.

The rage on her face confused him. "Jo? What is it?"

"You son of a bitch!" she growled at him.

"Hey! Wait a minute now—"

"Wait? You go to hell, you son of a bitch!" She stormed towards him.

For a moment, Thom felt embarrassed. Things like this didn't happen to him. And certainly not in front of two police detectives or in a crowded lobby "Look, Jo—"

"Don't you dare talk to me," she spat at him. "No more of your lies, no more! You played me like a real fool, Thom Mitchell!"

"Hey," he cut in, getting angry himself now. "I never played you for anything. What the hell are you talking about?"

She got closer, close enough for him to smell the lavender scent of her cologne. "You just stay away from me. Don't talk to me. Don't come near me. I am not going to be treated like some groupie that you can use and then throw away."

"I never—"

She cut him off swiftly by slapping him in chest with the newspaper. She raised her arm back to do it again but he caught her wrist and wrestled the paper neatly from her fist. He waved off the two detectives who had tensed up and were ready to rush her.

She pulled her wrist from his grasp with a low moan. "Just leave me alone!" She whirled on her heel and ran, leaving him completely confused as to why she was so upset.

Never do *what* to her again. Why had she said that?

"Mr. Mitchell?"

He remembered the newspaper, still rolled up in his hand. He slowly flattened it out and found his answer. With a dawning horror, he saw the headline and it was bad enough. But the picture hit him in the solar plexus with a sledgehammer—*he and Missy on the sofa, his arms wrapped around her in what looked like a lover's embrace.*

"Mr. Mitchell?"

There he was, in black and white. *Son of a bitch*, she'd called him. And no wonder. What she must think of him right now. Thom grew very aware of the people around him, all staring at him. Pairs of eyes, accusing him of treating her like the wrapping on a hamburger—to be used once and thrown away. They stared at him, making him feel dirty and—

"Mr. Mitchell?"

Garrison was watching him, a look of concern on his face. Thom nodded and followed them out. He needed the excuse of answering their questions to give him a chance to think about what to do next or how to make this right with her.

18

MALCOLM WALKED INTO his hotel room, shut the door, and tossed the envelope on the table. He poured himself a good stiff scotch. Sure, it was too early for the hard stuff, but he had a feeling he was going to need the drink. A quick look at his watch and it was going on 11:00 AM. Okay, so it wasn't that early—they'd had a late breakfast. He stared down at the envelope and dropped onto the sofa. While Thom was off answering questions for the "toy cops," he could finally find out about the faxed information, see what he had. After a sip, he slipped one finger into a gap under the envelope's sealing flap and ripped it open.

Mitch was damned good at what he did and any information he dug up was going to be of the juicy kind. It certainly got what he wanted out of Sandy; she didn't fight Thom's divorce and had kept her mouth shut ever since. He opened the envelope and pulled the pages out. With drink in hand and his legs propped up on the table, he read slowly through the report. Each page got better and better. The pictures were grainy from the fax printer but still just as juicy as the prose.

"Well, well, well," he said. "Looks like Ms. Hayes has been a bit of a naughty girl here. Hmm...."

When he'd finished, he picked the pages up and stuffed them back into the manila envelope, then tossed them on the cushion beside him.

"So, all I have to do is keep Thom busy," he said to himself. "I know my Thommy; he'll want to make a bee line straight for that bitch. I won't let him. I need him to think she's cooling off. I'll tell him I tried to talk to her and she's refusing to see him."

He took a sip.

"'Let her calm down, Thommy,' I'll tell him. 'Let her calm down and we'll go see her in the morning.' Yes, yes. That'll do it. We'll go golfing, we'll go shop for the kids, for the graduation gift. We'll have dinner. And then, I'll send him to his room to have a lay down. In the meantime, the bitch and I shall have a long talk. A *very* long talk."

He patted the package on the sofa, then drained the scotch from his glass.

"I'm betting that this time tomorrow, she's gone for good. And the plan will proceed."

He looked at his watch. He had time for a quick nap. Everything was going quite well!

"Thommy, come on. Eat your dinner."

Thom just tossed the fork down on the table. "I'm not hungry."

Malcolm shook his head. "You can't relax on an empty stomach. Eat your salad at least."

"Mal, get off my ass. I'm not ten years old."

"No?" Malcolm noted the look on Thom's face. "You've got that temper tantrum look, like you want to kick something. I'd prefer it not be me." He put up with Thom's glare for about two seconds before turning back to his steak.

"How *could* she?"

"How could she *what*?" Malcolm asked, keeping his voice even.

"We've been shopping, golfing, hiking. I've spent more time with her than—I mean, we *talked*. I told her things that I've never told anyone. How can she take one look at a frigging picture and just condemn me like that! How?"

"Thom—"

"No, I mean it," he demanded. "I never gave her one reason to think I was only after a quick piece of ass. I *never* treated her like a groupie or a whore."

"No?"

"No, I didn't. And you know what? Fine! Screw her! I was not making a pass at Missy. Missy was upset and I gave her a hug. That was it! Nothing more! How the fuck dare she accuse me of this! It's not right."

"Thommy, the woman is insecure." Malcolm took a long sip of his iced tea. "Okay, I don't know why she's being an idiot. Maybe *she* doesn't know why."

"Bullshit," Thom exploded. "She knows why and she's pissing me off. Fine! I don't need this shit. I can have any woman I want."

"Yes you can," Malcolm answered. Inside, he was dancing. This was going to be way too easy. Fuel Thom's anger and he wouldn't make *any* attempt to go to that woman's room. This was just the icing on the cake. "You've got your pride."

"Damn right, I do!" Thom gulped his own tea, spilling some down his shirtfront. He made a haphazard blotting with his napkin before throwing that in a fit of pique.

"Thom, I tried to warn you."

"Don't, Mal."

"I did, my friend. I told you she was bad news."

"Mal..."

He knew he was flirting with disaster but there was more than one way to feed this. "Okay, all right. I'm sorry. But I'm telling you, you're better off. Before she really broke your heart."

And in that instant, the wind went out of Thom's sails. He seemed to deflate before Malcolm's eyes. "Mal?"

It almost broke his heart to see it. *Almost.* "Yeah, Thommy?"

"I love her."

The sentence, so baldly and simply stated, seemed to hang there in the air between them.

"Let her go, Thommy. You don't want someone that can't trust you, can't believe you when you tell the truth."

Thom's face turned scarlet again. "Damn right!"

"Then, here's what we're going to do." Malcolm signaled for the server to bring the check. "I have to go make a few phone calls, take care of some business. I want you to go back to your room."

"And?"

Malcolm signed the check with his room number. "I think we need a guy's night. How about we get some snacks and watch a pay-per-view movie. Something with Schwarzenegger or Stallone in it. Something he-manly, with car chases and sexy women."

Thom grinned at him. "Sounds good. I'll call room service and we'll have food brought up. Chips and dip, popcorn, the works."

"I'll meet you up there."

He watched Thom head on up, and then reached down to pick up the envelope on the chair next to him. He was going to go have a chat with Ms. Hayes, get this settled once and for all. He looked forward to it immensely.

In fact, this was going to be quite enjoyable.

19

JO HAD A very long day doing absolutely nothing. She had worked herself up into such a temper that eating was useless; her stomach always got acidic when she was upset, so lunch and breakfast turned out to be nothing more than coffee and soda. She tried to work on the briefs she brought with her but she could focus on nothing past a few sentences, no matter how many times she tried. She finally stuffed them back in the briefcase and put it back in the clothes closet.

TV was useless; there was nothing but game shows and soap operas. Then, when those were done, the talk shows. Maury and Rachael and Montel. And it was the same crap on every one of them. *I'm in love with my baby's nanny! I'm in love with my nanny's sister. My husband left me for another woman. My wife left me for my brother!* She finally turned the damn TV off and went to sleep.

But she dreamed of Thom, his blonde hair blowing in the breeze on that mountain trail. His eyes watching her as they ate lunch, his eyes that were brown pools of warmth. His voice singing to her that song about mountain thyme and loving the woman so much.

When she woke up, she was still as exhausted as when she went to sleep—only now she was even angrier. She ordered more coffee and spent a lot of time pacing, cursing under her breath. She spent a lot of time calling Thom Mitchell every evil name she could think of. How dare he! *How dare he!* And yet, she couldn't help but wonder what he was doing that very moment. Wondering if he even thought of her. Did he miss her?

"I trusted that bastard! I thought he really cared," she muttered to herself. "Kissing that girl and she's half his age! That son of a bitch!" She stopped in front of the hanging mirror. "That bastard son of a bitch!"

Her reflection wasn't angry; it was morose, hurt, and the voice was calm and reasonable. *Now, now, Joanna! Calling the man you love names!*

"I do *not* love him," she told her reflection. "I don't!"

Come on, now, Joanna. You can't just hate someone. Flip side of love, remember?

"Bull!"

She tried the TV again but this time it was just sappy love stories, sitcoms, and reality shows. She tried to focus but she could only manage five minutes and then was up pacing again. And each time, the face in the mirror watched her with something like regret in its eyes.

"What?"

You never really gave him a chance to answer, did you?

"What, give him a chance to lie some more?"

You've been hanging around Larry too long, it said. *Did you ever stop to think that he's never lied to you in all the time you've been together? Why would he start now?*

That was a damned good question. He'd been open and honest every time they'd been together. He'd told her things that no one else knew.

"But the picture...."

She was sorry she'd hit him with it now. She wanted to look again, see it. She closed her eyes and summoned up the sight.

The picture is taken through the plate glass window in the lobby. Thom and Missy are on the sofa. Her lips are pressed to his, but were they?

"Oh hell," she told the mirror. "He didn't tell me anything. He never told me what happened. He didn't even tell me he'd kissed her. Why not? Why not tell me the truth?"

Did you really give him a chance?

"Of course I did. Didn't I?"

She'd slapped him with the newspaper after making accusations that were vague. He'd said nothing. He never denied or acknowledged anything.

"Oh come on, he knew. He *knew!*"

But did he? He seemed more shocked than guilty. Even when he got angry, it wasn't a guilty kind of angry.

"Brilliant lawyer I turned out to be. Good thing I stick to contract law. I suck in criminal litigation!"

Now what? What should she do? Go confront him again? Let him explain this time? Would she even be able to believe him? He was awfully good at the sweet talk, convincing the listener to buy ice cubes in winter.

But he never lied to you, did he. He explained about that night at the fundraiser. He told you things that were none of your business, never pulled a punch, never answered your questions with anything but brutal, self-deprecating honesty.

"I have to talk to him," she told the reflection. "I have to. I have to hear what he has to say. I have to know. I need to hear him explain it."

And why do you need that? the reflection asked. Because you do care. You care a great deal for someone that you say is a son of a bitch...and a few other names. So why do you care?

The realization hit her hard in the heart. "Holy shit, I really *do* love him. I'm in love with Thom Mitchell."

She dashed across the floor to the phone, plucking the receiver from the cradle. She had to find him somehow. She had to. But as her finger pressed the pound key, there came a knock on the door.

"Thom! Please let it be Thom!"

She dropped the receiver back onto the cradle and made her way to the door. She threw it open to find that it wasn't Thom. It was *him*! She sneezed four times in rapid succession as she reached for the kleenex in her pocket. She blew her nose, stepping back just a bit to get away from the smell of his cologne

"He's not here, Mal," she told him.

"I know he's not." Thom's manager pushed the door open the rest of the way and walked past her. "I'm not here to see him. I'm here to see *you*. You and I are going to have a little chat!"

He walked into the suite, over to the bar. He helped himself to the pitcher of water, sniffing at it before taking a drink. He eased his muscular frame into one of the plush chairs. His eyes were watching her intently, almost daring her to throw him out. He said nothing, just sipped the water, waiting.

For a moment, she was shocked into inactivity but found her voice finally. "No, no," she said in mock protest, "please do come in and make yourself at home." She shut the door, turning back to her guest. "My room is your room, by all means."

"Spare me the sarcasm, Ms. Hayes."

She glared at him. "What do you want?"

He smiled at that. "Oh good, do be a bitch. That makes this so much easier."

"I'm only a bitch to someone who makes me uncomfortable."

"And I make you uncomfortable?"

She sneezed again, blew her nose, and kept silent.

He crossed one leg over the other and just stared.

This was absurd. "Well?" she demanded, panting slightly.

Draining the water glass, he just stared at her.

"I think you need to leave," she grumbled at him.

The Cheshire Cat stopped grinning long enough to finally show its sharp teeth. "No, not until you and I have an understanding."

"About what?"

"I think you mean 'about *whom*.'" He began to flick at his nails, as if he were cleaning something unpleasant from them.

"Thom?"

With a voice oily and confident, he answered, "Yes, Thom." He looked back up into her eyes. "I've been with Thom for a long time. We're close. *Very* close. He's my best friend and he means a great deal to me."

She nodded, wary at his meaning. "I know you care about him. I know he cares about you."

He worked his jaw before speaking again. "You have no clue what Thom or I care about. But I know *you*. Oh, yes I know you. I know what you'll do to him. Trust me when I tell you, it won't happen."

"Excuse me? What are you talking about?"

"You, some little hard ass lawyer from some podunk town in Michigan." His hand came up to silence her protest. "Oh trust me, I know the right people and I've had you thoroughly checked out, Ms. Joanna Hayes. Ms. Joanna Davidson Hayes."

Oh! That's where this is going. She simply stared.

"I believe the grounds for divorce were, um...infidelity on your part?"

"Roger was...wait a minute, that's none of your business!"

"Oh, it *is* my business. Very much my business," he answered smugly. "I know you filed that he was abusive and alcoholic, but I also know you slept with his business partner. *His business partner!* My, my, aren't we the little whore."

No, there was no way he could know that. There was no way! How? How did he know? Did he guess? How did he know about this?

"Go to hell," she spat at him.

"I suppose that Thom told you his second wife slept around on him? With his business partner in the restaurant he co-owned?"

She couldn't speak. All she could do was stand, shaking with her hands at her sides, balling into fists.

He threw a manila envelope down in front of her. "Now, we surely wouldn't want Thom to find out about that now, would we? Hmm?"

She felt the first tears start to spill over her lashes. Staring at the envelope, she said, "I was...I was lonely. Roger was a bastard, he...he hit me. David...David cared. He was going to help me get my divorce."

"Oh, of course," that man purred again. "Bet he said that to a lot of women before taking them to bed."

David had been a one-time thing, when her soul was in pain and she was at her wit's end. He hadn't liked Roger either but needed the partnership to go on for financial reasons. When he'd found another firm to join, he'd filed the papers for Joanna and when the divorce was final, they never saw each other again.

"No," she whispered. "It wasn't like that."

"You're a whore." He practically jumped out of the chair, still grinning. "You slept around on your husband and you'll do the same thing to Thom."

"You don't know shit, buddy." She was trying so hard to keep it in check; she was *not* going to cry in front of that bastard. She wasn't! "And you have no clue as to what I'd do or not do about or to Thom."

"Well, I'm going to stop you," he said smugly. "You stay away from Thom; stay away from him or he'll find out about you. I promise you that."

"You son of a bitch, you don't have anything to say about Thom and I!" She dug her nails into her palms, letting the pain keep her focused. "And I wonder what he'd say about this little ambush of yours. Hmm? St. Malcolm, the asshole."

"Oh, he won't find out."

He laughed in her face, stepping close enough for that wretched cologne to set her sneezing again. She grabbed the bridge of her nose, stopping the fit. "You can't stop me from telling him!"

"Oh yes I can," Malcolm told her, genuinely amused. "You see, I have no problem producing all of this evidence for him. And I will show him, Ms. Hayes. You can take that to the bank. You can have this particular package but I can produce another one for him. He'll know."

He would too; she didn't have to be psychic or know the bastard's mind to know that he meant every word. She let go of her nose and simply stared at her feet, her heart sinking fast.

"As long as we have an agreement, Ms. Hayes. And I see we do." He took the glass and left it on the bar where he found it, then left her standing in a quivering mess. He said no more, closing the door behind him. Only then did she burst into tears, letting the pent up rage and frustration pour out of her. She covered her face with her hands and just sobbed; aching, racking cries that came from the core of her.

She wiped her streaming eyes and blew her nose again, slowly getting control of herself. She stared at the envelope laying on the table, feeling a rush hit her. She wanted to pick it up and burn it, but she was afraid it would burn her instead. She wanted to know what was inside it. She wanted to destroy it without ever knowing. She picked it up, pulled the clasp apart, and opened the flap.

She fell onto the sofa, looking at one page after another. Obvious photocopies, the pictures were of that day at David's home. Someone had to have followed her, someone with a lot of money and a really good camera. The pictures captured everything. Every kiss. Every piece of removed clothing. Every inch of her skin. Every thrust of his hips. The transcript of the conversation—the bastard had taped their conversation and lovemaking. Was there a damned videotape out there now?

The tears flowed again. Who? If it had been Roger, he would have used it at the divorce. But he didn't. So who had done this? And why? She could only guess. But, God, if anyone should see this, find out about it. That bastard! What if he decided to show this to Thom anyway? How could she ever face him again? She found that she didn't give a shit about evidence. She took each page and ripped it to shreds of confetti. When she was done with each page, she tore the envelope to bits. She'd ruined the best thing that had happened to her in a long time and now her past was rising up to ruin what was left of her self-esteem.

The knock on the door pulled it all back inside of her.

Who is that? Now what?

She grabbed a tissue from the box on the coffee table and blew her nose. She was still wiping her eyes when she opened the door.

20

THOM GOT AS far as the elevator. There was just so much in his head right now; he'd bared his soul and lost his temper, been shot at, made out a fool in the papers, lost a lady that might have been the one. He looked down to see his hand was shaking and he knew why. He knew the symptoms—the taste in his mouth, the craving for something with at least a hundred proof. He wanted a drink so badly that he could almost smell the scotch. The need was gnawing at his insides, threatening to make his stomach turn inside out. He didn't want to go back to his room just yet; he certainly wasn't ready for Malcolm. He needed to be alone. He needed to think, sit some place quiet and just think.

Some place no one would expect him to go. Some place where he could fight an old demon and defeat it. He headed back the way he'd come, making a right turn into the bar.

He'd almost forgotten what the atmosphere was like—dark, intimate, pulsing with secrets and lies. The cool of the darkness contrasting with the hot spot as he sat on the stage, guitar in hand and music in his soul. Making love in an almost private way. The days before he met Angie. The nights after he did, when she would still come and listen. When they would sit at a table in the back with their friends and the booze flowed like water. The good times, the laughter.

He looked around for a place to sit, tossing out his order to the woman behind the bar. "Scotch, neat. Water back."

He sat down in a corner seat, in the darkness where no one would see him from the door. The bartender brought his drink and he tipped the lady well. She left him to his own devices after an all too knowing look.

Yeah, yeah, I'm that son of a bitch. Now go away.

She did just that.

He had no business drinking. Here he was an alcoholic, sitting with a live wire attached to a time bomb and ready to go off at any second. But damn it, he'd earned this one. He needed this one. And yet, he couldn't lift the glass to his lips. He ran his forefinger around the rim, just feeling the texture of it against his skin.

Why? The only thing in his head right now was 'why?'

What the hell was wrong with him? Why her? Why Joanna? He kept asking himself that same question and he kept getting the same answer—*no answer*. And yet here he sat—so head over heels, burning inside, over the moon in love with her and she hated his guts. All because of that goddamn picture and that dumb kid.

That's not what it looked like. It was just an innocent hug. I just kissed the side of her forehead. She didn't even give me a chance to explain, to tell her what really happened.

Missy was a cute kid and that was the extent of it. Why couldn't Jo see that? She was like his daughter; she was damn close to Lisa's age. Why would anyone think he was trying to pick up a child; that was just sick and disgusting.

Jo, you're wrong about this. I'd never do that to you. I don't...I mean, I learned my lesson. I know what it feels like to screw around on the one you love and then have it done to you. You're a lady. You're special.

"I love you," he whispered. He said it out loud again, this time meaning every word of it. "I don't believe it. After all this, I love her. I *am* in love with her."

He didn't want the drink anymore. He pushed it to the side and drained the water glass instead. He had to get to her, make her listen. He had to explain it to her, make her see the truth. He'd said it to Mal, now he had to say it to her. And he wasn't going to stop until he did.

He got up quickly and dashed to the elevator. It was an interminable amount of time before the doors finally opened. He jumped in and pressed the button for her floor. The climb seemed to take forever but the elevator finally stopped at the destination. He didn't even wait until the doors fully opened. He squeezed through and loped to her door.

But the moment he got there, he got tied up in knots again, a pressure building in his chest and threatening to blow him apart. He stood for a moment, trying to practice what he would say. He had to get it right. But his palms were sweating and he was afraid that if he waited any longer, he'd just lose his nerve.

He knocked on the door, three hard raps. He waited.

The door opened.

"Joanna, you have to listen—" He took one look at her swollen, tear stained face. "Jo? What's wrong?"

21

"Jo? What's wrong?"

She couldn't talk; she just burst into tears. He said nothing; he simply pulled her into his arms and closed the door behind them with his foot. He held her close, stroking her hair and humming a tuneless melody. She just held on, crying it all out on his shoulder. She was finally down to the sniffles when he took things in hand.

"Shh," he said, comforting her with a light back rub. "Come on now, enough. You'll make yourself sick. Let's go sit on the sofa and you can tell me all about it, if you want."

She nodded, taking deep breaths and wiping her eyes with the heels of her hands. Thom walked her to the sofa and helped her sit. Unmindful of the parallel, he took a fresh glass, pouring water from the same pitcher, and brought it to her. It was in her to refuse it but she was thirsty. She gratefully accepted it and drank it down. He fetched the box of tissues from the bedroom, then sat down next to her and pulled her close until her head was on his shoulder. Stroking her arm, he waited until she blew her nose and wiped her eyes before saying anything.

"You want to talk about it?"

Did she? Did she really want to spill everything to him? Tell him that his best friend was a jerk? What man would ever believe that? "No. I really don't."

He kissed the top of her head. "Well, if you do, I'm here."

There was something so soothing about the way he was stroking her arm. Everything was just draining out of her. She was melting against him, no way to stop it. "I know." She turned up to his steady, warm gaze. "It's just...."

"Shh," he said, stroking the side of her face now. "You don't have to tell me anything if you don't want to."

His face was so close to hers, the warmth of his brown eyes washed through her. She wanted to kiss him, long and deep. But she was afraid to; afraid he'd get the wrong impression. Afraid that he didn't want her like she wanted him. Afraid that he didn't feel anything for her. Afraid that being in love with him was going to get her hurt badly.

He made the decision instead. His head bent down and she felt the touch of his lips on hers. It was so soft at first. Just the touch, then release. Then he kissed her again, a touch and a release. When she opened her eyes, she looked into his face—he seemed to be as astonished as she was.

"Don't stop," she whispered.

"I can't," he whispered back.

It turned out that he wanted it too. The next kiss was deep, pressing his lips upon hers and tasting them. His arms came around her, pulling her so close that she couldn't breathe. It didn't matter; she pulled him tighter. She felt the tip of his tongue teasing at her lip and met it with her own.

Then, without warning, he pulled back. "I can't do this."

"Yes, you can," she said, breathless from the kisses. "I want it."

"No; no, I can't. Not here. Not on the sofa. That's too cheap."

She stood up, took his hand in hers. "Come to bed, then."

He followed her into the bedroom willingly. They barely

made it through the door before he spun her around, kissing her again. She put her arms around his waist, pulling him as close as she could. She could feel the bulge behind the zipper of his jeans.

"I want you," he managed to whisper in between kisses.

"Yes," she answered.

She slowly unbuckled his belt and plucked at the buttons of his jeans. He moaned softly when she reached inside the denim material to take him firmly in her hand. His breath was raspy and short as she worked her hand up and down against his shaft. He lay still as she brought him closer and closer to the brink, watching his face as she pleasured him. He took it as long as he could, finally stopping her hand to hold it to his heart, then he sat upright.

He pulled the blouse out of her trousers and she stopped long enough for him to pull it over her head. He unhooked her bra, tossing it to the floor, and began to kiss her breasts. He teased them with his tongue, making her want more. He gave it to her; he scooped her up in his arms to lay her on the bed.

Their clothes were off before either one could speak again. He had her on the bed, lying at her side and exploring her body as he kissed her lips. One hand found its way to where she was now wet and firm, and the fingers danced inside. His thumb pressed where she was pounding, making her catch her breath. His erect member was throbbing; she could feel the blood pulsing in every engorged vein. She wanted him inside her, filling her. She reached out for him, wrapping her arms around his shoulder and her legs around his hips.

They moved together, panted together. They moved as one being, rising and falling. All she wanted was to have him inside of her, wrapped around her. There was no tomorrow, there was no yesterday. They were caught up in the now, the bubble of contentment that included no one else but them. She was on fire and it was going to be a hell of a conflagration. But it would be glorious.

When he finally exploded inside of her, she was still trembling as her own orgasm burned through her, lighting her up like a roman candle. He fell against her shoulder, his chest heaving as he struggled to breathe. She held him close as her heart started slowing up again, the frantic beating becoming less and her breathing becoming normal.

When he tried to move, she wouldn't let him; the feel of him inside of her was comforting and satisfying. They stayed like that until they both could breathe again. She let him move then, feeling the lethargy fill every part of her body. He rolled off to her side, pulling her close in spoon fashion. She lay with her head on one of his outstretched arms, his hand lying comfortably on her breast. His cheek lay against her hair. For a moment, she thought she heard his soft snores. She closed her eyes and started to drift off herself until his voice pulled her back.

"You know I wanted to do that the night I met you."

"I know," she said, secretly gleeful. And a little sorry that she'd missed her chance that night.

He kissed her ear. "Better late than never, huh?"

She put her hand over the one fondling her breast. "Oh yeah."

"You're amazing, Joanna Hayes. Absolutely amazing."

Every part of her felt molten and warm, like that putty she used to play with as a child. She felt molded to his body, every part of her fitting so close. She wanted nothing more than to fall asleep but the voice inside her head wasn't going to let her.

I suppose that Thom told you his second wife slept around on him? With his business partner in the restaurant he co-owned? You're a whore! You slept around on your husband and you'll do it to Thom!

She jerked out of her doze, her eyes wide open. He moaned a little and settled back against her. But her mind was made up. She had no choice. He deserved to know before she let this go any farther. "Thom?"

"Hmmm?"

"Are you awake? I have to tell you something."

He sighed and kissed her ear again. "I'm awake."

She was probably making the biggest mistake of her life but she'd started this. She had to follow through. "Thom...I told you that I was married once."

He raised his head, waiting.

"His name was...*is*...Roger. He wasn't a very nice guy, Thom. He...well, anyway."

"Is he a lawyer too?" he asked her, his voice still husky from their lovemaking and his sleepiness.

"Yeah. He is."

"What happened?"

"I became friends with his partner, David. God, David was everything Roger wasn't. He was kind and understanding. He knew what Roger was. He helped me get my divorce and cut through the legal crap with my money. He...he...."

"Did you sleep with him?"

She nodded. "Yeah. While I was still married."

Thom was quiet for a moment, as if he were thinking. Then he asked, "Did he mean something to you?"

"Yeah," she confessed. "He did. He was a sweet man, a good friend."

"Did you see him again?"

"No. After the divorce, he just seemed to fade away."

He kissed her cheek. "Did it help you?"

"Yeah. It did," she admitted. "Gave me the courage to leave the son of a bitch I married."

He turned her face to see him. "You didn't have to tell me that, you know."

"Yes I did. Because I want you to know. I never slept around on my husband. Except for that time."

"No, you didn't. Have to tell me, I mean." He kissed her lips again. "And I care about none of it. Go to sleep now."

He pulled her close again, wrapping his arms around her. She felt him relax into the safe haven of sleep as he softly snored against her cheek. It lulled her, comforted her. She closed her eyes, mentally burying the past in the drawer where it belonged, and drifted off as well.

22

THEY HAD AWAKENED sometime in the very small hours of the night, the room still filled with moonlight. Thom had taken her again, making love with a glee that he thought had been lost in the shuffle of his life, somewhere. His appetite had been whetted; he had a new craving, a stronger one. One stronger than the booze, that craving that always stayed under the surface of his thoughts. A hum that only he could hear until it drove him crazy sometimes. At his age, once a night was a great accomplishment. But with Joanna, it was different. He felt insatiable, eager for more.

They slept again but she woke him at sunrise, eager for more herself. This time she rode him hard and put him away very wet. She rolled him on his back and settled on top, working her hips in motion with his. Every time he was close to a climax, she'd back off and distract him with something else. She kept it up until he was throbbing and close to implosion. Then, she started the final thrusting, pulling him deep inside of her. This time, he climaxed in every part of his body, glowing like a neon sign in the darkness. And this time, he was sure there would be no repeats until he'd had eight hours of sleep and at least one meal.

She fell asleep in his arms again, but he could only doze. He would rouse himself to make sure she wasn't a dream; that she was still there with him. He would touch her and she would sigh in her sleep, a smile playing on her lips. He would doze off again only to wake up again. After a few hours of that, he gave up. He'd promised Malcolm they'd hit the course this morning and his gods called, demanding to be obeyed.

He watched her as he dressed; one arm curled under her head and the other around her breasts, the hand tucked under her chin. The sweet smile hadn't left her face. He found that he had one on his own.

He had to go; but he couldn't just go off and leave her. He had promised that he would never treat her that way. So, he sat down on the bed next to her. Taking a tendril of her red hair, he tickled her nose with it. She wrinkled it a few times before one blue eye opened, still sleepy. The smile broadened when she saw him there.

"Hey, handsome."

He tucked the hair behind her ear, running one finger around the curve of it. "Good morning back, sleepy."

She stretched and shifted her position until she was lying on her back; it was like watching a cat as her arms came straight down and her back arched. When she had finished, she lay back on the pillows and reached a hand out to his arm.

"You are the most amazing man I've ever met," she said. Her face was slightly puffy, something he'd always found sexy in a woman.

"Am I?" He covered her hand with his own. "I was just thinking the same thing about you."

She purred in that drowsy, still satisfied way. "You were?"

"I was. How beautiful you look in the moonlight. How I can't keep my hands off you." He leaned forward to kiss her lips, her free hand creeping to the back of his neck to hold his mouth close to hers. When the kiss ended, he was breathless again. "Darlin', you better stop that or I'll miss my tee off time."

She blinked a few times and sat up. "You're going?"

"Shh," he crooned to her. "I promised Malcolm we'd get in eighteen holes this morning. I have to go."

Her face changed, a shadow fleeting across it.

"What is it?" he asked.

In that instant, she was smiling again, as if the expression had never been there at all. She stroked his cheek and answered, "Nothing. Just a bad dream."

"Want to talk about it?"

She shook her head. "No. I don't. Besides, it's gone now. It can't hurt me. I won't let it."

He nodded. "Ok, I won't push. But if you want to talk—"

She laid a finger on his lips. "I know. I'll tell you."

He kissed the finger, and then got up off the bed. "What are you planning on doing today?"

"Oh, I was thinking of doing some more shopping. Presents for friends back home."

"Sounds like a good plan, darlin'," he said, grinning. "Tell you what; how about you and me and Malcolm hook up for lunch and we can discuss hiking a peak or two tomorrow."

It was a slight hesitation, the shadow back and gone again. "Sure, sounds great. Say...1:00?"

He winked at her. "I'll see you then." He leaned over to kiss her once more, savoring the feel of her lips against his. Standing up, he added, "You go back to sleep. I'll see you later."

"Go kick his ass," she teased.

"Oh, count on it!"

Thom was ravenous. He called Malcolm on the cell to

invite him to breakfast and they'd go play the course afterward. Unfortunately, he found several reporters were waiting in the lobby for him.

"Hey, Thom, how's the new girlfriend? What's her name?"

"Mr. Mitchell, I'm from *The Mountain Ear*. How does it feel to have someone shooting at you?"

"Hey, Thom..."

"Hey, Thom..."

He just smiled and pushed his way past. "Sorry, guys, I never answer questions on an empty stomach. Maybe later."

They followed closely behind him before the hotel manager managed to wedge between Thom and the lot. The dining room was declared off limits to reporters unless they wanted to eat. And he knew personally that each one of them had already availed themselves of the continental breakfast, so they were invited to leave Mr. Mitchell in peace. He turned around to escort Thom to the dining room with no fuss.

"Mr. Mitchell," he apologized, "I am so sorry. Unfortunately, there was no legal way for me to keep them out."

"Isn't this private property?"

"Investors, sir. And they agreed that if these *gentlemen* paid for rooms, I could not keep them out. We're completely sold out now. I am truly sorry."

Thom shrugged. "Nothing you can do then."

"I've hired security, sir. That should be *something*."

Thom thanked the man and went to the start of the buffet. He was just loading up the plate when he felt Malcolm's presence beside him.

"Not hungry are you?"

Thom managed to laugh and rub his middle with his free

hand. "My belly thinks my throat's been cut. I'm starving."

Malcolm picked up a plate and got in line with him. "How was your night?"

"Great, fantastic! How was yours?"

"It's been a while since someone stood me up. I'm not sure *how* I feel about that."

Thom ducked his head, the guilt kicking him hard in the chest. "Mal, I'm sorry. I really am."

"What happened?" Malcolm asked drily.

Thom scooped up a cup and filled it from the coffee urn. He waited for Mal to get his and lead them to a nearby table, secluded behind a standing mural.

"So?" Mal asked him.

"I spent the night with Joanna."

"Ah."

Thom plunged right ahead with it, trying to get it all out and in the open. "I don't know what it is, Mal, but I know that I love her, that she is the most incredible woman I've ever met."

Mal said nothing, simply eating his food. His coolness didn't escape Thom's attention at all; Mal wasn't even trying to hide it.

Thom dropped his fork on his plate and sat back. "What?" he asked curtly.

Mal just held up his hand. "Thommy, far be it from me to advise you on your love life, okay? Do what you want."

"But?" Thom sat back in the chair, a cool civility in his words. "Come on, Mal, don't stop now. Not when you've spent the last twenty years doing exactly that, advising me on my love life."

Mal took a slow sip of the hot coffee and set the cup down. "Thom, the truth is you don't know anything about her. All you know is what she tells you."

"So, what?" Thom was starting to get more than a bit irritated. "I know more than you do. At least I've spent more than five minutes with her!"

"You've spent a grand total of a week with her," Mal bit back. "I could understand if you'd spent a month or a year—but a week? And that makes you an expert on this woman, does it?"

"You don't know what you're talking about," Thom grumbled. Mal had a point, but *he* wasn't going to admit that. "I know how I feel and that's all that matters."

"And by coincidence, all of a sudden you're in danger of some kind. Mugged one day, shot at another. And funny how she just happens to be there by your side both times. You make a great alibi, buddy."

Thom picked up his fork again, slowly and deliberately cutting into the sausage patty. He kept his voice even but he couldn't completely keep the anger out. "You're wrong!"

Malcolm sighed and started eating again.

Thom hunched his shoulders, his stomach in knots. "Mal, I'm sorry. I don't like to fight with you."

"I don't like to fight with you either, Thommy. I'm just worried about you."

"I know you are." Thom relaxed, giving his belly time to do the same thing. "And thank you for that. I know you care."

Malcolm nodded. "I *do* care. And I want what's best for you."

"Then, just be my friend, okay? That's what I really need. A friend."

Mal offered up a conciliatory smile. "I don't want to talk about *her* anyway."

Thom was grateful for the change of subject. His belly was totally unknotted by now. He launched into his breakfast again.

He nodded in his friend's direction and asked, "What's on your mind?"

Mal wiped his mouth with his napkin, pushing his plate to the side. "Thom, we need to talk about...." He pointed to the window and beyond.

Thom could see a portion of the front lawn. The news trucks and vans were still there. Even if he couldn't see the men and women who'd driven them, Thom knew they were out there waiting for him. "Shit!"

"Exactly," Mal agreed. "There's a fiasco waiting to happen out there and we're going to have to stop it."

"I don't know about this, Mal." Alarm bells went off inside his head.

"Thom, if we don't take the bull by the horns, they'll get worse. Which do you want, their speculations getting more outrageous or just tell them the truth—"

"I don't like that either."

"Then, keep to the shooting and the mugging, and leave the women out of it."

"They'll ask," Thom insisted. "You know they will."

"You don't have to answer."

Thom snorted. "Right. And really have them up my nose. I don't think so. I'll have to say something."

"Fine, whatever you want to say," Mal conceded. "But I say, the less you talk about Missy and Ms. Hayes, the better."

The flips in his gut returned and his head was starting to pound a little. He reached up to rub his temples, then his forehead. "Fine, whatever."

"I'll write up a statement for you and schedule it for this afternoon. Say, two this afternoon? That'll give you some time to rest and decide what you want to say."

Screw it, he thought to himself. Mal was right; he was going to have to do this. "All right. But I'll write up my own statement."

"Whatever you want." Malcolm sipped his coffee, making notes on a small notepad he'd pulled from his pocket. "Oh, and something else."

Thom groaned. "What now?"

"You're going to have a bodyguard. And I'm hiring a car and driver for you, too."

Thom immediately got defiant about that. "What?"

Mal turned a pained look in his direction. "Do I have to fight you on this one too?"

That balloon deflated very quickly and Thom shook his head. "No, I guess not. The hotel manager can only get enough security to keep the hotel covered. Me? I'm on my own."

"Fine, then," Malcolm answered. "I want at least one bodyguard with you. And if you go anywhere, I want you in the car. I want to know you're protected."

"Mal, they can't go hiking with me."

"The hell they can't," he argued. "And if they can't, then you don't go."

"Mal—"

"Thom!" It was Mal's turn to glare at him. "You are obviously a target. I am going to make you *less* of a target and that's that! Let me do my job!"

Thom felt completely drained of any fight whatever now. He had a moment to question the whole situation again. It was just supposed to be a quiet vacation, what the hell had happened? And so quickly?

Mal seemed to sense it. He backed off. "Thommy, relax. It'll be okay, I swear. I'll...I'll work something out, okay?"

Thom nodded, not able to talk.

"Look, go back to your room and relax. I'll call you in a bit after I've set up everything, all right?"

"Yeah, sure. I'll call Jo."

Thom left the room, managing to get past the half dozen in the lobby without answering or acknowledging. Going to his room would be a damned good idea. He needed to think. He needed to talk to the one person he could get a straight answer out of.

He needed to make a phone call.

23

MISSY FINISHED STUFFING the menus with the new inserts and stacked them up on the concierge's desk. It was a breath of fresh air, taking care of the menial tasks. Mr. Waterhouse had been very sympathetic, trying to keep the reporters and photographers away from her. Oh, he'd been pretty pissed off at first. But he'd listened to her as she explained what had really happened, believed her only because he'd never known her to tell a lie. So, he'd given her a break from waiting tables, paying her full salary plus what she would have made in tips by having her take care of the dining room chores and working in the office. Until it all died down, he promised.

It wasn't quite that easy with Walt. One look at that damn picture and Walt had stormed out of the house, saying nothing more to her. That was the last she'd seen of him.

Sarah patted her on the back. "That's great, Missy. Do me a favor and go get the linens out of the closet?"

"Sure."

Missy carried the linen basket into the closet, a smaller room off the dining area that the staff used for storage. They had enough to start lunch, but she needed to fold more napkins to cover lunch rush and a change before dinner. Plus bring out enough tablecloths to cover lunch accidents and to replace all of the tables for the evening shift. It was boring work but it was quiet. It would give her a chance to think.

Missy pulled two stacks of cloth napkins from the shelf and walked around to the folding area. It was tucked back behind a partition, out of the way of the door drafts, to keep the folding process from getting disturbed. She took one from the stack and began by placing the tips together, folding each until the added ring made the whole napkin bloom like a flower. She placed it in the basket, and then went on to the next.

Her mind kept drifting back to this morning, Walt at the kitchen table with that stupid paper in his hands. That had to have hurt him so badly, to see that stupid picture. And, he hadn't given her a chance to explain things to him. She had to get him to understand that it wasn't what he thought it was. She had no interest in Thom Mitchell. Okay, he was a nice guy. But he was an old man; she wasn't attracted to old men. She sighed to herself, slumping a little for a moment. Did that mean she was in love with Walt though? Thom said she was. But was she?

The smartest thing she'd ever done was get out of her parents' house, going to school in another part of the state. Missy loved New Hampshire; enough to never consider leaving it, even to go to college. Being on her own had freaked her out at first, moving into the dorm and knowing absolutely no one. She came close to flunking out of her first term. Getting the job and meeting Walt had been the two highlights of an otherwise shaky start to college. Walt had made it okay; Walt had soothed her nerves and helped her find her feet. Walt had—

The door slammed open, rapping against the wall. It unnerved her enough that she almost yelled out, but something inside her told her to be silent. The hairs on the back of her neck rose up as she heard the door slam closed, again.

"Damn it all to hell." It was a man's voice. It took her a moment to recognize that it was Thom's manager.

She heard faint tones pressed in a sequence. Then, it was quiet until he spoke again.

"Derek, it's me. We have a problem."

It got quiet on his end as he listened to the other person. He had the volume turned up enough that Missy could hear a male voice but not was being said.

"Yes, I know, but we're going to have to make changes to the plan. No, I don't care about that. Look, it's not going to work, what we started. We need to alter things."

It was quiet again. Missy edged as close to the end of the partition as she could without being seen, peeking around the edge. She watched the man pacing like a caged lion.

"No, you don't understand. That woman is a menace. She could screw up everything. I can't have that." He listened again. "Yes, fine. Wilde would be perfect. You have a secluded spot? Alright, then what?"

What the hell is he talking about? What's he doing?

"I need your two goons to show up on time. I need a bodyguard and chauffer—and get a car! Limo. You know where to get it. Make sure Mike and Neil are dressed appropriately. I want Thom comfortable with them. He's got to be able to trust them."

Trust them? Of course, after the mugging and getting shot at, Thom needed some security. That makes sense.

"Good, then that's the plan. I'll tell you the rest later. I have to think about this. Just be ready."

She heard the click of his heels as he left the room. It seemed strange to her that he had come into the closet to make a phone call, but then again, it was private. He probably was trying to get away from the reporters, too. She went back to folding linens and worrying about Walt.

24

THOM BARELY GOT his door open when the phone started ringing. The light was blinking; he'd have to get the voicemail when he was done. He picked up the receiver and put it to his ear.

"Yes?"

It was a husky female voice that he knew well, a slight Midwestern accent in it. He'd been married to the woman for fifteen years. "Thom? Is that you?"

"Angie? I was just getting ready to call you, honey."

He heard a loud exhale on the other end of the phone. "Jesus, Thom, you scared the hell out of me. I've only been trying to call you since last night."

"Why?"

Once again, the ex-wife had to get a dig in. "*Why?* Do you ever read a paper or watch the news? You're all over it!"

Thom flopped onto the sofa, laughing as he did. "Oh, that."

"Oh, that," she repeated. "Thom, I swear to God, you live in your own dream world. How can you not know what's going on out there, what they're saying about you. And who is this girl?"

He wanted to laugh at her. For as long as he'd known her, she had been brutally honest with him. It was one of the reasons that their friendship had outlasted the marriage. He always knew where he stood with Angie. He could always trust her to tell him the truth about anything, but the woman had an ability to be painfully blunt.

He rested his head against the back of the sofa. "Missy is just a friend, Ang. It's not what you think and it's not how they're making it out to be."

"Thom, you're kissing her. How is anyone getting that wrong?"

"No, Angie," he wearily protested. His head was starting to pound. "I mean, yes I kissed her but I kissed her on the cheek! For crying out loud, she's Lisa's age. I'm not *that* hard up."

"Thom, the press is all over this. You've been on *Entertainment Tonight*. It's national!"

"I know, I know." He got up, taking the cordless handset with him into the bathroom. With one hand, he fished the aspirin out of his toiletries bag. Cradling the handset between his ear and his shoulder, he kept on talking while he shook three aspirin in his palm. "Look, Angie, nothing is going on with her. She's a kid. A sweet, funny kid."

"A kid you were flirting with."

"I was not," he protested.

"Thom, you always flirt," she fussed. "And then it totally amazes you when the women take you seriously. You really need to pay more attention. People get hurt that way."

Angie could be a real nag when she was upset. It was better just to humor her. "Fine, Ange, whatever. Yeah, you're right. You're always right."

"Don't patronize me," she grumbled. "You know I hate that."

"And I'm not in the mood to get my ass chewed off." He needed a change of subject if he was going to have to get her off this kick. "Look, why were you calling?"

"Did you forget Lisa's graduation?"

He swallowed the aspirin with a slug of water, grimacing from the taste. "No, I did not forget. I have my speech ready. Give me a little credit."

Lisa was going to be an honors graduate in two days and Thom was delivering the keynote speech. On top of that, he was going to be receiving an honorary doctorate in Environmental Sciences. It was a double dose of pride for him; a doctorate for a man that had dropped out of college was a big thing. But he was even more proud of his daughter, for all that she'd accomplished. .

"Thom, are you even listening to me?" she barked.

He blinked, clearing his sore head. "What?"

"I *said*, remind Malcolm to book your flight."

"Oh yeah, sure. I will. He probably has already."

"Is he coming?" she asked.

"No, he won't be." He hesitated, debating whether he should ask or just do it. But in this case, permission was easier to ask than forgiveness for the social faux pas. "But, uh, you mind if I bring a guest?"

"A guest?"

He laid back down on the sofa, propping his legs up on the coffee table. "Yeah, I've met a really lovely lady, Ange. She's... she's something else."

Angie laughed, finally sounding anything but pissed at him. "I thought so. But I take it that it's not this Missy person?"

He felt the grin come over his face. "No. Her name is Joanna, Joanna Hayes. I met her in Nashville doing that fund raiser."

"Oh yeah? What's she like?"

He regaled his ex with the new lady's attributes. At least with

Angie, he could talk to her and know she wouldn't automatically pass a jealous judgment.

"She sounds lovely, Thom."

"She is, Angie. She really is."

"You sound like you have feelings for her."

"Yes, I do." He had loved Angie very deeply; her insistence on the divorce had cut him in two. It was hard to sing the songs he wrote for her after that, harder still to see her or talk to her. They lived in the same town, knew the same people. It had taken the better part of ten years and a second divorce to get back on speaking terms with her. They could never go back, but they had become deep and close friends. She advised him and he counted on her honesty. "You know, she's a little like you."

"Oh? How?" She sounded skeptical at that statement.

"She tells me the straight up truth too."

Her laugh was gentle this time, affectionate. "Well then, I like her already. Definitely bring her, Thom. I can't wait to meet her. You know the kids will love her too, if you do."

"You think so?"

"Anyone who makes their Dad happy is aces in their book."

"Ange?"

"Yes, Thom?"

"You don't think—um, do you think I'm rushing things?"

"Why?"

"Mal says I'm pushing it because I've known her for only a week." He heard the exasperated sigh and imagined her rolling her eyes at that.

"Thom, I don't know that I'd put too much stock in anything Mal bitches about."

Thom slapped the pillow beside him in frustration. "Angie,

come on."

"No, I mean it," she insisted. "You know exactly how I feel about that man. Just because *you* don't want to acknowledge it—"

"What's to acknowledge, Angie. He's my friend. He's been my best friend for a lot longer than I've known *you*."

"And how well do you *think* you know him, Thom? If I thought you'd listen, I know a hell of a lot more than you do."

Thom shook his head, sitting up suddenly. "No, I won't listen to a bunch of bullshit untruths and exaggerations," he grumped, instantly sorry he'd sat up so fast. The pounding had returned. "You don't like him, fine. But he's like a brother to me and I won't have this."

"Thom, you really can be naïve, sometimes," she said, huffing in exasperation.

"I choose to call it loyal, darlin'."

"That too." The friend part of her came back as she went on. "Thom, seriously. I think it's great you've found someone. I really do. But be careful about Malcolm. Please? I just don't trust him."

"Alright, Angie, okay. But you're wrong about this. Mal is a good guy."

"Whatever."

He decided to change the subject again, but this time out of genuine curiosity about his daughter. "How's Lisa holding up?"

"Nervous, but happy. She's already accepted at Johns Hopkins, Thom."

"That's my girl, future medical doctor!" He grinned from ear to ear. "You tell her I'll be there with the digital camera and a lot of memory cards. And I'll have a video camera too!"

Angie's laugh was full and throaty this time. "Oh lord, really put the pressure on her. She's still fussing about her hair."

Thom laughed with his ex-wife. "I'm sure. But you just let her know I'll be there, proud as hell about my darlin' girl."

"I will."

He started to say goodbye when she interrupted him.

"Thom?"

"Yeah?"

"Didn't you ever wonder why that little issue with the senator just disappeared? Why all of a sudden, the flack was gone? How it was just an accident? Or why that guard died three days later?"

He held the receiver away for a moment, staring at it. What the hell did that have to do with anything? Why was she bringing that up now? He put it back to his ear and said, "No. Why should I?"

"I gotta go, Thom. Lisa's back with her friends. I'll see you tomorrow."

"But, Angi—"

He was talking to a dead line. He hung up the phone and sat for a moment. Why had she dredged that up again? It had never occurred to him to doubt Malcolm's handling of that. Why should he? It made no sense. Thom shook his head. Angie had put Mal at the top of her shit list for reasons that only she knew. And Mal had stayed there, no matter what.

He let it go. He changed clothes, grabbed pen and paper, and took off to be with Joanna while he wrote his statement. He gave it no more thought that day.

25

"GARRISON? WHAT ARE you doing here? It's eight am. You never come in this early."

The precinct's self-styled hippie looked up from the desk. "Hey, man. What's shakin'?"

Tony Morris took off his suit jacket and carefully arranged it on the cedar hanger. He slipped the hanger on the hook of a coat rack, next to his desk. He brushed it down to remove any of the lint that was still on it before turning seating himself at his own desk.

"I repeat, what are you doing here so early?"

Garrison ran his hands through the curls on his head and stretched. "Figured I'd get a jump on the case, you know? I mean, who'd wanna whack this Mitchell cat?"

Tony finished wiping his chair off and sat down carefully, trying not to crease his trousers. He took the alcohol pads out of his desk and began to disinfect every square inch of his desk, phone, and computer keyboard.

"And?" When he received no answer, he glanced up to see that Garrison was staring at him. "What?"

"Just thinking about all those poor germs that we'll never have a funeral for."

"Ha-ha, very funny."

Jim laughed and shook his head. "Man, you are what we call

a frigging clean freak."

"No," Morris disagreed. "I am what one would call healthy and I intend to stay that way. With half of this office suffering a cold and the other half recovering, I do not intend to be a statistic."

"Right," Garrison answered with a shrug. "Whatever."

Tony pulled out his vitamins and poured a cup of water from his private bottled stash in the drawer. "Not to be a killjoy or anything, but the feds took this over."

Garrison's answer was a raspberry. Obviously, he didn't care. Tony reflected, then why should he? "So, what are you reading?"

"Well, I'm checking out this cat Mitchell, okay?" Garrison began to pull page after page of Post-its from the computer monitor. "I mean, we talked to everybody this dude knows. He's got no enemies. I mean *nobody* said anything against him. Cat's got like two ex-wives, okay? *They* didn't have any bad shit to say about him."

"So?"

"So, don't you find that just the least bit weird?"

Tony sat back in his chair and crossed arms. "Why should I? We've met Mr. Mitchell. He's a stand up guy."

"Yeah, but someone took a whack at him. *Twice.*" Jim waved one sticky note in the air. "This cat beats his ass and takes off, still don't know why." He waved another one. "This cat tries to shoot him, still don't know why. Does that sound like a man that ain't got any enemies to you?"

"No, it sounds like a man who has enemies that he doesn't know about."

Jim grinned back. "Yeah, see, that's what I'm thinking. But that doesn't fit. I can dig the mugging theory. *Maybe.* But who's gonna mug a pop star on the deck of a big, fancy hotel like that?"

Tony shrugged.

Garrison was on a roll. "But it *wasn't* a mugging, right? I mean we found that length of rope on the lawn and that mask a little ways away. That ain't a mugging."

"We don't know that, Jim."

"Come on," Garrison whined. "What else could it be? You got any better ideas?"

"Okay, go on."

"So I say somebody was trying to snatch the dude."

"And the Hayes woman interrupted the event."

"Right, right. And then there's this shooting thing, man—"

"If it's the same guy," Tony interjected.

"Okay, okay, yeah, but I think it is," Jim answered with enthusiasm. "Come on, I mean, who's gonna go out of his way—"

"Or *her*," Tony corrected. "We don't know gender on this."

Garrison sighed and his shoulders slumped. "Yeah, okay, but the point is, whoever fired that rifle was going for somebody in that party. I'm thinking it's Mitchell."

Morris nodded. "We don't know that the shooter was only aiming at Mr. Mitchell. The trajectory only shows that whoever was shooting aimed in that direction."

Jim wagged his curls at that. "Dude, whoever it was plugged two in his jacket. Someone followed him out there on that mountain and aimed for him, man. I'm thinking Mitchell was the target."

Tony couldn't find any fault in that logic and said so.

"Gets better, man." Jim pulled a folder out of the mess of paperwork on his desk. "Check this out." He tossed the folder to Tony, who caught it.

"What's this?"

"Ballistics report. That rifle? Was used in another shooting."

Tony glanced up, brow furrowed, then opened the folder and began to read.

"Shell casings we found in the ravine match the casings they found at the Mullins estate, when that guard got nailed—one Scott Amber. They found a couple of the shell fragments, too. Striations match the slug the coroner pulled out of the corpse."

Tony held up his hand. "Wait. Amber worked for Senator Mullins. I remember that case. Turned out to be a murder for hire. Didn't they put that creep away?"

Jim laughed and rubbed his hands together. "Now you got the *real* weird shit going down. They put *a* jackass away. I'm thinking not the *only* jackass. You dig what I'm saying?"

Tony nodded, grinning broadly. "I think I do, partner."

Jim was practically dancing in his excitement. "So like I got this call last night from ballistics. They said the report was done and they'd have it on my desk. And they said I'd wanna read this and get on it. So, I came in early. Figured we can check it out."

Morris nodded. "I agree. What are you thinking?"

"This jackass we got, his name's Eric Roberts. I'm thinking we can shake him down for the name of *this* putz."

"Might lead us to who hired the shooter?"

"And the shooter, man. We got a frigging murder for hire ring right here in Carroll."

"You're reaching, Garrison."

Now Jim's eyes were glittering. "You sure about that, dude?"

Morris chewed on his lower lip. "Let's see if the two cases are connected first. You check out...." He pulled up the information.

"You check out this Eric Roberts at the pen. See what he knows. Let's see if they're related. If they are and he can give us the goods, then I'll see if the DA can cut him a deal. But I want you to go talk to him first."

"Stick me with the dirty work, huh?" Jim had a mischievous grin.

"Your questioning technique is better than mine," Morris conceded.

"You just hate prisons."

"Very true. But I also have a better rapport with our lady DA and I can get what we need."

Jim laughed again. "You just wanna put the moves on her."

Tony gave his partner what he hoped was a bored and irritated look. The teasing about his private life was nothing new. And the truth was; he really *did* want to 'put the moves,' as Jim would crudely put it, on Allyson. They'd managed to keep their affair very secret and it was nothing that Tony wanted spread all over the station.

"I want to have an intelligent conversation with an individual in power," he answered tersely.

Jim shrugged. "Okay, okay, don't get flipped out over it. I'll go hit the big house."

Garrison grabbed his leather jacket and headed off. Tony looked down at his watch. If he called her now, she'd still be at home. They could talk privately and maybe have a little special time. He put his jacket back on, grabbed the folder, and made sure to let the Desk Sergeant would know how to get in touch with him on his cell as he left.

26

SHE KNEW WHO it was the moment she heard the knock. Jo ran to the door, threw it open, and launched herself into his arms. "About time," she whispered. She covered his mouth with her own in a deep and penetrating kiss.

Thom's arms wrapped around her and he gently pushed her backwards into the room. She heard the click of the door as it locked in the frame. She jumped up in his arms, wrapping her legs around his waist. They never made it to the bedroom. He took her as she leaned back against the wall, her arms wrapped around his neck as she moaned into his mouth. It was quick and glorious; they clung to each other, still using the wall to hold them both up until he could catch his breath.

"You okay?" she gasped against his neck, her feet finally hitting the floor.

He softly laughed, his breath tickling the flesh under her ear. "I think so, but if I don't sit down, I'll *fall* down."

"Come on, then," she told him. She led him to the sofa and eased him down on it. She collected his jeans and her undies, and tossed both on the empty chair. She picked up the pages and pen that he'd dropped, no longer forgotten, and brought them to the coffee table.

"Come back here," he told her.

"Coffee first, *then* me."

"No, screw the coffee. Come back here."

She got the coffee anyway, setting the two cups on the table. She lay down beside him, her thighs still moist from the lovemaking. The smell of it made her hot for him again.

"God, that's what I call a quickie," he muttered.

She giggled, opening the buttons on his shirt so that she could touch his chest. His heart was beating, rapid and hard, against her fingertips. She just wanted to listen to it, feel it. Anything to remember that he was real, that he wasn't a dream. That he was here with her. "Just think what later's gonna be like."

He kissed her forehead. "Later? Lord help me, I'll be a puddle."

"Nope. A greasy spot!"

He kissed her again, holding her close. He closed his eyes and laid his head back on the pillow. She watched him, watched his brow furrow. She kissed the divot in his chest and stroked the skin as she spoke.

"Thom?"

One eye opened, looking down at her. "Yeah?"

"What's going on?"

"A lot of craziness." His blinked a few times, then reached up to rub the side of his face with the hand that wasn't holding on to her. "Jo, we need to talk. About a few things, I guess."

"All right." She waited for him to speak. The set of his jaw and the deep furrow in his forehead told her this was going to be a deep conversation.

"I need to tell you something. At the risk of opening a wound. But, I need—"

Her fingers danced over his lips. "No, you owe me nothing."

He kissed the tips and pulled her hand away. "Yes, I do."

He started talking. He told her about Missy and the kiss, what had really happened. What she'd said to him. What she'd wanted. And with every word, he was watching her reactions. He held nothing back.

Jo listened, torn by so many emotions and her mind was racing all over. She felt guilty as hell for doubting him. She wanted to smack the shit out of a bunch of nosy busybodies masquerading as news reporters and photographers. Then she felt sorry for Missy and Walt, wondering what they were dealing with and if it was this bad for them. It had to be. Somewhere in the middle of those thoughts, she noticed it was quiet again.

He had stopped talking. He was watching her. Waiting.

Joanna got up on her elbow, looking down into his face, that handsome face that still held the trace of the young man he'd been. The fullness of his lips that held the memory of youth before age began to thin them, the dimples that deepened when he smiled. The dark brown eyes that missed nothing, that sparkled when he was happy and filled with tears when his heart was broken. She'd stepped on it a few times already, with her suspicious nature and her paranoia about men in general. She traced the shape of that glorious mouth with a finger.

"I never should have doubted you to begin with. I am such a fool."

"But—"

"No, I am. In the short time I've known you," she confessed, "you've never told me one lie, never made me believe something that wasn't true. Never led me on. And I never stopped to ask you what happened, give you a chance to tell me." She glanced back into his face, stroking the fine hair on his chest. "Why did you stay around? Why didn't you just move on?"

He smiled, one hand against her back to keep her from tilting off the sofa and the other reaching up to his chest. In a very simple gesture, he patted the place over his heart.

She understood. "Me too, Thom. Me too."

"I promise you something," he said.

"Yes?"

"I will never hurt you. I will never have other women instead of you." His free hand rested on hers where it had been curled against his heart. "I learned that the hard way, Jo. I screwed around on Angie; Sandy screwed around on me. I...."

He cocked his head, staring off over her shoulder. "Isn't it funny how things come back to haunt you? Pains you gave become yours. Love you shared is given when you least expect it. I loved Angie. I did." His gaze returned to hers, solid and still contemplative. "More than I can ever say. And I blew that so bad. Then, when Sandy came along, I thought I had a second chance. Turned out that it was some cosmic revenge on Thom." He smiled at her. "I never counted on this, on falling for someone so hard. Especially knowing someone for only a week."

She nodded. "I know. I loved Roger more than I can ever tell you. But it wasn't meant to be, Thom. And that's okay. Maybe it was just to let us know who we were really meant for."

"You think so?"

She kissed his chest, smiling against the cloth of his shirt. "I do."

Tom sighed and nodded his head, satisfied with that answer. "I have a press conference this afternoon. Mal's setting it up."

"All right, then," she answered. "I'll be there."

"No," he said simply. "I want you to stay here, in your room."

"Why?"

He kissed her fingers, and then eased her around so that she was sitting on the coffee table and he was on the sofa opposite her. He passed her one of the cups and then took his own.

"Why, Thom?" she repeated. "Why can't I be there?"

"Jo, you ever had a press conference?"

She shook her head. "No, why?"

"You ever see those TV shows about sharks? How, when there's blood in the water, they all go nuts?"

She shook her head again. "I don't watch TV."

"I watch all those nature shows. That one channel that has a week where all they show is programs about sharks and what makes 'em tick." He sipped the hot brew. "It's called a feeding frenzy, see? And they go crazy, trying to feed, circling the carcass. And sometimes, they feed on each other, if some poor shark doesn't move fast enough."

"You think this press conference will be like one of those?"

"Count on it," he answered with a rueful expression. "They'll ask me a lot of personal questions and most of them will be none of their business. Questions that I'm not going to answer."

"About what?"

"Hopefully, just the shooting and the mugging. But they'll also ask about that kiss and who Missy is. And if you come, they'll want to know about you too."

"Oh," she said. "What are you going to tell them?"

"I'll figure it out as I write it." He smiled at her. "But I want to protect both of you. You don't need to have the sharks feeding on you. Trust me on this. Please?"

"I trust you." She leaned forward to kiss his lips. "So, what time is this little shindig?"

"Mal originally said two o'clock." He pointed to the chair

where his pants were. "I've got my cell phone there. He'll call me when it's time."

"Well then," she said. "Sounds like we'll be eating in. How about you write that statement and I'll order food for us. We can eat and maybe take a nap."

"That sounds great."

She reached over and picked up the pen and paper from the chair, laying them down on the table. He gulped back the rest of his coffee and started writing. By the time she had phoned down for room service, he was lost in the words. Periodically, he'd reach up into the blond hair and scratch the same place in the crown of his scalp, as if the scratching helped the ideas flow. Then, he'd write another flurry of words on the page, crossing out some and inserting others.

She didn't disturb him until the food arrived and she'd laid it out on the table. She quietly walked over and sat next to him. He had moved from the couch to sitting on the floor by then, writing on the tabletop. He was lost in reading what he'd written. When she sat down, the cushion moved behind him and the trance was broken. He looked up into her face and smiled.

"Got it done?" she asked.

"Yeah. All done."

"Good, come eat."

He folded the papers and laid them down on his jeans. He walked over to the table, still half-naked, and seated himself.

"Well, your appetite hasn't changed at all."

He grinned around a mouthful of seafood chowder. "Good sex, you know."

"Uh huh," she muttered, feeling secretly pleased at that.

"Right."

"It's true. Making love with you is…is…."

"That bad, huh?"

"No. That good." He reached out for her hand. "Jo, you make me feel so young, so desirable. It's been a long time."

"I do desire you, sir," she answered. "Very much."

He took a bite of the lobster salad, closing his eyes in ecstasy. She watched him, amused at the way he approached food—the same way he approached hiking, golf, and making love—with his entire being. She wanted to lick the mayonnaise from his lips, the childlike smile he had right now was turning her on in ways she never imagined. How could she not be in love with that man?

"Oh shit!"

That startled her so badly she dropped her fork onto the table with a clank. "What? What's wrong?"

"I almost forgot. I can't believe it."

"What's wrong with you?" She lightly slapped his arm, making him laugh. "Don't do that! You could give a girl a heart attack."

"Look, I have to take a trip tomorrow."

Something inside her deflated and Jo had to work hard to hide her disappointment. "Oh. Um. Are you coming back?"

She had to have been unsuccessful, because he giggled like a child, spitting out some crumbs. "Of course I'm coming back. My daughter's graduating the day after tomorrow. She's finished her pre-med and I'm going to go see my baby walk across, Magna cum Laude and Valedictorian of her class."

She took a quick drink of her iced tea to cover her embarrassment. "Oh, well. Um, congratulations."

He took a long drink from his glass, sitting back with his chest puffed out. "I'm giving the key note speech since they're gonna give me a degree too."

"Oh?"

"Honorary doctorate in ecological sciences," he added, suddenly modest. "But still...."

"Thom, that's a big deal," she gushed. "They don't just pass out degrees for shits and giggles, you know. You've earned it, I'm sure of that. I'm proud of you."

He grinned at her, obviously warming under her praise. "Yeah?"

"Yeah!" she repeated, smiling back at him. She meant every word of it; it *was* a big deal.

"Then, how would you like to go with me?"

Jo's jaw dropped. "Are you serious?"

"Yeah," he answered. "I want my kids to meet you. I want to share this with you." He stopped, then hesitantly added, "If you want to go, that is."

She squealed with delight and jumped over in his lap—almost tumbling both of them to the floor. "Yes! Yes! Yes!"

"Great!" He laughed like a little kid, high pitched and throaty. He hugged her fiercely, still laughing as he outlined the plans. "Then, we'll fly out tomorrow as soon as Mal can get our tickets. I'll introduce you around and we can come back the day after the ceremony."

Jo felt a bit overwhelmed. He was taking her to meet the family. That meant serious. She wasn't quite sure how she felt about that but she did know one thing, he'd done the impossible; he'd completely swept her off her feet and then some. "Wow," she sputtered. "Um, okay!"

He looked sheepish, shy even. "Unless you'd like to do some sightseeing. I hear Syracuse is a beautiful place."

"We're going to New York?"

"Yeah."

She kissed him hard before jumping up. "I'll get a small bag packed and ready to go."

"Sit and eat, silly. We're going tomorrow. You got time."

There came an odd noise from the chair where their clothes lay. She cocked her head, listening to the weird buzzing. "What the hell is that?"

"That's my cell," he said. He jumped up and dug it out of his pocket. "Yeah? Mal, what's up? Oh. Now?" His shoulders slumped and he exhaled with a weary sigh. "No, let's get this over with. Now is good." He listened for a few moments. "Sure, okay, good. I'll be glad to meet them. Listen, Mal. If I don't like the—. Good, okay then. I'll talk to them."

She stood up from her chair, walking to stand close to him. Not that she was trying to eavesdrop, but that he looked as if he needed a little moral support.

He listened for another moment or two, massaging between his eyes with his free hand. "Listen, Mal. I need you to do something for me. I need you to get two plane tickets to Syracuse for tomorrow." He turned around to smile at Jo. "Yeah, Lisa's graduation. No, Jo's going with me. So get me two first class tickets for a morning flight." He listened a little more. "Yeah, well, it's what I want. Make the reservations for me and I'm on my way down." He clicked off the phone and stuck it back in his pants pocket.

"Gotta go?"

"Yup." He pulled on his jeans, wriggling into the close fitting denim. "I'll be back right after, okay?"

"Okay." She smiled at him, letting him know that she'd be waiting here for him.

He kissed her again, this time practically taking her breath away. With a quick squeeze of her bum, he told her, "Keep that warm for me."

"You got it, champ," she answered with a grin.

After he left the room, she turned on the TV to a local channel. They were right outside the building, one of the largest gatherings she'd ever seen. They looked more like the mob at a stoning than a muddle of reporters. And she was suddenly nervous.

27

"How do I look?"

Mal looked him up and down. "Like you just got laid."

Thom gave him a dirty look. "I do not. I stopped and changed my sweater so I *wouldn't* look like I just got laid. That was a cheap shot!"

"That's a cheap sweater."

Thom crossed his arms over his chest and stood with his head cocked to one side. "Jo picked this sweater out, thank you. And it wasn't cheap," he grumbled. "Mal, spill it. What's wrong?"

"Nothing. Where's your statement?"

"Here." He snatched the paper away from Mal's groping hand. "Tell me what's wrong."

Malcolm stopped in mid-grab. "I just want to get this over with. So you can get back to your life and I...can get back to mine."

"Malcolm." Thom watched for something, some kind of sign that would help explain things. "Did I do something?"

Malcolm's answer was terse. "Nothing."

Then it dawned on him with a jolt. He shook his head at his own stupidity and sighed. "Oh, man. Mal, is this because I'm taking Jo to Lisa's graduation and not you?"

Mal looked shocked now. Something else played across his face but it was so quick, Thom wasn't sure he'd seen anything. But at least he had his answer now.

"Uh...what...?" Mal stuttered.

Thom rested his hands on his hips. He felt low enough to walk under a snake's belly. He'd had no idea that Mal might have been looking forward to this. "I am so sorry. I never meant to hurt your feelings. Please, forgive me."

"I...uh, well...."

"It was just that, well, I talked to Angie this morning and she wants to meet Jo. You know how Angie is. She's gotta check out all my lady friends; make sure they're good enough. And the kids are just as bad."

"Yeah, I know...."

The guilt set in at that point. Thom could see the disappointment in Mal's eyes. And why not? Mal was part of the family too. "But it won't be the same without you there, buddy. Why don't we talk about this after the conference, okay?"

It was a small smile, but it was still a smile. Malcolm pointed the way to the front doors and opened them. Thom stepped out onto the deck with a gazillion flashbulbs going off in his face. He stopped in front of the bank of microphones, held up a hand for silence, and received it.

"Folks, thanks for coming," he said, grinning and turning on the charm. "I want to read a quick statement and then, I'll answer a few questions for you."

Everyone settled and the murmuring stopped. The only sounds were the natural noises around them and the incessant clicking of the camera lenses. He slipped his reading glasses over his nose, cleared his throat, and began to read.

"I guess you folks have heard the gossip, so I'm here to tell you what's really going on." He gave a pause for dramatic effect and went on. "I got here about a week or so ago to have a month long vacation before launching into my next tour. I love New Hampshire; it's my home. Vacationing here requires no second thoughts and I can think of no nicer place than the Mt. Washington hotel.

"Yes, it's true there have been a couple of incidents while I was here. There was a mugging attempt a few days ago. I'm still wearing the black eye, as you can see. The guy got away with nothing. And then, day before yesterday, someone did take a few shots in my direction. I'm sure it was just some guy out hunting, not paying attention to where he was aiming. We saw wild deer in the area, so that may have been what he was gunning for. I don't know, maybe he slipped. But the point is I'm fine."

Thom scratched an itch under his nose, looking up over the rims of his glasses. They all seemed to be watching, waiting. He looked back down to the page, finishing with the last paragraph. "I was with friends and our hiking guide. He got us under cover and off the mountain safely. He then contacted the authorities just as a matter of courtesy, nothing more." He looked up again, smiling and folding the paper. "So, there's no story here. I think we can all just let it go. Okay, I'll take some questions now."

There was a chorus of "Thom" and "Mr. Mitchell" and a sea of hands. Thom took a deep breath and pointed to a tall gent in the back.

"Adam Wheeler, *The Mountain Ear*. Mr. Mitchell, isn't it true that the police are reporting the first attack as a botched kidnapping attempt?"

"I know nothing about that," Thom answered, still smiling.

"But the police have a mask," Wheeler continued. "They found a ski mask and a—" The man looked down at his notes.

"—a length of a synthetic rope found on the lawn. How do you explain that, Mr. Mitchell?"

"Mr. Wheeler, this *is* a ski resort." Thom chuckled along with the other reporters. "I'm sure you'll find a whole lot of lost ski masks out there."

Wheeler wasn't letting go of this one. "Mr. Mitchell, the police are saying that the shooting was not a random hunting accident. They have a ballistics report that indicates—"

"Look, Mr. Wheeler," Thom interjected. "Like I said, I'm not a cop. I don't know what's going on there and you're gonna have to get that information from them. All I know is it was a random thing."

"The police aren't calling it random."

"Cops have been known to be wrong before, my friend."

"Mr. Mitchell. Liz Borden, *Entertainment Weekly*. A photo's been circulating showing you sharing a pretty deep kiss with a young lady here at the hotel. Any romance going on?"

Thom spared a glance over his shoulder at Mal, who was tight lipped and expressionless. He turned back around. His own smile was starting to slip a little; he hadn't wanted to get into this but he had known it was coming. He was ready with an answer.

Thom turned on every ounce of that 'folksy, saccharine' persona that he was accused of having. With an 'aw, shucks" demeanor, he answered, "That was hardly a deep kiss and the angle that picture was taken from is very misleading. She was with me on the hike, along with her boyfriend and my lady. It was a terrifying experience for all of us and what you think you saw wasn't what was going on. It was a moment of affection for a very scared young lady who was real upset."

"Alan Davis, *Rolling Stone Magazine*. That looked a little more than just a friendly peck on the cheek, Thom."

Thom laughed along with the rest, except his laugh was a little forced. "Folks, you should know by now that you can't always trust what you think you see. Trust me; it was just a friend giving another friend a hug and a moment of support."

Another hand shot up, followed by a woman that looked more ghoul than reporter. Thom arched a brow at her, indicating that he'd take her question.

"Carol Stuart with *The National Enquirer*. Who was the other woman you were with? A lovely redhead, to be sure. You two seemed to be quite cozy."

He took his reading glasses off, stuffing them in the case and back in his pocket. "Ms. Stuart, let's leave the ladies out of this, shall we? Yes, that was the woman I'm seeing right now, and I don't want her bothered any more than I want Mi— Uh, the young lady in the picture bothered."

"Can we have the young lady's name?"

"No, I don't think so." Thom shook his head and held up his hand to indicate that no more questions would pry that information out of him. "I won't let you put her under a microscope. There's nothing there."

"Mr. Mitchell, don't you have a home in Nashua? Why did you choose to stay at the same hotel that the young lady works at if there's nothing going on?"

What a dumb ass question. Thom bit down a sarcastic retort. "The young lady is a very, *very* recent acquaintance. And since I come here once a year, I don't think it's for the romance."

"But why not go home?"

"Hey, I live in hotels," he confessed with a shrug. "I like to get waited on. Nothing wrong with that."

"Mr. Mitchell, why isn't your girlfriend out here with you? Maybe there's more with this younger woman than what you're telling us?"

He'd had enough at that point. Smiling, he nodded to them and waved. "Thanks for your time, folks. Have a great afternoon." He turned on his heel and walked off the deck, back into the hotel. He took it for granted that Mal had come inside with him and he wasn't wrong.

"Thom, that was a big mistake. You didn't turn them off at all."

He sighed, one hand on his hips and the other rubbing his forehead. "Tell me about it. *Shit!*"

Mal clapped him on the shoulder. "Come on; let's go back to my suite. I've got the two men I want you to meet."

Neither of them said anymore about the botched press conference as they took the elevator up to Mal's floor. Two men were waiting inside of Mal's room, both standing up as Thom and Mal walked in the door. Mal immediately began the introductions.

"Thom, this is Mike Rudner. He'll be your driver."

Thom reached forward and shook the beefy hand held out to him. Rudner was a tall man who looked as if he would be more comfortable in the gym than anywhere else. His blond hair was long enough to be pulled back into a ponytail and he had piercing blue eyes. One look at the man and Thom knew he didn't want to be on the wrong side of this one.

"Pleased to meet you, Mr. Mitchell."

Thom nodded. "Likewise."

Rudner continued, "I've been a chauffeur for about twenty-five years and most of my clients have been affluent or in the public eye somewhere."

"Oh?" That got his attention. Maybe Mal wasn't off the mark. This kind of experience would make him feel better and get him off Thom's back. "Can I ask who?"

"I've worked for the Governor on occasion, when he's been in the area. I was one of the drivers for Senator Mullins. I've also had the privilege of chauffeuring Dan Brown and a few members of the Kennedy family when they were in the state." Rudner clasped both his hands before him, standing at attention. "I've had training in defensive and protective driving, and I'm certified through the New Hampshire state police."

Thom nodded. "Right on." He looked into the man's face, trying to find some sign of recognition." You worked for Phil? I don't remember you."

"No, sir. I don't remember you either. I left Senator Mullins' employ a few months before his accident. I was going through some additional training at the time."

That made sense. Thom nodded and looked back to Malcolm.

Mal gestured to the other man. "And this is Neil Butcher. He'll be your bodyguard."

Butcher stepped forward and held out one mammoth sized paw to Thom, whose own hand was swallowed up in the massive fist. Butcher was equally tall but a hell of a lot brawnier. His black hair was cut very short, green eyes peering from a husky face. Butcher was a burly guy; more like a naked bear to Thom's mind.

"I'm CIA trained, sir. Former employee of Pinkerton agency, I've been out on my own for about fifteen years. My last job was working for a PR firm here in the state. I have my references if you need them."

"You licensed to carry a gun?" Thom asked.

"Yes, sir. And I'm a third degree black belt in the martial arts. I'll keep you safe, sir."

Thom nodded. "Great, okay. Then, you guys are hired." He flashed a smile at Malcolm to show his approval, and then turned back to the two men. "So, did Mal fill you in on the rest of my schedule for the next couple of weeks?"

Rudner nodded. "Yes, sir. We'll be accompanying you out of the state for personal business and then bring you back here to finish your vacation. We'll be your shadows."

"Uh, well, not *that* up close and personal, guys. I do require a bit of space."

"Yes, sir," Butcher answered.

"Okay, then."

Malcolm took over. "Gentlemen, I've gotten you the suite attached to Mr. Mitchell's. Here are your card keys. Why don't you go settle in while we talk and then, you can meet him back here."

Both men took their card keys and, after nodding to Thom, picked up their bags and carried them out the door.

Mal exhaled, shaking his head. "And getting that suite wasn't easy. I had to do a *lot* of persuading to get that journalist to bunk with his camera guy."

Thom didn't answer. He was still trying to reconcile the need for these two men with the desperate desire for his freedom. He hated this; he felt more like a prisoner than ever before. But Mal was right; he needed the protection. Whoever the gunman was, he'd missed—but just barely. Thom rubbed his chest, trying to ease the sudden fear and panic that threatened to knock him down.

"You okay with 'em, Thommy?"

He nodded. "I don't want 'em to begin with, Mal, but I guess they're necessary evils."

"Yes they are," Mal agreed. "And I *do* want them to begin with. The press hammered you with the truth, my friend, and you came across like you were covering something up."

Thom sunk into the chair. "Tell me about it."

Mal plucked a carafe off the bar and poured a cup of hot tea, handing it to Thom. He opened a bottle of brandy to pour a dollop in the tea, but Thom put his hand over the cup and shook his head. Mal raised an eyebrow. Right now, Thom's nerves were on fire, but the idea of adding the brandy made his stomach roil.

"Pass, Mal. I'll take it straight up." Thom took a sip from the cup and sat back. "So, about tomorrow."

"I booked a charter for you, Thom. We can take off whenever you want."

"Good."

"About Ms. Hayes going with you," Mal started, his tone of voice suggesting that he was about to ask something very unpleasant.

Thom knew he wasn't going to like whatever it was. "What?"

"After that conference out there, I'm thinking you may not want her on the plane with you."

"Of course not," he snapped. "And why would I want to take her with me? What *was* I thinking?"

"First, get rid of the tone in your voice and I'll answer that." Mal hesitated but went on. "Thommy, you really want them seeing you with her? After they tried to pry information about

Missy out of you? They didn't want to let it go at all. Imagine what they'll do to Ms. Hayes."

Thom saw his point immediately and backed down again. "They'll chew her up and spit her out."

"Exactly." Mal reached down and plucked a piece of paper off the table, handing it to Thom. "So, I went ahead and booked her on a separate flight. Delta to JFK, which is where you'll be landing. I've rented you a car and you can meet her in one of the hospitality rooms. Those have a back exit you can use and Mike can get you to the hotel where everyone's staying, with no muss and no fuss."

Thom stared at the paper that listed the flight information. On one hand, he'd wanted her with him. He wanted to hold her hand, talk to her while they flew. He didn't want to spend one more moment away from her than he had to. But on the other hand, when he'd described it as a feeding frenzy to Jo, he knew he wasn't far off the mark. Thom nodded. "Fine. I don't like that either, but let's do it. I don't want her attacked by the paparazzi."

"Good, the ticket will be waiting at the airport and her flight leaves at 10:40 am. I've booked it under her name. And Mike and Neil will get you to the charter. I figured about noon? Will that be too early?"

Thom shook his head. He didn't look forward to telling Jo. But it was better this way. A lot better. Then, he remembered something else. "Mal, listen. You know you're welcome to come with us. Lisa will want you there too."

To his astonishment, Malcolm declined. "No, Thommy, I think I'd better not. I've got this mess to calm down. Someone has to stay and keep them off Missy."

"Yeah." Thom nodded. Once again, Mal was two steps ahead of him. "Good, you make sure they stay away from her. Help me get this shit to die down. I want to enjoy the rest of my vacation."

"I understand," Mal told him. "You spend a couple days with your family and I'll take care of this. Irony of it all, though—it's selling records, Thom."

Normally, the idea of selling records would have pleased him a lot. But not this way. "Mal! How can you worry about that right now?"

"Because it's my job," Mal answered hotly.

"Whatever." Thom threw up his hands. "I don't wanna talk about this anymore."

Malcolm brusquely agreed. "Look, you don't worry about the rest. Let me handle it. Just relax."

"Whatever. You want to do dinner tonight?"

Mal clenched his jaw a little, but shook his head. "No, I've... I've got some calls to make. As a matter of fact, I'm off to use the computer room here in the hotel right now. See if I can cool things off with the label, too. How about I drive with you to the airport?"

"I'll call you about nine or so. After Jo leaves and I can grab a quick shower. I'll eat with her and we can go get some coffee or something before I head off to the airport."

"Sure, Thommy. Don't forget, we'll have to wait until Mike gets back with the car."

"Right. I won't." He turned and headed out. He was still a bit miffed at Mal's attitude right now. But he also wanted to get back to Jo. "See you in the morning, then. Tell the guys I'll be in Jo's room tonight."

He turned around and headed back to his lady.

28

HE WAITED UNTIL Thom had closed the door before having his temper tantrum. Nothing destructive; he threw pillows and cursed anyone he could think of, mostly the Hayes woman. He dropped to his knees and threw punches into the sofa until he was exhausted and his shoulders were aching. His racing heart began to slow, his lungs heaving as if trying to draw air through a leather veil. His body was calming, but his fury wasn't.

Thirty years. They'd been together through thirty years and a great many CDs, TV specials, and tours. Thirty years and Thom still didn't know the first thing about him. Still didn't have one damned clue. It was always 'let Malcolm take care of it.' Let Malcolm make that phone call. Let Malcolm clean up the mess. Let Malcolm take the fall.

Let Malcolm book the hotel room so I can get laid.

Let Malcolm give up everything.

He threw one more pillow before standing up again. The worst of it had left him with just the cold anger now. That, he could use. He'd told a lie to Thom, just another of many that he'd told in thirty years. He'd booked no flight for that dizzy bitch. And he'd be damned if he was going to. He drained the cup of tea that Thom had forgotten, and then poured another— this time, heavy on the brandy.

"So what the fuck do I do about this?"

He'd come too far, kept Thom's ass out of the fire too many times to let that stupid bitch get in the way.

"She's not going, and that's that!"

But what to do. How to manage it.

It was just like that Mullins thing again. Getting Thom out of that little mess had been costly in more ways than one. A drunk driving incident that almost turned into a mess with a senator. The first time he'd availed himself of Derek's services. Except Derek's idiot brother had almost screwed everything up by getting caught. Fortunately, a $100,000 payoff did the trick. It could have been worse.

But what to do now. He had them separated, but he had to fine-tune the plan. Thom couldn't know that she'd been taken. He had to believe that the stupid twit had left him. Hell, she'd fought with him enough. It couldn't be *that* hard. Could it?

Then, it came to him. That fast and that easy. He punched the number into the cell and waited for Derek to answer.

"Yeah?"

"Okay, here's the new plan. The redheaded bitch is on an earlier flight than he is—so *he* thinks. I've already volunteered Mike to drive her. He's strong enough; he can have her tied up in no time and take her up to you."

"That's cool. We snatch *her* instead. But what about your boy?"

"Oh, I can charter a plane without one hitch. Just have Mike back here in time to take us to the airport. I think I'll go along with him after all."

"My guys can do that. You still want 'em on the trip?"

"Yes." Malcolm poured another tea and brandy. "It'll keep up appearances. We go through the motions, little Ms. Hayes disappears, and he thinks she just got tired of him."

"You want me to beat a 'Dear John' letter out of her?"

Mal gave that one serious thought. It *would* make things easier. "Well, don't *beat* it out of her, but I think a bit of coercion would be fine. That press conference and the picture would be justification enough." He thought a little more. "Yes, get me a 'bye-bye' letter from Ms. Hayes. I'll arrange it so someone 'conveniently' finds it on her pillow or somewhere in the room."

"Let me do that. I'll put it in there and get rid of her clothes too. Make it look like she's split from the hotel permanently."

Malcolm sipped the tea. "Good. That will do nicely."

"I take it you don't want her back?"

He stopped, confused. "What do you mean?"

"You know; no witnesses."

"Tempting, but no. I don't want her dead," Mal decided. "We may discuss taking her back to Nashville later. For now, leave her secluded. We'll only be here another three weeks. Keep her hidden away that long, then Thom is gone and she's history as far as he's concerned."

The other voice sounded almost petulant. "So, can I have a *little* fun with her? Come on, three weeks up here? Alone?"

He understood *that* need. "Well, if the dear slut amuses you, by all means. I'm sure she'll satisfy you. But just be careful; that one's practicing to be a barracuda. Don't want something bitten off."

There was a deep laugh on the other end. "I'll tell Mike and Neil the change of plans. The cabin's all ready for our *guest*."

"Good. And no screw-ups, like you have so far. I want nothing to trace back to any of us. This should go smooth as silk."

"It will be."

The silence ended the conversation. Good, that took care of that. He contacted the front desk and got a recommendation or two for a charter service. He was lucky, the first one he talked to flew out of the same airport. He set it up for a noon flight. There would be two passengers, thank you. Booked it under *his* name. What the hell, it would be his alibi.

He contacted the desk again on his third call. The call was transferred to Ms. Hayes' room. He gave the lie so easily that it was almost embarrassing. He explained it to Thom, who said he'd explain it to Ms. Hayes. Thom was the one who suggested sending the bodyguard, just in case anyone in the press added two and two and came up with girlfriend. This was going too easy.

He hung up the phone and lay back on the sofa. All of this plotting and planning had left him tired. He let every inch of him start to relax, let himself drift closer to the nap that would restore him, ease his frazzled nerves.

29

Jim Garrison made the drive from Carroll to Concord in a little under an hour. He parked his motorcycle in the prison parking lot and went inside for a chat with the warden. He'd called in a few favors to get this interview. Normally, the inmates were kept under guard in the visitation room, but Jim needed private time. So, a couple of phone calls later and he was sitting in this room, waiting for the guard to escort the prisoner up.

It was only five minutes before the door opened and Eric Roberts was escorted inside, manacled at the wrists and ankles. Two guards ushered him in and seated him at the other side of the table. The cuffs around his wrists were attached to a steel eyelet to prevent any tantrums.

"Thanks, guys," Jim told them. "I can take it from here."

"We'll be outside the door, detective," said one guard.

"Yeah. Warden says you got as long as you need," said the other.

"Hey, right on." Jim gave a cheery wave and the two guards stepped back out, closing the door behind them.

Roberts' face was expressionless as he slumped over the table. Jim watched him for a moment or two. He was pretty good at body language, figuring out the other guy's bullshit. He watched the prisoner, sizing him up and trying to puzzle out what would make the successful play for what Roberts actually knew.

"You smoke?" he asked the prisoner.

That was enough to get the guy to look up. "Yeah. What's it to you?"

Jim took his pack out of his shirt pocket and his lighter. They weren't supposed to smoke in that room, but fuck it. He scrounged a tin can out of the trash and filled it with water from the fountain.

"Look, I'm gonna un-cuff one hand. So we can smoke. You fuck me over and I'll have those guys on your ass before you can say my name. Dig?"

Roberts nodded and Jim pulled his cuff key out of his pocket. They were standard issue handcuffs, so the key fit. He unlocked one side, and slid pack and lighter to the man. Roberts shook out one cigarette, lit it, and returned everything. Jim lit his own smoke and sat down across the table.

Roberts took his time, sizing Jim up as well. "What do you want with me?"

Jim tipped the chair on the back two legs and took a drag off the cigarette. "I need some info, man. I need to ask you some questions and get some serious answers."

"Yeah? Well, you know what the good book says? Says 'silence is golden' and 'ignorance is bliss.' Get your answers somewhere else. I don't know shit."

"See, I think you do," Jim insisted. "And I'm in a position to do *you* a favor if you do me one."

"Like what?"

"Well, I happen to know you're doing a stretch of twenty five to life for man-one. I also know you've done twenty."

"So?"

Jim shrugged. "So. You tell me what I want to know and I'll go to the DA and get you outa here with time served. Get the parole board to cut you some slack. I'll tell 'em that you fully cooperated."

Roberts' eyes lit up like a movie marquee. "What do I gotta do?"

Jim leaned forward, but not so close as to be within arm's reach of the prisoner. "I wanna know all about the Mullins job; I wanna know about that guard that got whacked."

Roberts sat back as far as he could. "Can't help ya."

"Yes, you can, buddy. Because if you *don't* tell me, I'll make sure you *never* get out of this joint. I can fuck that up with the parole board too."

They sat in silence while Roberts thought it over. Jim could see the wheels turning in his head to take the deal or not. Was it worth it? What should he do? Roberts finished the cigarette before he spoke again.

"Can I have another one?"

Jim pushed the pack and lighter back. "Tell me about the Mullins job."

"This a genuine offer? I'm not spilling my guts if you're fucking with me."

"I'm not fucking with you." Jim put his smoke out in the can and pushed that over too. "I already called the DA, and I'll call the parole board when you tell me what I wanna know."

Roberts thought again. "Okay. Look, I don't know too much, but me and my brother got called on a job. We were supposed to shut this guy up because he had some shit on this drunk driving thing, see."

"What drunk driving thing?"

"Some shit about a car accident with this Mullins asshole. Only, there was some other shit that the man wanted hushed up."

"*What* other shit?"

"Beats the fuck outa me. Derek said this guard needed taken care of because he had the goods on what really happened. And he was gonna go rat out on everyone with the truth. Somebody didn't want witnesses; me and Derek got hired to do the guy."

"You remember who?"

"Nah, I didn't get to meet the hitter. Derek handles all that shit, man. I'm just the trigger."

"You didn't catch a name? Nothing?"

"Sorry, man."

"What happened to the gun? Report says they never found the rifle."

"Derek snagged it. The cops on the estate nailed me. Derek grabbed the gun and split out the back where there wasn't no cameras."

That made sense. Jim nodded along. "How'd you get nailed, man?"

"I ran the wrong way. Two pigs at the front gate."

Jim pulled out his pad of sticky notes. "Says your fingerprints were all over the place, guard says you had blood spattered on your shoes. How'd you get blood on you if you were using a rifle?"

"I stepped in the shit. I wanted to make sure dude was a corpse."

Jim pulled off the top three stickies to write on the fourth. "And you never saw this cat? Never heard any kind of a name at all?"

"Nope."

"Come on, man," Jim cajoled. "I can't go to the parole board with this crap. I need a name."

"I don't have one, I told ya," the inmate protested.

"Derek didn't say shit? Never mentioned a pay off?"

Roberts' eyes widened. "Hey, wait. Yeah. Derek said something about this cat making the drop of the cash. A...a... *Ross*! That was his name, *Ross*!"

That caught Jim's attention. "First or last name?"

Roberts shrugged. "Dunno, man. But that's what Derek said. Said Ross would make the drop and we could split with the cash."

Jim put his sticky notes back together. "Right on, then. That'll do it. If I need anymore, I'll come back."

"Hey!" Roberts was staring hopefully. "You gonna do it?"

"Yeah," Jim answered. "I'll talk to the DA and the parole board, just like I promised."

He replaced the lighter with a pack of matches and handed them, along with the pack of cigarettes, to the prisoner. He crossed over and slipped the cuff back on Roberts' wrist. He winked at the prisoner. "We'll keep that part between you and me, dig?"

"Yeah."

He opened the door. "You can take him back now." The guards came back in to collect Roberts. "I gave him a pack of smokes, guys. If you wanna check 'em for contraband."

"Yeah, we have to," the short one said. "But he can have 'em back if they're clean."

"Come on, Charlie," the taller one said. "Jimmy's a cop. He knows the rules."

"Yeah, right." Charlie slipped the pack back into the pocket of Roberts' orange jumpsuit along with the matches.

Jim nodded his thanks. "You'll be hearing from the board, man. Thanks for the info." The three men barely made it to the door before Jim called out, "Hey, Roberts."

The prisoner stopped, looking over his shoulder.

"I'm pretty sure neither one of those sayings is in the Bible, man," Jim said. "In fact, it was Thomas Gray that said, "If ignorance is bliss—"

"Then 'tis folly to be wise," Roberts finished, grinning. "Yeah, well, can't win 'em all, man."

Jim returned the grin. "Guess not."

Roberts glanced at both of the guards before turning back around to face Garrison. "Listen, man. One more thing."

Jim lifted his chin, hinting at the man to go on.

"Derek came back one more time after I got put in here. Said if I kept my mouth shut about the shit, that Ross guy would pay us off plus a hundred g's worth. Said it was my insurance money."

"But you told me anyway. Why?"

"Parole, man. So I can spend it. Besides...." Roberts reached up and flipped a pendant out of his shirt. "I found the Lord, man. Time for me to get my shit straight. You coulda left me in here and I still woulda told ya."

Jim nodded. "Praise the Lord, man."

"His wonders to behold," Roberts added and turned to leave.

Jim watched them lead Roberts out and back to his cell. He stared at the notes in his hand. *Ross.* There was something coincidental in that. But what? He decided he'd run it by Tony when he got back to the precinct.

30

THOM GOT OUT of the shower, toweling his hair and body dry. The best part of hotel living was the endless hot water. Well, that and the six head shower they had in the suites. He wrapped the towel around his middle and set up to shave. He could see her moving about in the bedroom; every time she passed the doorway, she was walking over to check out yet another outfit. She'd step before the full-length mirror and hold the hanger up to her shoulders, examining the dress and how it would lay. How she looked.

"I liked the blue one," he said, not even sure she'd be hearing him. But it felt good just saying it.

She smiled, showing she *had* heard him, and turned around to pick up the blue dress again. She stood before the mirror, fussing with the pleat of the skirt, the lay of the neckline, the gathering in the sleeves. She turned her head, as if that would change the way it looked.

"Give it up, darlin'," he told her. "You'd look beautiful in nothing but a potato sack."

"Thom," she whined, "this is important. I'm meeting your kids. I want to look perfect. I want to *be* perfect."

"You will be," he assured her. He turned on the electric razor and went about to the task at hand, stealing glances as she stood applying her make up now.

"Thom?"

He looked at her reflection, standing in her slip and hose and her eyes, oh so serious.

"Yeah, darlin'."

"You sure he's got the arrangements made?"

He stopped at that, turning around to see her. She was looking at him with a slightly furrowed brow, the look of someone worried. "I'm sure. Why?"

She shrugged. "Nothing. Just...nothing."

He tossed the towel back onto the floor and walked into the bedroom. He came up behind her and slipped his arms around her waist, kissing the space between her neck and shoulder.

"You better stop that, sir, or I'll never be ready on time."

He laughed against her skin and did it anyway. "Why are you worried about that reservation?"

"Promise you won't get mad?"

That stopped his kisses. "Of course I won't. Why would I be mad?"

"I don't...I mean...I don't think your Malcolm likes me very much."

"What?" He twirled her around to face him. "What do you mean? Of course he likes you. Why would you think that, darlin'?"

She wouldn't meet his eyes with that question.

"Jo? What is it?"

She hesitated before finally answering. "I just get the feeling that...well, he'd rather have you all to himself, that's all. I...he always seems so cold to me. And then, he said...."

"Said what?"

She shook her head again and threw her arms around his neck. He held her close, smelling the perfume she'd put on. Whatever it was, she wasn't going to tell him. He debated pushing the issue, but decided to let her tell him in her own time. It had to be a misunderstanding. Mal wouldn't be rude to someone; well, certainly not Joanna. Mal had a tendency to be a bit proprietary sometimes, but not— No, it was just a misunderstanding.

He ordered breakfast in the suite as they both finished dressing. They'd sent a male server this time; he set the table with the food and left after Thom tipped him. He and Jo sat down to eat.

"Thom?"

"Yes, darlin'?"

"You're sure, right?"

He reached over to take her hand. "I'm sure. You have a 10:40 AM flight on Delta. Mike is going to drive you to the airport and you'll pick up your ticket at check in. I'll be right behind you and we'll meet at JFK. Mal's arranged it. I'll meet you at the hospitality suite. Okay?"

Her smile was timid, at best. "I just...."

It hit him at that moment. He knew exactly what she was feeling. He didn't want to be separated either. To let her out of his sight for even the trip there would be totally insane. But he needed to hear her say it. "What, darlin'?"

She squeezed his fingers. "I feel like—you're gonna laugh."

"No I won't."

"I feel as if something bad will happen if I leave and you're not with me." She blushed, staring down into her coffee cup. "Isn't that silly?"

"No, it's not." He tugged on her hand, to pull her gaze up to his. "I don't want to be separated from you either."

"So, what do we do?"

It took only a second to decide. "Screw 'em."

She tilted her head. "Excuse me?"

"Screw 'em. The press, the paparazzi; screw 'em!" Just that easy, he knew what to do. "We'll just show up at the charter office and you'll fly with me. I can sweet talk 'em into letting me have that plane early. And if they won't, I'll rent one. I don't have my pilot's license for nothing, you know."

"But...but, my ticket."

"I don't care," he told her. "I just know that I want you with me. I have a bodyguard; he'll keep the reporters off us until we get in the car. And we can go in a side way to the airport. We'll be fine, darlin'. In fact, the car is picking you up at the kitchen entrance anyway." He grinned. "They'll never know we're in that car. What do you say?"

Her grin was answer and reward enough.

"Alright, then," he told her. "I need to get dressed and finish packing my overnight bag. You finish getting ready and I'll be back in...." He looked down at his watch. "Oh shit!"

She jumped and then smacked his arm. "Stop doing that!"

He laughed at her, at himself. "I keep forgetting to take this damned GPS off. I'll try to remember that and get my watch." He pulled his cell phone out of his pocket and noted the time. "I just have to change and throw a few things in the bag. Give me half an hour? That'll give us plenty of time to get to the airport and talk to that guy at the charter."

He kissed her lips, thinking nothing would please him more to make love with her once more before he left her, but he couldn't afford the luxury. He had to hurry. He left, heading up to his room. He barely had the door open and his card key in his pocket before the phone began to ring. It was enough to stop him in his tracks.

"Damn! I was supposed to call Mal," he muttered to himself.

If he answered, he'd have to explain what was going on and listen to Mal try to talk him out of it. It wouldn't be safe for him, Mal would say. It would expose Jo to the paparazzi, Mal would tell him. It would destroy her privacy and make their relationship public. Mal would try to convince him that this was needless and they'd be able to spend a couple hours separated.

Thom didn't want to be convinced. He wanted to be with his lady. He decided to ignore the phone and get dressed. He went into the bedroom, stripping off his clothes as he went. He opened the bag that held his shaving kit and left it laying on the bathroom counter. He went back into the bedroom and picked out what he wanted to wear for the trip. He decided on his jeans and that sweater she'd picked out for him. For the ceremony, he'd wear his black pinstripe suit.

He sat down on the bed, pulling on his black socks, as the phone began to ring again. The twinge of guilt turned into a stab. He stopped in the middle of pulling the heel up, letting his thoughts turn to his friend.

"First, I don't invite him and now, I don't talk to him," he muttered again. "Some lousy friend, I am."

But that prospect of Malcolm trying to talk him out of the plan loomed large. Those who spoke of Thom Mitchell called him a lot of things, stubborn being the chief comment. Angie used to chide him about that, about being so set in his ways that granite was more pliable. Thom had made up his mind and he wasn't about to let anyone change it. With a true sense of regret, he ignored this call too.

He was packed and ready to go. Tossing his last minute

toiletries into the shaving kit, he added that to his overnight bag and made sure everything was turned off. As he headed to the door, the phone rang one last time. Stuffing his card key into his back pocket, he turned back to the ringing phone. "Sorry, Mal. I'll talk to you when I get there."

He met her as she was coming out of her room.

"I just tried to call you," she giggled. "You must have just left."

"That I did," he told her.

They held hands on the elevator ride down, through the kitchen, and to the employees' entrance. There were five limousines parked in the back area, but only one came forward to the door to greet them. Thom held the door open for her as she walked out to hand her suitcase to his bodyguard.

"Uh...Mr. Mitchell?"

"Hey, Mike. Morning, Neil," he greeted them. "Take Jo's and my bags to the trunk and then, we'll skip the check in for Delta. Jo's coming with me to the charter flight."

Rudner nodded and took the bags. Thom's bodyguard was a little more flummoxed.

"Mr. Mitchell, sir. Are you sure? I thought we were going with Mr. Ross."

"Change of plans, Neil."

Jo took his arm and asked, "Thom?"

"Yes?"

"How do you know which charter?"

"There's only one there that Mal uses when we're in New Hampshire," he answered. "And I know the owner. I'll go in and talk to him, and the pilot can take us. He'll have to re-file his flight plan but that doesn't take too long." He kissed her cheek and held the back door open for her. "Or I'll file that plan and

I can fly us. By the time we get loaded up, I'll have called Mal to tell him the change of plans and we'll be on our way. Okay?"

She put thumb and forefinger together, raising up the other three fingers and thrust that hand at him. "Ooooooh-kay."

He helped her into the car and got in beside her. Neil climbed in next and sat in the jump seat. Mike got in the front seat and started the engine.

"Mr. Mitchell." Neil nodded to them. "We'll get you straight to the airport, sir."

"Good, Neil, thanks." Thom agreed. He put his arm around Jo as the car took off. He could see inside Neil's jacket and noticed that the man wore a shoulder holster. *Good, he's prepared*, he thought.

They were lucky; everyone seemed to be up on the front deck as they pulled around. Jo watched as they continued down the road past the vans and trucks. She smiled down at him. "They're not following," she told him. "They don't see us. This is great."

"Tinted windows, darlin'," he answered with a wink. The press might take a guess that someone important was in the limo, but on the off chance anyone wanted to follow, this stretch car would already be cruising down the road.

When Mike made a left turn, Thom sat up in the seat. He was a bit disoriented; they should have taken a right turn to head for the airport. He tapped on the glass between the areas and Mike rolled it down.

"Yes, sir?"

"Uh, we should have gone right. The airport's the other way."

The driver glanced up in the rearview mirror. His eyes were suddenly hard, steely. "Short cut, sir." The glass went back up.

Since Neil didn't disagree, Thom just relaxed. Sure, a short cut. No big deal. He and Jo sat back to watch the scenery. At least they were together. After another twenty minutes, the car pulled onto another road. This time, Thom was sure about something. They were *not* heading to the airport. He rapped on the glass again. This time, Mike didn't bother to answer.

"Neil, get Mike's attention, will you?" He turned back to his bodyguard. "This isn't the way to the airport."

Neil simply glared.

Thom felt Joanna freeze up beside him. "Thom?"

"Neil, what's going on here," Thom demanded. "I want you two to turn this limo around and take us to the airport right now. There was no answer and Thom was starting to feel a sense of dread in his middle. "Neil," he said as sternly as he could, trying to hide his growing fear. "I said tell Mike to turn this damned car around. Now!"

The bodyguard resembled a pitbull now, his grin suddenly ugly and cold. He said nothing, only pulling out the gun and pointing at them. "No, I don't think so. Sir."

Jo stiffened against him, one hand gripping the edge of the car seat. Thom's eyes darted around the car; he wasn't sure what he was looking for but he'd know it when he saw it.

"Uh, don't try it, Mr. Mitchell," Neil said. "The doors are locked from the front and you won't get out. The windows are locked as well. And this is a nine millimeter, just in case you were thinking of taking *me* out. I'll have that first bullet between your eyes in no time." He pointed the gun at Joanna. "Or maybe I'll just take out the lady here. That should keep you in line, I think."

Thom took a sideways glance at Joanna. She held his hand

hard enough to make his fingers turn purple from the lack of circulation.

"All right, we'll sit here. Quietly." He eased her hand to let go a little, all the while watching his bodyguard. "We won't do anything stupid."

"See that you don't."

They rode on in silence. But Thom's eyes never left the gun. Jo said nothing, didn't move. Thom just pulled her closer to him and held her. Another half hour and they pulled up another road and behind a decrepit gas station. There was an SUV waiting behind an old shack. They pulled up alongside of it and Mike turned off the engine.

"That'll do it," he said. "They won't find this car back here. We can head up the mountain now."

The locks clicked, the buttons rose as if by magic. Neil gestured with the gun. "Go on, Mr. Mitchell. You first. She can stay with me."

Thom took a deep sigh and opened the door. He stepped out of the car, looking around him. "Hey, I know where we are." He looked up over the roof of the limo. "We're at Wilde Mountain." He glared at the driver. "You're taking us up Wilde? Why?"

"Privacy," was the answer. "Get your ass over here."

Of the two of them, Mike was the shorter. Thom made a decision. As he stepped away from the car, he raised both of his hands as if he were going to put them behind his head. As he got closer to the driver, he went for broke and threw the first punch. He caught the stocky man unaware and jumped on him. Within seconds, they were rolling around on the dirt. Mike had a hell of a left uppercut and he popped Thom with a sucker punch to boot. Thom felt his head rock back but he had a few moves still in him. He drove his knee into Mike's gut, the air rushing out of the man's lungs. They rolled over again, Thom on top this time and now in control.

A shriek took him unaware. Thom stopped long enough to see Joanna dragged out of the car, but the lady didn't come easily *or* willingly. She fell against the bodyguard, stamping her heel against his instep as hard as she could. Neil fell back against the car, but that gave her an edge. In a move that would have made a wrestler proud, Thom watched her drive her elbow into the man's middle and follow it up with the heel of her hand against his nose. Blood gushed from Butcher's wounded face as she screamed curses at him.

Her mistake came when she lifted her foot again, raising her knee to slam it into Butcher's groin. He blocked the attack easily, throwing her off balance. Neil grabbed her shoulder and whirled her straight into the side of the car. Her head smacked the metal hard. As Thom pinned Mike down, he watched in horror as Neil repeatedly slammed his open palm against her cheek. On the second slap, he managed to split her lip. On the third, he cut open her cheek with his ring. Her mouth and face bleeding, Thom watched her eyes glaze over. She started to fall but Neil wouldn't release her. He continued to slap her. The sound of his hand cracking against the soft flesh of her face made Thom angrier.

Thom roared, sitting back and ready to spring forward. "You fucking bastard," he yelled.

At that moment, he felt two hands grabbing his shoulders and pulling him forward. Mike's head connected with his own, hard enough for Thom to hear the crack and the starbursts to fill his vision. Mike head-butted him again, driving Thom backwards onto the gravel.

The last thing he saw was Joanna slumping to the ground, her face bloody and puffed with the coming bruises. His sight went black as he passed out.

31

MALCOLM DIALED THE number while he put on his socks and loafers, waiting for Thom to pick up the phone. It went to voicemail; Thom should have answered by now. He tried that woman's room, no answer. That was a mixed blessing; at least she wasn't there. But then, where was Thom? He called the front desk. He was *not* prepared for what he heard there.

That chipper ditz at the desk told him, "Mr. Mitchell and Ms. Hayes left together."

Malcolm gripped the receiver hard. "They...did?"

"Yes, sir," she chirped with an annoying glee. "They passed by the desk on their way to the security exit."

"Are you sure?"

"Oh, yes sir. He waved to me as they left. I remember that distinctly."

Malcolm hung up the phone, suddenly frozen to the marrow. They left together. *Oh, sweet Jesus, tell me he didn't do something stupid...like go with her.*

Malcolm quickly pulled out his jeans and fished the extra card key to Thom's room from the pocket. He used the stairs to get to Thom's floor, to his room.

"Thom?"

He made a quick dash to the bedroom.

"Thom? Thommy?"

The suite was deserted, quiet.

"Oh shit!"

Malcolm made a quick search through the closet.

"Damn! His overnight case is gone. Shit! Damn it, Thommy; please...please tell me you didn't fuck this up!"

He pulled out his cell and dialed the number.

"Answer the damned phone!"

There was only the sound of a ringing line.

"Damn!"

He put the cell back in his pocket and sat down on the bed.

"Where the fuck are you, Thommy?"

Mal noticed the tiny light on the phone was blinking. *Voicemail.* There was a chance that his wasn't the only message. *Maybe...maybe....*

He pressed the button and waited.

"You have three unheard messages. To hear voice messages, press two now...."

The first message was his.

"Thommy, I have got a splitting headache. You mind sleeping in a bit? We can grab coffee and some danish or something from the kitchen on the way out. I just need to stay in bed a little. You mind? Call me about nine or so. I'll be fine by then."

Malcolm deleted that message.

"Thom, it's Angie. Listen, I just remembered something. Can you remember to bring your camera? I hired a professional photographer for the ceremony, but I love your work better. Besides, I want Lisa to have something from her father. Oh, and Dean Sowards said to tell you that they'll have a cap and gown for you, don't worry.

"Listen, Thom, I'm sorry about what I said about Malcolm. It's just...there are things you don't know about him. Things you don't know about me either. I guess maybe things that would make you hate me. But Thom, I have never done anything that would compromise you; you know that. Malcolm...Thom, if you only knew him, knew the things he's done. Just...look, I'm sorry I even said this, but one day, you have to know the truth. Bye. See you when you get here. Don't forget the camera."

"Bitch!"

How dare she! Fine, he could play that game too. Mal gladly deleted that one. He'd make sure she paid for this one. A little secret or two of *hers* exposed would put her right back in her place. She was not going to blow this arrangement to hell.

"Hi, honey. It's me." That woman was practically purring through the phone. "Listen, it's a long ride to the airport, I was thinking of getting a thermos of coffee to take with us. You think we'll have time to snag that from the kitchen? Oh, and we should stop somewhere and find something special for your daughter. It's her big day tomorrow. You need a present. You think we'll have time to find something here? Or do you want to wait until we get into New York? Hurry! I miss you already. I love you, Thom."

It wasn't the '*I love you*' that had frozen him to shocked silence. How many women had told him that? Too many—all of them, in fact.

Listen, it's a long ride to the airport....

Oh, sweet Jesus. He did it. He *did* fuck it up. Damn it, he'd gone with her!

"Oh shit, he...oh God, they got him too. Oh no! Oh God, no!"

He replaced the receiver, in a daze. His heart was pounding into his chest; his vision was blurred. He felt lightheaded and sweaty. His worst fear realized.

They got Thom too.

32

ADAM WHEELER SAT down at his desk and laid out the morning spread. He'd stopped at Starbucks to get his usual—two no fat, blueberry muffins and a quad venti mocha latte with an extra shot of espresso. Just what a growing boy needed—a growing boy with a pregnant wife, a mortgage, and a peaceful, quiet existence.

It wasn't too bad, really. Some would have called it boring; Adam called it freedom. He was a struggling novelist, waiting for that big break. The peace and quiet gave him free reign to exercise that twisted imagination of his, turning it loose on the bizarre and quirky stories that had become his trademark. He'd managed to sell a few of his short stories to local magazines and a handful to the major ones. It wasn't enough to live on, but it gave a nice little nest egg for the baby's college fund and the little extras that made life grand.

It wasn't until Thom Mitchell came onto the scene that he realized how mundane his life had actually become. With Jessie working her bank teller's job and his work with the paper, they came home, ate dinner, had a little conversation, and maybe took a walk around the block after dinner. Then he was off to his latest novel and she was in the living room watching the latest *Survivor* or *American Idol*. Or something equally inane. At the end of the night, after she'd served up the hot cocoa and cake, he'd read her what he'd finished and she'd listen. They'd go to bed, make love, and fall asleep.

God, it really *was* boring when he spelled out that way.

Mitchell changed that. Someone was after Thom Mitchell for some reason, and that was just the scope he needed. Something to take away the humdrum boredom with some action. All he needed was the angle.

Why would someone be after Thom Mitchell? The guy was white bread. Adam started in on his breakfast, simultaneously surfing the internet to find anything he could on the singer. He found the *official* website and started checking that out. Just what he thought, Mitchell was a vapid, pretty boy in his hay day. His hits were the touchy, feel good crap that made him the darling of the blue rinse set. He'd lost his status as a hit maker soon after grunge took hold of the industry and made the jump to country with more saccharine music there. Mitchell had gotten two more hits after that on the country charts and had maintained a cult following after that. Two divorces, three kids. Two drunk driving arrests—then something caught his eye. It was glossed over with barely a mention.

Thom's crusading for the environment had been joined and encouraged by many noted politicians, including the late Phil Mullins, State Senator from Keene. "I lost a great friend in that accident," Thom has said. "I just feel like I could have saved him, saved us all from that loss."

And the page went on to Mitchell's environmental activism but that one sentence got him. He read it again—*"I just feel like I could have saved him...."*

"Hmm, what do you suppose that means?"

"Huh? You say something, Adam?"

Adam looked up to see he wasn't alone anymore. Duncan

had sneaked in while Adam was lost in his research. The tall, geeky Duncan MacElroy was the closest thing that Adam had to a mentor and friend on staff. Duncan normally handled the *Emergency Services* beat, spending most of his time at the police station. Murders were relatively few, if any, in this neck of the woods. But vandalism had been on the upswing. Duncan was one of the few reporters that could make a snail crossing the road sound interesting.

"Uh, something I found here. Hey, Duncan, do me a favor."

"As long as it isn't illegal, immoral, or involve my ex-wife, I'm game."

Adam rolled his eyes. "Get over here, putz."

Duncan came to stand by Adam's desk. "What's up?"

"You know who Thom Mitchell is, right?" Adam queried.

"Sure. I'm a big fan."

"Read this for me."

Duncan pulled up a chair and sat down next to him. He sat quietly for a few seconds, reading the paragraph. When he'd read it, he reached over to commandeer Adam's mouse so that he could read the entire article. Then, he used the pointer to highlight the paragraph. Adam sat as quietly as he could but it was driving him nuts, waiting. Just as he was about to pull the mouse out of Duncan's hand, the man sat back in the chair and folded his hands over his chest.

"Well?"

Duncan had the most perplexed expression on his face. He sat, staring that the screen and biting first one corner of his lip, the other.

"Well?"

He waved Adam off. "I'm thinking, I'm thinking."

"Come on, man, don't start a new religion here," Adam huffed. "I just want to know what you make of that."

"Well," Duncan started. "It could just be wishful thinking. I mean, that sounds like something a really good friend would say, you know? The old 'woulda-coulda-shoulda' thing."

"But?" Adam asked, hopefully.

Duncan looked directly into Adam's eyes. "That sounds like a guilty conscience to me."

Adam grinned. "Me, too."

"But I don't understand how," Duncan added thoughtfully.

Adam stopped grinning. "What do mean?"

Duncan scratched the side of his face. "Well, it's just that Senator Mullins died in a freak one car accident."

"Huh?"

Duncan leaned forward and took control of the keyboard this time. He tapped the letters out very quickly, getting into the newspaper's archives. After a couple of minutes of searching, he pulled up the article he was looking for. He reached over and tapped the screen.

"See? Right there. I remember this."

"You'd better, Mac, that's your byline."

"Yeah, beauty, ain't it?" Duncan poked a finger at the article. "Read it, wise ass."

"Summarize it, butt munch!"

Duncan shook his head. "Butt munch. Geez!" He leaned back again, resting his hands on his chest again. "It says that they found a moose about fifty yards into the woods on that road. It says that Mullin was driving someone else's car and, evidently, ran smack dab into that poor moose, who then went into the woods to snuffeth!"

"Whose car?"

"Uh...." Duncan leaned forward again. "You know what, I don't remember. That was...geez, that was twenty years ago, kiddo."

"I didn't think you were *that* ancient," Adam teased. "Bet you remember the Civil War too. Or was it the War of 1812?"

"Watch it, junior. I remember dating your mama, too."

Adam chortled. "Yeah, right. So, he hit a moose. So what? He smacked the shit out of someone's car."

"Wasn't just that, my friend," Duncan admonished. "Take a look at that picture."

Adam looked again. "Shit, that car was totaled."

"Very totaled," Duncan agreed. "And, the only car on the road. Wasn't found until the next morning, when someone called the Staties in on it. By then, it was too late. The Senator was dead."

"Shit." Adam hit the print command. "But...."

"But what?"

"That just feels too simple," he answered. "And something inside says, it wasn't that easy."

Duncan grinned again. "You got good instincts, junior. And you're absolutely right."

"I am?"

Duncan walked over to his desk and opened the very bottom drawer. "I have no clue why I kept this shit all these years. I was real into this case too, until the cops closed it as an accidental death." He pulled out a stack of manila file folders and started going through them, one at a time. "But a lot of shit didn't add up, so I kept it. Just in case I might pull one of those cold case investigations."

Adam watched his friend methodically open and close each folder before tossing it on the desk again. "What are you looking for?"

"Well, I'm looking—*aha!*" Duncan came back to Adam's desk and proudly tossed a file folder on the blotter. "Here you go, Junior. Call it a present."

Adam opened the cover to find a copy of the police report. "Holy— Where did you get this?"

"Connections, my young friend. You read that and we'll talk." Duncan returned to his desk and started piling the folders back into the drawer. "Right now, it's time for me to earn my pay and see what the police have uncovered today." Duncan slammed the drawer closed, then pulled his digital camera and his small tape recorder from the drawer. He winked at Adam as he started out. "Have fun with that, Junior."

Adam immediately started reading every word on every page. Duncan had a gift for understatement; and his comment about things not adding up was definitely an understatement. It should have been a simple accident—moose wanders out in the road, car hits moose, then veers off and smacks into a tree. Senator sustains damage to heart, liver, lungs, and stomach; dies of internal bleeding. But that was just the original report.

For starters, the forensics lab had found evidence that didn't add up. The senator was driving but the blood was on the other side of the car. The passenger side was the part of the car that had sustained the most damage, having been crushed down and caved in to the dashboard. There was no air bag on that side, either. But the driver's bag was deployed. And there was no blood there, none! And yet, the senator was still crushed like a tin can.

Then, there were other fingerprints found all over the car. But they couldn't identify them. According to the report, the owner of the vehicle was ruled out because they didn't match his prints.

"But Mullin was the only one in the car," Adam muttered to himself. "This just makes no sense."

He read the reports, the autopsy results, everything. Nothing added up to a man killed in a car accident as the driver, when all the evidence clearly pointed to him being the passenger. The phone rang at that moment. Since he was the only one in the building still, he picked it up.

"*The Mountain Ear.* Adam Wheeler speaking."

"Junior, I remember whose car."

"Good, you old fart," Adam groused. "Because it's not in the report."

"I know. There's a reason."

"Why?"

"The gentleman's manager made sure the name didn't appear. Was professional courtesy at the time, the gent in question undergoing some serious shit. It was the reason he went into alcohol rehab very soon after, I was told."

"Oh?" Adam looked up from the file. "So?"

"So, his manager gave a hefty donation to the policeman's charity if they'd leave the owner's name out of the reports."

"And?"

Adam heard the soft chuckle on the other end of the phone. "Well, let's just say that as much as Thom Mitchell did for this state and saving the White Mountain Natural Reserve, everyone—including the police chief—felt it just as well to do that."

Adam felt his jaw drop hard enough to make the joints crack. "T-t-t-Thom? Mitchell?"

"The very same." Duncan chortled again. "So, you agree with me? There might be something more there?"

"Was Mitchell in the car?" he asked, still breathy from the shock of the revelation.

"His manager says no."

"What does Mitchell say?"

"No one ever asked."

Adam grinned. "Duncan. I gotta go. I think maybe *I* need to ask. Don't you?"

"Let me know what you find out, Junior."

Adam disconnected the call, still staring at the wrecked corpse of a small sports car. "Thom Mitchell...hmm."

He pulled out his own mini-recorder and digital camera. He stowed the file in his top drawer, locked his computer terminal, and headed out the door. He was on his way to ask!

33

MALCOLM PICKED UP the wrong phone and dialed the number. He realized his mistake and disconnected quickly. "No phone records, idiot!"

He pulled his cell phone out of his pocket and dialed again. There was no answer.

"Son of a bitch! You stupid son of bitch!"

Malcolm began to pace.

"Shit!"

He dropped into the chair and put his face in his hands. This had just gone totally balls up. That idiot, Derek.

Malcolm knew he was dead meat. Thom was going to kill him, that's all there was to it. Thom was going to kill him!

"Wait." He sat up again. "Get a grip, Malcolm, old pal. You don't even know if Thom was taken. Just relax and get it together."

He took a couple of deep breaths.

"Yeah, yeah," he said to himself. "That'll do it. That's it, get your shit together."

He surveyed the room, looking at things.

"Okay, I'm Thom's manager, okay. My prints will be here, it's okay. But *I* can't be here. Go back to my room."

He had already called the desk, so they could give him an alibi. He was here in the hotel when they had disappeared. That would count in his favor.

"Does a call that hasn't connected show up on the records?"

He would have to hope it didn't. Then, it struck him. It was okay. He'd made the call from Thom's room. If he wiped off the phone, they would think the kidnappers had used the phone and cleaned their prints off it afterwards. He took a washcloth from the bathroom and practically polished the handset. He hung it back over the towel rod as neatly as he could, and then made a hasty retreat from the suite.

The moment he had closed the door to his own lodging, Malcolm was dialing the cell phone. This time, he was successful. He didn't even give the man time to say hello. "What the fuck did you do?"

"Easy, simmer down."

"No, I will not simmer down," Malcolm spat through the phone. "I want some straight answers."

"Sure, pal. Ask."

"Did those two idiots take Thom? *Answer me!*"

"I'll answer you," the other man growled. "Just cool your jets and gimme a chance."

Malcolm bit down on his retort and did just that.

"Wasn't much of a choice, pal. Your man came down with his girlfriend, handed the bags to Neil, and sat his ass in the limo."

"But—"

"What was he gonna do? Tell the cat to get out? Pull his gun? You tell me."

Malcolm resisted the urge to scream at the man. He *did* have a point. "How is he?"

"The guys had no choice, man. He came out swinging and tried to kick Mike's ass. Mike put him down."

"He did *what*?"

"Mike had to ring his bell," the voice complained.

"He's a guitarist, you twit," Malcolm snipped. "He won't do that to his hands."

"Yeah, well he did. Mike knocked him out and Neil had to smack the bitch around. She was getting a bit feisty too."

"I'm warning you—"

"Oh shut off, asshole,"

Malcolm, stunned, did exactly that.

"My turn to talk, your turn to listen! You dig what I'm saying?" There was a brief pause on the other end before the other man went on. "Game's changed, buddy boy. Your man changed that and you know what? Suits me right down to the ground."

"Wh-wha-what are you talking about?" Malcolm stammered.

"I'll tell ya," the voice answered. "I'm thinking what you wanna pay us is nothing compared to what someone will pay for this dude."

"You—"

"I mean, he's gonna be worth a lot more than you're offering. Am I right?"

"But—"

"Yeah, I'm right. I'm thinking the stakes have changed, buddy boy. I don't think splitting five hundred large is gonna cut it. I think me and the guys want a little more."

It was *really* spiraling out of control now.

"You can't do this," Malcolm whispered.

"I *am* doing it, asshole."

Malcolm sat down slowly on the closest chair he could find. His knees barely held him as he did. At that moment, his insides had turned to liquid. He waited.

"We want two million. I'd ask for three, but well, that's a bit *too* hard to cough up. I figure a muckety-muck like you can get your hands on two mill pretty easy."

"You. Are. *Insane.*"

"No, asshole, I'm in charge now. You're gonna follow up with the scratch because you don't have a choice. And if you don't, someone will. I remember this cat's got two ex-wives. I bet they'll be more than happy to pay up."

"You son of a bitch, you can't do this to me." Malcolm could barely restrain his anger. He wanted to snatch up something and smash it against the wall. "I'll go—"

"To the cops? *You're* not even that stupid. Because I'll let our little pigeon know exactly who set this up. But then, we won't be here when the cops get here. Your man will be, but *we* won't. Then, we'll see who's fucked up and who ain't."

Malcolm swallowed hard. He had to think fast, come up with a plan. Better just to agree for now. "Okay, fine. Your way," he answered. "But I need some time to get it together. No bank is going to have that much cash on hand. And I don't want to raise any flags, make anyone suspicious."

"Fine," Derek purred. "I'll keep these two locked up and you got twenty four hours."

"No," Malcolm insisted. "I need more than that."

"Twenty four hours and not a moment longer, fucker. Or I start making phone calls to the old ladies."

"You can't, you don't know how to call them."

He heard the low chuckle on the other end. "No, but your man brought his cell phone. He programmed the numbers in. All I gotta do is punch a button. Ain't technology grand?"

"But—"

"Twenty four hours!"

"But you can't do that!"

It was too late; he was talking to silence. Malcolm held the cell away from his head to see that the call was disconnected; he was staring at the phone's background. He forced himself to slowly and quietly slip it into his pocket. It hit him full force and he began to shake. He gripped on to the chair arms to keep his hands from trembling. How the hell had this gotten away from him so easily. What the hell was he going to do now?

Three sharp raps at the door broke his concentration.

"What the—"

He took a very deep breath to calm his racing heart. Whoever that was, he would have to send the intruder away. He had to think. Maybe he shouldn't answer the door. That's it; he wouldn't answer—

"Mr. Ross, I know you're in there."

Who is that? He didn't recognize the voice at all, but it was definitely male. The unknown man rapped on the door three more times.

"Mr. Ross."

Malcolm stood up, took a deep breath, and straightened his shirt. He crossed to the door with several quick strides and opened it.

"Mr. Ross, Adam Wheeler of *The Mountain Ear*. I wonder if I can have a few moments of your time."

Malcolm plastered his most convincing smile on his face. "Of course, Mr. Wheeler, what can I help you with?"

"Uh, may I come in?"

"Why?"

The look of surprise on the reporter's face was worth it. But it didn't stop him. "Mr. Ross, I wanted to ask you a few questions about something I found out."

Malcolm tensed. "Found out?"

"Yes, sir. See, I've been looking into this shooting incident."

Malcolm's grip tightened on the doorknob. He kept his voice light, however, never betraying his sudden sense of doom. "Are you working with the Carroll police?"

"Oh, no sir," Wheeler told him. "But I'm curious as to why someone would want to shoot Mr. Mitchell. So I went to his website. Seems like everyone loves the guy. He has absolutely no enemies."

"Uh, no, he doesn't."

"But I found a reference to the late Senator Mullins on his site, too. I'm curious, why would Mr. Mitchell feel guilty about the senator's death? Do you know?"

Malcolm couldn't help it; he blinked. Several times. "Guilty? What are you talking about?"

Wheeler held out a small tape recorder. "He makes a statement on the site about how he could have saved the senator. Can you elaborate on that for me?"

"Uh, well, I'm sure it was just Thom talking—you know, regret for a friend's death. It was ruled an accident. Terrible thing about that moose."

"So, you're saying a moose caused the senator's death?"

"Of course, it's in the accident report."

Wheeler seemed to have expected that one. He smirked and dropped his polite posture. "And what about the irregularities?"

"What irregularities?"

"Well, the fact that the police report doesn't exactly jibe with a moose-caused accident. Care to comment on that?"

Malcolm felt the blood drain from his face. "Comment?"

"The blood was on the wrong side of the car. Almost as if someone else was driving. You know anything about that?"

"I don't know about that at all."

"And where was Mr. Mitchell? It *was* his car that was in the accident."

Think fast, Mal. Come on, that's what you get paid for. Spin this wool into a yarn. "Mr. Mitchell had...well, that was during his 'dark time,' as he calls it. He *is* a recovering alcoholic, as you well know. He'd been drinking quite heavily and, uh, had taken a taxi."

"Taken a taxi? And left his keys in the car?"

"Of course," Malcolm lied. "All the more easy to pick it up the next day, when he'd sobered up. Or, he was, um, still married to his first wife at the time. She would have driven him back to get the car—"

"But what was the senator doing in that car, sir?"

"I assure you, Mr. Wheeler, I have no clue. And now—"

"One more question, Mr. Ross."

Malcolm sighed. He might as well answer it; the son of a bitch would never leave if he didn't. "What?"

"The police report said it was a black tie celebration for a wetland that Senator Mullins and Mr. Mitchell had raised funds for."

"Yes, it was."

"Why would the senator leave his own party?"

"I really don't know, Mr. Wheeler." Malcolm stepped back, pulling the door before him. "Now, if you'll excuse me."

Wheeler seemed to have expected that. His free hand shot

out and stopped the door. "Mr. Ross, what aren't you telling me? I get the feeling you know something."

He was going to have to be abrupt with the man. "Mr. Wheeler, the only thing I know is that my friend had too much to drink and took a taxi home. Senator Mullins, for whatever reason, decided to take a ride in Thom's Porsche and had an accident. You're talking about something that happened twenty years ago."

"And still seems to be important now, don't you think?"

"If you'll excuse me."

Wheeler took his hand off the door and Malcolm closed it in his face. He leaned his forehead up against the wood and listened to the retreating footsteps.

Oh, dear God. Not that again. Not on top of this. I thought that monster was dead and buried.

Turned out, it wasn't.

34

Tony listened as Jim ran down everything he'd learned from Roberts. When Jim was done, he sat back and mulled it over. "And you don't think he was lying?"

"No, man, I don't," Jim assured him. "I checked him out, okay? Watched him the whole time. The only act I got off this guy was that he was pissed that his brother was running around free and he wasn't."

"See, that bothers me," Tony admitted. "Why didn't he give his brother up for a lighter sentence when he had the chance?"

"I checked that out too." Jim pulled his trusty pad of sticky notes and started peeling off the pages. "Our boy there has been a model prisoner lately. Eric got religion. He's been getting his shit together on the off chance he was gonna get out in five more."

"Oh?" Tony cocked an eyebrow. "Eric got born again, did he?"

"Yeah. And it's strictly legit, according to the warden and the priest. Seems our buddy is planning on entering the seminary when he gets out. *And* he's been acting in a lay capacity in the prison." Jim peeled off another sticky. "Plus, he's gotten his bachelor's degree in Religious Studies through an online university."

"And how did he pay for *that*?"

"Grants and scholarships. Point is that he did it."

Tony nodded. "And you think he's on the level."

"He's still a cocky son of a bitch, got a foul mouth and an attitude problem for a would-be priest, but yeah, I think he is."

Tony took a sip of his coffee. Jim was watching him intently, waiting for his response.

"Okay, we go on the prospect that he's telling the truth."

"Okay," Jim said.

"But he sure didn't give you much."

"Hey, he gave us his brother who was in on the shooting with him, places this Derek at the scene. And I'm betting that either Derek or a new partner is our shooter."

"Could very well be." Tony scribbled that on his notepad. "And all he got was the name 'Ross'?"

"Yeah."

"He never saw the guy or spoke with him?"

Jim shook his head. "Says Derek was the front man who did the wheeling and dealing. Says Derek came to *him* and set up that end."

"That makes it tough."

"Yeah, does. But if we get Derek, we can roll him to find out who this Ross is."

"Wait a minute." Tony leaned forward to look at the reports, neatly arranged on his desk. He carefully peeled back each piece of paper, scanning the pages quickly. "Ross, he said? He's sure about the name?"

"Yeah, he's sure. Why?"

"That's quite convenient, don't you think?"

"What is?"

Tony found it on the next set of pages, the statements they'd taken from the night of the aborted kidnapping attempt. He looked back up with a big grin.

"What?" Jim asked again.

"Seems that the beat boys had a little talk with a Ross after the kidnapping. A *Malcolm* Ross, Mitchell's manager and friend."

Jim's eyes bugged out of his head and his mouth dropped open. "You're shitting me."

"Nope. Here, read it for yourself." Tony passed the report to his partner and waited while Jim read it.

"Well, I'll be damned," Garrison muttered.

"Gets better. At least, *I* think so."

Jim looked up, brows knitted in a quizzical gesture. "How?"

"Call it my suspicious nature, but you notice Mr. Ross wasn't around either event?"

Jim's crossed arms and exaggerated sigh said he *had* noticed.

"He wasn't on the deck when the guy tried to kidnap Mitchell. He didn't go on the little hiking excursion."

"*Now* who's reaching for it," Jim pointed out. "That doesn't mean anything."

"Not by itself," Tony agreed. "But it's a hell of a coincidence, you gotta admit that much."

"Oh yeah." Jim started adding his sticky notes to the array of colored sheets attached to his monitor. "Makes me wonder, though."

"About what?"

Jim turned back to face his partner. "Who pulled the trigger this time? And, why? Money? And is the kidnapper the same dude? *And* if this Ross cat is involved, what's he stand to gain? Why have your meal ticket busted up or kidnapped."

Tony let that roll over in his mind. "Nah, you're right. That's really reaching for it."

Jim shook his head. "Not necessarily. You got anything else?"

Tony nodded. Jim had a way of keeping him focused. Which was good right now, it took the sting out of what he was afraid was a wrong guess. "I took the liberty of checking out Mr. Ross," he told Jim. "And contacting Mitchell's insurance agency. And did a little digging in a few other places."

"Yeah? And?"

"Mitchell named his kids as the beneficiaries of all of his policies. But he also named Mr. Ross as executor of his estate, if anything happened to him. Mitchell's kids will be *very* wealthy, but Mr. Ross gets the say on what happens to all those songs. Every single one of Mitchell's assets is controlled by Malcolm Ross."

"Wait, you saw the will? How?"

"A copy got filed with probate. I have a few connections that spilled the beans for me."

Jim cocked an eyebrow, giving his partner a rather dubious glance. "You know how much trouble you could get in for that?"

Tony just smiled. "Probably. Call it my need to know these things."

Jim nodded. "So, what do we do?"

"Think we have something here?" Tony asked.

"I think we got a lot o' shit," Jim answered. "What do we do?"

"Bring Mr. Ross in for questioning. I'll have one of the cars pick him up at the hotel and bring him here."

"Something else comes to mind, man," Jim added. "Another reason to bring him in."

"Yeah?"

"If Derek was the one to deal with this Ross guy, Ross should be able to pick him out of the mug shots," Jim said gravely. "We can tell him it's because we think Derek Roberts is the shooter."

"And if he picks Derek out, we have a link. Could be, could very well be." Tony nodded. It sounded good. "Get him in here."

Jim called for a patrol car to pick up Mitchell's manager and bring him to the station. Twenty minutes later, the desk sergeant escorted a very annoyed Malcolm Ross into the room. Tony stood up immediately shook hands with the man. He introduced himself, then his partner. Jim waved from his desk.

"Please, Mr. Ross, come sit down."

"Why am I here?" he demanded.

"I'm hoping you can help us, sir. We have some questions about the shooting—"

"And I told you, I know nothing about it. I wasn't there."

Tony put on his best soothing voice, trying to reassure the man. "Mr. Ross, no one thinks you had anything to do with it. We know that. But we wanted to see if maybe you could help us figure out who *did*."

He shot a look at his partner, who took up the narrative.

"Yeah, see, we were hoping you could answer some questions for us and give us some background here. It'll help us figure out who might have had a motive, see. Fill in some blanks for us."

Ross carried himself stiffly, hands clenched at his sides. But he nodded and sat down in the chair offered to him. His posture was ramrod straight, not relaxing a bit. "Go ahead with your questions."

"Yeah, sure," Jim answered. "I mean, this kinda thing never happens here, you dig? The kids knocking over tombstones or spray painting graffiti is the usual shi— Uh, stuff."

Ross nodded again. "Of course. The appeal for Thom and me was how idyllic this place is."

"Oh, you've been here before?" Tony asked.

"Of course. Thom is a native of the state."

"Then, he knew Senator Phillip Mullins."

It was the briefest of hesitations. "Yes, he did."

"Mr. Ross, did Mr. Mitchell know a—" Jim picked up the forensics report on the guard. "A Scott Amber?"

There was a twitch in the man's left eye. Maybe something, maybe nothing. But still— "No. No, he didn't."

"Did *you?*"

Ross took that moment to cross his legs and sit even straighter, if that was possible. He folded his hands in his lap. Tony took one look at the posture and thought to himself, *that man is hiding something or I'll eat the leather off his loafers.*

"No," Ross answered primly. "No idea who that is."

"Used to work for Senator Mullins," Jim filled in. "He got himself shot and killed a few days after the senator's wreck. Turns out the gun that killed him is the same gun used to shoot at Mr. Mitchell."

The folded hands quickly *un*folded and Ross picked at imaginary lint on his trousers. "And you think it was the same shooter?"

"That's what we think, sir," Tony told him. "So, we're hoping you could help us."

"Certainly, detective. Anything and I do mean *anything.*"

"Detective Garrison has the mug shot books over there."

"But, I told you, I wasn't there," Ross protested. "I didn't see anyone or anything."

"No, sir," Jim answered. "We know that. But you worked hand in hand with most of Senator Mullins' staff, right? To get ready for that big shindig?"

"Well, yes, I suppose so."

"Then, maybe if you check out the mug shots, you might recognize a face. Someone that *didn't* belong and might look familiar."

"Look, Detective Garrison, that was twenty years ago—"

"Certainly," Tony interrupted. "We understand. And faces change with age, hairstyles, things of that nature. But something might spark; there might be *something* familiar about the face."

"All we can ask is that you try," Jim said.

Tony watched the man as he sent off signals that were loud and clear. Tony wasn't sure what was going on but there was definitely something funny about Malcolm Ross. It was as if the wheels in the man's mind were turning faster than a hamster running in a cage. Tony half expected him to refuse. He was pleasantly surprised when Ross agreed.

Jim escorted him to the table, showed him the books, and even got Ross a cup of that gourmet coffee that Jim kept for special occasions. Then, they sat down at their respective desks to watch.

It took quite a while, almost two hours before they got their answer. Jim said he'd put the mug shot of Derek Roberts in the third book, on the second to the last page. Sure enough, Ross got a look on his face that signaled some kind of recognition. When asked, he denied knowing the man. But it didn't matter. Suspicion had just been raised. Malcolm Ross knew more than what he was telling. After five hours of searching through every mug shot in every book, the squad car carried off their first suspect in God only knew what.

The two detectives were now determined to find out.

35

ANGIE EXPECTED HIM to call about 1:00 PM or so, but with Thom...well, with Thom and his fluid sense of time, it could be 2:00 or 3:00. She waited, somewhat less than patiently, by taking care of last minute details. She'd gotten an entire floor for Lisa's friends and the family that were coming, which included Allan and his very pregnant wife. Tonight, they'd party in their rooms—with explicit instructions to be quiet enough that the old farts could sleep—and tomorrow, the party would be in the hotel ballroom.

As she sat, going over details, her mind drifted back to the phone call. This was going to be a first, Thom bringing a date. Thom never brought *anyone* to meet the extended family, *never*. This one must be pretty special. Angie had told the kids about their father's new lady. The concept wasn't unwelcome. They knew the situation between Angie and Thom. As Lisa had explained, they'd always go on hoping for Mom and Dad to get together again, but it didn't mean they expected it. As long as Angie and Thom were happy, that's what the kids wanted too.

Angie pulled out the guest list again, to go over the RSVP list, but her mind pulled back to Thom. She'd never remarried, never wanted to. As she had told one would-be suitor, she'd already married the love of her life. Angie had had relationships but nothing permanent and lasting. She'd never wanted them to be. Thom was a hard act to follow. But he was her friend now, not just 'for the sake of the children,' but because they could talk to each other. They didn't have to play games or hide secrets.

Which isn't quite true, is it, Angie?

She put down the pen.

No, it wasn't quite true. She did have a secret, a particularly ugly one. One that Thom would never have understood, one that would destroy any semblance of friendship they had. It certainly would have destroyed their marriage far earlier than it had. Thom and his old-fashioned notions of how marriage should be, how women should act. Whoever this woman was, Angie wished her the best of luck. Thom had grown a lot in the last few years but he hadn't changed a great deal.

The RSVP list would have to take care of itself. Maybe, one day, she might be able to tell Thom what only one other person knew, hope that Thom would be merciful to her.

"Why the hell am I worrying about this?" she asked aloud. She needed to be focusing on Lisa right now. Angie got up from the desk and put on her clothes. It was going to be typical upstate New York weather, still a bit of a chill in the air. She had a light sweater with her. She had a rental car, so she would be the one to drive to the airport to pick up Thom and Joanna. She was actually looking forward to meeting this woman.

He'd call around one or so. Angie had a nice leisurely lunch with her kids, talking about this, that, and the other thing. They finalized the plans for the parties, set up the sleeping arrangements of who would bunk in which room. They talked about baby plans for Allan and Lara. Looking down at her watch, she noticed it was 1:30.

She wasn't all that surprised that Thom hadn't called yet. That was Thom. But when 2:00 rolled around and still no call,

Angie was irritated. At 2:30, she'd developed a full-blown state of pissed off. She made the first call to his cell phone, only to connect with the voice mail. Of course, she left a blistering message before disconnecting the call and tossing it back in her purse. She ignored the looks her children gave her and they went on with their shopping.

If he doesn't get his ass here soon, he can just take a damned taxi to get here. I'm not his damn chauffeur!

Angie made the next call at around 3:15 and only because Lisa was becoming frantic. To tell the truth, so was she. Still no answer on the cell, she decided to try his hotel suite. She got the voicemail there too. Lisa wasn't the only one getting frantic. Even Allan was concerned now.

She sent them to their rooms, to take a nap before dinner. Angie went to hers. She tried Thom's cell one more time, then his room. Then she made the call she dreaded most. She dialed Malcolm's cellular.

"Well, well. Angie."

She swallowed the bile rising in her throat. "Where's Thom?"

He was his usual smirking, arrogant self. "What? No 'hello, Malcolm?' No 'good to talk to you, Malcolm, how are things?' What's wrong, you forget how to be civil?"

She sat down on the bed. "I'm sorry, Malcolm. I'm very concerned about Thom right now."

"Why?"

She cleared her throat. "Why? He's late. He should have been here hours ago."

"No, I mean why do you care?"

She sighed in exasperation, closing her eyes for a moment. That bastard still knew how to get under her skin, a human parasite. "That's a rather stupid question, Malcolm."

"You're divorced, Angie. What's the problem? Still looking for a little of the Mitchell fortune?"

She forced herself to keep civil. Getting pissed off at Malcolm was like spitting into a fan; it only flew back at you. Hadn't it always been that way? She came off the proper harridan and Malcolm came out smelling like a rose. "Malcolm, Thom and his girlfriend are supposed to be here right now. Is he coming or not?"

"He's on his way, Angela."

"He said he'd be here by now."

"So, he got a late start. What's the problem?"

She dug her fingers into the comforter on the bed. "The problem is...Lisa's upset that her father isn't here. We have a special dinner to attend and Thom is supposed to be here for that."

"Well then, I guess you *do* have a problem."

"Malcolm, I'm tired of dancing with you on this," she finally huffed at him. "Where is he?"

"As I said, Angela, he's on his way. You know Thom. He's more than likely stopped to do some shopping. He'll be there." There was something about his voice, something smug and false.

"Malcolm. What's going on?"

"I have no idea what you're talking about."

"Yes you do," she insisted. "You're hiding something from me. I know you."

"Or maybe *you* know something."

Now it was her turn to be vague. "I know a great many things, except the whereabouts of—"

"Talked to the police lately?"

That stopped her for a moment. She paused before she asked, "What?"

"Would you like to know where I've been for the last five hours, dearie?"

She didn't want to know, not really. But if it got her an answer about Thom…. "Where?"

"The boys in blue, Carroll's finest, decided they needed to snoop into the Mullins affair."

It was probably a good thing that she was already sitting down. The loss of her strength left her feeling boneless and spent. *Oh God, not that…not that again!* "How?" she asked in a breathy voice.

"How? How did they find out?"

She nodded, still in shock, before realizing what she was doing. "Yes. How did they find out?"

"I was going to ask *you* that. Considering that you and I are the only two who know the details. It was a small fishing expedition about another matter altogether but still tied in to that."

It felt like a large ball of something had wedged in her throat. She swallowed but it wouldn't budge. She took a deep breath; still nothing. "If…if you think I called them, you're out of your mind," she finally croaked. "I don't want that coming out any more than you do."

"Good," Malcolm declared. "Because you've got just as much to lose as I do."

"Not bloody likely," she spat at him. "I had nothing to do with it."

"No," he agreed. "But you knew. You knew all about it and

kept your mouth shut. That makes you an accessory after the fact."

Bastard! He was right. It did. "It also makes me dangerous. It means that if any harm comes to Thom, I have no problem going to the police about it."

"Now, why would you do that?"

"Because I don't trust you, Malcolm. After what you did, I don't trust you *not* to do it to Thom."

"Would you trust me to tell him about *your* little secret?"

A hand gripped her heart, squeezing tight. "You don't dare."

He wasn't laughing but he sounded as if he could break into one of those stereotypical villain's laughs any moment. He was too cocky about it. "Oh, but I do."

She had no answer. She didn't need one. He kept talking.

"I looked through their little mug shots. I answered their questions. If you didn't put them on it, then I won't worry. But if you *do* give them any ideas, I'll make sure Thom gets some information that I know you want suppressed. And trust me, I'll have no guilt in telling him."

She licked her lips, trying to keep them from sticking together. It was hard to do; her whole mouth had gone dry. "That sounds like you know where he is."

"Maybe. Maybe not. After all, he left the hotel to come see you."

"You *do* know where he is."

"I only know that if any trouble comes to me, honey, you'll have plenty. Now, go play with your children and let me get my work done."

"I want to know where Thom is."

"As I said, my dear, he's on his way. That's all you have to worry about. Now, if you'll excuse me...."

The line went dead.

"Oh sweet Jesus," she mouthed. "What the hell have you done?"

Maybe he knew, maybe he didn't. But something inside her turned over on itself. There was something seriously wrong and, as usual, that man was behind it.

"God, Thom, where *are* you?"

Her palms started itching and burning, a sure sign that there was trouble somewhere. She rubbed them together for a few moments, hoping that would stop the pain but it gave no relief. If she was right and Malcolm *did* know where Thom was, he'd spill the secrets so fast it would make her head spin. But what if—

"Mom?"

Angie snapped out of her daze. "Lisa. You're supposed to be taking a nap."

Her daughter flopped down on the bed next to her. "I can't sleep, Mom. I've just got this really bad feeling."

Angie put her arms around her daughter's shoulders. "Now, now, honey. Come on. You should *not* be worrying about a thing."

"No, Mom, I mean it," Lisa insisted. "Daddy should be here. He *should*. Something's wrong." Lisa's cherubic face suddenly paled and her eyes widened. "Mom, you don't think Daddy had a plane crash. Do you?"

Angie hugged her daughter tighter. "No, I don't, honey. We'd have heard something by now."

"But Mom...."

She put a finger to Lisa's chin and lifted the young lady's gaze to meet her own. "You listen to me. Your dad just got delayed by business, that's all. He'll be here. I know he will."

"But...but what if he doesn't make it?"

"He'll make it, if I have to go up there and drag his ass back here, he'll make it."

"But what if he doesn't?"

Time to admit the truth. "Then, something's wrong and I'll take care of it. Okay?"

Lisa seemed mollified for the present, but Angie's fears weren't as easily dismissed. She'd start calling the police on all levels and damn the publicity. If Thom hadn't made it by the end of commencement, she'd fly down there and take matters in her own hands. And if that meant ripping open the carefully preserved past, then she'd do it. And Malcolm Ross could go straight to hell!

36

"THAT BITCH!"

Malcolm indulged himself in the only fit of pique his self-control would allow. He threw the glass as hard as he could, glaring as it shattered against the wall. He stood still, draining his fury and gaining control again.

"Damn that woman. She's going to be another fly in this particular ointment!"

He immediately took to the stain on the wallpaper with a dry washcloth. Fortunately, he had a small brush in his suitcase so he used that to pick up the large pieces of glass. He swept them onto a folder from his briefcase and threw the shards in the trash. He'd call room service and have the maid vacuum later.

One good thing about the phone call—he could confirm that Angie hadn't alerted anyone to that nasty business. The police were fishing. How and why, he didn't know, but something had tipped them off. Whatever it was, it wasn't going to tie *him* to that Mullins business. As long as the former Mrs. Mitchell kept her wits about her and her mouth shut.

He poured himself a finger of scotch in another glass and downed it. Hell, it was after five *somewhere* in the world, even if it was still an hour away here.

"She'll keep her mouth shut. I have dirt on the saintly Mrs. Mitchell. Dirt that too many would pay good money for. And she knows it, too."

Yes, dear Angie, the poor put upon wife. The one who'd managed to escape the vilification of Thom's second ex. Now, Sandy had caught the full brunt of the fans' hatred and anger. They still burned up the internet, badmouthing the woman's character. But Angie? Angie had managed to become the glorified ex-wife who had endured and lost her true love. If they only knew.

He desperately wanted another drink. He wasn't about to pour it, though. He had to keep a clear head right now. The whole thing was about to end up in the shitter if he wasn't careful.

First things, first. Thom.

Derek wanted money. *More* money. The greedy little weasel was threatening to tell Thom everything if Malcolm didn't pay up.

The smartest thing Malcolm had ever done was tie up Thom's money in more places than Thom ever knew. The glory of being a manager was having that access. All Thom knew was that he was doing well enough that he could make the alimony and child support, pay for three kids to go to college, own an estate that was actually three lots in a gated community, *and* still have plenty of money in the bank. All *Thom* knew was that he wasn't hurting for cash.

What Thom *didn't* know was the extent of his wealth. Malcolm had seen to that. Thom was worth a hefty eight figures and that was *before* the decimal point; roughly, ninety percent more than he thought he was worth. Two million dollars? Malcolm snorted and poured the damned drink. Two million dollars was chump change.

It just went against his grain somehow. Paying the money at all just irritated the hell out of him, especially to that greedy little idiot, a local yokel who had delusions of grandeur. But there were worse things at stake, so he would pay. Hell, he might even be able to turn this around to his own advantage. After all, his loving friend, Malcolm, would save him from the kidnappers. But how to do it.

There was always the matter of cash. But, as he'd told Derek, no bank had that much cash on hand. It would take at least two weeks and too many people knowing. A check? Traced back to all parties concerned. He didn't care about himself, but Derek would sing like the proverbial canary. And Derek already knew where too many bodies were buried—metaphorically speaking. So, what other alternatives? The epiphany was almost staggering. Of course! *Of course!* He dialed quickly.

Derek answered, just as quickly. "About fuckin time."

"How is he?" Malcolm insisted. "You tell me how he is or forget this. I'll take my chances with the police."

"He's still out. Not a hair on his head's been slashed, ripped, or beaten."

"And there better not be."

"Or what, asshole?"

Malcolm snorted. "I didn't call you to get into this. I want to be sure Thom's okay. And I'm going to do it."

"Do what?"

"Pay you the money. I'll do it."

Derek chuckled. "I knew you'd come through."

"How *is* he?"

"He and the bitch are still sleeping it off. A bruise or two here and there but they're fine. We didn't fuck 'em up, okay?"

Malcolm felt the flood of relief. He'd expected a few bruises, to make it all look good. But since this wasn't going as he'd planned, he didn't expect Derek and company to keep the "no harm" promise either. Dangle the carrot of cash and they'd play along. "Good! Keep it that way."

"So?"

Malcolm flopped down onto the sofa, propping his elbow on its arm. "So...what?"

"Money, dick head. When do we get our cash?"

"You're not getting cash!"

"But, you said—"

"I said I'd pay you," Malcolm assured him. "I didn't say *how* I was going to pay you. But I know exactly how and it'll be to our mutual advantage. Just as long as you don't do something stupid."

"I'm listening."

Malcolm laid out the plan. "I can set up a numbered account in an offshore bank in the Grand Cayman Islands. I'll set it up so that all you'll need is the number and a password. Then, you can put whatever bloody name you want on it with whatever bloody ID you want and I won't know a damned thing."

"Go on."

"Once that's done, I'll want to reassure myself that Thom is truly all right. When I see he's unharmed—except for the bruises—I'll wire the money into that account and give you the information."

"No, I don't like that idea."

"What?" Malcolm sat up rapidly.

"I want the money *before* you get to see him. I don't trust you, Ross. You're as slimy as they come."

He couldn't help but laugh at that one. That was just too priceless. "You? You're calling *me* slimy? That's funny. Pot... kettle...*black!*"

"Kiss my ass."

Malcolm stopped laughing. "No, I don't think so." He leaned back again. "You want the money, you play it my way."

"Whatever," Derek growled again. "Why do you wanna see him anyway? He ain't stupid, he'll figure out you're in this."

Malcolm gave that one serious thought. That was quite true. "I said I wanted to see him," he finally answered. "I never said I wanted him to see *me*."

"Yeah, fine. We can put blindfolds on 'em, I guess."

"Good, then that's what you do."

"Whatever. But I want that account number and information before you leave."

"*After* the money is in there."

"No! You come see your man and give me that bank name and account number. Call it good faith."

Malcolm rolled his eyes and began to massage his temples with his free hand. "Fine! Whatever!"

"Then, you put the bucks in and I can call and confirm it. You don't fuck us over; your man and his bitch are free."

Damn, he hadn't counted on that. Joanna being free. And nothing brings couples together like a mutual kidnapping. He was going to be back to square one when this was over. *To hell with that,* he told himself. *I'll worry about that after I get* him back. "Fine. We're agreed."

"You coming tonight?"

"I can't."

"Why not?"

"Because, you insipid yokel, it's not that easy," he sniped. "I can do this via the computer but I didn't bring my lap top with me."

"How the fuck are you gonna do it then?" Derek demanded.

"The hotel has a computer room for business men. Ideally, they use it during business hours when they travel. Which means, it's perfectly anonymous. No one will pay attention to me. Besides, they're already used to me going in there during the day, so I won't have to sign in again."

"What's wrong with now?"

He felt like he was explaining toilet training to a chimpanzee. "They also let the staff and other guests use it, not to mention local residents. The room will be crowded and less private. Not to mention the fact that no one knows me. I'll have to sign in. Paper trail of sorts."

"So?"

"So," Malcolm impatiently went on. "If they trace to me, they can trace to you. Get it?"

"Yeah," Derek admitted. "Fine. Tomorrow will be okay, then."

"I'll have it done in the morning and then call you to get directions to where you are."

"I'll get you to the top of the mountain. You gotta have a four wheel drive to get up here and we're real secluded. It's easier if Mike or Neil picks you up at the old gas station down at the crossroads."

"Fine. That'll work then."

"Don't fuck me over, Ross. I can be pretty ugly if you fuck me over."

"I have no plans on it," Malcolm answered through gritted teeth. "You just make sure no more harm comes to them."

This might just get carried off after all. And he could still be the hero by ransoming Thom. Hell, he might just tell the cops anyway. Derek was the only one who'd seen or talked to him. No one would believe a soon to be convicted felon, especially if Mal had his alibi in place. This could work after all.

If he was careful and kept his own cool. If everything fell into place. If he could keep Angie's nose out of his business. If he could avoid that reporter and the cops...or at least snowball them for a while longer. If, if, if....

It was going to be a long night in the meantime.

37

THOM WOKE TO the feeling of a white-hot railroad spike shoved between his eyes. The very idea of trying to sit up made his stomach turn over, not to mention the fact that his entire body was one big mass of strained muscles and aching joints. He couldn't move if he'd wanted to. After very careful deliberation, he decided that he really *didn't* want to.

He also decided that he had bruises on bruises. The bastard had nailed him in the eye again; he could feel the swelling flesh and thought he might not be able to open it. The left side of his face was aching and a careful poking with his tongue told him that he had at least two teeth loosened. His jaw was throbbing. It was probably a good thing he wasn't that attractive anyway.

It took a moment to realize that he was lying on a plank floor, his head resting on a block of wood. The thought that it could have been much worse zipped through his mind. He could have woken up at the pearly gates with St. Peter. That sobering thought did nothing for his mood, which was growing blacker by the second.

With his eyes closed, his other senses started to come alive. He could hear birds; the hawks and eagles were screaming somewhere nearby. He could make out the chattering of a jay, probably a gray or blue jay. There were ravens and crows having a veritable gossip fest. The whole noise sounded like an Alfred Hitchcock movie. Somewhere in the background, he could hear the roar of water gushing and falling against the granite. It was distant, but still there. And the plaintive cry of a coyote.

He could smell the scent of pines mixed with the occasional spruce and balsam fir. The fresh clean air found only at a certain elevation. There was an earthy scent wafting through, as well. The smell of the wild things moving about, creating a home in the wilderness. The feel of the crisp air against his skin. He was in the woods somewhere. And considering that the last place he'd recognized was at the base of Wilde, Thom was willing to bet that's exactly where he was. Wilde Mountain.

Hell of a way to get here. Shit!

Wooden floor. Birds and coyote. The falls; those would have to be *The Maidens' Tears*. He knew those falls, remembered the story he'd heard as a child. This was Wilde all right. He had to be in some kind of cabin or cottage, an old one too by the feel of the floor. It was rough. Had to be old and only used to keep him here. There was the smell of stale air in the space; the place had to be thick with dust.

Time to open your eyes, Thom, old buddy. Come on, you can do it. Fine! But this was under a great deal of protest.

Left eye *was* swollen but not quite swollen shut. So he gingerly opened the other instead. He found himself staring across the rough-hewn floor. In his limited sight, he could see a kerosene heater warming the space. It was sitting in the fireplace, in the firebox. A slow rotation of his eye produced a modicum of pain but also afforded him a view of a door. There was a bit of light coming through from somewhere but he was too afraid of lifting his head to try to find the source. It hurt too much as it was.

He heard a moan behind him and remembered that he

wasn't alone. He was going to have to brave the pain and turn over. Thom girded his loins and started the slow process of rolling over onto his other side. It was an exercise in sheer agony as every part of his body screamed in physical unison. He tried to reach out to steady himself, and found out very quickly that his wrists were bound together. With a groan of his own, he managed to turn over on his other side. He stayed still for a moment, waiting for the pain in his head to subside before he whispered out her name. "Jo?"

He faced the window side now and could see where it had been mostly boarded up. There were still open places that allowed light to filter in. But there was no way they were going out that window; there might be a whole two inches between each board.

She moaned again and he turned his head gingerly. The side of her face that the son of a bitch had repeatedly slapped was swollen and red. There were the faint beginnings of bruising around her cheekbone and under her eye. She had a bit of blood dried against the corner of her lip and the flesh of her cheek. Wisps of her hair had been pulled out of the ponytail and some had matted in the blood.

"Jo? Are you awake?"

She opened one blue eye to stare balefully at him. "I refuse to answer on the grounds that I might be dreaming. At least I hope I am."

"It would be a nightmare, if you are."

"Yeah," she quietly agreed. "Does your head hurt half as much as mine does?"

"How bad does it hurt?" Thom asked.

"Oh, somewhere inside, some little midget is pounding out

the *Anvil Chorus* and I feel like my skull is the anvil."

"Then, the answer's yes."

"Wonderful," Jo answered. She laid her head back down against the lump she reclined against.

"How bad *are* you?"

She took a deep breath and let it out slowly. "Well, besides my face hurting, I think I'm okay." She opened both eyes now. "You, on the other hand, look like shit."

"Thanks," he muttered. "You're such a sweet talker."

"Thom."

"Shh, I'm teasing, darlin'."

"Are *you* ok?"

"How bad *do* I look?"

She surveyed him from top to bottom. "You've got a purple lump instead of an eye and it looks pretty bad. Can you open it at all?"

"Feels glued shut but I can open it a little."

"That side of your face is pretty swollen too. How are your ribs?"

"They hurt."

"That son of a bitch. I should have clawed his balls off instead of trying to kick them into his gut."

He really wanted to laugh at that but that would hurt worse. Instead, he told her, "Next time, champ. I'll even cheer you on."

She rolled over on her side and pushed herself up to a seated position. She was bound too and Thom could see that they were both tied up with either duct tape or some sort of strapping tape. Either way, the flat grey color stood out against their skin.

"Where are we?" she asked, surveying the room. Such as it was.

"Nearest I can tell, we're on Wilde."

She put her hands up to her face, trying to pull the hair back from the dried blood. She winced as she pulled the strands free. "Ouch." She tucked the lock behind her ear and gingerly prodded the wound. "Well, you wanted to hike it. Guess you're gonna get to do that, aren't you."

"Guess so. If we ever get out of here."

She looked around the room. "Think we've got a chance?"

"Always."

His heart warmed to see her turn a small smile his way. The smile was immediately followed by another wince. "Ouch," she whined. "Don't do that, Joanna. That hurts."

He struggled to sit up, groaning at the pain. But she was quicker. She managed to get onto her knees and crawl to him. She pushed him back down, stroking his wounded jaw.

"No, don't," she whispered. "You're hurt badly. You just lay still."

He did exactly as he was told.

"We'll get out of this," she told him. "You'll see."

"Probably," he answered. "But it'll be too late by then."

"What do you mean?"

"I'm laying here trussed up like a Christmas goose, my life is probably hanging in the balance, and the only thing I'm worried about is missing Lisa's graduation." That was the most depressing thing he could think of. He fixed his gaze on the ceiling, trying not to look at her. He felt like shit as it was, hurting as he did and now adding guilt to the mix.

"Thom...."

"My little girl is going to be a doctor. Did you know that? She's graduating pre-med. And I'm wondering if I'm gonna make it or not, now." He felt her hand, soft on his chest, the fingers gently touching him in a gesture of conciliation.

"Hey, now," she told him. "Don't you dare go getting defeatist on me here."

"I have to face facts, darlin'."

"Maybe." She leaned over him, resting her hands lightly on his chest. "But you don't know that we're not going to get out of here. Someone's going to miss us."

He felt as defeated as he sounded. "Who?"

"Your ex-wife, for one. Your kids. They'll be expecting us and I rather think we're overdue right now."

He tore his gaze away from the ceiling; the moment of self-pity replaced with something else—hope. "You're right. We are. She'll call Malcolm. He can tell her. They'll call the cops."

"Well, the police won't start looking for twenty-four hours but still, they'll miss you."

"Us," he corrected. "Angie knows you're coming."

She smiled with the unhurt half of her mouth. "All right. *Us!*"

He felt the tension relaxing out of his body. "They'll start looking. They may not know where, but they'll...." He sighed again. "And I'll still miss my little girl's big day. Just like I've missed everything else like this."

"Thom...."

"I have. I've been a shit father and I've missed all the important days, the important things for my goddamn career and...." He was close to tears and he was damned if he was going to cry in front of her.

She stroked his chin, her fingers barely touching his skin. "Hey, what brought this on? Hmm?"

He closed his eyes in answer. To be honest, he didn't even know.

"Look," she whispered. "Look at me."

He opened his eye again.

"Somehow, I don't think that's true. I don't think any of your children would ever call you a lousy dad. Far from it." She was smiling at him, trying to reassure him. "And even if that was true, now is not the time for you to be worrying about that. All we have to worry about is getting the hell out of here and off this mountain."

He smiled back at her, grateful for what she was trying to do.

"And I, for one, want to see that Neil bastard get that gun shoved in a very tender place," she said, slight anger in her voice. "And so far up that he'll need surgery to have it removed. I have to tell ya, Thom, your buddy Malcolm has lousy taste in employees. I hope you didn't let him hire your band."

It started as a chuckle in his chest, and then grew to a controlled guffaw. His face and ribs still hurt like bloody hell, but the laughter was better than any painkiller they could have given him. "As a matter of fact, *I* did," he confessed.

"Good, at least *you* know what you're doing!" She scootched down until she was laying at his side, her bound hands against his belly and her head on his shoulder. "I have no idea what time it is, but I know I'm about to pass out again. I'd like to sleep next to you, if that's okay."

He kissed her forehead. "Honey, if I could hold you in these arms, I would." He looked at his bound wrists, then at her. "You know, I bet I could."

He ignored the pain to turn back to her again. He managed to put his arms around her shoulders, drawing her in close. She rested her head on his shoulder again, a soft sigh of contentment slipping from her lips.

"Much better. Now, go to sleep and rest," he told her. "You

and I need to be rested so we can start figuring out a way to kick ass and run like hell. I'm not staying in this godforsaken place one moment longer than I have to."

She sneezed against his shirt and snuffled. "Me either. The dust is a bitch."

She kissed his lips before settling again, closing her eyes. His exhaustion finally stilled the guilt and depression inside of him and his eyes closed. He'd be pissed off later; for now, he was just too tired to deal with it anymore.

38

I T TOOK A little bit of persuasion and about a hundred dollars to find out the first piece of information. Adam paid it gladly. In exchange, he received a name and phone number. It was the best hundred bucks he'd ever spent, especially since it wasn't his money.

He dialed the phone number and waited for the answer.

"Hello? Marker residence."

Female. Good sign.

"Yes, my name is Adam Wheeler with *The Mountain Ear*. I'm looking for a—" He looked at the scribbled name. "A Eunice Marker."

"Speaking."

Let the games begin! "Mrs. Marker." Adam stopped, unsure of how to go on. He didn't know what to say or how to say it.

"Son, did you need something?"

"Yes, ma'am. I needed some answers."

"About what?"

"About the night Senator Mullins died." It got very quiet on the other end. For a moment, Adam was afraid she'd hung up on him. But there would have been a dial tone if she had. So, he waited.

"Why do you want to dredge that up again?" she murmured. "That's been over for a very long time."

"I know."

"Then, why do you want to hurt people? Rake that up and hurt people."

"Mrs. Marker—"

"You have no idea what you're playing with here," she snapped at him. "I didn't just lose an employer, I lost a friend. We *all* lost a friend. Senator Mullins was a good man and to die in such a senseless accident...."

In for a penny, in for a pound. "Mrs. Marker. That's precisely why I want information. Things don't add up about that accident." Only silence again. Adam waited, holding his breath.

"I always said that accident was too funny," she said finally. "That there was something funny about it. Just hitting a moose like that? I know those brutes can wreck a car but...."

"There were other things, Mrs. Marker. You were the housekeeper, right?"

"I was his personal assistant, but yes, I supervised the running of the house."

Okay then, he was going to get somewhere with this. "Ma'am, what do you remember about that night? About the party?"

"Oh my, it was a wonderful evening. The senator invited a great many of his colleagues and the governor was here. That wonderful Thom Mitchell even sang for a while. They raised quite a lot of money for the senator's environmental causes."

"Was there a lot of drinking?"

She sighed on the other end. "I figured you'd want to ask that," she answered reluctantly. "Yes, there was a lot of drinking that night. The senator and Mr. Mitchell seemed to be drinking more than the rest of the crowd—quite heavily."

"Was the senator drunk?"

"How can you say that?" she was quick to ask. "How dare

you insinuate that that lovely man was—?"

"Mrs. Marker, I'm not trying to destroy the man's reputation," Adam corrected. "I'm really not. I'm just trying to understand what happened."

He didn't bother to tell her that he was looking at the toxicology screen on the senator's blood alcohol level. It was at least five points higher than the state limit. The man hadn't just been drunk; he'd been plastered off his ass.

That calmed her again. "Forgive me, Mr. Wheeler. It still..."

"It still hurts," he finished for her. "I understand."

"The senator was quite jovial and certainly boisterous. Was he drunk? Well, I'm not qualified to answer that."

"What else can you remember?"

"Well," she started, then took a moment or two more to answer. Hopefully, she was finding those buried memories. "I remember that Senator Mullins and Mr. Mitchell seemed to be quite inseparable all night."

"Inseparable?" That got his interest. "How?"

"Once Mr. Mitchell was done singing, he and the senator greeted all the guests, talked to them. Why, Mr. Mitchell never left the senator's side. Nor did the senator leave Mr. Mitchell's. And I noticed they were egging each other on in their drinking and partying."

"When did Mr. Mitchell leave?"

There was another pause. "Well, I'm not really sure."

Now he was especially eager for the answers, but he held himself back so that he didn't tip his hand. "Did anyone see the senator leave?"

"That I couldn't tell you, Mr. Wheeler. I know that I surely didn't."

"How about Mr. Mitchell?"

"Sorry."

"Who *would* know?"

"Well, the late Mr. Amber would have known."

"And he was...?"

"He was that nice guard that worked here, the one that was shot a few days later."

Shit, there went that lead. "Would anyone else have known? Someone that *could* tell me?"

"That I don't know, Mr. Wheeler. We had mostly hired staff that night, helping out with the crowd."

"Hired? How?"

"Normally, there was only a minimal staff kept there. Myself, three maids, the cook, and two guards. The state police actually did the bulk of the guarding of the mansion."

"But that night?"

"Well, there were so many of the state politicians and the governor here. The senator's aide felt that having so many of those folks around, it would be best to have extra staff."

"So?"

"Well, we added on temporary servers and cooks to help me, and he called on the Pinkertons to add the guard staff."

"Was this Mr. Amber—was he a Pinkerton?"

"Oh no, he was on the senator's staff."

Adam nodded to himself. "Mrs. Marker, one more question. Do you remember which Pinkerton office?"

"Um, yes," she answered.

She gave him the information and Adam scribbled it down as fast as he could. "Mrs. Marker, thank you very much for this."

"Mr. Wheeler?"

"Yes, ma'am?"

"Senator Mullins was a real good man," she said, a very sorrowful tone in her voice. "If you find out that this wasn't an accident...well, if you do, make sure you fry the bastard that did this to him. He was a *real* good man!"

"I will, Mrs. Marker. I promise."

His next phone call turned out to be just as profitable. The man who ran that particular branch had also been there in 1994, the year of the accident. Turned out all of the guards—save one—had either retired, been fired, or left the job for something better. There were no records for them. But one man was still working for the company and the man in charge was more than happy to give his information. Adam was giddy to find out that the guard, C. J. Williams, was working two towns over.

He took a drive over. Sure enough, the man was just leaving. Adam pulled up beside the Jeep vehicle as Williams was putting his key in the lock.

"Mr. Williams? Mr. C. J. Williams?"

He turned around and watched Adam get out of his own vehicle, then approach. "That's me," he answered. "Can I help you with something?"

"Yes, sir, you surely can."

Williams removed the key and leaned back against the door. "Shoot."

"My name is Adam Wheeler, with *The Mountain Ear*." Adam flashed his press badge, then returned it to his back left pants pocket. "I was wondering how much you remember about the night that Senator Mullins died?"

Williams crossed his arms and simply stared. It was a hard look in his eyes and Adam felt decidedly like a bug under a magnifying glass.

"Sir?"

For the second time, he was accused of ulterior motives.

"What game are you playing, son?"

"Mr. Williams, I am not playing a game, I assure you."

"Then, what are you doing?"

"I have reason to believe that the senator's *accident* wasn't an accident."

The man turned his head and spat on the ground. When the steely gaze returned, Adam thought he saw something else—a glimmer of belief.

"What are you thinking?"

"I'm not sure," Adam told the man. It wasn't a lie, he wasn't. But he was getting the glimmer of an idea. "I think someone else was involved."

Williams nodded. "Okay, then, I'll tell you." He settled against the door again. "Now, you understand, I didn't see much, but I do remember the senator and that Mitchell guy coming out of the house, drunk as lords."

"Where they together or alone?"

"Oh, they were together all right. Making enough racket to wake the dead."

"What did they do?"

"Uh, well," Williams sputtered. "I remember they came out with a bottle of something and started swilling out of it. After that, I don't know. I lost sight of 'em when they went in the house."

"Who would know?"

"That would be Scott."

"Scott?"

"Scott Amber. He was the guy I got partnered with."

"Okay. Go on."

"Scott had the front of the house," Williams told him. "I remember he came back shaking his head, said they were gonna get killed sure as the sun rose."

"Wait," Adam stopped him, his hand up. "They?"

Williams reached up to scratch the back of his head. "Oh yeah, Scott said they took off in Mr. Mitchell's car."

"You mean, the senator *and* Mr. Mitchell?"

"Yeah, they left at the same time."

Adam wanted to be sure. "Together."

"Yup. That's what Scott told me."

Holy shit, they were in the—but that wasn't in the report. "Mr. Williams, uh...who was driving?"

"Don't know. Scott never said."

"Shit."

"Might be on the tape, though."

Adam felt something leap inside of his chest. "Tape?"

"Oh yeah, the video tape. We had the cameras going that night."

"You still have those tapes then?"

"Hell, yeah. Thought the cops were gonna come get 'em, but when they declared the whole thing an accident, they never did."

"So, you still...?"

"Sure. I figured, one day, someone would wanna see 'em. So me and the boss locked 'em up in the safe. You wanna come with me? I'll get 'em for you."

Forty-five minutes later, Adam walked out of the Pinkerton office with three video cassettes under his arm and a spring in his step. He was another bit closer with this mystery.

39

TONY WAS ON the phone when Jim arrived. He motioned with a finger against his lips for Jim to be quiet, and then pointed to the coffee pot. Jim nodded and poured two steaming mugs from the freshly made drink. He set one down in front of Tony, then sat in his chair and watched his partner as he blew across the top of the cup.

"All right then, sir. I can't promise that we can do anything but my partner and I will run over to the hotel and see what kind of information we can get. If she's been missing for twenty four hours, I'll be back in touch and we'll proceed from there." He replaced the handset in the cradle and stared at it, running one finger over the plastic. "What was that all about," Jim asked.

Tony sat back in his chair, folded his hands across his chest, and stared down his nose as he talked. "You'll be interested to know that I just spoke with a Larry Micarello, Attorney at Law, from Nashville."

"And I should care because...?"

"He was reporting a missing person, my friend."

Jim tilted his head, crossed his arms, and waited.

"Turns out one of his lawyers is missing up here. A Joanna Hayes."

Jim frowned. Tony waited, smiling. He didn't wait long. Jim put it together.

"Wait, that's the chick that was with Mitchell when the

shooter...."

"Exactly right, partner," Tony confirmed. "I got quite the earful from her boss. She was on vacation after working with Mitchell on a fundraiser in Nashville, something to do with abused kids. Micarello said he's been trying to get in touch with her since yesterday."

"And she's missing?" Jim drank a little of his coffee, then dove into the sticky notes on his desk.

"Yes she is."

"Think it's got something to do with this Mitchell thing?"

"I'd say they may be connected. Especially since she disappeared after we started investigating the shooting and mugging." Tony took a sip from his own mug and glanced at the clock. It was now 9:30. "So? Where've you been?"

Garrison was still sifting through the sticky notes on his monitor as he talked. "Hey, while you were hobnobbing with the rich and famous, I've been running a background check on our intrepid manager."

"Ross?"

"That's the bugger."

"What did you find out?"

"This guy comes straight outa college to work for this Mitchell cat. Majored in *Art History*, okay? And yet he's this bigwig manager, getting all these gigs for his boy. So I did a little more digging. Guess who he's related to, on his Mom's side of the fence. Guess!"

Tony shook his head; he had absolutely no clue.

"Fat Sally."

Tony felt his eyes bugging out of his head. "What? Fat Sally? The mob butcher?"

"One and the same," Jim answered smugly. "The dude sittin' in a federal pen for ten counts of racketeering, six counts of murder one, four counts of extortion, and a partridge in a pear tree."

"Holy—"

"Shit," Garrison finished for him. "Yeah."

He quickly recovered his composure, motioning Jim to go on. "What else did you find out about?"

"This Ross guy knows all these bigwigs in the families and the Teamsters and some real shady organizations. He also knows a lot of important people in the music biz, in politics."

Jim tossed a folder over to Tony, who started leafing through it.

"I got all those off the internet last night. Any pictures I found, he's always hanging right with Mitchell, but he's gabbing it up with some big dude. All these governors and mayors and senators and shit."

And a few male recording artists that seemed to be a little on the chummy side, standing very close to Mr. Ross. Tony went through them, one by one. The pictures were intimate and secretive. Mitchell standing close but alone while Ross was head to head with someone else. Almost as if they'd been plotting something.

"So, we're headed to the hotel?" Jim asked.

Tony felt his focus pulled from the pictures back to his partner. It also brought back the errand he had to do. "Hmm? Oh, yeah, we should. Check around; see if we can find any information from the staff. She may not even be missing."

"You think she's not?"

"Very possible. Micarello made it sound like she was out here to do some work, try to get Mitchell in the fold with her firm."

Tony shook his head. "Hey, if I were on vacation, I would not be thinking work. She may have just turned off her cell phone and unplugged the hotel phone."

Jim stood up and pulled his leather jacket back on. "Then, let's go see."

Tony didn't get very far before his phone was ringing again. This time when he picked it up, it was his second surprise of the morning.

"Carroll Police, Detective Morris speaking."

There was a sharp exhale, almost a sigh of relief on the other end of the line. Then a female voice burst out, speaking rapidly—the voice of someone scared.

"Detective, thank God. My name is Angela Mitchell and I want to make a missing persons report on my ex-husband."

"Uh...okay, Mrs. Mitchell, relax. That's what we're here for."

An alarm bell went off in his head at the name, *Mitchell*. It was just too convenient. He tossed a quick look up to Jim, who'd sat down again.

"Who exactly are you missing?"

In the same clipped and hurried tone, she answered, "His name is Thom Mitchell, the recording artist. He's missing and I'm scared. Thom never misses anything to do with the kids, *never*."

He pulled his pen out again and began to jot notes on a separate form. Two in one day, the alarm bell was really going off now. Especially after the first phone call.

"How long as he been gone, ma'am?"

"He was supposed to be here last night. He and a friend, a...a...oh hell, he just said her name was Joanna. Anyway, they were supposed to fly in to the Syracuse airport. I waited for his phone call and it never came. I called the airport and they said they had no flight scheduled for that charter service. Something is wrong and I think Thom's in trouble. You have to do something! Please!"

Tony switched to his best 'I'm your friend, I'm here to help you' voice and did his best to try to calm her down. She was too close to real hysteria.

"All right, Mrs. Mitchell. When was he due in?"

"He was supposed to be here about one p.m. or so but he never showed and I've been calling and—"

"Well, that's not really enough time to—"

"You don't understand," she shrieked through the phone. "He's *missing* and I'm scared."

He lowered his tone, speaking more softly than before. "Mrs. Mitchell," he said, keeping his voice as calm and even as he could. He looked directly into Jim's eyes as he spoke again. "That's not what I meant. What I mean is, normally we have to wait twenty-four hours before we can declare a missing person. However, since this is Mr. Mitchell, we'll get on that immediately. All right?"

That calmed her down. "Thank you, detective, thank you."

Jim cocked an eyebrow, seemingly asking what was going on.

"Good. We know where he was staying. My partner and I will head over there and poke around, see what we can find out."

Jim nodded. He understood.

"Mrs. Mitchell, I need a phone number where I can call you, let you know what's going on."

"No."

That jerked him up short. "No?"

"I'm on my way, detective. My daughter is graduating in a

few hours, something her father isn't going to see evidently. Can you imagine how she's feeling?"

"Yes, ma'am," he told her. "I think I can."

"Good. Because right now, this is one of the most important moments of her life and I have to tell her the bad news. Now, how do you think that makes *me* feel?"

"If that were me, pretty angry."

"And very scared. No, Detective, I'm not going to wait for you to do anything and call me. I'm coming to you. After the ceremony."

She was digging her heels in. Tony did his best to do the same. "Ma'am, I have to caution you against this move. I can't let you get in the way of our investigation."

Mrs. Mitchell was not accepting that answer. "I don't give a damn, Detective. I'm coming. And you won't stop me. Maybe all I can do is stand there and watch but at least I can tell my children what's happening."

"All right," he acquiesced. "As long as you understand that you can't get in the way. And please, I don't want a media circus here."

"No, neither do I."

That eased things considerably. Tony said goodbye and disconnected the call.

"Well, that sure made things a lot more interesting." Jim was amused. "I take it that we're talking about our missing person and our shooting target?"

Tony curled a corner of his mouth in a half grin. "Like you said, one and the same."

Jim rubbed his hands together. "Man, when it rains, it pours." He stood up again. "Come on, let's book it over there."

Tony nodded and did the same, easing his suit jacket over his frame. The pictures caught his eye again. "That connection is less speculative now, Garrison."

Jim nodded. "I'm thinking something else, partner. I'm thinking this Ross guy is lying about a lot of shit. And I'm wondering how much he knows about this."

"Me too."

"So, we talk to him again."

Tony stopped just long enough to print off the pictures of Mitchell and Hayes before they headed off to the Hotel.

40

"M ISSY! HEY!"

"Hi, Rod. What's going on?"

The guy behind the desk made a quick sweep of the lobby and sitting area, holding his hand straight out in front of him. "You see this madding crowd, don't you?" he asked with a wink.

Missy shook her head. "English majors. Gimme a break."

Rod laughed with her. "Got today's menu?"

"I sure do."

Missy laid out the two bound menus on opposite sides of the desk, then took the dry erase board and the black marker. She started sketching out the menu and decided to add one of her trademark drawings. They always seemed to get notice and sell the special of the day.

"So, Missy. How's it going?"

Her answer was a deep sigh.

"That bad, huh?" Rod was a great guy, one of those guys that was a woman's best friend.

"Bad enough losing a day's tips," she told him. "But now Walt's pissed because he believed that stupid story in the paper."

"Did you tell him what really happened?"

"I haven't been able to get hold of him. His cell's turned off and Deke said he was with a customer and he'd give Walt the message."

Rod nodded, an expression of sympathy on his face. "That

really sucks."

"Tell me about it."

Rod put a hand on her shoulder, then slid it around to the other shoulder. "Look, Miss, trust me on one thing, okay? Being a guy, I can say without a doubt that that story just punched Walt in the ego a little. Not you. Okay?"

"Yeah, well his ego is peeing all over me, Rod."

"Yeah, but that's just because he's not thinking right now. Or maybe he's thinking too much. What do *you* think?"

She mulled on that for a second or two. That really was Walt to a 't,' always over-thinking things. Like he was always waiting for the other shoe to drop. It was one of the reasons they fit together so well.

"Well?"

She smiled at him. "You're right. I bet he is."

"Missy, I've seen him with you. I know he worships the ground you walk on." Rod patted her shoulder and pulled his arm back. "I know when he's calmed down a little, he's going to be ready to listen to you. Hear what you have to say."

"Think so?"

"Know so."

Rod leaned forward, his arms opening to give her a hug, but the phone interrupted them. With a wry grin, he picked up the receiver, holding it to his ear. He barely got the name of the hotel out before she heard a woman's voice screaming at him. He managed to sputter now and again but it was going to be one of those very one-sided conversations that usually ended up with "I'm sorry, ma'am," and "Perhaps you'd like another room, ma'am." Missy tuned it out. She'd wait for the narrative.

She bent back to her drawing. The lunch special was going

to be the house lobster salad and clam chowder. She set to making illustrations of some small lobsters and clams, dancing at the bottom of the menu board. When life went to hell in a hand basket, drawing was something that calmed her nerves and settled her down.

Missy was only half listening to Rod when the motion from the elevator caught her eye. It was Thom's manager. He pulled a notebook out of his pocket and rushed into the computer room. She knew she should finish the menu board. She knew it was none of her business. She still found herself drawn to the doorway.

He was sweating as he sat there, waiting for the connection to be established. She watched him, curious as hell. Watched his fingers keying in some address into the browser. Once, he looked back towards the door. She managed to duck back before he could see her. She waited a few seconds before she chanced another peek and saw him working the keyboard again.

She couldn't see the exact page but she knew it was some sort of business. It had that look to it, professional and crisp. She watched as he keyed furiously, acting as if he had some place to be and in a hurry. He glanced back one more time and she avoided being seen again. But when she looked back in the next time, he was shutting the computer down. She dashed back to the front desk, barely making it as the man left. He gave her a cold look, not even responding to her smile or nod, then ran out of the lobby to the parking area.

"Yes, ma'am. I understand. Of course, of course...I can't...yes, ma'am. But I can't do that, ma'am. It's called privacy, something our patrons pay for. Yes, ma'am, I can take a message." Rod scribbled across a notepad. "Yes, ma'am, I'll see he gets this. No

ma'am, I can't tell you that either. Yes, ma'am, I'll do just that."
Rod disconnected the call with a heavy sigh of relief.

"What was *that* all about?" Missy asked, her attention still
on...*what was his name? Oh yeah, Mr. Ross.* She was curious
about what the guy was up to. But she wasn't going to get an
answer right now, so she went back to her drawing. "Sounds
like she sure had an earful for you."

"You'll never guess who that was."

"Um, you're right. Who?"

"She said her name was Angie Mitchell," Rod answered.

"Thom's ex wife?"

"You know about her?"

Missy waved a hand, dismissing the question. "What did she
want?"

"Oh yeah, that's right," he said, grinning. "You like his music.
I guess you'd know, then."

She restrained herself from throwing the marker at him in
exasperation. "Rod!"

"Okay, okay, keep your shirt on." He filed the note in the
cubby for Thom's room. "He'll get that when he's back." He
turned back to Missy. "She was screaming at me to tell her
where Mr. Mitchell was and wanting to speak to him."

"What did you tell her?"

"The truth. Mr. Mitchell isn't in the hotel."

"He's not?" Missy asked, looking away from the board. "Wait,
he's not due to leave for couple of weeks. Where is he?"

"Can't tell you," Rod answered. "He and Ms. Hayes left
yesterday and that's the last anyone knows."

"He didn't say where he was going?"

"Missy." Rod straightened up his posture, taking a serious

tone. "That's none of our business and you know that. Discretion is our motto at the Mt. Washington."

She rolled her eyes. "Yeah, real discrete, if you're telling me."

Rod grinned at her. "Yeah, well."

"Come on, you know something."

"Yeah, okay. I do." Rod leaned closer, lowering his voice. "He told Mr. Guilford, when he checked in, that he was going to upstate New York for the weekend but he said he'd be back. He asked us not to give his suite to anyone while he was gone."

"And that's all? He didn't say why?"

"That's it, Missy. That's all I know."

He stood up again, nodding in the direction of the front doors. She didn't have a chance to look before the two men approached the desk.

"Detective Morris," the tall one said, flipping open a leather case and flashing his badge. "This is Detective Garrison."

The other guy, curly headed and looking a bit unkempt, did the same. She remembered them. They'd been here before, questioning everyone after the shooting incident. Detective Garrison must have recognized her, too. He nodded in her direction, then focused back on Rod.

"How can I help you gentlemen?" Rod asked, a very professional cant to his voice.

"You've got a guest here, a...." Morris flipped open a notebook. "Ms. Joanna Hayes. We need to speak to her."

"I'm sorry, sir," Rod told him. "She's not in the hotel at present."

"Do you know where she went?"

"Not our place to ask, sir."

"Look, dude," Garrison cut in. "This is a police thing, you dig me? It's real important you answer the questions. Don't make me get a warrant, man. Just shoot us the answers."

Rod wasn't an idiot. He sighed, nodded, and answered. "All I know is that Ms. Hayes left the hotel yesterday morning."

"Was she with anyone?"

"She left with Mr. Mitchell."

"Did they have any bags? Any luggage of any kind?"

"If they did, I didn't see, sir."

"Is your manager in?" Morris asked.

"Yes, he is."

"Get him, please."

Rod nodded and left, going into the back. The two detectives turned away from her while they waited. Missy picked up the menu board and continued drawing, slowly moving within earshot.

"Well, that confirms that, man."

"Yes, it does."

"What do you think?"

"I got this feeling in my gut that says it's serious, Tony."

"Yeah, me too."

"May I help you?"

Both men turned to Mr. Guilford and flashed the badges and names again. The hotel manager simply nodded and repeated his question.

"I understand that Mr. Mitchell and Ms. Hayes are not in the hotel."

"That's correct," Guilford confirmed.

"Did they say where they were going?"

"Detectives, it is not our policy to question our guests as to where they go or how," the man explained in a rather haughty tone. "We do not ask and they do not tell."

"But they left?" the one named Morris asked.

"Look, dude," Garrison broke in. "This could be a serious matter. We're here investigating...ah, what the hell, you probably need to know. We're here investigating a possible missing persons report. On both of 'em."

Guilford's face turned pale as he swallowed hard. He nodded his co-operation to them. "Mr. Mitchell has left to attend to a personal matter and he is scheduled to return in three days."

"What about Ms. Hayes?"

"That, I cannot say."

"Was she with him?"

"Yeah, she was," Rod interjected. "They were holding hands, so I kinda figured they were headed out to—come on, *you* know."

"Romantic getaway?"

"I guess."

"Did they have luggage with them?" Morris asked.

"I don't know." Rob was being hedgy; even Missy could tell. "I didn't see any. Maybe."

"Dude, they did or they didn't," Garrison insisted.

"Yeah, they did." Rod shot a look at Missy, shrugging his shoulders.

Both detectives turned to each other, whispering for a moment. Then, they turned back to the desk. Morris barked out, "I want to speak to Mr. Ross. Ring his room."

"Um, excuse me." All of them turned to Missy and she cleared her throat to continue. "I think I can answer that."

"You're the other chick that got fired at," Garrison said. "I remember you. Uh...Missy, was it?"

She nodded.

"What is it, Missy?"

"Mr. Ross isn't in his room," she told them.

The detectives exchanged another look before addressing her again. "How would you know that?" Morris asked.

"Because I just saw him leave." She pointed to the computer room. "He went in there and was working for a few minutes. Then, he shut everything down and left through the parking area." She shook her head at Rod and Mr. Guilford. "Which is weird because no one ever shuts the computers off during the day."

Garrison smiled at her. It helped calm the butterflies in her belly.

"Did you get to see what he was looking at?"

"No, sir," she answered. "I was too far away. I just know he was in there, typing. I didn't want him to know I was snooping, so I ran back to the desk when he started to shut down."

"You remember which computer he was at?"

"Yeah. Walk in the door, first bank to your right, third one down."

The men turned back again.

"You think he left any kind of clues?" the one called Garrison asked.

"He'd have to," the one called Morris answered. "We can check the history; see what he was looking at."

"Let's go then."

Garrison turned around and nodded to them. "Thanks for your co-operation. If we need anything else, we'll call you."

Morris pulled out cards and handed them to the three. "If you folks think of anything else, you call, okay? Could be nothing, could be important, but you let us know."

"Of course, Detective," Guilford answered.

The menu board was forgotten. Missy watched the detectives rush into the computer room and disappear behind the door. She wanted to go be nosy again but her feet were nailed to the spot. She didn't even turn around to pay attention to Rod or Mr. Guilford. They were muttering to each other and Missy thought she heard something about the earlier phone call.

Wait! She started adding it all up. The ex-wife calling about Thom's whereabouts. Now, the two detectives asking about where Thom and Ms. Hayes were. Asking those questions. Wanting to know. Something was wrong. Something was very wrong.

The two men dashed out of the computer room and took off at a gallop. As they left, Missy heard a snippet of Morris' phone call—words to the effect of "surveillance" and "airport."

Yes, something was very wrong. But what to do. She couldn't just stand around and wait. What to do, what to do.

"Walt!" she murmured to herself. "Walt will know. I gotta tell Walt. He'll know what to do."

She stopped long enough to let Sarah know that she was leaving for the day, a sick stomach—not entirely a lie. She jumped in her car and drove off to find Walt.

41

I T WAS A stupid dream. The damned rehab hospital again and he was back in the therapy room. It was his turn to talk, to tell them about why he'd come. But nothing would come out of his mouth. Thom stood there, opening and closing his mouth like a stupid fish and he couldn't speak a word. Why was that? What...no, he knew why. To talk about something that was hidden in the blackness. To talk about the screaming, the sound of metal on metal. That's what they wanted him to do. But the curtain was so heavy and his head was splitting.

Then, he realized something was tugging at his wrists. He looked down to see Phil's hands tugging at him. "They know," was all he said. But that was impossible. Phil was dead. He looked down at his wrists again. This time, it was Angie. "They know," she said as she tugged at the material wrapped around his wrists.

"Who? Who knows? What do...hey, what are you doing?"

"Getting this damn tape off of you, what else?"

Thom forced his eyes open and realized he wasn't in rehab. He was on the floor with a couple of boards propped under his head for a pillow. He blinked his eyes a few times, trying to see through the dusky haze. They'd evidently stirred up the dust from the thickly coated floor. What little light that managed to shine through the boarded up windows showed the proof as dust angels swam in the beams.

Jo was working feverishly on the thick duct tape around his wrists. Her face was still showing the marks of the bruises, puffy around that one cheek. But, in his eyes, she was still the most beautiful sight in the world.

"Hey, darlin'."

She smiled at him. "Hey, yourself. Hang on, almost got this."

He watched her as she used the rusty nail to slice through layer after layer of the metallic colored tape. "Where did you find that?"

"Stuck in one of the boards over the there," she said, her voice slightly nasal. She nodded her head in the general direction of one of the fairly dilapidated walls. "Took forever to get the damned thing out, let alone cut myself loose."

"You didn't sleep at all, did you."

She shook her head. "Nope. I was too pissed off."

"Remind me never to get on your bad side."

She grinned at that, pulling the last piece open. She gingerly pulled the tape from around his wrists, tossing it to one side. She helped him sit up and lean back against the wall, then lightly chafed at his flesh to get the blood stirring again.

"Jo?"

"Yes?"

"You look like hell, honey."

"And here I thought I was ready for the *Next Top Model* spot. She sneezed once, wiping her nose against a sleeve in a very unladylike manner. "I feel worse than that, Mitchell. A lot worse."

He chuckled lightly and held out his freed arms, shoulders a bit tender from being bound for so long. "Come here." He pulled her into his arms, cradling her against his chest. Her cheek nestled against his skin, her head just under his chin. He kissed her forehead, heard her sigh ever so softly.

"Won't," she muttered. "I won't."

"Won't what?"

"Cry. I won't cry."

Thom kissed her hair and laid his cheek against it. "You can if you want."

"No, won't do any good. Just make my nose more stopped up than it is now and I don't have my meds."

He held her tighter against him. "Okay. Whatever you want."

"I'm scared, Thom."

"I know. Me, too."

It was quiet for a while as they held each other. He surveyed the room instead. Whoever brought them to this place obviously didn't live there. There was nothing but busted up kindling and pieces of old furniture lying about. So much for being in the lap of luxury. At least the kerosene heater was still going. But that would give out eventually. Maybe they could use the bits and pieces for a fire. But Thom didn't plan on staying that much longer if they didn't have to. There had to be a way out of here.

But how to get out. The window was as good an option as they might have but it was boarded up from the outside, it seemed. And the windows were those multiple paned kind. He'd seen them on those Cape Cod houses. *Well, at least they're not stained glass or those glass bricks. We'd never get out then.* It would be hard. But they'd have a shot at escape.

The sound of a dull thud broke them out of their embrace and made Jo sit up again. Thom could hear the sound of muffled voices outside of the door. He couldn't make out what they were saying but he could recognize the sounds of more than two people out there. They seemed to be very unhappy.

It grew quiet again. Then, there came a click at the door. They both jumped up and Thom barely had time to pull Jo behind him before the door flew open. He recognized the face of his now *former* driver, Mike. But the other guy, he didn't know. This new man stood a good six feet tall and had thick, shortly cropped, black hair. He was just as burly as Mike but there was something familiar about him. He had a pleasant smile, yet his eyes were blank, devoid of any emotion at all. Thom shivered inside.

"Well, Mr. Mitchell. You're up and about. Free, I see. And your girlfriend there."

Thom felt Jo's hand tighten on his arm. He stroked her fingers, trying to reassure her, and said nothing.

The man just grinned more broadly. "Not the...uh, well, not quite the accommodations you're used to, are you? Hmm?"

Thom struggled to keep his voice even, non-threatening. "What do you want from me?"

"Well, see, there's our problem," the man answered, reaching up to scratch the back of his head. "We didn't want you at all." With a jovial, almost giggly voice, he added, "But since you're here and all that...."

"Let us go!" Thom said. "Just let us walk out of here and we won't—"

"Tell the cops?" The other man mimicked Thom's stance, hands on hips and legs slightly shoulder width apart. "Well, we'll see. For now, you got a visitor. One that doesn't want you to see him just yet."

Thom squinted in the darkness, trying to place the face. He was so familiar. Thom knew he'd seen him somewhere...

but where? When the man turned around to talk to Mike, he suddenly realized where.

"I know you," Thom said to him. "I *know* you."

The man looked slightly amused at that. "Oh?"

"You were in the hotel that day. I ran into you." Thom tilted his head, remembering. "Or rather, you ran into me. Shoved me into a table."

The man just grinned.

"Oh shut off," Mike growled. He tossed a glance to the new guy. "Come on, Derek, let's just do this."

"Right," Derek cheerfully agreed. "Neil! Chairs, if you please."

Neil came in with two ladder-back chairs and plunked them down, facing the window. Thom had an idea to jump his former bodyguard but squashed it quickly as Neil and Mike both pulled guns out of their pockets. Brandishing the weapons, they pointed down at the chairs. Thom decided a fight wasn't in anyone's best interest so he nodded to Jo and they both sat down. Immediately, Thom felt a hand roughly grab his shoulder and the gun stab into the back of his neck.

"Good, well done," Derek said to them. "Now, just one more piece of business."

Derek stepped into the other room and came back with a roll of duct tape. He tore off a strip and covered Jo's eyes with them. She immediately started protesting, so he tore another strip and covered her mouth. Thom pulled out of Mike's grip to stop him and got the back of Derek's hand across his mouth for his effort. He fell back into the chair and didn't move again.

"I said sit there," Derek grumbled. "If you behave, there's some breakfast in it for you. Otherwise, you can eat dust for all I care."

"Jo, just be still," Thom told her. "Just…just stop and be still. It'll be over fast."

Jo stopped struggling and got quiet.

"Now, that's the ticket," Derek said with a grin. He turned back to Thom. "I'm going to cover *your* eyes, now. You behave too, you hear me? Don't make me do something nasty to the lady. Deal?"

Thom licked his lips once, closed his eyes. He felt the duct tape pressed against his skin, across his eyes and the bridge of his nose, then his forehead and cheeks, then his temples. He forced himself to remain calm and still, forced his breathing to stay even and relaxed. The grip on his shoulder tightened once, then relaxed enough to stop hurting.

He heard Derek's footsteps as he left them to go back to the door. "All right, come on. You wanted to see him? Here…now you can see him."

He heard a different set of footsteps now. The click-click-click on the floor of some kind of heels. They clicked into the room and stopped.

"Well?" Derek asked. "See? Still alive. You see for yourself." It was quiet for a moment. "Yeah, so what. We had to get his co-operation. What's a few bruises? He'll heal. Now gimme what you promised."

The heels clicked closer to where Thom was sitting. His breathing speeded up, then he took a deep breath and held it as the heels stopped right in front of him. Fingers touched his chin, left his head up. But the gun in the back of his neck told him not to move. His head was turned one way, then the other, then released altogether.

He let go of the breath and took another one, breathing

through his nose this time. There was a faint scent of a cologne in the air, something familiar almost, but it was hard to tell. Jo sneezed twice, the brunt of it coming through her nose and followed by a soft moan. It pissed him off but there was nothing he could do for her. Hopefully, this would be over soon.

The heels clicked away from them quickly. He needed to stop whoever that was; he needed an answer.

"Wait!" Thom shouted.

The heels complied.

"Who are you? Why are you doing this to me?"

"He don't wanna talk to you," Derek snarled.

"I don't care," Thom told him. "I want to talk to *you*, you son of a bitch...whoever you are! Why are you doing this to me?"

There was no answer and the heels weren't moving.

"I'll get out of here, you know. I will. And I'm gonna find you." Thom waited and got no answer to that. "I will. And when I do, I'll see you locked up for the rest of your life!"

There was a moment of silence before Derek spoke. "Get out, go on. Don't be a stupid asshole. Just get out!"

The heels clicked out the door and it was quiet again.

"Get the chairs and let's go. Come on. Mike, lock the door behind you."

The chair was roughly removed from under him and Thom fell hard to the floor. He heard Jo's muffled "oomph" as she fell beside him. Fortunately, their hands were still free. He ripped the tape from his face, then turned to gently pull it from her mouth and eyes. The door locked behind him.

He scooped her into his arms, holding her as they both recovered from the treatment. He smoothed her hair and stroked the part of her face that wasn't bruised. There was a tiny rivulet of blood in the corner of her nose, most likely from the sneezes. He had nothing to use as a tissue, so he wiped it away with his finger. She clutched him tightly, breathing slower and slower until she was calmed again.

"Thom?"

"Yes, darlin'?"

"Damn, my head is stopped up now. Friggin' cologne."

"I know, honey. I'm sorry."

"Thom?"

"Yes, Jo?"

"I really hate that guy! All of them!"

"Yeah," he answered. "Me too."

They stayed that way, waiting.

42

MALCOLM WAS FURIOUS. The sight of Thom's bruises had put him into a seething rage. *How dare they harm him! How* dare *they!* He had no choice; he had to pay them whatever they wanted. He didn't give a damn about that woman; they could do what they wanted with her. But Thom? Damn, this wasn't going right at all! He waited until Derek had shut the door.

"So?" Derek asked.

"So what?" Malcolm asked back. "You *said* he wasn't hurt. You *said* you wouldn't do anything to him. I told you to take the woman, not him, and you fucked that up. Now, I find he's... you—"

"Look, Ross! I *said* my guys had to get a little rough. They did what they had to do. The bastard came out swinging. So did the bitch."

"That is no reason—"

Derek was fast. He had Malcolm backed against the wall with Mal's shirt bunched in his fists so fast that the manager had no time to react. He connected with the log façade hard enough to knock the wind out of him and stars to burst in front of his eyes. Derek was standing nose to nose with him, so close that Malcolm could feel the man's foul breath against his skin.

"Now, you're gonna listen to me, old chum," Derek began in a silken, deadly voice. "And considering that it's three to one here and I got the goods locked up in that room, you're gonna listen real good. And do what I tell you."

"You weren't supposed to—"

The thug slammed Malcolm against the wall again, this time much harder. This time, he hit his head, crossing his eyes. But Derek pulled him back, slapping the side of his face. Malcolm blinked a few times to clear his vision.

"I don't give a damn what I was or was *not* supposed to do, dude. Now, are you ready to listen?"

Malcolm, wisely, just nodded.

"Now, me and the guys want our cash. That's all. After that, the bitch is your headache and so's he. But, see, he knows what we look like. Knows Mike and Neil. So, I'm left with two choices. One is to kill the fucker—"

"*No*—"

Malcolm steeled himself for another shove against the wall. Derek just smiled at him.

"I see that won't be your choice, then," Derek said with a sneer. "Then, the only other choice is enough money to split this sorry place and live in luxury."

Malcolm nodded again, saying nothing more.

"Good boy!" Derek let go and back off a pace or two. "So, you got the account?"

Malcolm calmed himself, smoothing the front of his shirt down. He reached into the breast pocket and pulled out a business card, then held it up in front of three pairs of very anxious eyes.

"It's an anonymous bank account in the Caymans. Registered with only a number. Give them that number and they'll confirm it."

"And the dough?"

Malcolm was still enraged on the inside but he wasn't going to make the mistake of showing it again. "I've seen him. He's alive and relatively unharmed. I'll go wire the money now."

"Two million bucks, got it? Not a penny less!"

"Two million, yes," Malcolm agreed. "On the condition that you don't lay a hand on him again. Understood?"

"I ain't promising shit," said one of the other thugs in the room. "He comes at me again, I'll rip his friggin' head off."

"Mike!" Derek barked over his shoulder. He turned back to Malcolm. "I'll keep 'em off the old dude. But you better come up with the cash before the end of the day or I ain't promising shit!"

"You'll hear from me!"

It was a game of chicken—who would flinch first, Malcolm or the creep in front of him. They stood, locked in a stare down. Obviously, Derek didn't know whom he was dealing with. Or if he did, he gave no sign that it mattered. Malcolm gave a momentary thought to throwing that little card out, as well. He could have these three taken care of in a flash. And just might before this was all over. In fact, that wasn't a bad idea. Get rid of the loose ends that would tie him to the kidnapping. Thom would never know or suspect. Transfer the money back and all was well.

So, Malcolm flinched. He nodded, his head barely bobbing up and down. He turned on his heels and went back to the hotel. When this was all over....

It took a while but the one called Derek was true to his word. Joanna heard the click of the lock and the door swung out. That despicable bodyguard came in holding a gun on the two of them, followed by Derek with a bag from a local fast food place and two cups of coffee. The driver filled the kerosene heater and lit it again. She felt Thom grow tense beside her.

"Now, now, Mr. Mitchell. I see what you're doing and you really don't want to do that."

The gun swung in her direction, pointed straight at her head. Derek grinned at them. "He's a damned fine shot." He set the bag and coffee on the floor a distance away from them. "And trust me, it'll hurt. You ever see someone get gut shot?"

"You don't dare," Thom growled.

"Oh, I *do* dare. Unless you just want to see the shit running out of a gaping hole in her gut, I suggest you be a really good boy now."

It wasn't worth it. She'd been smacked around, locked up in this extremely filthy place, had about an hour of sleep when she wasn't trying to free them from that duct tape—that was enough. She was exhausted, bruised, and just flat out of fight. She put a steadying hand on Thom's arm. "Let it go, Thom. Just let it go."

Both men grinned now.

She couldn't help but stare Derek in the eye, though. And add, "For now."

His grin disappeared. "You want to walk out of here, babe, you'll do what you're told and just shut up."

"Except we won't walk out of here, will we?" Thom asked.

"I'd say your chances are real good, Mr. Mitchell. See, they'll find you—about a day or so after we've split the country."

"Alive?" Joanna asked, a bit amused at the raised eyebrows the men turned in her direction. "Just a fine point in the contract, you understand. Will they find us alive?"

"Always the lady lawyer, huh? Derek's grin returned. "Yeah, alive. Keep up the smart ass shit and I may change my mind."

This time, Thom put his hand on *her* arm. He nodded to the three thugs and pulled her back beside him.

"Good. Keep it that way." Derek pointed down at the bag. "There's your breakfast."

"And what do we do about a toilet?" Joanna asked. "I need to use the bathroom."

"I'll get you one of those campin' toilets. We got one out here."

"Thank you."

He called to Neil, who brought it in and set it in the corner. The three men backed out of the door and Joanna heard the lock click home. She and Thom relaxed again.

"Why don't you use the toilet and I'll get breakfast set up," he told her.

"I hate this! There's no privacy!"

He smiled at her. "Yeah, I know." He reached into the bag and pulled out a wad of napkins. "Here, one to blot and one to blow your nose with."

"Thanks."

With a wink, he added, "I promise I won't look."

True to his word, he picked up the bag and coffee and took them next to the window. He laid out the food, all the while having his back to her. With a resigned sigh, she dropped her trousers and relieved herself. She had nothing to clean her hands with—not that it mattered anyway, considering the conditions. She just wiped her hands on one of the napkins and tossed it into the chemical toilet, followed by the napkin she blew her nose on. She crossed over to the window and sat down next to Thom.

"So? What did we get from the Kidnapper's Kill It and Grill It?"

Thom snorted. "Well, we won't starve. There's a couple of egg and sausage sandwiches, a hash brown apiece here. And the coffee."

She looked at the food before her and pushed it back. "I can't, Thom. My stomach is so upset right now, I'll just throw it up."

He paused in mid-bite. "Jo, you gotta keep your strength up."

"Maybe in a bit. Just the coffee for right now."

"You could stand some sleep, you know."

"In a bit."

She drank her coffee while he tore into his food. The sun was starting to come up higher in the window. It had to be getting close to midday.

"Been thinking."

She glanced in Thom's direction. "Oh? About what?"

"How we're going to get out of here." He took a sip of his coffee. "Those boards are on the outside. And the damned window opens out. But I was thinking, if we can break a few of the panes, we could knock those boards off. Then, the window would open. I can help you out first, then follow."

She wasn't feeling *that* optimistic. "You have no clue where we are right now, do you."

He grinned at her. "Well, I know we're on Wilde. I figure, we can hike our way out of here. Or at least to one of the shelters. There are always shelters up in these mountains. Stocked for hikers that get lost. If I can find a trail, then we can head off and find a shelter."

"And do what? You know they'll follow us."

His face got serious again. "Yeah, I thought about that too. That's the only fly in the ointment." He took another bite and began to chew it methodically.

An idea occurred to her and she brightened at the thought of it. "Wait. A missing person's report!"

He stopped slurping his coffee, a quizzical expression on his face. "What?"

"Thom, if we've been gone long enough, your ex-wife will file a missing person's report."

"Have to be missing twenty-four hours, darlin'."

"And how long have we been missing?"

He held up his arm and looked down at his watch. She watched his face screw up, then suddenly brighten. His face was like a little child's, beaming broadly in that "look what I done" sort of way.

"What?" she asked. When he didn't answer, she asked again, "What? Come on, what?"

He held up his arm so that she could see his wrist. "I kept forgetting to take it off."

She looked closer—*the GPS.* For a moment, she was so taken aback that she couldn't grasp the idea of what that meant. Then, it dawned on her. She remembered what Walt had told them. "The tracking device!"

"Yup," Thom said cheerfully. "It's constantly monitored, darlin'. By the National Forestry Service. And I bet that good old Walt has a monitor in the shop."

She grinned in response. "What do we do?"

"This!" He turned around and smacked the back of his wrist on the ground, then turned to face her again.

"And?"

"I just set it off, Jo. Now, all we gotta do is wait. Someone picks up the signal and sends a search party up here. We're as good as saved."

She hadn't known how wound up she was until the tears burst out. He said nothing, just pulled her close and let her cry. He sang that song again, about the thyme and heather, and sang her to sleep in his arms.

43

ADAM STOPPED LONG enough to get a cup of coffee before taking the three videotapes into the multimedia room. A former desk editor had managed to convince the owners that they needed a room that could handle the new technology of DVD, CD, etc. They'd spent an obscene amount on the equipment to do so. Considering how much he'd grumbled about the lack of pay raises during that time, Adam wasn't complaining about it now. These videotapes were three quarter inch, a special kind. Miraculously, there was a three quarter inch machine in the room.

The tapes were marked with the date only. No idea of which one was the first, last, or in the middle. He turned on the video machine, stuck in a tape at random, and sat back to watch the show.

"Wheeler, what are you doing?"

"Hey, Joe. What's up?"

His boss sat down in the other chair and stuck his boots up on the nearby desk. "Not a damn thing. Got everyone out, running for stories. Thought to send you on one but I didn't see you out there."

"Already on one," Adam answered. He nodded to the screen.

"So I see. What's going on?"

"Remember that tip I got? About Senator Mullins?"

"Oh yeah, the car accident."

"Yup, that's right."

"So, what's this?"

The screen was split into four pictures. Each from a different camera's viewpoint. There had been a camera faced toward the front of the mansion, capturing the steps, the front porch, and front door. There was another camera inside that pointed towards the foyer and the doorways to at least two of the rooms. Yet another camera outside filmed what appeared to be the back porch and the lawn, showing off the party area. The last camera focused on the driveway, right outside the garage. There was a date and a running clock at the bottom of the screen.

There was nothing on this tape. This one had to be the beginning of the day. They were setting up the outside pavilion. He watched a limo pull up in front of the house, letting the Senator—and a woman that Adam presumed was his wife—out in front. The inside camera just showed the staff getting ready, dusting and cleaning. The back yard camera showed the tables being set up, the bar being stocked. In other words, nothing. Adam flicked the fast forward button and kept watching while he talked.

"These are the security tapes from the last evening Mullins was alive."

"Okay," Joe said. He sat back further in the chair and crossed his arms. "And what are you hoping to find here?"

"I'm hoping to find something that will shed a little light on that accident."

"What do you mean?" Joe asked.

"Something isn't right, Joe. Too many unanswered questions, too many puzzle pieces don't fit. And I got a hunch."

"What hunch?"

"There was another party in this; someone was with the senator in the car."

"Who?"

"I'm not ready to say yet. But I can tell you that it's someone still alive and it may blow up in that someone's face."

Joe sighed.

Adam could see him out of the corner of his eye, just sitting with his arms crossed and that look of contemplation on his face. He was taking this seriously, at least, staring at the floor and nodding his head. Joe pursed his lips and chewed on the lower one for a moment with his brows furrowed. It was another moment or two before he looked back up again.

"There's no story here, Wheeler. Besides, you'll be opening up a can of worms that you really don't want to get into."

Adam hit the pause button, sitting up abruptly. "What are you talking about? Of course there's a story here."

Joe shook his head and pointed to the screen. "All you got there is a bunch of party bullshit and society frippery. It's old news, Adam. Why do you want to upset the family again over a bunch of shit that happened twenty years ago?"

"Because there's someone who's still alive that's tied to this."

"You don't know that. You said *a hunch*. Which means you got nothing concrete. In the meantime, I got a missing persons report that you could be writing up for me."

"Who's missing?"

"According to MacElroy, your buddy, Mitchell."

"*Thom* Mitchell?"

"Yup. Heard the two detectives talking about it. Of course they weren't talking to him, you understand. But MacElroy heard them. Seems the first Mrs. Mitchell called in a missing persons report. Right after one was called in on a...a...." Joe fished for the name. "A Joanna Hayes, whoever *she* is."

"Uh...uh...."

"No, Wheeler. I need you to help MacElroy cover this. You know Mitchell; he doesn't. I need you to cover that side of it."

Adam heaved a sigh.

"What?" Joe stared at him. "Look, if you can convince me why this is relevant, okay. I'll let you go on. But I'm telling you this is a dead issue...no pun intended."

"Because I think Mitchell was the other guy in the car," he blurted.

Joe's eyes widened and he sat for a moment, saying nothing. It was enough for Adam to go on.

"I started checking Mitchell out and found a reference to Mullins. I also got a copy of the police report and found out all about the accident. Joe, that was just flat out weird. So, I started checking some stuff out. And found out it was Mitchell's car that Mullins was driving that night."

"I'm listening."

"So I talked to a couple people working that party. The housekeeper says that Mitchell and Mullins were like twins all night, getting shit-faced as hell. They never separated. Then, I talked to one of the guards on duty. He didn't see much but he says he remembers Mitchell and Mullins left the party together."

"That doesn't mean Mitchell was with him."

Adam shrugged. "The guard said that they got in the car together!"

Joe nodded. "That could be a side bar with this recent crap, too."

"Yeah," Adam agreed. "It could. Please. Let me keep working on this."

Joe chewed on his lower lip again. Adam waited. He'd said all he was going to be able to say. There was nothing else. Either Joe would allow it or Adam would have to work on it in his off time—which would really piss off his wife. But he was far too deep in this to let go now. He waited, hopeful.

Joe stared at the screen again, then back at Adam. He breathed out through his nose like a bull getting ready to do battle with some poor matador. Adam steeled himself.

"All right," Joe finally answered. "Keep up on this. And keep me informed of any developments." His finger jutted up in the air, punctuating his parting shot. "BUT! I reserve the right to pull the plug if this is going nowhere."

"Yes, sir," Adam agreed. "You got it!"

"Go on then. I'll pull Dickens from the school beat and stick him on the missing persons."

Joe left the room and Adam hit the play button again. He turned off the fast forward and settled back. He had no idea when the important part would come up and he didn't want to miss a thing.

44

"WALT! MAN, COME on and sit down. You're making me tired just watching you."

Walt stopped in his tracks. He'd been running all morning, doing anything to keep from thinking. He didn't want to think, didn't want her in his thoughts at all. It hurt too much and he'd have to remember—

"Walt."

Walt dropped down in the chair. Deke was going over an invoice of shoes that had just arrived from the supplier; something that Walt would normally be doing while waiting on customers.

"Wanna talk about it?"

"Nothing to talk about," Walt replied grimly. "I mean my life just went into the shitter, my lady has a thing for another man. It's all pretty fucking peachy, thanks! Why do you ask?"

"Oh yeah, the infamous Mr. Mitchell."

Walt jerked his head around. "You know about that?" Then he realized. "Of course. The whole world knows. She takes a great picture, doesn't she? Damn good kisser!" He plucked a rolled pair of hiker's socks and started twisting them in his hands. "The son of a bitch! How can she want *him* instead of me? How?"

Deke calmly reached over and took both of Walt's hands in his. He loosened the fingers and took the socks away. "Dude, we can't sell those if you mess 'em up."

Walt put his head in his hands instead, running his fingers through his black hair. "What's wrong with me, Deke? I mean it, what is so friggin' wrong with me?"

"What are you talking about, man?" Deke put the socks back on the display. "Why do you think something's wrong with you?"

"I saw that picture and it's like she cut my balls off that fast. She and that old man were kissing!"

"And?"

"I love her, Deke." He felt the tears and covered his eyes. "What is wrong with me?"

He sat trying to get control of his emotions. He forced himself to slow down, get calm. He counted to ten in about four different languages, trying to focus on anything but her.

It was quiet until he heard the scrape of wood. He looked up to see Deke pulling a bottle from under the register. His friend pulled out two glasses and brought everything over to the desk. Deke poured two short amounts into the glasses and handed one to Walt.

"Deke—"

"Medicinal purposes only, dude. Besides, we got no customers in here. I think you need that right now." Deke slid the bottle back into the cubby and closed the door. He reseated himself and went on. "Now. You say you love her?"

Walt took a ginger sip, feeling the raw warmth slide down the back of his throat. "Oh yeah."

"She ever slept around on you?"

"What?" He thought for a moment, taken aback by the question. "Uh...no, I don't think so." He thought some more.

"No! No, she never has."

"She look at other men?"

"Probably. But if you think I'm not checking out the bikini clad chicks at the hotel, you're nuts."

Deke nodded sagely. "Fair enough. All looky, no touchy. That's fair." He gulped down the contents of his glass. "After all, it's not like she's a dog or anything."

Walt shook his head. "Oh God no, she's amazing, she's beautiful. Those legs and that great—" He caught himself up short. "Green eyes, that's what I mean. She's got those amazing green eyes and she has that sweet smile."

Deke nodded. "Never called you names? Never said you suck in bed? Never tried to fuck with your head or make you look bad in front of her friends?"

"Of course not! Why would she do that?" Walt gulped the rest of the scotch down. "She's too kind to do that, she's not like that at all. She's good hearted and witty and funny; we like to hike and she knows things. She's brilliant. She...she...we love the environment and—what are grinning at?"

Deke started to laugh, an infectious sound that was both merry and warm. Walt felt foolish for a moment; like there was a joke that he wasn't privy to. Then, the scotch did its thing and he felt the warmth inside. He chuckled along, waiting for the answer.

"Walt, my friend, don't you get it?"

"What?"

"She kicked your ego in the groin." Deke put his elbows on the desk and rested his chin on his fists. "Trust me, Walt, that is not a fatal thing. Shit happens, you get up and move on. Fix it."

"Yeah, I guess."

"No 'guess;' it does and you do. Trust me on that." Deke sat back again. "So, what's the one thing that *really* bothers you?"

He really wanted to plead ignorance but the truth was that he did know what was bothering him. "I want to marry her."

"Even after she kissed this guy?"

"Yeah. I do."

"Then, ask her."

"She doesn't want me."

"Why? Because she kissed this old fart? When she could have young, handsome, virile you?"

Walt opened his mouth to answer.

The bell on the door pealed as the door burst open with a fury and Missy ran in. Both men stood up immediately and Walt started forward. Missy flew at him, her eyes wild. She was babbling at a thousand miles an hour. He finally clapped his hands together in front of her face to get her to calm down. She was shocked but she got quiet.

"Missy, what is it? Come on, slow down and tell me."

"It's Thom; he's missing!"

"What?" He took her by the shoulders, speaking to her as calmly as he could. "Who said he's missing?"

"Two policemen...no, no. It started before that. Thom's ex-wife called. She said he was supposed to be someplace yesterday and he didn't show up. Then, those two detectives started talking to Rod and Mr. Guilford. They started asking all these questions about Thom and Ms. Hayes."

"What kind of questions?"

She gulped air, still upset. "Where did they go, how long had they been gone, did they take luggage. That one detective said it was two missing persons reports. One on Thom and one on

Ms. Hayes." She clutched Walt back. "He's in trouble, Walt, I just know it. We have to do something."

Well, *someone* had to take control. "Missy, there's nothing we can do." He looked over his shoulder at Deke, who merely shrugged.

"Walter," she protested, almost hysterically. "We *have* to. He's in danger, I know it! We can't just sit here."

Let him fry for all I care. "Michelle, listen to me." Walt gave her a light shake. "Stop it, right now. And listen."

It was enough to calm her again. She was listening.

"You have no clue where they are. Even if they *are* in trouble—which I highly doubt—how are you gonna do anything? You don't know if there's any kind of danger."

"What? Walt, how can you—"

"Did they take bags with 'em?"

"I don't...I mean...Rod said yes, they did."

"Then, they're off somewhere getting laid, Missy."

She shook loose from his grasp, her brow furrowing. "You... you don't know...his ex-wife called. She was frantic."

"What do you expect her to be?" he asked. "Would you want *your* ex to know you were off shagging somebody else? I damn sure wouldn't."

"That's...that's just cruel, Walt. To make that poor woman scared like that. Thom wouldn't do that. He's a nice guy."

"Yeah, right, real nice."

"Walt, you have—"

"I don't *have* to do anything, Missy." He felt himself tensing up, powerless to stop it. He was now being deliberately cruel to her and he knew it. "Look, Missy, the old fart doesn't want you. He wants Jo. And they're off getting a little, away from the press and his groupies. Give 'em a break, will ya?"

She looked like she'd been slapped and for a moment, he wanted to take it back, say he was sorry. But then, she turned red. "Walter Beaton, I swear to God, you can be such an idiot sometimes."

Now it was his turn to be shocked. But she didn't give him a chance to say anything.

"You're so damn sure. All the time. It's exactly what it is, totally black and white, and that's how it is, isn't it. You can be so damn stupid sometimes!"

He got what she was talking about. "I know what I saw."

She did something very un-Missy-like. "You saw shit, Walter! You saw nothing and you don't even have the decency—"

"Uh, excuse me. As much as I love this little Peyton Place drama...." Deke was bent over the computer, staring at one of the programs. "Walt, you better come see this."

Walt took a deep breath and came around the desk and looked down at the monitor. He recognized the program now, the same one the rangers used. It was the one they used to monitor all of the GPS traffic of their customers. It was part of the service Walt and Deke provided, just in case.

"Someone's GPS just went off. See that?"

"Yeah," Walt said. He sat down at the desk and tapped in a few commands. The computer pulled up the longitude and latitude of the signal. "Hey, that's Wilde. Who the hell went up there?"

"Is there a number there?"

Walt read it off to him and then looked back at his partner. "Well? Is it one of ours?"

Deke nodded. He turned back to look at Walt. "And you'll

never guess who you sold that too."

A rock landed in his middle. "Oh shit. Let me guess—Thom Mitchell."

"One and the same, mate."

With one breath, Missy yelled out, "We gotta go, Walt, we gotta, we gotta go save him, come on, let's go now, hurry!" She turned on her heels and made a dash towards the door.

Walt was quicker. He had her arm in his hand and pulled her back. "Whoa, there, darlin'. You just hold up a moment there."

"Walt, his GPS went off. That means there's trouble!"

"No, it doesn't."

"What?"

"Those things are sensitive, Missy. *Very* sensitive. He probably just whacked his arm against a tree while he was walking. He and Jo may have lain down to...." He let that trail off and watched her face. When her eyes widened, he knew that she'd gotten his point. "Either way, there may be nothing wrong."

"You don't know that. Walt. Ms. Hayes barely got through the trail we did, so why would he take her up Wilde. You've never even taken *me*."

"Missy—

"I know he's missing! Even the cops say so. So, now we know where he is. We can rescue him."

"So, let the cops do it. Or better yet, the rangers. They're already out there; let 'em do their jobs."

She shook her arm out of his grasp and pulled away from him. "Just because you're jealous, you're going to let him die out there, aren't you?"

"Missy—"

"You are! You are just being stupid and you're gonna let him die." She put her fists on her hips. "Well *I'm* not! If you won't go with me, then I'll go alone."

"Missy—"

"I'll go save him...*them*! I know first aid and mountain safety. I'll just go by myself!"

"Missy—"

"And you can't stop me, Walter Beaton!"

Before he could, she was gone—the door rudely flung in his face and the streak of her white shirt as she ran.

"Shit," he muttered to himself.

Behind him, Deke was making a tsk, tsk noise with his tongue. Walt turned around and waited.

"Dude. If the cops are on this...," he said, repeating Walt's thoughts.

"I know," Walt said. "What do you suggest?"

"Look, it'll be a while before the rangers can get coordinated, you know that. A couple of hours, at least. Wilde's a bitch."

"And?"

"Well, you got the co-ordinates. You can go with her, check it out. Then, when it turns out to be nothing, you can take her away for the rest of the day. Go fix it."

"You think it's nothing too?"

Deke crossed his arms, tilting his head to one side. "No, I think there might be something here. But the rangers are gonna send a spotter plane first. You'll already be there on the ground." Deke tossed a hand-held to Walt. "Take that tracker and you can pinpoint the signal."

Walt caught it deftly. "Yeah. What the hell. If they're in trouble, I can radio in."

"Good, take your gear and go check it out."

"Yeah, all right."

"Radio in at...." Deke peered down at the clock. "It's 11:00 right now. Take you about forty-five minutes, maybe an hour to get to the main fire road, then another hour or two to hike to those co-ordinates. You can radio in about...say, about 3:00 or 3:30? That'll give you plenty of time to find 'em."

"Make it 4:00. That'll give me some extra time, just in case."

"Ok, 4:00. If I don't hear from you by 4:02, I'm sending the rangers to that location, if they're not already on the way."

"Sounds good."

Walt grabbed all of his gear and threw it in the back of the four by four. He added the radio and strapped his own GPS onto his wrist. He stopped long enough to pick up Missy at her apartment—after she had changed into her hiking clothes—and they headed off toward the base of Wilde Mountain.

45

"LOOK, CAN YOU just check again? Please? Name'll be either Thom Mitchell or Malcolm Ross."

Jim flashed his toothiest grin, making sure his shirt gapped just enough in the front to give her a bit of a show, and leaned over the counter. The young girl blushed, ducking her head and giggling. He waggled his eyebrows and gave her a wink.

"Sure, detective," she answered, trying out her *sexy* voice. "Give me just a few minutes. I'll even run a search on the airlines. See if *they* have something."

"Thanks, darlin'."

Jim stood up again and, hands in the back pockets of his jeans, caught the look on his partner's face as he stepped up beside the counter. Tony just shook his head, chuckling silently.

"What?"

"Nothing," Tony answered. "So?"

"She's looking for me, gonna check out all the majors. Maybe they didn't take the charter."

"I highly doubt that," Tony said. "While Ms. Hayes may use public transport, I don't see Mitchell doing that."

"Yeah, you're right." Jim drummed lightly on the counter, the pads of his fingers beating out a rhythm. "Maybe they got rerouted somewhere else for some reason."

"Maybe."

He faced his partner again. "But, what if they didn't?"

"Then, we've got a serious problem."

"Maybe you can run rental cars. Maybe they decided not to fly, maybe they drove."

Morris shook his head. "Thought about that. And I will before we leave. But, don't you think Mitchell would have called his ex-wife and told her?"

Jim scratched behind his ear. "Yeah, you'd think he'd do that. But if he's got a thing for—"

"Detective Garrison?"

Jim whipped around and flashed the pearly whites again. "Yeah, babe?"

"I checked our databases again. We don't have a charter for either Mr. Mitchell *or* Mr. Ross. I also cross-referenced with all of the other flights that took off yesterday and neither name shows up on any of the manifests."

"How about a Ms. Hayes?" Tony interjected. "A Ms. Joanna Hayes."

She typed into the keyboard and waited. "No, sir. That name doesn't appear either."

Jim sighed. "Damn." He smiled at the lady again. "Hey, thanks a lot, ma'am."

"Lorrie."

He winked at her. "Thanks, Lorrie."

"Are you married?" she asked, giving him that coy look.

He heard Tony's pained sigh behind him and ignored it. What the hell, she was pretty and he was still single. Jim sent his partner on to check out the rental places. He walked away from the charter desk with copies of the manifests from all the airlines at the airport for the last 36 hours and Lorrie's phone number. He ran into his partner as Tony was leaving the Hertz counter, tucking a notebook into his jacket pocket.

"Hey, dude, any luck?"

Tony shook his head. "Nothing. No reservations for a rental under the name of Mitchell or Hayes. The rental under Ross' name is the one he's driving here and the unmarked said it was sighted at the hotel parking lot this morning."

"Crap! There went that idea."

"We know they didn't take a plane, there's no rental information," Tony ticked off. "We got bupkus, buddy."

Jim laughed and held up the sheets of paper. "Not me, dude. I got copies of the manifests."

"Why?"

"Oh, check up and see who actually showed up on the other end. Just a hunch that may go nowhere. But you never know."

"You're spinning your wheels, Jim."

He grinned, holding up the sticky note with Lorrie's phone number. "Not really."

Tony huffed, rolling his eyes. "I don't believe you. We're here on business and you're scoring a make out session?"

"Hey," Jim snorted. "I'm single and over the age of twenty one, thank you. If I choose to have carnal knowledge of that luscious lady, it's her choice, my privilege, and none of your biz, dude."

It was Tony's turn to laugh. "Garrison, you ever met a woman that you *didn't* go to bed with?"

"Yeah, your mama," he answered with a grin.

It was that kind of camaraderie all the way back to the station. Jim took it with a lot of his normal good nature. His chief philosophy was that it never hurt to look like a rock star, it scored high with the babes. It was the biggest reason that he didn't want to get the regulation haircut. The chicks dug the curls, he would say with a grin.

He sat down at his desk, sorting his sticky notes. "Hey, what can I say? Little Jimmy's going on pussy patrol, man."

He looked up to see Tony get a serious look in his eye, flashing that warning shot at Jim just as he heard the polite cough behind him. Jim turned around to see a very well dressed woman standing in the area they laughingly called the "reception desk." She had short brown hair, cropped at the jawline, with incredible hazel eyes. She was short and petite; probably full of piss and vinegar, too; the type that would freeze you out in the board room and set you on fire in the bedroom.

Tony glared at Jim for another second before going towards the woman with his hand out. His face melded into a very amiable grin as he turned on the charm.

"Ma'am. I'm Detective Tony Morris. My rude partner there is Jim Garrison. How can we help you."

She gave Tony a very odd look but put her hand out anyway. "Angela Mitchell. We spoke on the phone earlier."

Oh hell, Jim thought, *the ice princess is here.* He immediately kicked himself in the ass for that one. He was judging her on the basis of looks and he didn't even know her yet.

Tony was still talking to her. "Mrs. Mitchell, we weren't expecting you until late afternoon."

"I decided my daughter's father was a bit more important than my attending a party. I saw my daughter graduate—and took pictures for her father to see—and caught the first shuttle to New Hampshire." She turned a rather haughty look in Jim's direction. "I wanted to be here to make sure everything is being done to find my ex-husband."

"Well, ma'am," Tony said. "We don't really have anything yet. We've only just started."

"And what exactly *do* you have?"

Tony threw him a look that said "save me" and Jim decided to turn on the Garrison charm.

"Mrs. Mitchell, won't you have a seat? Tony can get you some coffee and we can talk."

That seemed to satisfy her for the time being. She sat down in the chair next to Jim's desk. He gave her a limited amount of the information they had, vague and without some details.

"And he left the hotel in a limo?"

"Yes, ma'am. We just wanted to make sure the airport and rental car places came up dry before we started checking out limo rentals. You know, in case...uh...."

"I understand, detective," she said. "And then, what?"

"Well, if we find that limo, we can find out who rented it and then go talk to him or her."

"Oh, I know *exactly* who'll have rented it. Malcolm Ross."

It was the way she said it that raised the hackles on the back of Jim's neck. "You don't sound like a big fan of the guy."

She accepted the cup of coffee from his partner and stared into it. Tony stood next to her, listening.

"No, detective, I'm not."

"May we ask why, Mrs. Mitchell?" Tony asked.

She blew across the top of her coffee cup. Jim could almost hear the wheels grinding in her head, like she was trying to think of something...or censor herself.

"Mrs. Mitchell," he repeated.

She had a slight grimace on her face. "Detectives, I'm sure you understand the need for discretion in this matter, yes?

We may be divorced but that doesn't mean that I want my ex-husband hurt."

"Of course," Jim told her.

"I don't like Malcolm Ross. I never have."

"Why?" Tony asked her.

She locked gazes with his partner. "Because, Detective Morris, the man is untrustworthy. You don't know him like I do. He'll do anything, say anything...and he doesn't care if it's legal or not."

"How so?" Jim asked.

She looked down, staring into the cup. When she began to speak, it was a slow halting voice; as if she were choosing her words *very* carefully. "It was early on in Thom's career. While he was still struggling to pay off the debts of his group. You remember them. *Manchester*."

"Yes," Tony answered. "Pop group, real popular in the early eighties."

She nodded.

"I remember a problem with a hall, labor problems. The employees threatened to go on strike, something with a union mess."

She nodded again.

Tony narrowed his eyes, watching her. "You know something about that?"

She looked up at Tony. "Yeah. Malcolm used his family connections to break the strike. His *family* connections. He put in a call to some Teamster friends and the two leaders were in the hospital for three months."

Jim whistled through his teeth. "How do you know this, Mrs. Mitchell?"

"The same way I know everything about Malcolm Ross. He told me, whether I wanted to know or not." She sighed, closing her eyes. "He found out something—something I did, something I wanted buried—and he decided that in order to insure my silence, he'd...." She swallowed hard. "He'd tell me everything. Every shady deal, every time he did something under the table."

Jim sat back and just let Tony take this one. Tony was staying cool and she was responding to it well. She sipped her coffee.

"What things did he tell you?"

She set the cup on the edge of Tony's desk and went on in monotone. "How he'd managed to blackmail the president of Thom's record company into letting him control what songs were released on what CD, what music was put in the vault, who would produce. He lets Thom record anything he wants, but the music doesn't always make it on the CD."

"That's not exactly criminal, Mrs. Mitchell...unethical, maybe—"

"He knows where Thom is," she blurted out.

Jim tensed. Tony sat down in his chair, then leaned forward as if he were honed in on every word she was saying.

"He *knows*?" Tony asked.

"He never denied it. I asked him and he never denied it."

"You spoke to him?"

"Yesterday. I called to ask him where Thom was. He was his usual evasive self. He threatened to tell...." She shook her head. "It doesn't matter. But I said, 'you know where he is,' and he didn't deny it. I *know* he knows."

Tony blew out a breath. "Mrs. Mitchell, did you know that Mr. Ross was named executor of Mr. Mitchell's will?"

Her head snapped up, the anger back in her eyes. "He was *what?!*"

"He's the executor of Mr. Mitchell's estate."

"The hell he is! I have a copy of Thom's will! I can assure you that he named *me* executor of his will."

"According to what's been filed, Mr. Ross is."

Jim could practically hear the growl in her voice. She bared her teeth in an almost feral movement.

"Then Mr. Ross duped my husband, detective. Thom gave me the copy that he *thought* was filed with the probate court. He has asked me to be executor of his estate until his children— all three of them—are of legal age and can make those decisions for themselves. Then, I will be acting with the second Mrs. Mitchell in an advisory capacity only."

Jim caught Tony's eye. They might have just established motive in this mess. If they could just tie Ross to Derek in some concrete way. Jim decided to risk it and tip his hand to the lady.

"Mrs. Mitchell, one more thing. Do you know why Mr. Ross might have set up an account in the Grand Caymans?"

"An account?"

Jim pulled out the printout from the computer room at the hotel. "Yes, ma'am. I don't have all the information but looks like Mr. Ross went to the website for the Wellington Fiduciary Trust and set up an account."

The woman's face took on a hard line. "You talk to Malcolm Ross, gentlemen." She stood up. "I want my ex-husband found alive. And that man knows where he is. I'd stake my life on it."

Jim and Tony stood up with her. It was Jim who reached out this time. He held his hand out and she placed hers in it. He could feel her shaking, from anger or fear, he didn't know. He covered her hand with his other and looked into her eyes. "Mrs. Mitchell, we're gonna find him. We're gonna find him safe and sound."

She nodded, her hand lingering in his. "Thank you, detective."

"You got some place to stay, in case we need to talk to you?"

"Yes, I booked a room at the Mt. Washington. So I can be close. My daughter and son will join me tomorrow."

"Good. You tell the desk clerk that we'll probably be calling as things progress."

She straightened, her shoulders squaring off. "Oh no, detective. You misunderstand me. I intend to be part of this investigation. I know my way around Carroll; I was born here. I know who to ask and how to get information."

"Ma'am, you need to let us do our jobs," Tony said. "If you get in the way, if you interfere at all, you could blow our case."

Jim watched her eyes turn steely as she stared his partner down.

"From what I've seen, sir, you have no case. You have a lot of 'what isn't' and none of 'what is'. Well, I intend to get you something." She turned smartly on her heel and headed towards the door. She stopped at the threshold long enough to give her parting shot. "You'll hear from me after I've had a nap and some food. And I'll want to know *everything* you have on this case." With that, she walked out.

Jim and Tony both heaved a sigh of relief and dropped into their chairs. The lady had just turned the heat up on them.

46

ADAM ENDED UP pushing the fast forward button again and letting it run. It was the smart thing to do. This was an eight-hour tape. He had no idea when or if what he wanted to see was going to be here. He rubbed his eyes and just focused on the flow.

He took a break for a bathroom stop and get another cup of coffee, mostly just to give his eyes a rest. He walked around the office a few minutes before he headed back to the room. He put the fast forward on again, and sat back to sip coffee. It wasn't that much longer before something caught his eye. His feet hit the floor, his thumb hit the button, and it was all he could do not to yell out *"eureka!"*

The camera out on the lawn captured the slow walk that Mitchell and Mullins were making. From the way they were walking, it was obvious that the two were completely bombed. No one seemed to pay attention to it, just moving out of their way. Both were carrying glasses and Mullins was carrying a bottle of something. He'd periodically fill the glasses and both would gulp back the contents, then move along.

Mitchell seemed to be the worse off. He stumbled quite a bit, bouncing off people or furniture. The senator was always there to straighten him up or laugh along with him. They worked their way down to the middle of the screen, then down to the front of it before they stopped.

They stood there for several minutes, barely holding each other up, miming conversation with others or each other. At one point, Mullins pointed off in a direction. Mitchell threw back his head and laughed, pointing in that direction as well. They both took another drink, then Mullins pulled Mitchell along by the back of his collar. They disappeared from view.

Within five minutes or so—according to the clock at the bottom of the screen—the camera picked up action in the garage. Mitchell and Mullins appeared, their walk even more pronounced and wobbly. They stopped by one car and stared at the wall. The quality of the video was grainy at best, so Adam couldn't be sure of what he was seeing. But it looked like a lot of keys on a peg board. Mitchell reached up and grabbed a set and the two meandered off, still holding each other up and still fumbling around in a drunken way.

The next time they appeared was in the camera pointed to the front entrance. The senator stood, visibly weaving now as Mitchell ambled off camera. Adam watched the man lean against a pillar, barely able to hold himself up. Another several minutes passed before a very shiny sports car lurched forward and stopped. There was no mistaking Thom Mitchell as he got out of the driver's side and came around to open the door for the senator. Mullins got in the passenger side and Mitchell closed the door behind him.

There was only one moment where a guard—presumably the late Scott Amber—came up behind Mitchell before he came around the car. The guard tried to take Mitchell by the arm but it was no good. Mitchell shook loose and actually seemed to sober up as he walked away. They talked for a few moments before the singer got back into the driver's side and pulled off. The guard, dismissed, merely waved and went back to his duties.

Adam watched that section several times. No mistake. Thom Mitchell was behind the wheel of the Porsche. There was always the chance that they'd stopped somewhere and traded places. But after viewing the police report and autopsy, after looking at the forensics report, there was only one conclusion to be made. Thom Mitchell left the scene of a drunk driving accident and left the senator to die. The only question was why.

And right now, only one man had that answer. With Mitchell's disappearance, that left his manager. Adam packed up the tapes and locked them in his desk drawer. He grabbed his mini-recorder and headed off to find Malcolm Ross.

47

WALT DROVE IN stony silence. He had that grim set to his jaw; the one that said 'don't screw with me.' So it was a quiet ride for the first twenty minutes of the drive.

Please don't let it be too late.

"I just want you to know that I don't give a flying fuck at a rolling donut about Thom Mitchell."

For a moment, she was taken aback by the severity of the tone. "What?"

He barely moved his lips as he talked. "I don't care about him. You want to save him, that's your problem."

"Walt—"

"I'm going to help Jo. He may know what he's doing but she doesn't. I'm going up there for her and he can go straight to hell."

It was the familiar way he used her name, as if they'd been close for a long time. He said it with such affection. That stabbed Missy in the heart with a good dose of reality.

"I guess...I guess we'd better save them both, don't you think?"

It was quiet for a little bit longer. They were almost there.

"I want to know one thing, Michelle."

"What is it, Walt?"

"Why?"

She closed her eyes and waited. "Why what?"

"I've never been anything but good to you. I've never cheated on you, never lied to you. I've loved you from the first moment

I saw you."

"I know."

"Then, why?"

"Why what, Walt? I didn't kiss him. He wasn't kissing me! I was upset, okay." She twisted her hands in her lap, trying to say it the right way. Trying to make him understand. "Come on, we were shot at. Some jerk barely missed us. I was freaking out. All he did was hug me, kiss my cheek. That was it! That was all there was!"

They were at the turn off, but instead of turning right to go up the mountain road, Walt cut the wheel sharply into the abandoned gas station. He stomped on the brakes and jumped out of the vehicle, slamming the door behind him. She followed.

"Don't walk away from me, Walter!" She came up behind him and turned him around to face her. "What is it with you? You want to know but you won't give me a chance to tell you. What are you so afraid of hearing?"

He tensed up for a moment, his shoulders stiff and his jaw set. "Maybe the truth."

"That *is* the truth, Walt. There was nothing going on. There never could be." She was close to tears, trying not to look away or do anything that he could mistake as evasion or falsehood. "He's a friend, Walt. More like...like an uncle who takes you out for ice cream when you get an 'A' on a test or shows you how to blow bubbles in your chocolate milk. That's the only way I see him!"

"I wish I could believe that."

She got closer now, close enough to stand toe to toe. But she wouldn't touch him. She couldn't. But she was determined. She kept her voice level but firm. "I never lied to *you* either," she said. "I'm not gonna start now."

The expression on his face changed. The anger was gone, replaced with confusion. But he wasn't looking at her anymore.

"Walt?"

He gently nudged her aside and walked around her. She turned to follow him and saw exactly what he was looking at. The limo had been pulled around to the back of the lot, hidden behind the building. If they'd not pulled off the road to have this argument, they'd never have seen it.

Walt walked over, trying the doors. None of them were locked, so it was easy to peer inside.

"I saw this limo in back of the hotel," she said. "It's the one that was shuttling Thom and Ms. Hayes around. And Mr. Ross."

"Yeah," Walt answered. He was already in the front seat, poking around. "I want to know why it's *here*, in the middle of BFE." He looked up at her and gestured toward the back seat. "See what's there."

She stepped into the wide passenger area, amazed at the roominess. Nothing seemed undisturbed or out of place. Until she looked down. There, under the seat, was Ms. Hayes' purse. "Walt!" She held it up for him to see through the clear glass partition. "It's her purse. All of her stuff is still in here. And a book."

They both stepped out of the car, standing and looking around. Walt saw something else and trotted over to it. She closed the limo doors before following him. He had hunkered down in the gravel.

"What is it?" she asked.

"See where the gravel is missing here? In these long grooves?"

"Yeah. So?"

"Someone's spun out here. Like they were in a big burning hurry to get somewhere and the tires kicked out all the gravel, leaving these trails."

"Can you tell where they went?"

He nodded and stood up. "Yup." He pointed up towards the mountain road. "They've gone up Wilde. Exactly where we're going."

"Then, we need to hurry."

He nodded again and took her arm to guide her back to his four by four. She tossed the purse into the back seat as he put it in gear and hit the gas. They made slow steady progress up the road, passing the lower parking area for the picnic grounds that weren't open yet. It was the only part that saw any real tourist traffic. The rest of the mountain was fiercely steep and treacherous. Only the most devoted, serious hikers and climbers ever went up that far. There was another parking area but it was small, seeing precious few cars there.

Halfway up, he was forced to slow down and put the four wheel drive into gear. They passed the small climber's parking lot and kept going. They were a mile from the summit when Walt finally stopped the vehicle.

"Walt? What is it?"

He pointed to a side road. "That logger's road. See the gate?"

It had been pulled wide and left standing to the side of the road, as if it had been hurriedly thrust open.

"Is it not supposed to be like that?" she asked.

"No, it's not." He examined it, tapping two fingers on the steering wheel as he peered through the windshield. "That used to be for the logging company to get back and forth to their campsites. When they got thrown out by the government, the rangers took it over and they only use these for fire access. That gate is supposed to be kept locked at all times."

"You think it means something?"

"I know it does, Missy." He pulled up past the road and found a flat place to park. He pulled into it and turned off the motor. "We're going to have to walk. You got your boots on?"

"Yeah."

"Good. You get the safety bag there and I'll get the other gear. Just in case."

She knew the other bag in question was his rappelling gear, the sat-com radio, and his GPS tracker. The safety bag would have a first aid kit, water, chocolate, and granola bars. They each grabbed a bag and crossed back down to the road. Walt pulled out the tracker and turned it on. She looked over his arm to see the steady green pulse.

"Now," he said. "The closer we get to that busted GPS, the faster that'll pulse."

"Okay, I see it."

"Missy, maybe you better walk behind me. Let me take the point. Okay?"

She knew better than to argue with him. She did as he asked and they took off hiking down the road. He kept watching the sides as well as ahead, moving as quietly as he could and peering down at the tracking device in his hand. She kept up with him, neither of them talking. He seemed to be concentrating and she didn't want to disturb him. They'd traveled a long pace before she smelled it. He must have too, because he stopped and was still.

"Walt?" she whispered.

The tracker in his hand was starting to pulse even more

quickly. He pointed ahead. They were close.

It was another fifteen or twenty minutes of hiking before they saw the cabin. It was a large thing, with a window peering out from the front. It appeared to have at least two or three rooms inside the structure. It was very odd that someone would be living out here with no water or electricity. It didn't even look like it would have indoor plumbing of any kind.

Walt suddenly pulled her back into a stand of beech and brush, then laid his hand over her mouth. He put a finger to his lips to motion her to silence. She nodded her understanding and he let her go. Peeking through the branches, she saw why. A man had come out of the cabin and was standing, taking a leisurely bathroom call off to one side. He had turned away from them, so he obviously hadn't seen them in the bushes. One good look at the man told her who it was—the guy that Thom had hired as his bodyguard. But what was he doing out here?

They waited until he'd finished and gone back inside. She felt a tug on her arm and turned her head to see Walt waving her to follow him. They made their way through the growth to the back of the cleared area.

Walt motioned her to stay where she was and she nodded again. He quietly dropped the bag beside her and, after looking around, sprinted off to the back of the cabin. There was a single window on that wall. A few of the slats had come down, leaving open spaces that one could see through. She watched Walt peer in between the slats. From where she was standing, she could make out the shocked expression on his face, soon followed by an angry one.

She also saw, too late, the man come around the other

corner. Before she could call out, a hand was over her mouth and another arm came around to pin hers against her sides.

"I thought I saw a little birdie flying through the trees. Looks like I caught it."

Before he knew what was on him, the burly man had snuck up on Walt and had put him on the ground with a sucker punch to the belly. He pulled a gun and pointed it directly at Walt's head. The man holding Missy let go of her mouth to reach down and pick up the two bags they'd brought. He lifted her off the ground as if she weighed no more than a sack of potatoes.

"Hey, Derek, look what I got!"

Derek gave a disinterested look in her direction before grunting. "We got company. I'm sure the lovebirds will be real glad of it."

He motioned with the gun and Walt turned around, a resigned look on his face. He led the way as Derek poked him with the gun.

"Put me down, you son of a bitch," Missy growled. "I can walk!"

The man who'd caught her chuckled. "Yes, you can, little bird. Just don't get cute or I'll have to clip your wings for you."

The minute she was on the ground, she took off running to Walt. He reached out and put his arm around her shoulders as she grabbed his waist. They were both pushed toward the front of the cabin. They turned the corner just in time to see the bodyguard step outside.

"You find them where I told you?" he asked.

"Yeah," Derek answered. "Good catch. Looks like we got two more 'guests' with us."

"Hey, dude, check it out."

Missy turned around to see the man who had held her was

the limo driver that Thom had hired. He had Walt's sat-com radio in his hand. He handed it to Derek, who made a face.

"Well, well. Look what we got." He looked up at Walt and Missy. "I'm guessing you're just here by accident. And I really don't care. But this"—he gestured with the sat-com—"means I've got a problem. I can't have you calling anyone right now. For obvious reasons."

He threw the radio down and stomped on it with his hiking boot, shattering it in shards and pieces. Missy's heart sank in her chest.

Walt pulled her closer to him. "What are you going to do to us?"

"Behave yourselves," Derek said, "and you'll walk out of here. Let us finish our business and you all can leave fine. I just want our money."

"Move," said the limo driver. He grabbed Missy's arm and shoved her inside. "Go on, asshole, get in there."

Walt followed behind her, taking her shoulders to steady her. Derek walked up to the only other door in the room and unlocked a pad lock.

"I want you two back from the door or I start shooting. You got company!" He slipped the bolt back and pushed the door ajar. He motioned with the gun to Walt and Missy. "Go on, shake a leg."

Missy's legs threatened to give at that moment, so Walt took her arms and helped her walk. He was scowling at the man as they passed him to enter the room. She barely heard the lock closing again when she saw who else was in there.

"Missy? Walt?"

She was staring at Thom and Jo. Well, that answered *that* question. They'd found the missing persons.

48

MALCOLM HAD CALMED down considerably when he made the turn onto the long drive into the hotel. It was going to be okay. He was going to be able to do this. So what if he'd originally wanted to get rid of the nuisances up there. He decided it would be better off if he just paid the money and got Thom and that woman back. He'd be the hero, Thom would be grateful, and they could go back as before. No one ever needed to know anything about *anything*! Malcolm was still large and in charge, as the saying went. It was going to be fine.

And then he found out differently. He hadn't traveled very far before he saw the phalanx of news vehicles lining the road again. Local news, national news. What the hell was going on now? He parked the rental and made his way to the front entrance. There on the deck, he found the reason for the renewed interest—Typhoon Angie had arrived at Mt. Washington.

She was holding court like the Queen of England. Poised and collected, she stood answering questions and acting every other inch the aggrieved wife. Forget the fact that she'd walked out on Thom. Forget the fact that they'd been divorced almost twenty years. She still staked her claim on his soul and she gave nothing back. The viper even had the gall to be weeping.

The last thing Mal wanted to do was being seen by the press...or by her. He had no clue why she was here and didn't care. He ducked behind a pillar and made a quick, quiet dash for the door. He made it inside, just in time—she was thanking them for coming. He closed the door behind him and breathed a sigh of relief.

"Mr. Ross!"

He turned to see that hateful local jackass—what was his name? "Oh God."

"Adam Wheeler, *Mountain*—"

"*Mountain Ear*, yes I know. What do you want? I'm really bus—"

"It's about Senator Mullins' death."

Malcolm froze in his tracks.

"I saw the tapes, Mr. Ross. I know who was *really* driving that night."

Malcolm wheeled on the man. "You know nothing."

"I know Thom Mitchell was drunk off his ass," the reporter continued. "I know he was behind the wheel when he and Senator Mullins drove off."

It was so hard to breathe, so hard to think. He felt as if someone had punched him in the stomach and left him speechless.

"I want to know what really happened that night, Mr. Ross."

Mal had to get away. He couldn't think. He was garroted and unmanned. He had to find some place to hide, to get control again. "No!"

"No? Mr. Ross—"

"No, you don't know shit, buddy. Now get away from me."

He tried to make his way around the man but the reporter was persistent. Wheeler stepped into his path. Malcolm could see a small tape recorder in his hand.

"Mr. Ross, you can set the record straight or I start printing what I have."

Malcolm lost it. Between the incompetent bunglers he'd hired and this son of a bitch who was threatening everything, he lost it completely. He grabbed Wheeler by the lapels and drove him backwards into the wall. "You print one word and I'll have your ass on the street the next day. I'll sue your fucking paper for every dime it's worth and I'll see you ruined beyond all hope."

For that brief moment, the look of surprise and terror on the reporter's face was delicious.

"You...Mr. Ross...*let me go!*"

A chorus of voices assaulted him. Both the desk clerk and that insipid hotel manager saw him at that moment and both came out calling his name. He felt one hand on his shoulder and shrugged it off.

"Mr. Ross, please," that weasely manager said. "This is not the place for this! I run a respectable establishment."

He relaxed his fingers and allowed them to pull him away. But only so far. He shrugged them off again and put his finger in the reporter's face. "I mean it! Not one fucking word, you understand me?" He turned again, practically running for the elevator. He had to go, had to run away. The goddamn money would have to wait. They'd be in and on him in a flash if he wasn't careful.

"Malcolm!"

Damn, she'd seen him. He made the dash.

"Malcolm, stop!"

His hand was poised on the button.

"Malcolm! Don't you run away from me, you bastard." She grabbed his arm and turned him to face her. "I am talking to you!"

He willed his racing heart to slow down...and failed. He wiped his mouth with the back of his hand and got control of his breathing instead. "Angela, my dear, always a pleasure to be tortured by you."

"Spare me the flattery, you bastard. Where's Thom?"

"I'm sure I don't know." He grinned at her. "Considering his current romantic situation, I'm sure he's not alone." He watched her face tighten; he was laughing inside at the secret pleasure he always got in digging at her.

"I will not get into games with you, Malcolm," she said, her jaw clenched. "I want to know where he is and he damned well better not be hurt."

"Angela," Malcolm spat back. "Even *if* I knew where he was, I damned well wouldn't tell you shit! Considering how much money he's spent to get away from his harpy ex-wives."

That caught her off guard. Her mouth flew open.

"Thom is a fine musician but a lousy judge of wife material, if you ask me." He pressed the button for the elevator. "Personally, I hope this new piece of ass turns out for the best." He leaned into her, as if confiding a secret. "I think she's got potential, actually. She gives a great blow job."

"And how would *you* know?" Angela sniped. "I never had you pegged for the tuna taco type."

That took him aback.

"Oh come on, Malcolm. You really think I'm that stupid? You'd have been happier if Thom was playing 'hide the salami' with *you* all this time." She snorted. "I guess you just weren't man enough, were you."

Malcolm sniped back. "Honey, I'm more woman than you'll ever hope to be and more man than you'll ever hope to get!

Spare me!"

The door opened on an empty car. By now, the media had managed to see the two of them and were rushing in their direction. He quickly stepped into the elevator and pressed the button for his floor. Unfortunately, the harridan stepped in with him and the doors closed behind her. Thankfully, on the reporters.

He huffed a loud put upon sigh. "Angela, what the fuck do you want?"

"I told you. I want to know where Thom is."

"Don't we all, my dear," he answered with a feigned boredom in his voice. Right now, all he wanted to do was get away from this bitch so he could think.

"Except, you *do* know, Malcolm."

"Angela, go away; you're boring the shit out of me."

"I'm not going anywhere"

"Whatever."

She started to look smug at that point. "Did you happen to notice the company I was keeping?"

"How could I miss it? Holding court again, I see."

"The press. They know already. I was only too glad to call them out."

The doors opened and gave him the excuse he wanted. He grabbed her arm, hard enough to bruise—he hoped—and dragged her along. Ignoring her protests and insults, he slammed his card key into the lock and waited for the green light. It took two tries and a very hard shake of the bitch before the lock clicked and he opened the door. He threw her roughly over the threshold and slammed the door behind them.

"Angela, my dear," he whispered through clenched teeth. "I

know you're not that stupid."

"No? Well, I call it being smart. And safe." She straightened her clothing before glaring at him, rubbing her arm where he'd grabbed it. "They already knew he was missing. All I did was call a press conference with the details that I had."

"And you damn well mentioned my name, didn't you?"

"No," she answered defiantly. "Not yet. But I will if you don't tell me what I want to know."

He shook his head. "And that Wheeler bastard?"

"Who?"

"The one who just stopped me downstairs. The one who said he saw the tapes." He was sweating, losing control again. "I have no idea what tapes he's talking about. I didn't even know there *were* tapes."

"I didn't know either. I don't know what *you're* talking about."

"He knows about the Mullins business," Mal growled. "And only one other person knows the details. That would be you." He advanced on her, glowering down at her face. "So, you tell me—what did you tell that Wheeler shit?"

She started to back away. "I didn't tell him anything. I don't even know who he is."

"Oh yes, you do."

"No," she said, panting now. "I don't know. I only went to the police. I wanted to know what *they* knew. Get them looking for Thom."

"You mentioned my name to them too, didn't you!"

"No! No, I never said anything. You—"

He backhanded her across the mouth. She whimpered but never lost the rebellious look on her face.

"I believe you," he said. "You know why?"

She shook her head.

"Because if you *had* mentioned my name, if you *had* told them anything about Mullins, you'd be sitting in a jail cell right now."

"No, I wouldn't!"

His hand shot out, grabbing her by the throat. "Oh, yes you would." He got close enough to smell the cologne on her skin. "Let's see...concealing evidence, harboring a fugitive, accessory after the fact. So many other charges, if I have the time to think about them. Oh yes, Angela, my precious, if I go down, you go down with me."

He felt her swallow, her throat moving under his fingers.

"And believe me, I'll rat you out with Thom too. Some information that I'm sure he'll want to know. We'll see if he finds you half as saintly as you pretend to be."

"Let me go!"

"After we have an understanding." He waited until she'd stopped struggling. "No more press conferences. No more going to the police, you hear me?"

She glared at him and kept silent.

"And you avoid that Adam Wheeler asshole. He's trouble. And he'll get Thom in jail with us. You really want that?"

She looked shocked at that but she was still listening.

"No, I didn't think so. So, you be a very good girl and shut up. Stay in your room." He kissed her cheek and whispered in her ear. "Yes, I know where Thom is. And I'll get him free. But if you fuck this up by talking to anyone else, I'll see you hang along with us. Understood?" He stepped back, his hand still gripping her throat. "You've got just as much to lose, little bitch. And you'll fry us all!"

He let her go, watching her sidle along the wall like a kicked dog. She was rubbing her throat as she made her way to the door and let herself out. That was okay. He knew she'd follow his orders, keep her mouth shut. After all, seeing Thom in jail was nothing compared to losing their relationship.

He helped himself to a glass of scotch and soda. "Stupid bitch still thinks he's going to come back to her." He took a healthy gulp from the glass. "I'll give it a little time to cool off down there. I can go transfer the money and get out to save Thom."

He took a look at his shaking hand. "It'll be okay. It'll be fine. I'm still in control. It's still my game."

Angie's throat was in agony, her chest still heaving. She'd gotten damned lucky. She blindly made her way to the elevator and punched the button. She just wanted to go lay down and think about this. Was she making the right move here? *Would* he tell Thom?

"Mrs. Mitchell, right?"

She whirled around.

"Yeah, I thought so." The man came towards her. "My name is Adam Wheeler, I'm with *The Mountain Ear*. We need to talk."

Oh God. Hell had come with a fury. Now, what?

"Look, Mrs. Mitchell. You can talk to me or talk to the cops. But you stand a better chance with me."

Angie stood, frozen. *God, what to do, what to do.*

"Look, I saw that tape. I saw Mr. Mitchell get into the car with the senator. I saw Mr. Mitchell drive off." He stepped closer. "All I want is the truth. I can help you. I can help Mr. Mitchell by printing out what happened."

Angie shook her head violently. She couldn't, she wouldn't.

There was too much at stake.

"If I tell the cops what I know, Mr. Mitchell goes to jail. Is that what you really want?"

Her heart was pounding in her chest. She was being torn apart by all of this. If she told anyone, Malcolm would have her killed. He might even harm Thom. Malcolm knew where Thom was but if she said anything.... Thom! Thom could go to prison for this. If she talked, Thom *would* go to prison. But at the same time, if she told the truth.... If she finally let this all go, she could get out from under Malcolm's thumb, make Thom see the bastard for what he really was.

If she told the truth...if she told someone. Maybe Thom wouldn't go to jail if someone else knew what had happened that night. They could all breathe easier. No more secrets, no more lies.

But he said he'd tell Thom about....

Not if she told him first. After all these years, it was time that she came clean about a lot of things. She took a deep breath and raised her eyes to look into the man's. She wanted to believe.

He seemed to understand that. "Please. You can trust me."

Something jingled inside of her. It told her that she could. With everything. "All right, Mr. Wheeler. I'll tell you what you want to know. Come with me. I'll tell you everything."

She led the way into the elevator and escorted him to her suite. After making an order with room service, Angie sat down and started to talk.

49

TONY GLANCED OVER to the young man at the other desk. They'd called the desk clerk in, just to see what he could find. One never knew, they might get lucky and this kid had seen something.

"You got him checking out the mugs?"

Tony nodded. "Yes. Just in case."

"Cool." Jim sat down at his desk, rearranging his sticky notes. "Thing that bugs me is, how were they grabbed? I mean, didn't that Mitchell cat rent a car?"

"It was a limo, sir," said the young man. "I saw 'em."

Both men turned back to the desk clerk.

"Rod, right?" Jim asked.

"Yeah, Rod Hadsell."

"Rod, you saw 'em leave?"

"Yeah," the young man answered. "I was on my smoke break. We have to take our breaks off the kitchen, so the patrons don't see us smoking. Mr. Guilford says it's not good for bus—"

"Rod. Dude," Jim interrupted. "I get the point, man. You saw 'em split?"

"Oh yeah. They handed that bodyguard guy the bags and got in the limo and it took off."

"Limo?" Tony reached for the phone book. There were only three limo companies close enough for hire in Bretton Woods. One of them was here in Carroll.

"Yeah, big black one."

"Any other info you got? You remember the plate?"

"Oh yeah, sure," Rod answered, smiling. "Was a custom plate. Said RubyToo."

"RubyToo?" Jim cast a hopeful glance at his partner. "You sure that's what it said?"

"Yup."

Tony nodded in the young man's direction. Jim nodded, understanding what he wanted, and crossed over to sit with Rod. Jim would keep him distracted while Tony made the phone call.

"Ruby's Limo Service, how can I help you?"

"Detective Tony Garrison, Carroll Police. This Dave Ruby?"

"Speaking."

Tony laid it out in a few sentences. Mr. Ruby was only too happy to volunteer that one of his limousines *had* been rented this week. By a Malcolm Ross.

"Has your driver returned with the car yet?"

"Driver? He didn't want a driver. Said he had his own."

"His own driver?"

"That's what he said," Ruby confirmed. "I didn't argue."

"Okay."

"And to answer the rest of your question, no. The customer hasn't returned the limo yet. It's still out."

"Still out? You mean stolen?"

"Naw," Ruby grunted. "He rented it for two weeks. If it ain't back at the end, *then* I report it stolen. Besides, damn thing's got GPS; that damn satellite shit. I can find it if I need to."

"Okay," Tony said, jotting down the information. "Any way I can get copies of the rental agreement and signatures?"

"Come on, detective, you know you gotta get a warrant for that."

"Call it a personal favor, Mr. Ruby. Maybe I can help you some day."

"Yeah, whatever."

" Oh, and the credit card slip," Tony added.

"That won't do you no good. Credit card was in another name."

"What's the name on that?"

"Detective."

"Come on. It's not going to land in your lap. Do me the favor."

There was a bit of heavy breathing on the other end, nothing being said. Tony waited.

"All right, detective. What's the fax number? And you owe me one!"

Tony grinned. "Sure, no problem."

He hung up the phone and crossed over to the fax machine just as it started ringing. While he waited for the whole thing to print out, he took a peek over at Jim and the desk clerk. Jim was pointing to something in the book. The young man was nodding and pointing as well. He watched and waited. Jim grinned broadly and grabbed the book up.

"Lou, do something for me. Give Rod a ride back to the hotel, okay?"

"Thanks, detective."

Jim grinned at the young man and nodded. "I'll call you if we need more, dude. And you call me if you remember anything else."

"Sure."

Tony pulled the sheets off the fax machine. Sure enough, the name scrawled at the bottom was Malcolm Ross. Ruby hadn't lied about the credit card receipt. The name on the credit card was for a Darren Reese. He sat down at his desk.

"Old man Ruby says one of his limos is out. Turns out, it was signed for by our old buddy, Mr. Ross."

"Is that his John Hancock?"

"We'll have to check against the hotel book. See if it is."

"I got one better," Jim answered, beaming. "Turns out that Rod got a good look at two new employees of Mr. Mitchell. Rod says they were staying at the hotel too. Hired by Mr. Ross himself."

"Yeah? And?" Tony asked.

Jim swung the mug shot book around so that Tony could see them. His fingers were poised over two sets of pictures.

"He just ID'd Neil Butcher as the bodyguard and Mike Rudner as the driver." Jim handed the book over. "Read who their known accomplice is."

Tony read the information under both pictures and fingerprints. Sure enough, they had a connection. "Derek Roberts."

"Yup. And even better news."

"I can't wait, buddy."

"The slugs that match up to both the murder and the shooting of Mitchell? The gun used is an assault rifle only made in Russia. Part of a shipment that got confiscated back in '87. Except a few disappeared before the trial."

"Okay...and?"

"They tracked 'em down to a dirty cop that pawned 'em off at this place in Manchester. I checked the records. Guess who bought that gun?"

"Was this before they even *kept* records?"

"It was before the right laws came up, man. But this guy kept records. Just in case, he said at the time."

"Let me guess...Derek Roberts," Tony said.

"Nope. Malcolm Ross."

"Mal—" Tony's jaw clamped shut. "The rifle is *his*?"

"I'm thinking either his or someone forged his signature. And I'm betting that we call the bank that card is drawn on? That we got a match for old Mr. Ross!"

Tony grinned. It was finally falling together.

"I got the phone records too." Jim pulled a handful of papers from a manila file. "Ross has been using his cell a lot the last couple days. Lot o' calls to one of those prepay cell numbers."

"No way to trace that," Tony answered. "You know that."

Garrison shrugged. "Yeah. But it's still kinda weird, don't you think?"

"Why should I think that?"

"Because there was one call made from Mitchell's phone to this same number. Lasted less than a minute—long enough to dial and hang up."

Tony stared at the papers. "You think...."

"I think since the bulk of the calls are from Ross's phone except for that one call, I think Ross is the one that made it." Garrison grinned. "And I think when we tie all of this up, this phone belongs to our bad guys and Mr. Ross is in cahoots with 'em."

"I think you're right, Jimmy," Tony said. "We got him."

"Yup," Jim agreed. "We got him."

"Think we need a squad car?"

"I'm thinking maybe a couple wouldn't hurt," Jim answered.

"Just in case."

Tony made the phone call and arranged for an escort. He grabbed his coat and followed Jim out the door. It was time to bring in their prime suspect.

50

JOANNA HAD A problem. Since childhood, she'd been plagued with allergies. Some were worse than others. Simple things could make her sinuses painfully clogged. Other things made her skin itchy and her face swell up like a balloon. It wasn't a long list of things that she was allergic to, but it was a crappy one. Oh, the usual things like dust and pollen, pet dander. The moment that Thom mentioned hiking, golfing, and being outdoors, she'd pulled out her trusty prescription of antihistamines and taken them religiously. She was covered.

But the worst was cologne and perfume. If she got within a close proximity, she'd begin to sneeze and her eyes would run as hard as her nose. Often, it was enough to give her a serious migraine. It didn't matter how much the person put on—a drop was just as bad as marinating like a steak in the stuff. Sometimes the meds worked, sometimes they didn't. It depended on the blend. Either way, it made things uncomfortable.

The man who came in had a very distinctive cologne—a combination of a heady musk and a cloyingly sweet flowery scent. It smelled like one of those designer scents and closed her sinuses up tighter than a drumhead. The sad part was, the scent was too familiar. Something had fit into place inside of her head about the first time she'd smelled it. And her reaction to it.

The heels, too; they clicked across the wooden floor. The sound of very expensive, handmade shoes. She remembered hearing them click across the floor at the hotel; the same click across the wood. The problem was how to tell Thom. It wasn't the kind of news that one just blurted out—*hey, I think your friend is the one that set this up*. She wanted to be wrong. She knew she wasn't.

But when the time came and she'd managed to stutter her way through, all he did was stare at her. She waited, sitting on the floor. He had been standing in front of the kerosene heater, listening.

"Thom?"

Nothing.

"Thom, talk to me. Tell me I'm wrong. Tell me anything. Just say *something*."

For a moment longer, he didn't comply. Then, with a slow shake of his head, he ran his fingers through his thick blond hair and tilted his head back. What she didn't expect was the low chuckle that came out of him.

A bit indignant, she asked. "What? What's so funny?"

"You think...." He turned around to look at her. "You think *Mal* is doing this? Are you *serious*?" Well, he wasn't angry at her. Just amused. That was a start. Insulting, but a start.

"Thom, I recognized the cologne. When he came close to us. Maybe my eyes were taped shut but my nose wasn't. I could smell him. I smelled that stuff he wears."

Thom snorted. "Please."

"What kind of cologne does he wear?"

"That doesn't matter—"

"What kind?" she insisted.

"It's a special made blend, okay?" he retorted. "Is that what you want to know?"

"Yeah," she bit back. "Because everyone wears that scent, it being so common and all."

Thom shook his head again. "Jo, I've known the man for over twenty-five years. And you're wrong."

"Am I? What about his shoes?" She bristled, her pulse pounding in her temples, making the headache worse. "I recognized his shoes. The heels as they clicked on the floor; only *his* shoes make that sound."

He shook his head and spoke with that same condescending voice he had when he was speaking to those reporters. The one that said, 'you're being irrational and delusional, honey,' and 'you really need to get over yourself.' "Oh, dear Jo—"

She glared at him. "Don't you 'oh, dear Jo' me, dam—"

The door slammed open at that moment. She was just barely able to make out who was being shoved through the door. "Missy?" she asked. "Walt?"

Walt lurched forward, shoved from behind. He whirled around to say something to whoever had shoved him when Missy flew into his arms. Her eyes were huge, the look on her face was one of horror. Jo watched as Walt guided Missy to stand behind him.

"I'm warning you," Walt grumbled.

"Yeah, warn this," Neil said He flipped Walt off and slammed the door in his face.

The door was locked again and the four of them were alone.

"Are you two okay?" Jo took a few steps towards the girl, to try and help calm her down. "Missy."

Missy shook her head before burying her face in Walt's chest.

"Walt?" Thom tried next. "Not to sound ungrateful but what are you two doing up here?"

Walt sighed, Missy still pressed against him. "Your GPS went off," he answered rather curtly.

"Are you two okay? Did you get hurt?"

Walt shook his head. "No, we're okay. He roughed us up a little, nothing big."

"Missy?" Thom asked.

"She's fine," Walt sniped. "I said, *we're* fine."

Thom backed off, raising his hands up in surrender. He came back to stand by Jo, watching the younger couple.. "Yeah, okay. I was just making sure she was okay, that's all."

"Yeah, well she's not your problem."

Jo took his arm, cutting off any further reply from him. "Thom, we have a bigger problem. How are we going to get out of here?"

"I don't know, honey."

"Don't worry about it," Walt said, cradling Missy in his arms. "I've got a backup plan."

"What kind of backup plan?" Jo asked.

"With all due respect, Jo, I have a more important question." Walt jutted out his chin in Thom's direction. "Why are these guys taking a poke at you, man? What did you do to piss 'em off?"

Thom's hands went to his hips, legs spread in a defiant stance. "What did *I* do?"

Jo stepped between them. "Thom did nothing, Walt." She turned back to face her lover. "This is all Mal. Malcolm did this. I just don't know why."

Thom huffed, frustrated. "I'm telling you that you're wrong, woman. He had nothing to do with this."

She whirled back around on him, tired of his ostrich routine. "And I'm telling you he did. The cologne, those shoes. No one else in Bretton Woods has shoes like that."

"Damn it, Jo, you're wrong!"

"Excuse me, but she's not wrong." Missy, at last, looked up from Walt's chest. "I heard him talking on the phone to someone. I was in the linen closet, getting ready for lunch rush and he came in. He didn't see me, but I heard him."

"What was he talking about?" Thom asked.

Missy swallowed hard, stepping away from Walt at the same time. He was reluctant to let her go, but did anyway. She looked over her shoulder before braving Thom. "I heard him talking to someone named Derek. And when we were being brought in here, I heard one of the guys call that leader guy Derek."

"That means nothing, Missy," Thom insisted. "It's a common name."

"But I heard your manager tell this Derek guy to get the limo and the two guys—a bodyguard and a chauffeur. And he told him that you had to be comfortable with them or it wouldn't work." She balled her hands into fists at her sides, as if she was trying to work up the courage for the rest. "And I heard him say that Wilde would be perfect."

Jo risked a look at Thom's face. He looked floored for a moment, his mouth hanging open and standing hunched, almost defeated. She wanted to touch him, reassure him. She wanted to say something that would help him understand. But he saw her looking at him and straightened up quickly. Mr. Stubborn had returned.

"No, you're wrong, Missy. You're both wrong."

"No, I'm not," Missy argued. "I know what I heard."

"No you didn't," Thom argued right back. "You misinterpreted. You misheard."

Walt stiffened at that. "Wait a minute, pal."

"Look, don't you 'pal' me," Thom bit back. "That man is my friend and I've known him a lot longer than you. And I know what he's capable of."

"If Missy says she heard it, she did."

"She's lying then."

"Fuck you, buddy!"

"Jesus H. Christ, Mitchell! Get your head out of your ass for one moment, will ya?" Jo slapped her thigh. So typical—first she wanted to comfort him and then she wanted to slap him. *Men!* "You just don't want to admit that it's true."

"It's bullshit," Thom argued. "I'm telling you people, you don't know what you're talking about. You're wrong, Missy."

Walt growled, stepping forward and reaching for Thom's lapel at the same time. Missy and Jo moved to step in the middle to try and stop them. The room had erupted into shouts and was about to devolve into fists. The loud bang shocked them all. Neither of them had heard the lock or the door until Mike had fired the pistol into the ceiling. Bits of wood and plaster floated down around them and Jo covered her head instinctively. It took a few seconds for the dust to settle before they all turned back to the door.

Derek was standing, grinning from ear to ear. "Well, I'd love to thank you for the entertainment but you're giving me a headache. Now, shut it!"

Walt was closest. He tossed his head in Thom's direction, making his black hair jump. "Look, I don't give a damn what you have with *him*, but let *me* go. Let me take the ladies and we'll go. We won't tell anyone."

"You asshole—"

"Looks like old Mitchell there didn't like that idea much."

Walt glared back over his shoulder. "I really don't care." He turned back to Derek. "Please, just let the ladies go then. I'll stay. But let them go."

Joanna felt Thom bristling beside her. She placed her hand on his arm again, willing him to be quiet. She knew he wanted to be up there negotiating their release, except he *was* the prize now and they all knew it.

"Let the ladies go," Thom agreed with a bit less grace than he probably should have had in the situation. "You've got me. Let the ladies go. Him too."

"And they said chivalry was dead," Derek said sarcastically. "Well, too bad. You're all stuck here. Neil."

Neil appeared from behind Derek, carrying a large box. He set the box down in the far corner, away from the group.

"Now then," Derek went on. "Since we have extra guests, I decided you lot would need extra provisions. And you could fend for yourselves. There's food, toilet paper, and another can of kerosene in there."

"Wait," Missy said. "You can't leave us here."

"Oh, we're not leaving, sweety," Derek answered cheerfully. "Not yet. Not until the phone call comes about our money. When we're gone, we'll let the money man come and get you." He waved the other two men out behind him. "Then, you're free and we're out of the country." Derek turned to walk out, then thought better of it. He faced the group again, the same tiger-like grin on his face. "Now, do behave yourselves in here. Any more of this nonsense and I'll have to let Neil and Mike have some fun. You wouldn't want that now, would you?" He turned to leave.

In the flash of an eye, Walt leaped forward and grabbed the man in his fists. "Son of a bitch!" he yelled and laid a punch on Derek's shoulder.

Derek either didn't feel it or he concealed it well. But his arm came up and around, propelling him in the turn. His ham-sized fist caught Walt under the jaw and knocked him backwards. Mike came running in, followed by Neil, both with guns drawn.

"He's mine," Derek told them and moved in.

The bulky man began punching Walt, who was keeping up for a time. The crack under his jaw had only momentarily dazed him. But another lucky punch knocked him into the wall, banging his head against the wood. A fist into his belly drove the wind out of him and Walt sank to his knees. Jo made to run to him but Thom gripped her arm and held her back. Missy started to jump in and a gun was pointed at her head. She stopped immediately. Derek backhanded Walt across the mouth and Walt was knocked out.

Missy glared at the former bodyguard and ran anyway. She dropped down beside Walt and started crying, calling his name and holding his head in her arms.

"You bastard," Jo spat out.

Derek got up, wiping his hands on a handkerchief he'd pulled out of his pocket. "Keep that up, honey, and the food and fuel go out with me. Now, stay in here and be good little children. Understood?"

The three men left the room, locking them in again. Until that moment, Jo had kept a kernel of hope alive in her heart. Seeing what the man had done to Walt, who was more athletic and muscled than Thom, that hope began to fade. They were going to die up here, regardless of Derek's assurances. They were going to die.

51

TWICE, MALCOLM STARTED for the door and twice, he stopped. Those reporters would still be downstairs and he was not ready to face them yet. That damned Wheeler punk was asking about the Mullins accident. Who else knew about that? No, he couldn't go down. Not just yet. But damn it, he had to go. He had to get down to the computer room and wire that money to the Caymans. If he didn't, he felt reasonably sure that Derek would just kill Thom—the bitch too—and forget any assurances to the contrary.

Then, he picked up the cell twice. All he had to do was call his Uncle Sally's right hand guy. Damn it, he was the nephew of an important Mafioso. All he had to do was say the word, ask the favor. It would be done and those louts would be strewn in bits and pieces all over the Presidents. He could have Angela taken care of. Hell, do that Hayes slut too. All of his headaches cured in a single phone call. He put the phone back in his pocket both times. No, that wasn't the best idea. Too many more complications would arise from that phone call.

In twenty five years, he'd managed to rise to be a major player in the music industry and do it on his own merit. Sure, he called on connections sometimes. But he never out-and-out asked for anything, never put his own ass out there on the line. If he asked this favor, he knew what they'd want in return. He'd spend the rest of his life playing lackey on the inside.

Anytime someone needed something fixed or wanted Thom to play a casino for free. Anytime, *the boys* needed a place to stay or money to launder. Malcolm *knew* people and he was a connection just like anyone else.

Angela was a loose cannon. Maybe she hadn't contacted that reporter. But that didn't mean she hadn't contacted *somebody*. For all he knew, she could have made a confession on DVD or an MP3 and stuck it somewhere. She was the type that watched too many crime stories. 'In the event of my untimely demise, that little silver circle gets delivered to the police.' Stupid cow, he didn't put it past her.

He reached up and massaged his temples. It was all falling apart. It wasn't supposed to be like this. It was just supposed to be a simple kidnapping; the bitch would be gone and Malcolm would have Thom back to himself. Maybe he'd never be Thom's lover, but Thom would love him. It would be enough.

It was falling apart. And he had only one way to keep it from totally unraveling. He'd have to risk it, he'd have to go down there and put the money in the bank. Malcolm grabbed his card key and left the room. He grabbed the elevator down, gripping the railing all the way. His stomach was starting to churn from all the stress. He was overdue for a Maalox cocktail. But when the doors opened, he froze. He had a clear site of the computer room from the elevator. Two cops were standing right in front of the damned doorway, talking to a TV crew. The bright lights were throwing the shadows back on the wall.

"Damn," he muttered. He stepped back and punched the button to his floor. His chest was starting to pound as he flew back into his room, slamming the door hard in the frame. He was panting, trying to catch his breath and damn near hyperventilating while doing it.

"God, what do I do? What do I do?"

No one saw him, so that was good. But what now? He paced and paced, from one wall to the opposite. He wanted a drink but didn't dare. He wanted to scream but didn't want anyone hearing him.

The money! Well, he couldn't go down to the computer room. He grimaced and pulled out his cell phone; of course, he could phone the transfer in. He laid that on the small sofa table while he pulled his wallet out of his pocket. He'd written the phone number of the bank down for Derek, then written it down for himself, including the account number and pin. He pulled the card out, then stuffed his wallet back in his pocket. Mal dialed the number to the Zurich account, laying the card back on the table.

He went to the window to try and get a grip, look out at the mountains—like Thom did when he was upset—and maybe, just maybe, the sight would give him calm. He waited while the automated answering service went through the options of pushing one for this and two for that. He took deep breaths and rested his forehead against the glass. This *was* calming; everything would be clearer.

It turned out to be anything *but* calming. He had a room facing the front of the property. Looking out, he also happened to look down. There was already one squad car but now another joined it, with an unmarked car leading the way. All three pulled up in front. Malcolm could just catch the edge of the drive where they'd parked. Sure enough, those two detectives were down there. They stood, waiting for the cops, then talking with them. The dark haired one pulled something out of his pocket.

Malcolm had a real good idea what that was. Now, he felt like a trapped animal. He had to get that money in that account. But he also had to get the fuck out of this hotel.

"Side entrance," he muttered to himself. "The security entrance. That old man'll go right to the cops to help, so he'll be away from the guard station. I can go that way. If I'm not here, they can't question me. I can go get Thom out and this will be over. I can go get Thom and cover my tracks and...and...."

The police made their way to the entrance and out of Mal's sight line. That was it, he was screwed. He disconnected the call. He had to move and move now. Without any further thought, he ran out the door.

They would be coming up the elevator. He thought he might be lucky, that there weren't more than the four uniformed men. The two detectives would be coming up the elevator, with two of the cops. Maybe...just maybe...maybe he could take the stairwell. Yeah, he could take the stairwell and miss them. He'd worry about the other two when he got to the lobby.

Mal turned left instead of right and headed to the door marked with the red exit sign. In less than a minute, he was through the door and on his way down the steps. He reached the second floor landing and stood, waiting and listening. Good, they weren't coming up the stairs. He'd been right after all. They were using the elevator.

He remembered that the parking lot was on the other end of the hotel, so he cut through the second floor. He ran across the length of the wing, running as fast as he could, until he hit the other stairwell. He was through that door and dashing down the next flight of stairs as quickly as he could. The door led straight to the hallway that fed into another. It was well after lunch; 1:00 PM, actually. He looked straight across and saw the exit door. The parking area lay beyond that door, he could see cars through the huge windows. He'd been right about the security guards. They were gone; they had to be with the cops.

Malcolm grinned and walked as quickly as he could. When he burst through the door, the smell of the air was the cleanest and most free thing he'd ever smelled in his life. He was sweating profusely, his heart was pounding and his lungs were burning, but it didn't matter. He made a beeline for the rental and managed to drive off without being seen.

52

"CARROLL POLICE DEPARTMENT, what's your emergency?"

"My name's Deke Murphy. My partner's missing and I want to report it."

"And how long has he been missing, sir?"

"Since around lunch. He went to rescue someone out on Wilde. A customer bought a GPS from us and the signal got activated up on Wilde Mountain. Walt was supposed to radio in about 4:00 p.m. but I couldn't wait. I started calling *him*, like about three or so, only he's not answering."

"Sir, I'll dispatch a car to your location."

"No, don't. He ain't here. I *know* where he is."

"Well, sir, if he's lost on Wilde Mountain, you need to be calling the rangers for that."

"I did. Ain't just that though. See, we sold that GPS to that singer dude. That Thom Mitchell guy. Walt's girl, Missy, said he's missing. Said your cops were talking about it at the hotel."

"Sir, you have information on the whereabouts of Mr. Mitchell?"

"Yeah. That's where Walt went. To find Mitchell. They're up on Wilde. Only Walt ain't checked in and...well, I'm thinking this is some heavy shit."

"All right, sir. I'll pass the information on to the detectives. I'm going to dispatch a car to your location for more information. Do not leave the area. Understood?"

"Yeah, no problem. Just hurry. I got some bad vibes going here."

53

"LOOK, DUDE, YOU know what this is?" Jim insisted.

Tony put his hand on his partner's shoulder. Jim stepped back, his hands in the air. Tony took the warrant and laid it out in front of the Hotel manager.

"This is called a search warrant, sir. It gives me the right to go through that room. Now, let's not turn this situation into a lot of unpleasantness, shall we?"

Guilford looked down at the paper, running his finger back and forth on the lines. He sighed, nodding his head. "All right, detective. Let me get the master key." The fussy little man disappeared into the office.

Tony turned back to his partner. "See, you just gotta know how to talk to people."

Jim blew a raspberry.

Within ten minutes, Tony and Jim were in Ross' room. Tony pointed the way into the bedroom area while he and Jim began poking around the sitting area.

"I'd love to know where he split to," Jim muttered. "It's too convenient for me, man."

"I agree, partner. *Very* convenient." Tony pulled out the latex gloves, pulling them on his hands. He tossed a pair to Jim. "Here, put these on. Just in case."

Jim caught them in mid-air. "Yeah, no contaminating the scene. Just in case."

There was nothing in the desk. Tony didn't really expect anything. But he had to look as a matter of course. He heard a sudden hissing intake of breath and turned around to see his partner at the sofa side table.

"Well, check out this shit, man." Jim held up a small business card. "Man, I can't even pronounce this but it says Zurich, Switzerland underneath."

"Oh?" Tony walked over.

"Yeah, and there's a phone number on the back. And...looks like an account number." He handed the card to Tony.

Tony turned it over a few times. He looked up at Jim. "Tell you what. You call the number on the back and I'll call the number on the front and let's see what we have here."

The luck was with them. Both numbers turned out to be banks, the one on the back was in the Grand Caymans. Wellington Fiduciary Trust. Jim found out that yes, they did have a website. Yes, that number was one of their accounts. They had no other information they could provide because of banking regulations. They'd need to see his warrant. Jim didn't push it. But then again, he didn't have to. The bank Tony called had been a lot more co-operative. They had an account under the name of Thom Mitchell with a second signer—Malcolm Ross. The account had more than thirty million dollars.

The boys in the bedroom were finding interesting things. One of the uniforms found a copy of some paperwork that had to do with Mitchell; copies of the will, the insurance policies. Whatever Mrs. Mitchell had been told, these copies said something else. Sure enough, Ross had been named executor and beneficiary of the policies. Anything happened to Mitchell, the family was not going to be happy. Tony wondered if Mitchell even knew about this.

The other found something just as interesting. In going through Ross' briefcase to catalogue the contents, he found the receipts for the credit card used to purchase the limo. The final nail was hammered into Ross' coffin but good.

His cell started vibrating in his hip pocket. Tony reached in, pulled it out, and pushed the answer button. "Morris here."

"Detective, I just got a call about your missing persons reports."

Tony waved his hand to get Jim's attention. "What? The Mitchell and Hayes reports?"

"That's affirmative on Mitchell, sir."

He listened as the dispatcher relayed what she'd been told. "Wilde? You sure?"

"Yes, sir. That's what he said. I contacted the rangers and they confirmed a signal up on Wilde. The GPS matches the unit that Mr. Mitchell purchased. Looks like he got it at a shop there in Carroll; *The Mind of God.*"

"Are they on their way?"

"Yes, sir. Sending the scouting plane now, said they'll be following it up with a ground crew within the next two to four hours."

"Call 'em back. Tell 'em we're on our way to assist. I'm taking Reilly and Martin with us. I'll send the other squads back on patrol."

"Copy. I notified the captain, too."

"Good, thanks. We'll report in with any news."

Jim was watching. "What is it?"

"Looks like we may have found our missing pop star and his girlfriend." He told Jim, then gave the two uniforms their instructions. "Let's go, lads. I have a feeling our bad guys are up there, too."

They collected their evidence, thanked the manager, and left.

54

THE ROOM GOT quiet again, no one talking. After the earlier blow up, it just seemed to be the best thing. Jo and Thom sat close but they said nothing to each other. It was tense between them. Missy was curious but didn't ask. It just wasn't her place. Besides, she was more worried about Walt. He was still unconscious.

She cradled Walt's head in her lap, stroking his face and singing softly to him. She felt a knot in her stomach, the worry about him getting to her. She really wanted him to wake up but was afraid to try to bring him up yet. Just in case. When the hand touched her shoulder, she flinched a bit. But it was Ms. Hayes, kneeling next to her.

"Missy, are you okay?"

"I'll be okay when Walt's okay," she answered and went back to caressing his cheek.

"Would you like some soup, honey?"

Missy shook her head.

"He'll wake up, honey. Just give him a bit. He took a hard knock to the head."

"I think he's got a concussion." Missy sighed. "He did this for me, you know. He came up here for me. Because I wanted to be a hero. I wanted to...to...."

She patted Missy's back, smoothed the hair back from Missy's face. "I know, honey. I'm sorry it didn't work out that way."

"We heard the signal. The GPS. Walt says that it'll ring off in the rangers' stations too. You'll see, someone will come to help us."

"Of course."

Ms. Hayes went back to sit with Thom. Missy watched them out of the corner of her eye. They really did love each other. She just hoped that Walt would give her the chance to show how much she loved *him*. "I didn't lie to you, Walt. It wasn't what it looked like. I swear it."

At the sound of his name, Walt's eyes fluttered open. It took a few moments for the beautiful green eyes to focus on her. "Missy?"

"Shh, you be still," she whispered. "You have a mild concussion. But you're gonna be okay."

He nodded. "What time is it?"

"I don't know," she answered.

"Doesn't matter. Deke'll call in the rangers. When I don't call *him*. We'll have help here soon."

"Help?" Thom had heard that part. "Did you say help?"

Walt tried—and failed—to sit up, collapsing back on Missy's lap. "Yeah," he answered weakly. "All we gotta do is sit tight."

"Sit tight," Thom repeated.

Missy watched them settle back and get quiet again. Walt closed his eyes and drifted off. She just sat, stroking his forehead and cheeks, and prayed they would come soon.

55

WITH THE CABIN in sight, Malcolm dragged himself up the path. His rental had hopelessly bogged down about halfway up the steep path, forcing him to walk the rest of the way. It was enough to make him sorry he hadn't changed his footwear before leaving. His shoes were for parties, fine dining, accompanying a pop star to gigs and interviews; they were not for trail hiking. His feet were killing him and he was sure he'd gained blisters on his heels. It would be worth it when he rescued Thom.

He'd also had time to work up a good head of steam. Malcolm was pissed off, to say the least. Derek was a moron. He should have realized that after the Amber debacle, which was caused by cleaning up after the Mullins debacle. Derek and his idiot brother screwed that up too. He probably should have called his uncle on that one but it would have been the same complications, only earlier. So, he'd pay these three off, get them out of the country, and it was over. He'd have it all back. Then, time to spread more fertilizer and grow the garden back.

He pushed open the door and ambled in on his aching feet. The three kidnappers looked up in surprise but only Derek got to his feet.

"What are you doing here? This isn't the plan, you're not supposed to be here!"

"I didn't have much of a choice, you imbecile," Malcolm

snarled. "The cops are breathing down on my neck. They showed up at the hotel!"

Derek dropped his head, shaking it as he did. "You fucking idiot."

Mal gritted his teeth. "You're calling *me* an idiot? *I* didn't fuck this up, pal. *You* did that all by yourself."

Derek looked back up again. "How do you know they were there for you?"

Malcolm's jaw clamped shut with an audible click. He didn't. They could have been there to talk to Angie. "Damn it."

"And you panicked." Derek laughed. "Man, why don't you just paint a neon sign over your head that says, 'come get me, pigs, I'm guilty.'"

"You son of a bitch—"

"Face it, asshole, *you* screwed up." Derek edged closer. "If they didn't know you were guilty before, they damn sure know now. Jackass!"

Malcolm found his bravado and got nose to nose with the moron. "At least *I* didn't get my own brother thrown in jail. At least *I* didn't screw up a simple murder for hire."

"*That* wasn't our fault," Derek growled back. "You *said* he wouldn't be watched. You *said* you could get us in and out with no witnesses. So who screwed *that* up, huh?"

"I told you there would be cameras and security, you asshole. That's why I got you the goddamn rifle with the laser scope! So you could take care of him from a distance!"

"*Bullshit!* I took care of your fuckin' witness, asshole. And *you* fucked up with that senator all by yourself."

"You bastard!" Malcolm was seething, angry enough that his fists were shaking. "That's it! I want this done and the fucking lot of you out of the country. This...is...*over!*"

"Fine," Derek practically screamed. "Is our money in the account?"

"I couldn't get to the damned computer room. The cops were guarding it!"

Derek just smiled and stood back a bit. He pulled out his cell phone. "Here, be my guest."

"I can use my own, you idiot. If I use *your* phone to do this, they can trace the call and the transaction to me!"

"So what! It's a ransom, shit heels. You're ransoming 'em."

"And they trace it to your phone," Malcolm shouted. "Which connects you to me! And you're in the goddamn jail! Use your fucking head for more than a hat rack!"

Derek raised his fist but Mal was faster. He held up his phone. Derek got the point and backed off. Malcolm pulled out his wallet, to find the card with the numbers.

But it wasn't there.

"No...oh God, no!" He laid the phone on the table and began to empty his wallet, tossing schedules, phone numbers, and dollar bills aside like trash. It wasn't there at all. The card was gone.

Then, he remembered. The same thought had crossed his mind back at the hotel. Phoning the bank seemed innocent enough. Like Derek said, he was paying a ransom. He'd dialed the bank, waiting to get through the endless menu...setting the card down....

"Oh sweet Mother of God. No, oh God, no!"

"He's backing out, man. I told you he would."

Mal felt Derek come close, standing at his side.

"No he's not, Butch. Because he knows that if he does, I'll

take care of his buddy and friends."

Mal threw his glance back at Derek. "Friends? What friends?"

"Make the fuckin' call."

"I can't."

"Yes you can."

"No, you asshole, I can't. I left the card at the hotel!"

"So, what," Derek cajoled. "I got the four-one-one right here on this card. You call and you use this one."

Malcolm sighed his frustrations. "No, you insipid, imbecilic, son of a bitch!" He wheeled on Derek. "Don't you get it? If they search my room, I'm fucked. That card has the name of the bank in the Caymans, the account number, and they can tie me to you! You fool, we're done for!"

The man's grin reminded Malcolm of a shark, just before the attack. The teeth were white and ragged, looking larger than life. For a moment, he could almost imagine what it would feel like to have those teeth bite down into his flesh, ripping and tearing along the way.

"Looks like you're going down, dude!"

"YOU BASTARD," Mal screamed at the top of his lungs.

His fists came out, his fingers shaped into claws. He was going to kill the son of a bitch and damn the two men behind him. But as his hands flew out, as Derek reached forward to grab at him, they were both shocked in to stillness.

There was a heavy banging at the inner door, the one where Derek and friends were keeping Thom and the bitch.

"Malcolm? Mal? Are you out there? Is that you? You son of a bitch, is that you?"

Thom!

"Oh God, he can't know I'm out here."

"Mal!! I heard you! If that's you—"

"I gotta get out of here."

But it was too late. Mal turned to the door. It was time to face the music.

Walt's head was splitting but at least he could sit up. He was feeling a little better. Especially since Missy hadn't left his side. She was napping now, her head against his chest. Jo had evidently decided a nap was a good idea too. She'd lain down beside Mitchell with her head on his thigh. It was just the two men now, holding vigil and not speaking. Until—

"So?"

He looked over at Mitchell. "So what?"

"You're sure they're coming?"

Walt nodded. "I know they are, man."

Mitchell scrubbed his face with his hand. "I hate waiting."

"I know," Walt said. "Me too."

"It's not what you think, you know."

Walt tightened up in his chest. "I saw you."

"Look, she was upset. All I did was give her a peck on the cheek. Trying to comfort her, show her it was all over. We were safe."

Walt squinted in the dimmed light. "She...."

Mitchell had a small smile on his face. "She's like my daughter, you know? Gets worked up so easy. With Lisa, all I had to do was tell her it was over, tell her it was all okay. She gets worked up easy but she calms down easy. She just needs someone to be strong for her, you know?"

He looked down at the lady sleeping with her back tucked tightly against his leg. Mitchell reached out to stroke her hair.

"Now this lady, she's not like that. She's fragile but she's so strong. She pulled me back from that damn shooting. She took a standing ashtray and beat the fuck out of that mugger. She calls me Jared sometimes. Because...because she knows me, the *real* me. Not the pop star." He looked back up at Walt. "Do you really think I would jeopardize that?"

Walt watched the singer stroking Jo's hair with such tenderness, such love. He leaned his head back again, at peace at last. He believed. He'd have to let Missy know, make it up to her for not believing her. But first, he had to tell Mitchell. "I—"

They both heard the shouting, both turned to the door to look. After a few moments, Mitchell's face turned red. He abruptly stood up, which roused Jo from her doze.

"Thom?"

Mitchell ignored her as he walked over to the door. He stood, still as stone, listening. Then, he shook his head, his fists balling and relaxing, balling and relaxing. His lips were moving, muttering to himself.

Jo sat up, wiping her eyes with her grimy hands. "Thom?"

Missy was awake, blinking her own beautiful eyes. "Walt? What's wrong?"

"Shh," he whispered. "I don't know."

Without warning, Mitchell raised both of his fists and started pounding on the door. "Malcolm? Mal? Are you out there? Is that you? You son of a bitch, is that you?"

Out of the corner of his eye, Walt saw Jo's expression. It seemed to flow from stunned to triumphant to something that could pass for guilt to anger. And all through it, Mitchell was still pounding on the door.

"Mal!! I heard you! If that's you—"

"Thom," Jo called out to him.

That time, he heard her. He backed away from the door. Walt could see the moisture on his cheeks.

"That must be Mr. Ross," Missy whispered. "The police were asking about him at the hotel."

"Asking?" Walt whispered back.

She nodded. "I think they suspect him."

Jo came up to Mitchell; put her hands on his face. "Thom, look at me."

He never had the chance. The door opened and in walked a man dressed in a casual business suit. Mitchell's face went white and a look of fury crossed it. Walt looked back at the man coming in the door.

"Hello, Thommy."

56

HEARING THAT VOICE on the other side of the door punched Thom in the soul so hard that he was sure to be feeling the after-effects for the rest of his life. After vehemently denying it to Jo, he had to stand there, listen to that voice...and know that she'd been right all along.

No, man, he's here to pay the ransom, that's all.

And on the heels of that thought came another, an even darker one. *Quit being such a foolish ass and accept the fact that your best friend has been lying to you for years. Are you so blind that you can't see the truth when it's right in front of your eyes? Or is it that you've seen it all along and just didn't want to accept it?*

Everything came crashing down around his ears, every bit of it. Every lie he'd caught Mal in and accepted the explanation for. Every moment when he'd felt that Mal was holding something back from him. Every time he'd asked to see his bank account statements and he let Mal turn him aside. Every guarded look that the crew gave him when Mal was around. Every time Angie said not to trust him, not to believe everything he heard. It all came down with a severe implosion. A single finger pointing back to himself for being such a fool, such a naïve fool.

Guns? They were talking about guns? Guns meant killing. They were talking about a murder that Mal arranged. Whose murder? Why? Arrangements and deals. How long? How fucking long had this been going on? And why? Why did Mal want him kidnapped? Money? More guns? Why? Why did he do this? *How* could he do this?

And now, staring at the man as he stood in the doorway. Now that he was in the same room with the man that he *thought* was his friend. Even now, that part of him wanted to forgive Mal. And this time? This time, there couldn't be any redemption.

"Thommy."

"Don't *ever* call me that again, you son of a bitch," Thom spat out. "You set this up, didn't you. You set this all up."

"Thom, you gotta listen to me."

"I don't have to do shit," he screamed.

Mal shut up immediately, looking down at the floor. He breathed a great sigh and came into the room completely. How could Thom have missed it? The click, click, click of Mal's shoes. It had been there all along. Every time they'd walked across the hotel lobby, the ballroom floor at dinner. The metal studs in his heels, clicking against the wooden floors. When Mal looked up again, he looked over Thom's shoulder. He had to have caught sight of Walt and Missy because he had a quick, panicky look on his face. It passed quickly as he turned his gaze back to Thom.

Thom took a deep breath, slowly letting it out. He relaxed his hands, let them drop to his sides. He licked his lips and asked, "Why?"

Mal had to know that he was caught, that this was it. He had only one option, the truth. "Wasn't supposed to be you." He looked around the room. He pointed to the other side of the room now. "Just her. It was only supposed to be her."

Thom glanced at Jo. "I'll say it again. Why?"

"She's bad news, Thommy." He caught the glare that Thom was throwing at him. "Thom," he corrected. "I knew that from the first time I laid eyes on her, she was bad news. You deserved better. You always deserved better."

"And the fact that I love her? That means nothing?"

Mal chuckled. "Love. My friend, you fall in love like the rest of us breathe. It was always going to be an endless stream of women. Love? I really doubt that."

"Then, you don't know me like you thought you did, asshole."

Mal winced. "Asshole. After everything I've ever done for you? After everything we've meant to each other? That's a little strong, don't you think?"

"I think it's not strong enough," Thom answered. "How could you *do* this to me?"

"How? Oh God, the question is more like how could I not?" Mal tugged at his ear, a low chuckle as he spoke. "I kept your secrets, buried your bodies. I even committed murder for you. Did you even know about it? Remember a damned thing? About Mullins and that fucking guard of his?"

That caught him unaware. "What? Phil died in the car accident. The guard? What the fuck are you talking about?"

Mal chewed on his lip for a moment, shuffled a foot. "God, you are— What the fuck, you were drunk. No, you were past drunk, you'd swallowed so much Jack Daniels that your blood alone could have made a wino happy."

"The accident."

"Yes, damn it, the accident. Jesus, Thom, you really think Phil died in that accident?" Mal shook his head, stuffing one hand in his pocket and running the other through his hair. "Thom, you ignorant asshole, *you* were the one driving that night. *You* were the one who hit the fucking moose and went off the road into that tree."

The air left his body and Thom was left gasping. No, no, that couldn't be true.

"You called me on the cell, told me you were in a hell of a mess. Told me where you were. Told me Phil was bleeding and you needed help. I was the one that talked you out of calling the ambulance, you idiot. I told you I had called them. Remember?"

The black curtain across his mind was starting to lift a little. Words...voices...drifting in and out. His own voice, crying in that thickly drunk way that all alcoholics have in the throes of their illness. Maybe he didn't remember details but it was feeling so familiar.

"You had a concussion, Thom. You didn't sleep through a black out, you had a concussion. I had a private physician come to your house and check you out. Hell, Angela knew."

"Angie...knew?"

"She helped me! All I had to do was pull Mullins over to the other side of the car and get you in mine. Take you home and let Angela put you back together. I made her swear to the lie so that no one would suspect you at all."

"You...I fled the scene?"

"No," Malcolm answered with a huff. "I dragged you to the car. You were fucking out of it by then."

"Phil...."

"Was mumbling your name, Thom. He was so fucked up, he was dying anyway. He damned sure wasn't feeling anything. But he was mumbling your name. I couldn't have him dying in some emergency room and saying your name to anyone there. Too many questions and the answers would have put you in jail."

"Phil...."

"I left him there and let him die, to keep him from naming you." Mal's voice took on a pleading tone now. "Don't you see? Mullins knew you were driving. Hell, that guard knew. I had to take care of him. I tried money but he told me to go to hell. He was going to go to the police when the funeral was over. I couldn't let him live that long."

Thom's malaise and shock was wearing off. Bits and pieces of memory were coming through now, like stills and sound bytes. A radio in his head, talking about Phil's death at the wheel of his car. A stretch of back road through the mountains. A huge beast in the middle of the road. Then the thumps, the slamming of the car. Blood spraying across the inside of the car now. The vision of white as his face burrowed into it. *Thom... help...Thom...help....* Another voice now. *Scott...dead...Mullins' guard...shot...car accident....*

When he looked back up into Mal's face, there was only emptiness, guilt, and anger in his heart. "You killed them both. *You killed them both!*"

Thom rushed forward so fast that everything else in the cabin blurred. He grabbed Mal by the throat, shaking him so hard that the man was turning red and then purple, his teeth chattering. Mal grabbed at his hands, trying to free himself. Thom gripped on tight, shaking harder and harder, screaming, *"You killed them both!!"*

It took Walt, Jo, and Missy to loosen his hands and pull him back. The thugs had grabbed Mal, separating the two. The one called Derek had a look of pure amusement on his face. Mal shook free and came back to his original place. Thom wasn't so lucky, they weren't going to let him go.

"Why? Why, Mal? What the fuck did I ever do to you? What?

How could you do this to me?"

"Are you serious, Thom?" he shouted. "I did this to cover your ass. I kept you out of jail!"

Thom shouted back. "He wouldn't have died if you'd called the police, called the ambulance like you said you had!"

"And you'd be in prison for DUI and reckless endangerment, you idiot! He was dying anyway. That's vehicular manslaughter. One to twenty five in the pen! No career, no music, no fans, just a dead senator and the end!"

"So what?" Thom screamed. "My conscience would be clear. Look what you made me! *Look what you made me!*"

Mal suddenly stopped, panting as he stared at Thom. "Made you? What *I* made you? I only made you a success, superstar. The greatest single album sales nationally and internationally. I only cared for you like...like...."

"You never cared for me," Thom spat out. "All you ever cared for was the money and the connections; me, you don't give a damn about."

"That's not true!"

"Of course it's true. If my career was going nowhere, you'd have dropped me like a bad habit. I brought you success and fortune. I put you in the same place with senators and congressmen, with presidents!"

"No! That's not it, no!"

"Of course it is," Thom screamed again, spittle flying from his lips. "You don't give a damn about me!"

"Thom, yes I do, I've always cared about you."

"Bullshit!"

"I'm in love with you, goddamn it!"

The room was deathly still, the silence enveloping them all.

Thom didn't have to look around to see the shocked looks on their faces. He felt it on his own. He couldn't breathe, found that he didn't want to.

"I'm in love with you," Mal repeated again.

They let go of him but it didn't matter. Thom couldn't move a muscle. "Fuck you!"

Tears slipped down Mal's cheeks. "Don't you see? Everything I have ever done was because I loved you. Because I was in love with you. I saved your marriage, Thom. I helped you adopt those kids. And when you wanted your own child, even after the doctors said it would never happen, I gave you the gift of my...*I* was the sperm donor, not you!"

Thom felt the fury rising. "You...you...."

"*I* kept Angela in her place when she tried to hurt you. *I* was the one who found the evidence against Sandy when she was screwing around on you. *I* helped you get those divorces without having to pay out the ass in alimony. *I* hid your money in special accounts so that those bitches would never be able to touch it. Touch the legacy of Thom Mitchell!"

"Son of a...!"

"I preserved it all, Thom. The dream. I kept your dream going, I made it live." Mal was spitting the words out through clenched teeth. "All for you, all because of my love for you! I just wanted you to love me back a little!"

"*Now* who doesn't know about love."

Malcolm stared at him, verbally slapped, nothing coming out of his mouth.

And in his head, all he could see was Phil's sightless eyes and bruised face. The thought of his friend left to die on the streets alone was more than he could bear. The guard? Him too? Keeping his wives in line? Finding evidence against Sandy? Hurting Angie?

The anger welled up inside of him. With a growl, he leaped forward again and this time, he let his fists do the talking. He began to lay into Mal with all of his fury, punching and kicking. They tussled, Mal striking back as hard as he could, both of them bouncing off the walls of the cabin. In the background, he heard Jo screaming his name, begging him to stop. But he couldn't. Right now, he didn't give a damn about his hands. He just wanted pay back. He heard Missy yelling Walt's name over and over. He heard shouting and yelling.

Then, he felt Mal's hands around his throat as he was bounced off the wall again. Thom grabbed his forearms and started to squeeze, trying to drive his fingers into the meat. He punched with one hand, then pushed with the other.

Now he saw what Missy was screaming at. Walt was tackling Butcher, trying to take him down. They were brawling themselves, landing punches. Derek was amused, but the gun in his hand was aimed at Walt. Without thinking, Thom ducked Mal's next punch, tripped Walt to knock him down on the floor, then dove into the bodyguard's middle, just as the shot rang out. Both men landed on the floor, rolling away from each other.

Thom rolled on to his back and sat up, ready to do battle again. But Mal stood stock still, a shocked expression on his face. He looked down, his hand coming to his chest and pressing against the flesh. When he pulled it back, Thom saw the blood dripping from his fingers and running down the front of his shirt.

Jo seized that moment and pulled the kerosene tank out of the heater. A stream of liquid flowed before the shut off could cut on. The stream caught the flame and the dry kindling caught next. The fire began to spread as Jo pulled the cap off the tank and started dousing the walls. The three men started roaring, turning to run. But Walt and Thom were faster. Walt laid a hard punch on Neil who tripped over Mal's body and fell flat on the floor. Thom knocked the gun out of Derek's hand and landed a sucker punch in the man's middle. Jo was close enough that she bashed Mike in the face with the now empty kerosene tank.

There was nothing but shouting and the heat from the fire.

"Come on," Walt shouted, grabbing Thom's arm. "We gotta get out of here, come on."

Thom took Jo's hand as Walt herded Missy through the door. They took advantage of the panic and ran straight out the door and headed into the woods.

Derek finally shut the other two up. "We gotta get out of here, this whole thing is gonna go up."

The other two ran for the door but Derek stopped them.

"Neil, get him. Get the body out of here."

"Are you nuts, Derek? Let him fry in here! No evidence."

"Except the rangers will find a corpse. This cabin belonged to my old man, his name is on the deed. If they track the name, they find me. And if they find me, they find you."

Neil and Mike picked up Ross' body and the three of them made it outside again, coughing and sputtering. Derek turned back just in time to see the dry wood of the cabin completely in flames.

"Mother fucker! That'll raise the rangers."

"So?" Butch asked. "What do we do?"

Derek tossed the keys to Neil. "Take that asshole down to

the limo and dump him in it. He left that senator to die alone, let him do the same. By the time they find him, we'll be gone. Dump him in the limo and meet us at the old apartment. We'll split from there."

"What are *you* gonna be doing?"

Derek looked out at the footprints that receded into the undergrowth. "Well, asshole there didn't give us our money. So that means we can't afford witnesses." He turned back to Neil. "You get rid of that body. Me and Mike are gonna get rid of these four. Now go."

Neil picked up the corpse-to-be and slung it over his shoulders, carrying it to the four-wheel drive. Derek and Mike pulled their guns and went in after the escaping marks.

57

THEY ENDED UP taking Jim's four-wheel drive, the only thing that would make it up the logging roads. With two of the Carroll police and three state cruisers in tow, they were speeding down the road as fast as they could. Jim knew where he was going, so Tony was glad to let him take the lead.

About five miles out, they turned off the sirens and ran with lights only. Sound had a funny way of traveling up here, bouncing off the peaks and going far distances. If there were bad guys up on that mountain, the last thing they needed to do was clue them in with the sirens. They rode the last five miles in silence, not even talking in the car.

What grabbed Jim's attention was the speed at which the vehicle crossed the road in front of him. He saw it in the distance, as it darted across the two lane, and disappeared behind an old abandoned building. He put on his emergency flashers and hit the brakes, slowing as fast as he dared and still not set the tires squealing. The three state cars went flying around them. The Carroll cruisers stopped.

Jim jumped out of the car while Tony radioed the troopers and told them to circle back. He pulled his gun and motioned for his men to run around to the left of the building. Jim started around to the right. He walked as quietly as he could across the gravel, walking on the parts that looked as if they'd been tamped down by foot traffic already. He was only halfway back when he saw the truck that had cut across.

He slowly and quietly crept closer to the back side of the building. Tony joined him, both of them silent and watching. It was one of their suspects, working the trunk of a limo. They watched as Butcher worked the lock until it clicked loudly. The trunk lid popped up a couple of inches and Butcher opened it the rest of the way.

They ducked back as he ran back to his truck, the passenger side door. From where they stood, they couldn't see more than his head and shoulders. But one thing Jim did see was that he was tugging at something, exerting a lot of energy trying to pull something out of the vehicle. He seemed to pull something up over his head, hoisting it up on his shoulder. He stood back up and Jim heard the door slam, probably kicked closed.

When he came around the front of his vehicle, Jim got a real good look at what the man was carrying—a body. He watched Butcher lean down and hoist it into the trunk. He waited for a few seconds as Butcher was about to slam the lid down.

"Freeze, asshole, you're busted," Jim roared.

Butcher glared over his shoulder but remained motionless. Jim and Tony pointed their guns at the man, while the uniformed lads came up behind him. It was a matter of seconds before Butcher was on his knees with the cuffs around his wrists.

"Neil, buddy, bet you never thought you'd see me again," Jim said jovially.

"Fuck off, asshole."

"Now, that's rude. That's just flat out rude." Jim patted the man's shoulder. "And here we went to all this trouble to make you feel wanted."

"Jim," Tony called out. "You better come here and see this."

Jim peered into the trunk. "I'll be damned. The late Mr. Ross."

"Except he's not so late. He will be if we don't do anything but he's still living." Tony turned to call out over his shoulder. "Reilly, call the state boys back and then get an ambulance out here. I think Mr. Butcher can have a seat in the back of your car."

Jim hunkered down by their prisoner. "Okay, bud. Here's the deal. You tell me where Mitchell is and I won't kick your ass from here to Maine and back."

"You won't touch me, asshole. I got rights."

"Oh yeah, you got rights. Sure," Jim answered cheerfully. "You got the right to get your ass kicked by me. If you give up that right, you'll get it kicked by my partner over there. But since he's the one with the steel toed boots, bro, I think you're better off with me."

"I ain't telling you shit."

"It's called a deal, numb nuts." Jim holstered his weapon. "You tell me about Mitchell and his girlfriend and who shot that guy and you might just see a lot less time in the slam."

"Fuck you! I want my Miranda!"

Jim grinned. "Hey, Tony. You hear this? He wants his Miranda!"

Tony laughed. "Neil, I hate to be the bearer of bad tidings, but you're not under arrest. *Yet!*"

"Huh?"

Jim crouched down next to Butcher. "See, we're not exactly in our jurisdiction, dude. So, we can't arrest your ass. *But* we can detain you until the proper authorities arrive. So, I don't *have* to Mirandize you. Dig?"

"So you can't use this in court. It's hearsay!"

"Maybe," Jim answered with a shrug. "But you help me with

my case and I can help you with yours."

"Derek will kill me."

"We'll put you in another prison. Make it so you don't do your time in the federal pen. What's it gonna be?"

God, he loved it when they rolled over like a dog. Ten minutes later, the ambulance was on its way, one state car and the Carroll guys were staying with the patient and the prisoner. Tony, Jim, and the other two state cars were on their way up Wilde.

58

THOM HAD NO idea how far they'd gone. Given the fact that they weren't following any kind of a trail and considering the conditions they were tromping around in, he was willing to bet it wasn't very far. But he was starting to get tired. And Walt was pale, which wasn't surprising after Missy had confirmed a mild concussion for him.

They came to a small clearing and stopped to take a rest before Thom spoke. "Where are we?"

Walt shook his head gingerly. "I can't see direction in this thicket."

"Me either," Thom said grimly.

"They're right on us, you know."

"Yeah. And I think we have only another hour or two of sunlight."

Walt put a hand to his temple, massaging the skin. "I got an idea."

"What?" Thom asked.

"We split up. I'll take Missy and head out that way."

Thom nodded. "I'll take Jo and we'll head out toward the falls. First sign of a chopper, wave. We'll get help and get the fuck out of here."

Walt nodded.

"Walt? Are you sure you shouldn't be laying down?" Missy looked scared.

"I can't, honey. We gotta shake these guys." He looked at

Thom. "It'll be easier if we split up."

"Agreed," Thom answered. "You keep low, buddy. Okay? Take care of that lady of yours."

"You too...Thom." Walt put his hand out tentatively.

Thom smiled and took it, shaking it with a firm grip. "Good luck." He took Jo's hand and they were off.

59

DEREK MANAGED TO find the footprints of the humans amidst the tracks of moose. Their boots left far more distinctive patterns. Mike had pointed them out as they ran out of the burning cabin. Derek tracked them into the underbrush and they were chasing as fast as they dared.

Even with the density of the forest, sound traveled. Periodically, he would stop and just listen. Besides Rudner's heavy breathing, he could hear the sounds of brush being displaced. Somewhere ahead, the sounds of twigs snapping and limbs violently returning to a natural resting state of being filtered back to his ears. In fact, all he had to do was close his eyes and wait. And he could figure out the direction.

With that, Derek took off again with Mike behind him. He had a feeling that he knew exactly where they were going. All he had to do was get close enough...close...enough....

It got quiet. Derek stopped again. He had to have lost his bearings somehow. He looked down at the forest floor and saw the tracks not five feet off to the side. He put a finger to his lips and motioned for Rudner to follow him. Derek stopped listening and started tracking.

The terrain was a bitch, trying to get around large roots and rocks, steep inclines that suddenly turned and started in another direction with a steep decline. Derek followed the boot tracks, never walking *in* them but to the side. They were shuffling in their tracks, maybe to get away.

They won't, I know this place. You ain't going nowhere that I won't find you.

There was another clearing coming up. Derek followed the prints to a patch just outside. The foot trails split up in two directions.

"Looks like two of 'em headed off to the falls," he muttered.

"What about the other two?"

"Looks like they're head off to that old logging trail, heads up to Franklin's Notch and out to the station."

"So, what do we do?"

Derek thought a moment. Then, he answered. "You follow that set there and head up to the falls. I'll follow this set." He turned back to Rudner. "You got your gun?"

Mike nodded and held up the semi-automatic.

"Good. Shoot to kill. No witnesses."

They split up and headed off to finish the business at hand.

60

ADAM EASED INTO his car and just sat. This had to have been what the Templars felt at finding the Holy Grail. Or what Marie Curie felt when she discovered polonium. This was quite possibly the biggest story to hit this sleepy little burg and it was his, all his. He had the exclusive on the whole thing. Angela Mitchell had spilled her guts about everything. *Everything.* Why? Didn't matter. The fact was that she had. All he had to do was write this. His hands were trembling at the prospect. He reached down and turned the key, the motor catching and purring to a start.

There was a crackling noise as his scanner sparked into operation. He'd forgotten it was on, so he reached down to turn it off. He had to think. But the damn thing was auto-cycling through the channels.

"—Dispatch One, do you read?"

"Station D, I read. Over."

"D, we've got reports of a fire on Wilde. Repeat, reports of a fire on Wilde. Do you copy?"

"Uh, copy that, Dispatch One. Scrambling now. Out"

There was another garble of static as the scanner cycled.

"All squads, all squads. This is not a test. We have fire reported on Wilde, co-ordinates D12 and J16. Repeat, fire on Wilde, co-ordinates D12 and J16. Dispatching paramedic units and ground crew. I need the bird in the air. Over."

"D, this is Chopper Alpha. Bird is in the air. Repeat. Bird is in the air. Over."

"Copy, Alpha. Gimme a spotter QSK."

"Copy. Alpha out."

"Station D, this is Rescue CT104, we are on route. We had ground call. One man shot, possible situation on the mountain. Do you read?"

"Uh, 104, did you say shot?"

"That's an affirm, D. We have gunshot wound at the base. Over."

"Do you need LifeFlight? Over."

"That's an affirm. Over."

"Dispatching LifeFlight. Out."

Another garble of static.

"Uh, Station D, this is Carroll Police unit, D23. Detective Garrison speaking, do you read?"

"Copy, Detective, how can I assist?"

"We're headed up on mountain. Receiving GPS signal, I imagine you got it too."

"That's an affirm, detective. Rangers are dispatched to that location. Over."

"Good. I need you to put in a call to the State...." There was static on the line, then it cleared. "...we're gonna need at least three more squads. We have...."

"Detective, your signal is breaking up. Repeat last transmission."

"We have possible kidnapping victims on the mountain. Dispatch state police. Signal is fading, we're in...."

"Detective?"

Silence.

"Detective?"

Silence. Then more static.

"Station D calling Station SP20, do you read?"

It went on and on and on, like that. Dispatching police units and air ambulances, fire crews and volunteers. Whatever was going on up there, he needed to be there too.

But his story....

Screw it; this was another story. He'd have an exclusive here. Hell, he'd have *two* exclusives! He paused long enough to call the boss, to say where he was going. Adam threw his vehicle into gear and tore off. He'd just make it if he floored it!

61

WALT TOOK MISSY'S hand and they left Jo and Thom behind. He had no clue where those scumbags were and he didn't particularly care to find out. The goal was to evade them and get out of this section of the forest. If they could find an aid station or a rangers' station, they could find provisions and a radio. Walt's GPS had gone off with all the crap and the fighting. Someone was coming.

If his head just wasn't pounding so hard, feeling each beat of his heart. His stomach was starting to flip flop a little. He swallowed a lot and willed it down but it surely wasn't cooperating. He forced himself to keep going. All he had to do was get to the Notch. If he could get them there, they could take the trail to the rangers' station. Get help. He tripped on a root, stumbling a few steps to try and keep his balance. He felt the hand on his elbow, pulling him back upright enough so that he could grab the tree and steady himself. When he looked to his left, he saw Missy's concerned face.

"Walt?"

Her hand came to rest on his arm and he nodded. "I'm okay."

"No, you're not," she told him. "You're so pale and you're sweating."

"Come on, Missy, we're running. Of course I'm sweating."

"No, Walt. Not that kind of sweating." She pushed him back to lean against the tree. "Walt, your eyes look...I mean...you have a mild concussion, Walt. You need to rest for a while."

"We can't, Missy. We gotta keep going. We gotta hit that ranger's station. It's our only chance."

"How far is it?" she asked.

He blinked the funny filmy haze away from his vision and started to look around, to get his bearings. Nothing seemed familiar. He looked up, trying to peer through the leafy ceiling and find out which way was east or west, at least. The sunlight was diffused in the overhead. They were lost. He had no clue where the trail was, no clue where the Notch was. He willed himself to not panic. But his heart was trip-hammering in his chest.

He pointed in the direction that he'd meant on heading towards. "That way. We gotta go that way."

"Walt, please."

"Missy," he hissed. "If we don't keep moving, those bastards will find us. They got guns, remember?"

She paid no mind to his anger. "Then, let's slow down a little. Come on, Walt, you're not doing your head any good and you're only making it worse." She surveyed the area too. "Can't we do a zigzag pattern? Throw them off a bit?"

He leaned his head back against the prickly bark. Scratching at the back of his head, the pain seemed to keep him awake. He wanted so badly to do as she asked, to sit down and sleep a little. Let his head stop pounding. Let the queasiness in his belly abate. Taking her hand in his, he stood up suddenly.

"Come on, then. We'll zigzag. We'll slow down a little."

He really did try to slow down. But it wasn't long before they were moving fast again. They moved as quietly as they could, walking over dead tree bark and fallen twigs. The crackling sounded like gun shots. Sleep, God how he wanted to just fall asleep right now. But he had to keep Missy safe, had to keep her...keep her....

"Stop," he grunted.

"What is it?"

He pushed her by a tall birch and turned around to vomit into a bush. That done, his legs gave way and he sat down hard. His vision blurred.

"That's it," she muttered. "You sit right here. Don't move, okay? Just don't move."

No problem, he thought, leaning back against the tree. Truth was, he couldn't move if he'd wanted to. Maybe he could just close his eyes a little. Maybe...maybe he could take a little nap, to ease his head. The world greyed out as his eyes lost their focus, everything swimming in a blur of green.

"Walt? Honey, wake up? Walt?"

He blinked a few times but the gauzy feel to the world wouldn't go away this time. "Missy?"

"Shh," she whispered. "Here, drink this."

He felt the papery texture of bark against his lips and tried to jerk his head back. "What is that?"

"I hear a spring nearby, running water. I got you some. It tastes a little funny but it's clean."

"Missy, no...parasites. Need...need tablets."

"Yeah, well, Girl Scout training says if the water is running, your chances are better. So, drink a little. If I'm wrong, we'll dose with the Pepto later. Come on."

He did as he was told and promptly threw it back up. She sighed a little, but made him drink a little more. This time, smaller sips. This time it stayed down. She disappeared again, then came back with more. This time, she poured it over his head, letting it run down through his hair and into his shirt. That was going to be freezing cold later when the sun went down. But for now, it felt good. She disappeared a third time and came back with a bit more.

He was able to see that she'd fashioned a cup out of some bark she'd found. It was downright clever, to be honest. She pressed the makeshift drinking vessel to his lips again.

"Slow sips now, that's it."

"Mis—" He swallowed another small bit, then turned his head to the side. When he looked back, she had this odd look on her face. "What is it?"

"Why have you never let me do this?"

"What?"

"Take care of you? Like this?" She smoothed the hair out of his eyes. "You're always being so strong, so commanding. You never let me see this side of you."

Her eyes were so beautiful right now, gazing into his soul like that. The words just flowed from his mouth. "I don't know how," he said. "I've never known how."

With a sweet smile, she leaned into him and kissed his lips softly. "Then, perhaps I need to teach you."

A second later, they heard the report of a gun and the bark flicked off the tree over their heads. It was quickly followed by two more shots. More bark flicked off before they could move. Walt pulled himself back together and rolled over to his left side, yanking Missy down with him. He put a hand over her mouth to quiet her, then nodded with his head in a direction away from the pops of the gunshots.

He pushed her ahead of him, following along with her

gorgeous backside in his face. They crawled for a length along the floor of the forest, making as wide a distance as they could. Walt made it twenty feet before grasping the waistband of her shorts to stop her. Neither of them moved for a minute, then two.

She looked back at him. "Is he gone?" she whispered.

He shrugged. He listened a little longer. There was nothing. They'd have to risk it. He pulled himself up to a standing position, grabbing onto a branch to act as leverage. She stood up beside him, helping him. The world threatened to grey out again, so he pinched himself in the groin area. The pain brought him back swiftly.

"Come on," he whispered.

They took off again, always conscious that the gunman was behind them, stalking them. Walt kept them to the thicker parts, where the brush had grown wild in place and covered their exits. The son of a bitch had to be close; or maybe he was far, Walt couldn't tell. They had to keep moving.

It was another five or ten moments before Missy stopped. Walt was still feeling woozy, if less dehydrated, and not watching where he was going. He bounced into her, almost knocking her down. She merely smiled and steadied him. She pointed ahead. Twenty paces beyond was the trail. They'd found it.

"You wait here," she said. "I'll go make sure the way is clear."

"That's supposed to be my job," he grumbled.

"Just wait, Grumpy," she said and leaned him up against a birch. She quickly ran off.

He wanted to throw up again. The water was sloshing around in his middle, stirring things up. His head was really pounding now, he could feel the blood pulsing in his temples.

This was interminable. They were never going to make that damn station. They were never going to get out of here.

"There you are, asshole!"

One punch knocked him flat on the floor. Two hands reached down, grabbing his shirt by the lapels and pulling him to his feet.

"Fucker, you think you're gonna get away?"

Unmindful of his own splitting headache, Walt grabbed the other man's shirt and drove his palm into the man's nose. He relished the sound of the breaking cartilage and the scream of pain. He threw a punch, hoping to land it somewhere on the man's body, and missed completely. The kidnapper grabbed the fist as it flew past and yanked out and up. Walt felt his arm wrench out of his shoulder socket, dislocating it. He tripped and fell face first into the carpet of needles, decayed leaves, and twigs.

Moaning in pain, he rolled over. The man that they'd called Derek was standing in front of him, gun drawn and aimed right at Walt's head.

"You fuckin' son of a bitch, you broke my nose!"

"Should have broke your fuckin neck," Walt growled. "Asshole."

"Well, not a problem for much longer!" Derek flicked the safety on the gun. "Say goodbye, asshole."

Before Walt could come back with an obscene epithet, he saw a blur out of the corner of his eye. A tree branch flew up, knocking the man's arm straight up. His finger squeezed the trigger and several shots went wild into the air. Missy screamed a primordial sound and lunged at him. Her face had been twisted with anger and something almost feral. She swung the branch with precision, bashing the man as he tried to back away from her.

"You bastard, you leave him alone! I'll kill you! You leave him alone!" she screamed over and over.

For every blow she rained down on Derek, more blood squirted from another wound caused by the rough and sharp edges of the limb. She had worked herself into a fury and finally worked him down into a crouch. Derek stopped protesting, his face gashed, bruised, and dazed. With one last swing of the limb, she knocked him out as cold as a mountain lake. The force of her blow shattered the limb, leaving her breathless and speechless.

Walt could only lay there, watching her in amazement. It took her seconds to recover and she pulled one of her shoelaces to bind the man's hands. Tying them tight behind him, she rushed over to Walt.

"Shh, lay still, honey, okay?" she murmured to him. "I heard someone coming up the trail. You stay here."

He tried to call out to her but the water came rushing out of his mouth. He finished purging it, then lay back on the ground. He didn't have long to wait. Missy came rushing back with three men. Two were state police. He didn't recognize the third but obviously Missy knew him.

"Detective, here...he's hurt."

The curly headed man leaned down where Walt could see him. "Hi there. You're okay. I'm Jim Garrison. Me and the guys are gonna get you to the hospital. You're gonna be just fine."

Walt let the blackness take over and he dropped down into unconsciousness.

62

IT HAD BEEN several minutes since they'd heard the shots. Thom felt the hope falling into the pit of his stomach. Missy, Walt—those shots didn't forebode well.

"Shit! Damn!" Jo went down hard, clutching her ankle and foot as soon as she landed on her butt in the dirt.

Thom had been several paces ahead of her but stopped and dashed back. "Jo. Don't move!"

She swallowed a grunted giggle, still holding on to her wounded appendage. "Like *that* is a real worry, Thom. Seriously?"

He dropped to his knees and helped pull the shoe off her foot. "Here, let me look at this." He removed the pump and the thin sock, then began to gently massage the area.

"It's okay," she muttered through gritted teeth. "I think I just turned it."

They were out in the middle of nowhere, on a mountain he'd never climbed before and only knew legends of, on a hike that they were ill prepared for. Neither of them had on their hiking clothes or shoes —they'd been dressed for a plane ride to upstate New York. He rubbed his thumb over a blister on her heel. Her poor feet were taking the worst of it, more so than his. At least his loafers had the rubber soles to them. Her flats were hard, more for looks than anything else.

"Shh," he said, trying to comfort her. "You let me take care of this. Okay?"

She nodded. But she had the look of someone about to cry.

"I ever tell you about my kids?"

She shook her head.

"My daughter, Lisa, she's the one that graduated pre-med. She's beautiful. She was the youngest, until Shelle was born. We adopted Lisa when she was about ten months old." He continued massaging her ankle. "One of her parents was Asian, the agency thought Chinese. I knew when I saw her, she was my little girl."

"You must be so proud," Jo answered, stifling a noise that sounded like a grunt of pain.

"Very. My son, Alan; he was our first. We adopted him in Australia. Took a long time and a lot of legal red tape to wade through. But we got him. He's part aborigine, see. They had a lot to say about it. His mom was insistent. Angie fell in love with him right away."

"That's much better," Jo said. "Thanks."

He paid her no mind, massaging her foot now. "We both fell in love with those kids. I think that, of everything that's happened to me, my kids have been my constant."

"Thom? Why did you adopt?"

That was a sore subject. Maybe, at his age, he needed to just spit it out and accept it.

"We couldn't have children of our own," he answered. "I... uh, have a problem."

Her hand came up to cover his. She pulled it from her foot and held it close to her heart. He couldn't look up at her, he couldn't face her yet. She didn't wait for him to."

"It's okay," she told him. "I can see it hurts. You don't have to tell me."

Now he could look up. "We wanted children, biological children. But it just wasn't meant to be. So, we adopted. I've never been sorry about that, Jo. Maybe they didn't come from my loins but they sure did come from my heart."

She reached up and touched his cheek. The light in her eyes and the sweetness of her smile told him that it didn't matter. There was nothing wrong with him, no defect. He put that little bit to rest.

"And...you called him...her...Shelle?"

"Michelle. Our little girl, Michelle. Mine and Sandy's." The wave of depression fell over him again. "I guess she isn't mine either, now."

"But you still love her, right?"

He stopped and let that wash over him. Did it really matter? Now that he knew the truth? He held a picture in his mind, his little dark haired sweety with her big brown eyes and her adorable smile. Hearing her calling him 'daddy' and the feel of her arms around his neck. He remembered her birth, how the doctor had given him the scalpel to cut the cord. Then the child was placed in his arms, to bathe her in the warm water.

When he looked back up at Jo, the tears were mingling with the smile he wore. "Oh yeah, I still love her. I don't care whose sperm. *I'm* her father, her daddy. That's *my* baby, Shelle."

She touched his cheek, then wiped the moisture from his eyes. "Then, come on. Let's get off this damned mountain so you can get back to her. And Lisa. And Allan."

He kissed her palm. "And I'm gonna be a grampa." Sliding the sock back on her foot, he followed it with the shoe. "Can you do this?"

With a nod, she took his hand and braced with the other foot. He pulled her up, then held both hands while she took the first ginger steps. There was pain, he could see that in the lines on her face. But she was damned stubborn. She was walking. They'd just have to go slower still. Because of her inexperience and their lack of proper attire, they were already going slow enough. Now....

"Come on, the falls are this way. We can follow the stream back to civilization. Maybe one of the parking lots." Actually, he had no clue where it would lead them. But, if Bear Grylls said that following a stream or river would take them to a town and people, then that's what they'd do.

She nodded and they began to make their arduous way through the forest. The roar of the falling water was getting louder. Hopefully, they were so far ahead of those bastards that they'd be okay now. They'd just have to risk it in the clearing. They were scant feet away from the end of the forest when they saw the chopper. He was torn between running for it or waiting with her. But it was help. If he ran, he could wave them down. Another second ticked by before he felt her hand in the small of his back. As if she'd read his mind.

"Hurry! Run!" she said hurriedly. "Before he gets away."

He took off at a pace, trying to push his way through the undergrowth and the krumholtz trees. He decided a straight light would be faster but it certainly wasn't going to be easier. He emerged, dashing at a full gallop, running towards the end of the falls.

"*HEY! HEY! HERE, DOWN HERE!*" he screamed, waving his arms to get the pilot's attention.

It was no use, the guy had been looking another direction.

He flew off over his head. But Thom paid attention to which way the chopper had headed off. It was back towards the cabin that they'd run from. The authorities had arrived; the GPS had drawn them. He grinned. They could find another way back. It was going to be okay.

He opened his mouth to call her, tell her it would be okay. The words never left his mouth, the breath stopping in this throat. Jo was being led out of the trees by Mike, his hand buried in her hair. Her face was twisted in pain and she was limping. She had managed to get one hand behind her head, probably trying to get him to stop pulling on her hair. The other hand grabbed at his sweatshirt, trying to keep from falling on her twisted ankle.

"Hey, old fuck. Look who I found."

"You son of a bitch, if you—"

"Yeah, yeah," Rudner huffed. "If I hurt her, you'll kill me. If I do anything to her, I'm a dead man or a wounded man or you'll rip my fucking balls off. Yada, yada, yada." He pressed the barrel of the gun against her cheek. "Except, she'll still have her pretty face splattered all over the granite, asshole. And you'll still be bear food."

The bastard stopped a good fifteen or so paces from Thom. Jo was now grasping with both hands, her face showing more anger than pain now.

"What do you want?" Thom asked

"Money!"

"All right. Let her go and I'll get it for you. What was Mal going to pay you?"

"Two mill."

"Alright, then," he answered with a nod. His gaze was firmly fixed on Jo and after a few moments, hers was on him. "Two million dollars it is. Just let her go."

"No, no," Rudner answered, grinning. "See, she's my insurance. Derek wanted you two dead. No witnesses. But I figure now, all bets are off. We can still do this shit."

"No, no money unless you let her go."

"Kiss my ass!"

But Jo had other plans. She didn't kiss his ass so much as she planted her fist right in his groin. Rudner screamed like a little girl, then flung her aside like a useless rag-doll. Jo rolled out of the way, kicking at Rudner's ankles with her good foot. Thom didn't miss a beat. He ran full out, hitting his former bodyguard with his shoulder buried in the man's middle. They both flew backward, the gun dropping out of Rudner's hand.

Rudner hit the ground on his back, momentarily stunning him. Thom landed to the left and rolled away. He was quickly on his feet again and aimed a kick at the man's side but Rudner was quicker. The man grabbed Thom's ankle and jerked upwards, throwing Thom on his back. With one hand cradling his wounded manhood, the other hand pushed up from the ground. Thom ignored the pain in his back and pulled himself up at the same time. They attacked each other like two wrestlers in the ring.

He threw punches as hard and as fast as he could. Rudner caught him on the cheek a few times and once on his ear, setting that side of his head to ringing. Thom didn't let it stop him. He threw a kick at the man's knee, following it up with another left to his jaw. Both hands came up to grab Thom's shoulders and Thom felt himself being pushed backward. The damned rubber souls were sliding over the top of the moistened grass, the spray from the falls making everything humid.

"Fuckin' bastard!" Rudner pushed harder. "You...go...down!"

Thom felt his feet slip again, this time over a granite stone. He spared a look over his shoulder and saw he was too close to the edge. He laid a punch against Rudner's jaw, gripping the man's collar as he did. "The hell I will!"

Thom found a foothold on a small out cropping and wedged his foot in tight. It stopped his momentum and he pushed back against Rudner. But the man wrapped first one hand, then the other, around his throat and started to squeeze. His throat started to close and the air was harder and harder to pull. He didn't dare try to kick out or he'd go over. He buried his fingers into the meaty muscles of Rudner's forearms, trying to squeeze with his fingertips, to make the son of a bitch let go.

At that moment, he heard a loud bang and saw the confused look on Rudner's face as his fingers lost their grip. In that split second, he saw the fine spray of blood that exploded from the back of Rudner's head. The last thing Thom saw, as he and the dead bodyguard fell over the edge, was Jo holding the gun in both hands.

63

THE BLAZING CABIN became an instant hub of chaos. The detectives had barely arrived at the scene when a half dozen rangers arrived by transport. They were immediately followed by another dozen volunteers who set about battling the inferno. According to the acting leader, the GPS device that they'd found had stopped sending; his guess was that it had been destroyed in the fire. What he wasn't saying was that his best guess was that the wearer had been too. Tony mentally crossed his fingers and prayed that it was otherwise.

When the first shots sounded, Jim commandeered a few of the rangers and the uniform that had come with them. They took off at a lope in the general direction. Tony hoped there was some kind of trail back there. He hadn't been aware of saying that out loud until he got an answer.

"There is, sir."

He turned to see the makeshift leader standing at his side. "Excuse me?"

"There's a trail on the other side of that outcropping. We use it now for fire rescue personnel, but it used to be an old logging trail."

Tony nodded his approval. "Good, thank you." He turned back to the cabin.

Two more vehicles pulled into the clearing, to be waved to the perimeter. The man caught Tony's gaze and nodded.

"We got LifeFlight on its way. And we'll need to keep an area clear for 'em to land."

"What about that fire unit?"

"Almost here, sir. Should be coming up over the falls any minute now."

Tony nodded again. "Hey, what's your name?"

"O'Connor, sir."

"O'Connor, as soon as that blaze is out, I need to see inside. Get the state forensics guys in there."

"Yes, sir. It'll be some time for the ruin to cool off, though. You've got a few thousand degrees going there and we got maybe another hour or two of sun left."

"I'm a patient man," Tony told him. He turned back to the burning wreck. "I have to be sure no one is in there."

"Sir, with all due respect—"

There was a squawk in his pocket and he heard the distorted voice of his partner. "Tony—"

Of course, the sat-coms! He pulled it out and pressed the side button. "Jim! Jim, what's going on?"

"Man down, dude. Got one of the bad guys over here, too!"

O'Connor pushed him out of the way as the chopper rose up over the trees. The men scattered as the wind created by the blades started to flatten out the bushes and grass. Tony was almost knocked over by the sheer force of it. It came down low enough to drop the load of water it carried. Gallons rained down in one burst, flattening the structure. It turned out to be all that was needed—the flames were gone, replaced by the hissing steam. The chopper rose and flew off.

"—shit, oh shit, oh shit!"

"What?" Tony bellowed. "What's wrong?"

"Gunshot, didn't you hear me?"

"The chopper was...gunshot?"

"I heard another gunshot. Over by the falls. I'm on my way. We need a stretcher over here."

"I'll tell the chief. We'll get units dispatched. Jim! Don't do something stupid."

"Just get your ass here, partner. The shit's going down *now*!"

Tony called for two of the volunteers to take a stretcher down that back trail, then grabbed two of the state boys and a ranger to lead the way to the falls. Jim sounded excited. Jim *never* got excited without a good reason. Maybe it *wasn't* over.

64

I T TOOK HER a moment to realize what happened; everything was going so slowly. She'd acted purely on instinct and anger. The son of a bitch had threatened to shoot her. Then, he'd threatened to kill Thom, was throttling him. She had to do something.

Everything came in images after that, like photographs with sound and smell. Thom and that bastard on the edge. Her hand reaching on the ground. The gun in her palm. Both hands wrapped around the pistol's grip, sighting down the barrel at the back of that bastard's head. The feel of the pull of the trigger, the smell of the powder in her nostrils. Then, the whole tableau turned into a slow motion action—the two men taking a long, arduous, frame-by-frame tumble over the side and out of her vision.

Jo screamed as loud as she could. Her legs threatened to turn traitor to the rest of her body and will, her knees trying to buckle and her ankle refusing to hold her up. But she kept moving, kept screaming his name. She would have crawled to the edge, across the bare granite, if she had to. She barely managed to get to the outcropping without dropping in her tracks, sobbing as she made it there. She dropped to her hands and knees with tears falling down her cheeks. She had to see him one last time, had to let go in the only way she could. She crawled over to peer down.

And saw him, on a ledge just below.

He had fallen on his belly, slightly turned on one hip. One of his arms was outstretched and reaching over his head. The other arm, bent between the wrist and elbow, had fallen to his side. His legs were slightly bent at the knees. They didn't look broken, as his arm did, but she couldn't be sure. He also didn't look dead. Was he? Was he dead?

Her breath caught in her ribs, her mouth drying up. She watched, almost willing him to breathe. She forced herself to get quiet, listening...waiting. Then, she heard it. A small moan. She watched as the fingers of the outstretched hand flattened, then curled slowly. The hand tried to move, then seemed to think better of it.

"Thom! Oh my God, Thom!"

She had to get to him. Somehow she had to get to him. Tell it would be okay, tell him the things she had to tell him. She was not going to let him die. It just wasn't going to happen. Damn it, she was supposed to be sitting in a restaurant in New York, not playing billy goat on some damned mountain.

"Oh, screw it!"

She pulled off her shoes, the slick bottoms would be useless and dangerous. She pulled off the thin socks, same reason. She'd have to be careful, do this slowly. The sand and the moisture from the falls were going to make that damned granite slick as glass. But she could do it, if she was careful. She pulled up every bit of information that Walt had told them, everything she'd learned in that first hike.

"Shit, I have no clue what I'm doing. What the hell am I doing?"

So thinking, she crawled over to the right side of the outcropping and started down. With a fistful of turf in her hand, she used her feet to feel her way down the first boulder. Her ankle was thudding with her pulse, the pain was enormous. But she did her best to ignore it; she'd deal with it later. It was fairly dry, with vines and small tree things sticking out around it.

"Fuck this, I need a hand hold."

She grabbed one with the other hand and slowly let herself down towards another. She kept on her back, walking crab-like, keeping friction going between her feet and palms, and the rock's surface. Slowly, she let go of the tiny tree and continued down the face of the rock.

She was reaching the bottom of the boulder, unable to see down. She stopped, looking around for another route. To her left was another outcropping of weeds and those small trees. She decided to go for it. She crept to her left, the hand outstretched to grip it. Her fingers a scant few inches away when her foot slipped and she started to slide.

Her heart was thudding in her chest, her panic trying to overcome her. She started a quicker descent as the edge of the boulder flew at her. Her feet finding no purchase, she knew she was gone. And then, at the last possible second, just as her feet were sticking over the edge, her palms stopped her. She waited, panting and trying not to faint. Waited until she'd gained control again, then reached over to a small crevice in the stone.

She slipped her fingers in it, tightening her grip. She reached up over her head to find another one. Slowly, she moved to where she could grasp the vegetation. One good tug told her it could hold her weight. She gripped it like a drowning man would take a life preserver and settled her foot on another boulder. This one was half buried in the ground and sturdy. She stepped on it, hugging the face and letting herself calm completely.

"Not bad," came a voice over her head.

Her fingers closed impulsively on the grips. She had a split second of panic before realizing that this voice was not the same one. She hazarded a glance up to see a curly head peeking over the ledge. "You scared the shit out of me," she grumbled.

"Sorry." He looked past her. "Are you sure you should be doing that?"

"I have to get to him. He's hurt, maybe dying. I can't let him die."

"Uh, not what I meant. There's rangers up here, you know. And another LifeFlight chopper is on the way."

At that moment, she heard another groan below her. The ledge was in sight, only another ten feet or so and she'd be there. She made the mistake of looking down the three hundred foot drop beneath the ledge, finding the broken body that had fallen down to the bottom, dashed against the granite floor. But that wasn't her concern. It was the fact that Thom was moving—one leg and the outstretched arm moving towards the edge. If he managed to slide to his right, he'd be joining his former bodyguard.

She looked up again. "I can't wait."

Another head peered over. "Hang on, okay? I'll get a stabilizing rope down."

"Look, I don't mean to sound ungrateful, but I don't have time. He's moving. Do what you have to do but leave me alone for a few minutes; okay? Please? Don't distract me. This is hard enough as it is."

"Go slow, okay? You're about ten feet away and you should have some good foot holds on the way down."

"Thanks."

She spared a look, trying to find those foot holds. She put her first foot down, gingerly trying the rock, then slowly putting the rest of her weight on it. Only when she was sure that it was holding did she let go and find another hand hold. It was long and taxing, she had to go very slowly and seemed to be taking forever. Her now swollen ankle wasn't helping matters. She bent back two nails on one handhold and the pain was excruciating. It wasn't enough to stop her.

The new voice turned out to be a ranger. He called down that his name was Bill and told he was an expert at this. He also began to give her directions on where to step and when to grab. The curly headed man was quiet but he stayed where he could see her, watching. She kept going, hearing but not really listening. She was focused on what she was doing, focused on Thom.

She didn't trust the ledge to hold them both. As she settled down to the side, she put her hand on his calf and just held on to the small tree. "Thom. Thom, can you hear me?"

He groaned, trying to reach his hand back to her. She was able to get a good look at him from where she was. His face was bloody from scrapes and it looked like his cheekbone might be broken. Maybe his jaw too. Blood dripped from a cut on his forehead. He was also breathing raggedly.

She turned her face upward. "I think he's broken some ribs. His arm is broken. He's bleeding a little."

The curly headed one called down to her, "Keep him still. Don't let him move around, okay? LifeFlight is gonna get you out. They'll bring the basket down for him and lower a harness for you. Just keep him still."

"Got it, thanks." She turned her attention back to the

wounded man. "Shh, now, you stay still, honey. It's okay, I'm here. I'm going to stay here."

He groaned again. "Jo...?"

"Yes, Thom. It's Jo, it's me."

"Jo...hurt."

"No, Thom. I'm fine. You're the one hurt. You've got to be still. They're coming to get us out of here. We're rescued."

"Hurt...Mal...lied."

She stroked his leg, letting him know she wasn't going anywhere. "I know, honey. I know. And he did things. Evil things."

"Lied...killed."

"Yes, Thom. He did. But that's not your fault."

"My...fault...no...."

"No, my love. It's not," she reassured. "Now, you don't think on him. You think on us."

"Us?"

"Yes, us. Because you're going to need someone to take care of you. Heal you. Nurse you back to health."

There, the tease of a smile on his bruised and battered lips. "Us?" he repeated. "Love...me?"

"Oh yes," she answered. "I love you very much."

"Love...you...too."

The chopper was very loud, the wind coming from the blades almost blew her off her perch. She decided she had to risk the ledge being able to hold them both, to keep him from being blown off along with her. She crawled up to his side, shielding him with her body. She watched the ropes lowered , followed by the two men rappelling down on them. Between the three of them, they got Thom in a cervical collar, then a backboard to keep him steady. Together, they turned him over and loaded him on the basket.

One man went up with the basket, holding the side to keep it from tipping. She watched, her hand shielding her face to keep the debris from flying into her eyes. When they were safely aboard, she turned to the other man and let him fit the harness on her. They rode up together before they were helped into the chopper body.

Once strapped in, the chopper headed off in the direction of the hospital. It was finally over.

65

J O FLIPPED THE pages of her magazine without reading a word
on any of them. Damned hospital emergency rooms were all
alike; if you weren't family, you stayed out in the reception area.
And since she wasn't family, she sat and waited for someone to
get off their scrub suited ass to come out and tell her what was
happening.

The moment the chopper had landed on the heli-pad,
they'd been whisked into the emergency ward. Thom had been
wheeled into one area while she'd been plunked down in a
wheelchair and taken into another. They ran a small fortune in
tests—ultrasound, CT scan, x-ray, you name it. She was poked,
prodded, palpated, and processed. After a while, she had her
ankle bound up, she was given crutches to walk with for two
weeks—doctor's instructions—and she was pronounced fit as a
fiddle—with only badly sprained ankle and the residue bruises
of her beating—and released.

When she'd asked about Thom, however, the volunteering
of information was under-whelming. They weren't at liberty to
say, they didn't have all the results yet—was she a member of
the family? No? Sorry, that information is privileged, have a seat
in the waiting room, someone will be out shortly. Well, no one
had come out in the last two hours and she was getting more
than a little frustrated and just plain old pissed off.

The swinging doors opened just as she was about to turn

on some poor unsuspecting ER nurse. She froze in the act of jumping out of the chair, waiting to see who would emerge. She released the held breath when she saw Walt being wheeled by an orderly, Missy walking beside them. With everything that had happened, until that moment, she'd forgotten about them.

The young girl saw Jo and waved at her. Jo waved back and waited until they were closer.

"Hey, you two," she said. "I'm so glad to see you. We heard the shots."

"That son of a bitch tried to shoot Walt." Missy looked down at him, coaxing his brown hair back out of his pale face.

Walt looked up at her with a sweet smile but he looked terrible, haggard and in pain.

"...mild concussion, dislocated shoulder, bruises, but he's okay to go home." Missy smiled down at him again. "I'm going to take real good care of him. Nurse him back to health."

Jo slowly sat back down in her chair, using one of her crutches to keep her from an ungainly sprawl. "How are you doing, sport?"

"Been better," he answered. His speech was a little slurred but he was still in there.

She took his hand. "I never thanked you."

"For what?"

"For teaching me all that stuff about hiking and climbing. Came in very handy."

"Any time. You'll have to tell me, sometime, what you mean." He squeezed her fingers. "I heard Thom is here. What happened?"

She filled them in with the salient points. When she was done, he slowly nodded his head. "How's he doing?"

Jo shrugged. "No clue. They won't tell me."

"They will." He smiled again; tentative but still a smile.

"Walt, honey, we need to get you home."

"Yeah," Walt answered.

Jo patted Walt's arm and smiled up at Missy. "You two take care."

"Are you leaving, Jo?" Missy asked.

"Soon," Jo answered. "I've got to get back to work, my life. I was only going to be here for two weeks. And that ends in about three days."

"You'll come by the shop and say goodbye, right?" Walt asked.

"Walt, you're going to need a week to recover, darlin'," she answered with a smile. "You let Missy take very good care of you. I'll be back sometime. You'll see me again."

She watched them head off, losing them after they were through the outer doors.

"Ms. Hayes?"

She turned back to the nurse who'd come up behind her. "Yes?"

"He's asking for you. You can come on back."

"Thank you."

Instead of being taken back to one of the ER cubicles, she was escorted by the hospital security to another wing entirely. The nice gentleman didn't say much more than "just relax" and "we'll be there momentarily." He pushed her in a wheelchair to the right room and then, inside.

Thom's face brightened the moment he saw her. It made everything flutter within her, tickling and rising to a peak. Just the sight of him made her want to plunge her fingers in his hair and paste her lips to his. Even lying in that bed, still showing the bruises and casts, still pale as the sheets he laid on, she never wanted anything more than she wanted him right now. She pulled herself up out of the chair and sat down on the side of the bed.

Turned out that his cheek and jaw *hadn't* been broken. His hand came out to her and she took it in hers. He pulled her down into a deep kiss, tasting the sweetness of his tongue inside of her mouth. It seemed to go on forever and that was just fine with her.

"Uh, Dad? Should we leave?"

Jo jumped, a bit shocked at the sound of another voice in the room. Blushing, she saw three young faces watching the two of them. The young man's was full of amusement, while the two young women seemed a bit astonished. *Ah, youth*, she thought with a smile. *They think we old farts don't get any.*

Thom chuckled. "Jo, I'd like you to meet my two oldest; my daughter Lisa and my son Allan. And that's Allan's wife, Lara."

She smiled as they shook her hand.

"I was just telling Dad that we got the graduation on the digital camera," his daughter said. "If he couldn't be there, he can see this."

"Oh yeah!" Allan reached into his shoulder bag. "Here, brought you the DVD and your degree. I accepted it for you."

"Well, thank you, son." Thom took the offered presents, lingering over the diploma. He flipped it open with his good hand. "Look at that."

"That's real too, Dad," Allan said. "It's real."

Thom's only answer was a smile. His face was a little drawn.

"Are you in pain?" Jo asked.

"No, honey, I'm fine. Pain killers are a wonderful thing." He darted his eyes up over his shoulder. "That IV is taking real good care of me."

Allan's very pregnant wife put her hand on her husband's arm, getting his attention. "Allan, honey. Maybe we should go. Let Jo and your Dad have a little time together."

"Sure," Lisa agreed. "Dad, we're gonna go back to the hotel, okay?"

"We'll be back tomorrow, to take you home."

"Okay," he cheerfully agreed.

The kids all kissed him good-bye. They also made sure to kiss Jo's cheek as they left. "Welcome to the family," Lisa said as they filed out.

"Family?" She turned back to Thom. "I'm family now?"

He put the diploma aside and reached out for her again. "Yeah, family. You saved my life, don't think I was so out of it that I don't know that."

"Well, don't think I was going to let you just fall off that ledge."

"Never."

"Are you alright?"

"Doc said I have a few broken ribs. Broke both the bones in my arm there." He lay his head back on the pillow with a slight grimace. "Cracked the noggin but it could have been worse. Said my concussion is fairly mild, considering. I figure to be out doing the cha-cha in a day or two."

"Stop!" She kissed his fingers. "I'm serious."

His eyes twinkled merrily. "So am I." Then his face sobered up. "Listen. Just so happens, I'm looking for a lawyer."

"Oh?"

"Yeah, a lady lawyer. Someone who might be interested in living with me, traveling with me. Being the woman of my dreams." His gaze captured hers. "Someone who likes the outdoors but needs a little help in the hiking department. Someone who likes popcorn and chocolate bars together. Someone who'll tell me to shut up when I need to and make me sing 'til she smiles."

That melted her. "Oh yeah?"

"Yeah."

"Well," she answered. "Might just be I know someone interested. I'm getting tired of Larry's bullshit anyway. And I was thinking a change of scenery might be good. That is, if you're looking for a *live-in* lawyer."

He kissed her fingers. "Yes, I am, as a matter of fact. How do you feel about leaving the heat of Nashville for the cool of New Hampshire?"

She nodded. "We'll take it slow."

He rested his head back on the pillow, sighing with relief. "Yes. I think I need to."

"So do I."

She leaned forward to kiss him again, wanting only the taste of him in her mouth to make the rest of the day fade away. She never got close enough, as there came a knock on the door. She turned her gaze to see the petite, dark haired woman standing.

"Who is it?" Thom asked.

The woman came into the room. "It's me, Thom."

"Angie, darlin'." He grinned at her. "Jo, this is the first ex-Mrs. Mitchell. One of my dearest friends and mother of those two hellions you met earlier."

Jo nodded her head.

"Angie, this is Jo, the one I was telling you about."

The lady stuck her hand out and Jo took it. It was a warm

gesture. The way Thom addressed his ex-wife let Jo know that it was over romantically between them. She relaxed a little.

Thom went over his litany of ills and ailments. Angie listened, nodding when appropriate. Maybe it was just Jo's imagination but something seemed a bit dark about the woman. Besides her hair color, that is.

"Are you going home then?"

Thom nodded, still holding Jo's hand. "Absolutely. I'm done with hotels. Why don't you and the kids join us? There's more than enough room in that old house. Was your home too, you know."

"Us?" Angie asked.

"Yeah, Jo's moving in." He flashed the dazzling smile at Jo. "We're gonna try each other out for a while."

Angie nodded and smiled, seemingly happy with that answer. "Good. I hate it when Thom's alone. And now that...." Her face went pale.

"Ang?" Thom sat up a little, grimacing at the pain in his ribs. "What is it?"

"Malcolm is in the prison ward, Thom. They evidently operated on him for a gunshot wound and then put him there pending arrest."

Thom's brow furrowed. "And how would you know that?"

Angie licked her lips. Jo watched the pain etched in her eyes. She suddenly felt sorry for the woman, without knowing why. Whatever it was she had to say, it wasn't going to be pleasant. For her *or* Thom.

"Thom, I have to tell you the truth."

"The truth?"

"Yeah. Things I should have told you long ago. Answers

you deserved. I think it's time I *did* tell you. Now that the shit's about to hit the fan."

"Maybe I should go," Jo said.

She made to stand up but Angie Mitchell just held her hand up. "No, I would like you to hear this too. I'm going to have to tell this in a court of law anyway. I might as well get used to it now."

Thom lay back against the pillow, still holding Jo's hand. Angela took a sip from a nearby glass of water and started talking.

66

Jo SAT WITH Thom's foot in one hand, between her knees.

"I feel like a big baby," he grumbled.

"Oh hush, you've got a broken arm. How are you going to do this? Hmm?"

She bent over and picked up the loafer, then guided his foot in it. With one finger, she tucked it neatly in and adjusted the back of the shoe around his heel. She repeated the process on his other foot and sat back to admire her handiwork.

"Now then, sir."

Before she could say more, she heard a knock on the door. Jo turned her head to see the two detectives that had been at the scene, followed by the reporter, Adam Wheeler. He'd already been in while Thom was eating breakfast. Thom agreed to an exclusive interview with the young man, telling him everything, after he'd issued a formal statement to the rest of the press. It made sense—Wheeler already had the important elements to the story. Thom would fill him in on his side of things.

Jo had made up her own mind about the issue, as well. She immediately stepped up to the plate, acting as his attorney. "All set up, Mr. Mitchell. We're ready when you are."

Thom nodded. "Thanks, guys. How do you want to work this?"

Detective Morris stepped up and proceeded to explain. "I think that...well, maybe we should let you speak first. You have a statement, you said?"

Jo rested her hand in the small of Thom's back as he nodded. Yes, he had a statement; she'd typed it out for him on her laptop and printed it on the hospital's printers. A very open statement that left nothing out. "Thom, are you sure about this?"

He smiled at her. "I have to do this, darlin'. My conscience dictates and I obey."

Detective Garrison also nodded but he did so with a smile. "Partner here has an in with the DA, man. You come clean, testify for the prosecution, and you're square."

"No, I don't think so," Thom said.

Garrison crossed his arms. "Look, Mr. Mitchell. I know you did rehab over this and you did your penance, man. Maybe you didn't know it at the time, but you did. You gave up driving and drinking. Now, you're gonna put the guy responsible behind bars."

"I killed my friend."

"No, sir," Morris said. "The way I see it, you just drove drunk. Yes, he was hurt badly. You'd have done some time for drunk driving and leaving the scene. But I also know you made a phone call. You trusted someone to do the right thing for you. He dropped the ball, sir. Not you."

"Thom," Jo whispered. "They're right."

"I know. I just feel like there should be more."

"Then, we'll figure it out together. Phil Mullins was well loved here. You'll have a backlash," she told him. "But I'll help you. Right now, this is a start."

"You think so?" His voice was so plaintive, the look on his face so touching.

She kissed the corner of his mouth that was unbruised. "I know so."

"Mr. Mitchell?"

Thom swallowed hard enough that it was audible, but he bravely faced the young reporter. "Yes, Mr. Wheeler?"

"I'll tell you what," he said. "You let me help too. I know how to write it."

"You give your statement, Mr. Mitchell," Morris said. "We'll handle everything after that. Don't worry."

"And no questions, honey," Jo reiterated. "You just give the statement."

"And I get the exclusive after that, right?" Adam asked hopefully.

"Yes you do," Thom agreed. "I promised. And I trust you."

"You won't regret it, sir."

"Then, let's go. I want to give my statement and go home. After we get our things out of the hotel."

The orderly met them with the wheelchair. Jo helped Thom gingerly sit down, then adjusted everything so he was comfortable. She was scared for him; this was a hell of a risk. But he'd decided this on his own. She had her cane and ambled along behind them.

They hadn't slept much the previous night. And it was no wonder. After Angie dropped her bombshells, Thom had kept completely silent. The only indication that he was upset was his lips disappearing into a thin line on his face. He hadn't made it all that easy for the woman but he hadn't made it outright impossible. He accepted her apology but it was clear that he was not happy with her. Angie had broken down into tears, which melted him somewhat. But not enough. He invited her to come stay with the kids and then asked her for some time alone. He used the excuse of feeling tired. Jo knew the difference. She was pretty sure Angie did too.

Thom had waited until he was sure she was far enough away, then broke down in tears. Jo sat next to him, letting him cry and holding his hand. He wept for the loss of his marriage, the loss of a friend. When his tears had dried, he talked long into the night as he remembered the man who'd died. That wound would begin to heal. The breach with his ex-wife was something else entirely.

The press conference went better than Jo had hoped. Better than Thom expected. He stood up at the podium and smiled at the flashing cameras. He introduced the two detectives and explained that they would take all the questions. He started out with his usual folksy manner, then switched to his statement. The moment he started talking, it got dead quiet. People were shocked. He told as much as he could remember of that night, explained who orchestrated the cover up. But he also took responsibility for his actions.

"Phil was my friend," he said. "Someone that meant something to me. To know that I had a hand in his death has caused me a great deal of guilt and sorrow. I've stopped drinking and I've attended rehab. But that's not enough." He paused, collecting himself, before going on with his carefully worded statement. "I intend to help the police give Phil the justice he deserved that night and his family deserves now. That's all I have, so I'll let the police take over."

They'd actually applauded as he left the podium. He sat back down in his wheelchair and he was rolled out, Jo tagging along behind.

"Think that was okay?" he asked, needing approval and reassurance. So like a child.

"It was perfect, my love," she told him.

He gave Wheeler the exclusive; everything he had told the rest plus a lot more. "I'm going to do a series of public service announcements," he told the reporter. "I don't want anyone doing what I did. Ever again. I owe Phil's memory that. And something else."

"Yes, sir?"

"I want to open a rehab center. Right here, near the Presidents. Where folks can come get the help they need, take therapy in hiking and being part of nature. Right here."

Jo smiled and held his good hand through it all. Wheeler got his exclusive and left happy. Jo called for a cab to take them back to the hotel where her rental was. The plan was to go upstairs and pack up their things, then leave. They only got as far as Thom's door.

Missy was sitting on the floor, waiting. "Thom, Jo!"

"Missy, darlin'." Thom's face brightened, then he frowned. "Wait, is Walt okay? Are *you* okay? Is something wrong?"

Missy sighed as she got up from the floor. "I don't know, Thom. And that's the truth."

"What is it?" Jo asked.

"I know he believes me about the picture and the kiss. But there's something else," she answered."

Thom handed Jo his key card. "C'mon you two. Let's go inside and get out of the hall. Missy, you can tell us what's wrong in there."

When they were in and seated, Thom asked Missy to go on.

"I got him home, got him in bed. But, you know Walt. Or, maybe you don't." She sighed. "He's not real big in being taken care of."

Thom nodded. "I can understand that. He's independent, trying to be strong."

"He's also stubborn as hell," she told them. "And a bit of a caveman about things. And I love him anyway. In fact, I love him because of all of that. If that makes sense."

Jo smiled at her. "It does indeed. So what can we do?"

Missy returned Jo's smile. "Well, I was hoping you could help me. See...." She blushed a bit, looking down at her hands in her lap. "Walt has asked me to marry him. A couple of times."

"And you told him no?" Thom asked.

She nodded. "I told you that day. I was scared. Not sure." She looked up at Thom again. "But if I learned anything over this, I've learned that I shouldn't have been scared at all. I love him, Thom. More than anything. And when that bastard was aiming at my Walt, to shoot him? Well, I realized what I had to lose and it wasn't going to be Walt."

Jo patted her hand. "Good for you, darlin'."

"So?" Thom added.

"I want to ask *him*, Thom. I want to put a smile on his face, to ask Walt to marry me. And then I want to set a date and marry my man. As soon as possible."

Thom smiled at Jo. "I think that Jo and I can help out with that, darlin'."

"Absolutely," Jo agreed. "And I have some ideas."

"Tell me," Missy said.

The three of them went to work.

67

IT TOOK HIS lady a couple of hours to get everything ready and she went to it with a fire in her. Who would have thought it, the lady lawyer was a romantic at heart. Thom took his pain pills and just let her. Hell, the kids had the keys to the house. He called and told them that he and Jo were running a bit late and they headed off with Angie in tow.

It was going to be a long damn time before he could trust Angie again. He supposed, in a way, he could understand why she had been an unwilling accomplice to Mal. It was a very bad time in their marriage and Mal hadn't left her with much of a choice. But she'd lied to him about everything. So many lies, so much deception. Had he really known her at all? The lies hurt more than anything else.

Jo, she made things better. She helped him know that it was okay. The PSAs were her idea. The clinic was his. Nothing was irredeemable, unforgivable. He had a chance to make things right. He had a chance to make it up to Phil. He'd do this somehow.

In the meantime, the lovely young lady that came back in with Jo was a sight for sore eyes. Missy had been dressed in a fetching silk dress that showed off the curves and the right amount of cleavage. Her hair was down, swept back from her face with barrettes. Jo had managed to put the twinkle back in her eyes.

"So?" Jo asked.

"Perfect," Thom answered. "If he doesn't fall in love again, he's an idiot."

Missy blushed and thanked them.

"So?" Jo repeated.

Thom was confused. "What?"

"Did you call him?"

"OH!" He grinned and picked up his cell. He flipped it open with one hand, using his thumb to dial the number.

A weary voice answered on the other end. "Yeah?"

"Walt. Thom Mitchell."

The voice brightened a little, but not that much. "Hi."

"Uh, listen, are you busy right now?"

"Um, look, Thom, I don't mean to be rude but—"

"Walt, this is kind of important." Thom furrowed his brow, shooting Jo and Missy a troubled look. What would they do if he said no? "Jo and I are leaving town and I have something for you before we go. Can you please come to the hotel? Please? Right now?"

There was a heavy sigh on the other end. Then, "Thom, you really don't understand—"

"Please, Walt. I promise I won't keep you long. We...well, you'll see when you get here."

There was a long pause; long enough to make Thom hold the phone away from his ear to make sure the call hadn't been dropped. "Walt?"

"All right," came the reluctant answer. "Where are you?"

"We'll be in the dining room. You just get here. Take a cab; you're not supposed to be driving yet. Just tell the kid at the desk you're here to see me and let him take care of the cabby's fare, okay?" Thom disconnected the call and stuck the cell in his breast pocket. "Okay?"

"Good," Jo answered. "Let's go downstairs. They can come get the bags."

They got a table in the center. That alone was hard to do since lunch rush was in session. It always helped to know the management. Of course, being Thom Mitchell still counted. There were the stares but no one jeered or booed him. In fact, more than a few shook his good hand and thanked him for finally coming forward. They wished him luck in making things right. Maybe it would work after all.

Missy disappeared, and he and Jo sat down. They didn't wait very long. Walt came in, his left arm in a sling and still showing the bruises from his ordeal. Walt saw them and came to the table. Thom gestured to a chair for him. Walt pulled it out and sat down with a slight hiss of air. He nodded to Jo, who smiled back.

Her mommy look was on her face in a heartbeat. "Walt, you all right?"

"No, Jo, I'm not."

"Why, honey?"

"I don't want to talk about it, if you don't mind."

"Sure," Thom agreed, looking over Walt's shoulder. "I really just called to say thank you."

Walt looked rather confused. "Thank you?"

"For coming to rescue us," Jo added. She rested her hand on his good arm.

"I didn't do anything," Walt answered glumly. "Remember? We got caught too."

Thom smiled. "All those hiking lessons, the survival tips you passed on. You realize we wouldn't be alive if it wasn't for you?"

Walt smiled back, glowing under the praise. "Really?"

"You kicked some serious ass, buddy. I owe you for that."

It was something the ladies always appreciated, seeing the blush on a man's cheek. Walt blushed and Thom could see the look on Jo's face when he did.

"I...you're welcome," Walt sputtered.

"So, I have a couple things to for you." Thom pulled out a cashier's check. "Turns out I'm richer than I thought I was. So, I'd like to show my gratitude and ask a favor to go with it." He handed Walt the check. "I would like to put a retainer on your services. On you *and* the shop. The clinic I'm planning is going to use hiking and climbing as a therapy to help substance abusers. I'd like you to be the official guide and your shop to handle all the gear we'll need."

"Are you serious?" Walt's eyes bulged out as he looked down at the piece of paper in his hand. "This...this is five figures, man!"

"Yes it is. Are you in?"

"W-w-well, sure!" Walt stammered. "I'm crazy, not stupid. Deke will freak out over this."

"Good!" Thom grinned and sat back. He was content to let Jo handle the rest.

Jo patted his arm. "Walt, there's something else. Something I think you're going to be very happy about."

She waved over Walt's shoulder. The confused look came back to the younger man's face, until he looked to see where Jo was gesturing. He turned, carefully, in his chair and saw the beauty walking towards him.

With all of the windows and sunlight streaming into the

room, she looked radiant. Her hair shimmering in the sunlight, the smile and the tears; she walked through the crowded dining room, garnering looks of appreciation and desire as she did. But her gaze was on one man and one man, alone. Thom gestured to Jo to pull her chair around to his. It was time to let someone else have the spotlight.

Walt's face was a study of a man deeply in love and not wanting to lose face. There was a great deal of emotion playing in that face. He was a captive audience.

Missy came around where she could be seen. "Walter Beaton, I have something to say to you."

"Missy...."

The room suddenly grew hushed, quiet. All eyes were turned to the center of the room. Even the wait staff had frozen in position. Thom smiled. This might work after all.

"Walt, you have no idea who or what I was when I came here. I was a scared little girl. I'd been used, tossed aside by so many men in so many ways. I thought all men were out for one thing and one thing only. But not you." She curled her fingers, as if she was trying to draw on something inside. "You talked to me, told me your innermost secrets. You shared things with me; your dreams, your hopes, your fears."

Walt was transfixed. He seemed caught in her words, as if he'd suddenly forgotten the rest of the room.

"You made me feel safe," she continued. "You made me feel like I mattered. You made me feel loved." Missy hiked up the hem of her skirt to just above her knees. With one hand on the edge of the table, she knelt down in front of her lover. It was only then, that she pulled a small box out of her purse and laid the bag on the table.

"Walter Beaton, I've not been a very good girlfriend. I'd like to make that up to you. I'd like to spend the rest of my life showing you how very special you are, how much you mean to me. How every day with you is like a day in heaven.

"I want to give you all of my tomorrows, every one of them scattered like diamonds in front of you. I want to go to sleep at night, watching your face in the moonlight. I want to wake up with you at my side. I want to know that you are mine, truly. That I am yours for as long as you want me."

She opened the box. Walt had a look of shock on his face was priceless. Thom grinned, squeezing Jo's hand. Missy pulled the gold ring from the box. From what Thom could see, it was a gold band with three diamond chips inlaid into the metal. Jo had gone with her to pick it out and help her pay for it. It had been their gift to the couple.

Missy reached out and took Walt's good hand in hers, holding the ring in her right.

"Walter Edward Beaton, after you have asked me so many times and I, stupidly, said I wanted to wait—I have finally realized that I am sure. I have always been sure. I will be more sure with every passing day. And I come to you now to ask you; Walter, will you marry me? Will you do me the honor of becoming my husband?"

Epilogue

Missing Pop Star and others found on Wilde
by Adam Wheeler

State Police confirmed the finding of international pop success Thom Mitchell and three others today on Wilde Mountain. Mitchell and hiking companions had been taken in a kidnapping that occurred outside of the Mt. Washington hotel, yesterday morning. Mr. Mitchell sustained as yet unknown injuries in an escape attempt. Both have been taken to Coos County Hospital for medical attention.

Mr. Mitchell's long time assistant and manager Malcolm Ross has been admitted to the hospital for a gunshot wound. Police are holding him in the prison ward, pending arrest for complicity in the kidnapping.

The state police have also confirmed the death of one of the kidnappers, Michael Rudner of Waterbury, CT. Taken into custody are Derek Roberts of Berlin, NH and Neil Butcher, of Manchester, NH.

***

Mitchell Admits Role in Mullins Death
by Adam Wheeler

After twenty plus years, there has been a break in the Phillip Mullins case. Police have long suspected wrongdoing in the senator's death but an unlikely witness has finally stepped forward with information that can bring about a swift justice.

Singer Thom Mitchell has come forward with evidence of murder, confessing to his part in the killing.

"I was a severe alcoholic at the time," Mitchell tearfully

confessed. "From what little I can remember, we went out driving, bombed off our backsides. I was responsible for the car accident that ultimately killed my friend. You have no idea how that haunts me now."

The singer was allegedly pulled from the wreckage by former manager Malcolm Ross, who is being held for murder, obstruction of justice, tampering with evidence, and other charges. Mitchell says that Ross told him that an ambulance and the police had been called, which proved to be a falsehood....

**

Mitchell and Ex-wife Given Immunity
by Adam Wheeler

Thom Mitchell and ex-wife Angela were granted immunity from prosecution in the trial of former manager, Malcolm Ross. Ross is being held on charges of kidnapping, extortion, vehicular homicide, murder one, obstruction of justice, and other lesser charges pending from the recent kidnapping of Mitchell and girlfriend, Joanna Hayes, along with the death of State Senator Phil Mullins and guard Scott Amber.

In a highly charged case, the Mitchells are expected to testify of the events surrounding the deaths. Thom Mitchell will also be giving testimony of his kidnapping....

***

Thom Mitchell Testifies in Ross Murder Trial
by Adam Wheeler

Thom Mitchell took the stand today, putting the final nail in the coffin of former manager Malcolm Ross.

Mitchell testified of a history of severe alcoholism that lead to black outs and serious lapses in judgment. He also gave sketchy details about the car accident that took Senator Mullin's life, alluding to being removed from the scene without his permission.

Mitchell is expected to return to the stand tomorrow, to continue. He is expected to tell the details and events of his kidnapping....

***

Angela Mitchell Called to the Stand
by Adam Wheeler

Former wife of singer Thom Mitchell stepped onto the stand today in the trial of former manager, Malcolm Ross. Ross is being tried for kidnapping, two counts of murder in the first, obstruction of justice, tampering with evidence, and other lesser charges.

Mrs. Mitchell corroborated evidence that Mr. Ross had orchestrated the death of beloved Senator Phil Mullins in a car accident that involved alcohol. Mrs. Mitchell testified that Ross had not only confided details to her of the accident and subsequent fleeing of the scene with her unconscious ex-husband, but extorted her silence by threatening to turn she and her then husband, Mr. Mitchell, over to the authorities.

Mrs. Mitchell testified that Mr. Mitchell was pulled from the car in a severely inebriated and unconscious state due to a mild concussion. She also testified Mr. Ross left the accident victim, withholding help from paramedics and police, which caused the senator's death.

***

Ross Found Guilty of all Charges
by Adam Wheeler

It took the jury less than four hours to find Malcolm

Ross guilty of all charges. Sentencing will follow, pending the outcome of the trials of Derek Roberts and Neil Butcher, both co-defendants in the kidnapping of Thom Mitchell and three others.

In a surprising report, DA Allyson has offered Ross a reduced sentence of fifty years to life instead of the death penalty for his testimony against the two kidnappers. Ross is expected to agree....

Ross Sentencing Today
by Adam Wheeler

Malcolm Ross, former manager of singer Thom Mitchell was sentenced today in the kidnapping/murder case. Judge Martin D. Riggs said that he was taking into account the fact that Mr. Ross had assisted in the case against Derek Roberts and Neil Butcher, in Mr. Mitchell's kidnapping.

"However, given the heinousness of these crimes and Mr. Ross' failure to report these events until now, I fully believe that while his penitence is real, it is not enough to pay for the years of pain and suffering he has given the Mullins family and the Mitchell family."

Judge Riggs struck down the plea agreement and gave Ross two consecutive life sentences for the murders, twenty five years for the kidnapping charges, and an additional ten years for the remainder of the indictments. All told, Malcolm Ross received a total of two hundred and fifty years without the hope of parole. Mr. Ross will spend the rest of his life in the state facility in Manchester....

Mitchell, Wild Mountain Thyme Stays Number One

Billboard released the top twenty list for the week.

Topping the charts for the fourth week in a row is Thom Mitchell's Wild Mountain Thyme, *selling another 150,000 copies this week. Recent notoriety has boosted sales and Mitchell is enjoying a resurgence in his career....*

Joanna came out of the bathroom, tugging at her dress. "Well?"

Thom grinned. "You look great, darlin'."

He looked relaxed, at ease with himself now that it was all over. Things were finally coming back together again. His arm had healed and he was back on the concert circuit. And in the ultimate irony, Malcolm's little kidnapping ruse had done what it was supposed to do. Thom was enjoying success again.

"Thank you, sir. Come here, let's fix that tie." She basked in the warmth of his smile, the glow of the look he was giving her. "I know what you're thinking."

"Yeah?" he asked with a grin. "What am I thinking?"

"That you would like to do the same thing today."

He caught her hands in his. "Would that be so bad?"

With a sigh, she leaned into him and kissed his lips softly. "What's the rush, sparky? I'm not going anywhere."

"Yeah," he said. "But I'd still like to make it permanent. We could, you know. Get the license, find the JP."

"Nice and neat? No thanks, buddy." She pulled her hands

free and set about fixing his bow tie. "Listen, I've played this marriage game once already and it was a fiasco. I'm not quite willing to put my head back in the noose. And since you've done it twice, I'm surprised that *you* are."

"Listen, darlin', when you get to be my age, you know a little quicker when what you want comes your way. I want you."

"Mitchell, you got me." She smoothed the lines of his jacket for him. "Now then, where's the guitar and we'll go rehearse before the ceremony."

He walked over to pick up the case while watching her. "So, you won't marry me?"

She smiled at him. "Thom, I'd follow you into hell itself. How about we just live in sin for a while; how would that be? We'll talk marriage later. Let's be really sure about this."

He grinned back. "Spur of the moment, huh?"

She nodded.

"Okay, let's get over to the church."

I will build my love a bower by yon crystal flowing fountain
And on it I shall pile all the flowers of the mountain

> *Will you go, lassie, go?*
> *And we'll all go together,*
> *To pull wild mountain thyme*
> *All across the blooming heather*
> *Will you go, lassie, go*

I will build my love a shelter by yon clear mountain stream
And my love shall be the fairest that the summer sun has seen

Thom left his guitar in the stand, next to the choir loft, then came to join Jo. He sat down at her side, waiting for the ceremony. It was going to be a moment or two, so she indulged herself in watching the crowd.

She caught a movement on the groom's side of the aisle and saw Angie being escorted in, on the arm of Det. Garrison. During the trial, Angie had asked for, and received, a police escort—which turned out to be the charming detective. The two had hit it off and begun dating. Thom had come to a sort of peace with her, forgiving her for the past. He'd also approved of her being with Garrison. It was time she moved on with her life, free from any guilt or sins she thought she had to atone for.

Angie smiled at them, the couple taking their places as the organ started the strains of the Bridal March. They all stood in unison, waiting.

The minister stepped out and Joanna felt as if her eyes were going to pop out of her skull. A chuckle at her side drew her attention to Thom, who was smiling broadly.

"Thom," she whispered. "Do you know who that is?"

"Preston Powell, host of *The Power Punch Hour*."

She was agog. "But...but...."

He took her hand in his. "He owes me a favor for that Easter special of his. I wrote the music."

Walt and Deke were the first out, stepping to the dais. Walt had certainly dressed the occasion, resplendent in a formal tartan of blazing scarlet, cool blue, and black threads—he'd opted for the look that had won his maiden's heart, his dress kilt and black tuxedo jacket. His hair hung loose around his shoulders, the smile on his face golden like the sunlight. He looked as if he was ready to run down the aisle and carry her to the altar.

They all turned towards the back, as the small flower girl walked down the aisle, accompanied by the wee lad acting as ring bearer. Missy's friend, Sarah, was next as her bridesmaid and followed by Missy's sister, Lana, as her Matron of Honor. They waited a few more seconds for the grand entrance.

Missy stepped through the double doors in the back, her hand in the crook of her father's arm. She was covered, head to foot in a white Chantilly lace; the same lace that decorated the beaded gown she wore. She was beautiful, radiant, effervescent. Jo was in awe, the child had matured into a striking woman. A sneak peek in Walt's direction and it was obvious that the man was head over heels. From the look in her eye, under the veil, so was Missy. It was about time.

"Do you, Walter Edward Beaton, take Michelle Laurel Summer to be your lawfully wedded wife, to have and to hold, to honor and to cherish, from this day forward until death parts you?"

"I do," he answered, his gaze locked with hers.

"Do you, Michelle Laurel Summer, take Walter Edward Beaton to be your lawfully wedded husband, to have and to hold, to honor and cherish, from this day forward until death parts you?"

"I do," came the teary reply.

Jo sniffed back her own tears, taking the offered kleenex from Thom. She spared a glance at him, looking back at her. The last few months had been incredible, making love, enjoying the hiking trails, the concerts and seeing him in his element. He was right about one thing; they were both old enough to know what they really wanted in another. And she knew without a doubt, she wanted Thom Mitchell more than anything else.

For a moment, she heard her own voice, vowing to love always, hold him dear, and make him first in her life. She could hear him saying the words, that there could be no other in his heart and no one would ever take that place from her. She wanted him. Not just in her bed but in her life. The idea that they could grow old together, enjoy his grandkids together, fascinated and soothed her.

"In so much as you have come before God and these witnesses, to give your hands and hearts to each other, you have created a bond that no man or woman shall ever be able to separate. And so, before the family and these witnesses and by the power vested in me by the state of New Hampshire, I now pronounce you husband and wife. You may kiss your blushing bride."

Walt lifted Missy's veil, then took her face in both of his hands and pressed his lips to hers. She pulled him deeply into her embrace and they shared a deep, abiding kiss.

Jo took Thom's hand in hers.

"Is that a yes, darlin'?" he asked.

"It's a maybe, Mitchell."

"I'll take that," he answered.

His kiss was soft and sweet. They had the rest of their lives to decide. For now, they'd just go pick that thyme and enjoy each other.

About the Author

Erotica and Contemporary Romance writer *Siobhan MacKenzie* is the bestselling author of the m/m erotica series, *His Man...* (*His Man Friday, His Man Saturday, His Man Sunday*). She has also contributed to the anthologies, *Stranded With the Billionaire* and *Gods and Goddesses Boxed Set,* among others published by Wicked Seductions Press. Other releases coming soon are *No Sooner Loved* and *Her Scottish Exile.*

Ms. MacKenzie is a member of the Erotic Authors Association and the Romance Authors Guild.

With Love, Siobhan
http://with-love-siobhan.blogspot.com/

Facebook Page
https://www.facebook.com/IAmSiobhanMacKenzie

Twitter
https://twitter.com/WithLoveSiobhan

Bonus Chapter

Call Me Gideon

By Jacqueline Druga

Without fanfare or disastrous preliminaries, Jesus decides now is a good time to return to earth. His purpose is pure, His intentions are good, and mankind's fate does not hang in the balance. Pure and simple, it is an experiment to see if He can make a difference by walking the earth as an ordinary man.

As an Average Joe, He surrounds himself with a small eclectic group of friends to help with His earthly endeavors. Their encounters and missions are comical and heartwarming. But will His presence on earth be so strong, that the experiment is an impossibility?

If His identity is discovered, will mankind embrace him? Or worse, will mankind reject Him, causing a repeat of history all over again?

www.jacquelinedruga.com

1.

EQUATE ME NO less than an observer. Who I am is not important. Though some may venture a guess on my identity, I played no starring role in the scheme of the story. My intervention was inhibited by will, not by the proverbial 'heavenly looking-glass' I chose to stand behind. It was better that way. To be in the midst of things was limiting. In my position, staying on the spiritual side afforded me an advantaged perception.

A spectator from beyond.

Enough said.

There was no major plot behind it all. The fate of mankind wasn't hanging in the balance. No one was being tested. Quite simply, a 'what would happen' conversation cascaded rather quickly into a 'let's do it' verdict. Rules were not completely set in stone. With an undetermined destination, the journey would be guided as freely as the will of man.

The 'where and who' aspects were the only definite factors that needed to be decided—where to begin and who to begin with. So, as elementary as the flip of a coin, or twirl of a finger over a map, the decision was made. I suspect some favoritism was shown in the selection of our chosen, perhaps even a bit of cheating. Nevertheless, the choice was final. Perfect.

It was done.

Outside of Cleveland, Ohio is the village of Lodi. The quintessential small town, with a low population and a gazebo set in the center of a Norman Rockwell community square. What made Lodi so ideal was not its atmosphere, but its honesty. No hiding behind an iron curtain of faultlessness. The people of Lodi made no pretenses of being perfect, nor were their lives contrived by revered Christianity. The Chief of Police padded the traffic tickets. The mayor cheated on his wife with the first grade school teacher, and the town's most regarded doctor was hooked on barbiturates that he prescribed for himself.

They were human. They erred. However, Lodi was not the starting point; Hedy McGuire was.

Our chosen.

Like the town of Lodi, Hedy never veiled who she really was. She made no qualms about disliking those who irritated her, but was dedicated to a fault to those she cared about.

Hedy was supposed to be a redhead, but best-laid plans often go asunder, and she was born a dull brunette. Something she changed quite often and annoyingly throughout the years. A ball of energy, Hedy acted frequently on emotions instead of thought. But unfortunately she constantly allowed her happiness to be overruled by the tragic events of her life.

Big Bruce's was the ridiculous name given to the ingenious place where Hedy worked as an assistant manager—her sixth job in two years.

Civilization constantly modernized itself, and Big Bruce found a successful niche in man's laziness. Bruce always claimed the 'powers that be' were working in his favor when he landed that huge business loan to start his endeavor. He was right.

The brainchild of Bruce's converted an old warehouse into a one-stop, one-roof, to-go entertainment complex. He boasted that it was "the only place you need to go to for all your 'bring home' needs." The center had four different carryout restaurants, a beer division, and a mini store; all of which encircled the state's largest selection of home movie rentals. People flocked from miles away and packed into Big Bruce's. Saturday night was by far the busiest. Between the hours of seven and nine pm, Bruce's was a zoo. Possible the worst time to begin the experiment—so to speak—was on a Saturday night.

Ignoring the advice to wait until after closing, with an unfounded urgency, he walked into Bruce's a little after eight pm.

Though updated slightly, his form was similar to that of which history depicted. His brown hair wasn't too long, his beard was thin but comparable with the average modern man, and he was on the smaller framed side. Wearing blue jeans and a t-shirt, he looked like any other customer. He preferred it that way. He didn't want to be the 'He' or 'Almighty', he just wanted to blend right in. No fanfare or special treatment. The first mission to accomplish was to reveal his true identity to the chosen one.

I hoped for a subtle approach

Hedy pushed a cart full of movies to the action section of the new releases. Timmy, a hardworking teenage boy, looked frazzled as he stood by an empty shelf.

"Here you go, Timmy," she said. "We can put these out."

Timmy reached to the cart and stopped. "These aren't new releases."

"Bruce said to put them out. People won't know."

"But they rush right over here when they see you putting up movies on the new release shelf. They'll know and get mad." He retracted his hand as if the movies contained some highly contagious virus. "Also violent. People here get violent."

"That's because people here are ridiculous. I wouldn't come here to get a movie if I didn't work here."

"Yeah, but it's a neat place, don't you think?" Timmy asked.

"It's an insane place." Hedy lifted a movie. "Stock the shelf."

Timmy looked at the title. "Grizzly Adams. Ah, now, they're gonna know this ain't a new release."

"Tell them it's a re-release." Hedy smiled. "Here, I'll even help you."

"Thanks. Now watch." Timmy raised a movie. "They stampede like buffalo."

Snickering, Hedy looked over her shoulder. The expression dropped on her face when she saw how right Timmy was. As if they were giving away gold, people raced their way.

Beating them to Hedy was a female co-worker who arrived just before the reaching masses. "Hedy!" The young girl sounded desperate. "I have a really, really, really mad customer up front. He wants management. Can you handle it?"

"Yeah, I'll be right there," Hedy answered.

"I'll tell him. Thanks." The young girl took off.

Shrugging, Hedy gave an apologetic glance to Timmy.

"Go on. Leave me," Timmy said.

"I'll be back. I promise." Hedy slipped through the people and found a free and clear pathway via the empty foreign films aisle.

It was then that our man seized his opportunity and made

his approach. "Hedy McGuire," he called out.

Hedy stopped and turned around. "Yes?"

He walked to her. "I need to speak to you. It's important, so I'll cut to the chase. When I was on this earth before they called me Jesus. Now, I ..."

Hedy lifted a finger. "Hold that thought." She spun on her heels, and then hurried away.

Subtlety gone. At that point I truly hoped he would hang back, wait until things calmed down, and then try again. But he didn't. He followed her.

A long line of people formed, held up by the irate male customer. Hedy was somewhat out of breath when she walked behind the counter. It was evident which customer she needed to deal with; he was first in line and apparently unhappy.

That didn't stop *him* though. Standing slightly to Hedy's left, our man made another attempt. "Hedy," he spoke her name.

Hedy ignored him and focused on the customer. "Sir, I was told there was a problem."

"Hedy." Stronger, he tried. "This is very important."

Hedy finally looked at him. "Then maybe you should see someone else. Someone not busy," she suggested.

"No, I need to speak to you and only you."

"I'm dealing with this gentleman," Hedy said.

"Hedy, I urge you right now; to not deal with him or give him what he seeks, and send him on his way. Now."

The burley customer slammed his hand on the counter to grasp Hedy's attention. "Handle me not him, damn it!"

Hedy glanced at our man. "Look, you're just gonna have to wait."

"Fine." He lifted a hand. "I'll wait. And watch."

Sighing out, Hedy returned to her customer. "I'm sorry.

Now, please, how can I help you?"

"You can fix the fuckin' charges on my account."

"Sir," Hedy spoke calmly. "I'll see what I can do. Let's take a look."

The young sales clerk intervened, and pointed to the computer screen. "This is his account. This is the charge."

Hedy read the screen. "Are you disputing the charge?"

"Hello! Yes!" he snapped.

"So you didn't rent 'Babes of Passion'?"

"Yeah, I rented it."

"Was it not late?" Hedy asked.

"It was late."

"I have two weeks late, is that wrong?"

"No, it's right." His tone was still hostile.

"Then this charge would be correct," Hedy said. "The policy for late fees on adult movies ..."

Slam! His hand hit the counter again. "I don't give a shit what the policy is, I am not paying seventy bucks! You hear!"

"Sir, you are way out of control. Now when you signed the rental contract you agreed ...."

"Look!" he fired a heavy point Hedy's way. "I don't care about the contract. I want those charges off!"

"Maybe we can come to some sort of compromise."

"No compromise!" he shouted. "You take off those charges or I swear I'll blow your fuckin' brains out."

"Removing the charges takes a manger's key." Hedy tried to make the situation lighter. She smiled at him. "And come on, I really don't think you're gonna blow my brains out over seventy bucks."

"Wanna bet." Without hesitation he stepped back, reached

under his jacket, pulled out a revolver, extended it forward at Hedy, and fired.

Stop.

Instantaneously all animation was suspended in a split second of time. Nothing or no one within the store moved. All noise ceased and Hedy found herself staring at a bullet frozen mid-blast, a mere two inches from her face. Breathing heavily and confused, she shifted her eyes to our man who tapped his hand on the counter.

He gave a simple 'I told you so' look, and then Hedy fainted and dropped to the floor.

The direct approach is often best, but nothing beats physical proof. Poor Hedy was the recipient of both. Even though man controls his own destiny, his own thoughts, there wasn't a doubt in my mind that he knew Chet Farmer—the irate customer— was going to fire that gun.

He knew.

Hedy was out. On the floor behind the counter, her face rested on the shoe of a fellow co-worker. She awakened slowly with the soft brush of his hand against her face. But when she snapped to realization, her eyes widened and Hedy scooted from him. "Oh, shit. Oh, shit."

Crouching, he reached out. "It's OK, calm down. Are you all right?" His hand took hold of her chin.

Hedy froze and locked into a stare with him. "Your eyes. There so green."

"Thanks." He smiled.

"Am I dead?"

"No. I wouldn't let that happen."

Hedy breathed out in relief, and then looked around. "Holy shit. What's going on?"

"You can say they're on pause."

"Why?" she asked.

"Well for starters we had to stop what was happening, and two ..." He sat down on the floor next to her. "I wanted to talk to you. I need to make sure you know who I am."

"Who are you?"

"I told you," he said. "When I was on this earth before, they called me Jesus."

"But you're not Jesus anymore?"

"I'm still Jesus, but that's not the name I'll use this time around."

"What is your name now?"

He shrugged. "Haven't decided. Do you have any ideas?"

Hedy gasped out an 'oh', then lifted herself to her feet. "This is too weird. Too weird." She glanced around, the stopped and saw the bullet. "Too weird."

He stood as well, and then pointed to the bullet. "You have to admit that it's pretty cool."

She snapped a look his way. "Why ... why ... why are you talking to *me*?"

"We'll have plenty of enough time later to discuss details," he replied. "But for now, you just need to know that you have been picked to know who I am, and that I am back."

"You're back," Hedy mumbled.

"Yes, to see what happens. But again, later we'll talk. Are you ready for me to start this again? People tend to get a little strange after they've been suspended for a while."

"No. No!" she said strongly shaking her head. "Wait. What if I don't believe who you are?"

"You will."

"No. What if I don't? What if I think you're some kind of whacko?"

"Correct me if I'm wrong, but I don't think just any whacko can do this ..." He motioned his hand about. "Possibly a great illusionist." He shrugged. "But not this good."

Hedy leaned to him. "What if you're not *Him*? But rather ..." she pointed down. "Him."

He snickered. "Hardly. But that's cute." He winked. "Hedy, I know you enough to know you'll believe. You can pretend you don't believe, but you don't pretend well. You run away well."

"What's that supposed to mean?" she asked.

"How you got here," he explained. "Three years ago when your husband and daughter were killed, you left no word, told no one what you were doing, you just got in the car, and you drove until you ran out of gas."

"In Lodi," she whispered.

"Lodi's been good for you though. Although ..." he smiled. "I don't know how good that one night stand with the chief of police was, but it did stop you from getting arrested when driving with a suspended license."

"Oh, my God." She wisped out, then froze. "Sorry."

He chuckled.

"But if you know everything about me, then why didn't you let that bullet hit me?"

"I don't know everything about you. But enough to know, despite how much you've said it, you don't want to leave this earth. Not yet. You're not ready. And you're especially not ready for a death that way." He indicated the suspended bullet. "We can talk later. Right now, we really need to start things again."

Hedy nodded quickly. He positioned her before the cash register, and then he walked back to the other side of the counter.

Index finger extended, Hedy touched the bullet. "Are you going to reverse things?"

"No. I'm starting them where they left off."

"What!" she blasted. "The bullet is right here."

"Don't worry," he assured.

"Ok. I'll have faith in you. I mean, you know what I mean." She inhaled deeply. "What do I do when you start it?"

"Duck."

"Duck?" she asked.

"Duck. Now."

"Shit!" Hedy dove behind the counter.

With a snap of his fingers, time fired back up, screams charged out, and the bullet continued its path. Only instead of hitting Hedy, it sailed into a glass wall, exploding it into thousands of pieces.

It was a good thing Hedy was already on the floor because she passed out all over again.

Call Me Gideon is available through Amazon.com.

www.ingramcontent.com/pod-product-compliance
Lightning Source LLC
Chambersburg PA
CBHW071630260626
47170CB00001B/40